INNOCENCE ON

TRIAL

Stephen Roth

Innocence on Trial © 2022. All rights reserved by author.

No part of this book may be reproduced or transmitted in any form or by any means, graphic, electronic, or mechanical, including photocopying, recording, taping, or by any informational storage retrieval system without prior permission in writing from the publisher.

Stephen Roth
122 Long Dr.
Stratford, ON
N5A7Y8

www.stephenroth.org

This is a work of fiction. All of the characters, organizations and events portrayed in this novel are either products of the author's imagination or used fictitiously.

Printed in Canada

Dedication

Dear Michelle,

When we first met, about thirty years ago, our connection formed instantaneously. You've pushed me to my best every step during our journey, including attending law school with a baby on the way. You sacrificed for my dream. I have searched the dictionary and have yet to find words that adequately describe what this meant to me.

It has been my deepest pleasure to join you in the fox hole of life, dodging the bullets that have whizzed over our heads. If I were to properly thank you, it would require words exceeding the length of this novel. I hope a simple thank you will suffice.

Thank you, my love.

INNOCENCE ON TRIAL

CHAPTER-ONE

Achilles

The human brain is a curious and wondrous organ, magnificent but mysterious – undoubtedly evolution's masterpiece. How is it that the mind can retain memories with absolute clarity from events forty years ago, yet forget last week's occurrences? Have you asked yourself that question? Lester Mobey often did, but he had reason.

However, that high-functioning computer within our head is also fragile, imperfect, narcissistic, and prone to severe lapses in judgment. Chameleon-like, it is just as capable of manipulation and deceit as a means to survival as it is of love and tenderness as a means to survival. It will be whatever it needs to be. These were Lester Mobey's conclusions after years of intensive therapy and decades of practicing his craft.

While settled into his favourite wing-backed chair, some forty years after his wedding day, the aging lawyer arrived at another verdict, although he probably knew it all along. The avid reader and military history buff sat alone in his study beside a roaring fire, as he was prone to do, celebrating his retirement and reading the words of the great Greek historian, Diodorus Siculus. Night combat was rare in ancient times, but the Spartans, who were overwhelmingly undermanned a thousand to one, proceeded with a daring raid in 480 BC, attempting to assassinate the Persian king, Xerxes the Great; the Spartans used the cover of darkness to even the odds and catch the unsuspecting Persians off guard:

> *They immediately seized their arms, and six hundred men rushed into the camp of five hundred thousand, making directly for the king's tent, and resolving either to die with him, or, if they should be overpowered, at least in his quarters. An alarm*

spread through the whole Persian army. The Spartans being unable to find the king, marched uncontrolled through the whole camp, killing and overthrowing all that stood in their way, like men who knew that they fought, not with the hope of victory, but to avenge their own deaths. The contest was protracted from the beginning of the night through the greater part of the following day. At last, not conquered, but exhausted with conquering, they fell amidst vast heaps of slaughtered enemies.

Siculus described one of the first documented examples of an enemy exploiting the cover of night to attack a sleeping and defenceless foe, easily slipping over an unguarded wall on its way to a crushing victory. Of course, since then, army tactics have evolved drastically to protect against these nocturnal assaults, leaving them with no real advantage in the modern world.

It was evident to Lester that the human brain, despite its brilliance otherwise, remained anchored in ancient times; and, unlike those primitive armies, had been unable to improve its defences against night attacks, leaving the formidable mind vulnerable and defenceless when it slipped into unconscious sleep. To Lester, that flaw compared to the greatest of all Greek warriors and the hero of the Trojan War, Achilles, who had that suspect heel, despite all of his might.

To this day, Lester did not invite sleep; like the Spartans, his demons scaled the wall at night to slaughter – and resistance proved futile.

CHAPTER TWO

Lady Justice

"Why are we doing this, Mom?" asked Tommy sheepishly, scrunching his face and looking down at his feet. His black dress pants, recently purchased second-hand from the local Goodwill Thrift Store, still hung an inch too far over his worn Adidas running shoes; despite the safety pin remaining in place, the trousers touched the floor.

Without answering her son, Linda Henderson made use of the convenient distraction, crouched down, pushed her long black hair away from her face and shortened the length of her son's pants by a half-inch. She had no reaction, not even a flinch, when pricking herself performing the alteration; the blood trickling down her right index finger went unnoticed.

The nausea setting in, combined with welling tears, momentarily paralyzed Linda, compelling her to remain fixed in a crouched position at his feet, prompting Tommy to ask her if she was okay. Again, without answering Tommy, she forced herself to her feet, managing an affirmative nod on the way up, a lie intended to calm her distressed son.

Now on her feet, Linda attempted to compose herself, knowing they didn't have much time, and wanting to be strong, a pursuit she was falling well short of at the moment. She was oblivious to the people continuously streaming by them, some in suits, some in their everyday clothes, and many in brand-new but ill-fitted garments intended to make a positive impression like Tommy.

Linda took a deep breath, tilted her head back and attempted to gain control. She was now an average-looking woman, thin from worry and improper diet, reflecting a sickly figure. As unruly as a rioting crowd, her long, straight black hair remained disheveled despite efforts to keep it in place. Although only twenty-six, more than a decade of heavy smoking had robbed her skin of the optimal blood flow and the vitamin C healing properties it so desperately needed, leaving it dry and blotchy. Those once dazzling and engaging eyes that looked out into the world had long ago been replaced with her current tired and sunken pair, the result of dehydration and endless sleepless nights.

How could I do this to my child, lamented Linda? No satisfactory answer existed – no answer as to whether it was fair to put a ten-year-old boy through such an ordeal. She struggled with this question over the last year, but inherent with any dilemma, she did not want to choose between two undesirable outcomes.

Finally noticing the blood, which had now meandered its way down to her palm, Linda retrieved a tissue from her purse and applied some pressure on her finger, although she was still numb to the pain. She dabbed her eyes with her shirt sleeve and looked directly down at her son, wanting to say something calming, but struggling to find suitable words.

Tommy pushed his red curly hair away from his sparkling blue eyes and looked back at his mother, their eyes finally meeting. In her opinion, he definitely had his father's eyes; but how could they sparkle and yet still look so sad? It was a question, if she was truthful, to which she already knew the answer, but when an answer is that painful, willful blindness is the only way to maintain your sanity.

Standing beside his mother, there was not an iota of physical resemblance to her. Rather, Tommy was the spitting image of his father, looking more like Alfred E. Neuman, the fictional character from Mad Magazine, complete with red hair, freckles, protruding nose and scrawny body.

"I don't know, honey," said Linda, finally replying, an underwhelming response given the circumstances, but it was the best she could do. The two of them had already had this same conversation many times over the last year; there was nothing further to be said. Linda bent down and wrapped her arms tightly around her son, who was now sitting on a wooden bench within the expansive waiting area, and whispered in his ear, "Honey, it's not your fault that we are here. It's not your fault." Then, she took her shaky hands, placed them on his slumping shoulders and gently squeezed.

"I love you, Tommy Henderson," she said passionately, guilt climbing aboard. "I love you more than anything in this whole wide world. Do you know that?"

With downward eyes and an expressionless face, her son nodded yes; he did know it. He knew that his mother loved him, but confusion and fear remained. Love is not the answer to everything, he concluded, a disappointing and weighty conclusion that belied his young age. It was nearly as regretful as Tommy's inability to believe in Santa Claus, his exposure to the callousness of life quashing his capacity to believe in fairy tales.

"I know I've made many mistakes, Tommy; and I'm not nearly perfect, but all I want is what's best for us," explained Linda. "This is difficult but you can do it!" she urged, her brown eyes fixed with intention.

Tommy bobbed his head up and down, unconvincingly, while gazing up at his mother and asking when they could return home. As she was about to respond that she didn't know, the bailiff exited the courtroom and announced that court would resume in two minutes. The ninety-minute lunch recess was almost over; Tommy was convinced it had only begun fifteen minutes earlier. Consequently, he stared at the clock to his left hanging on the wood-panelled wall, finding disappointment.

The panelling wasn't the fake variety found in the Henderson apartment; it was authentic, at least that's what Tommy overheard his mother advising fellow lingerers over the lunch break, not that he cared or could even tell the difference.

Howard King had been a bailiff in excess of twenty-five years, witnessing every type of trial imaginable; as he stared at Tommy and Linda, he appreciated the following days would be tough on them. If he could have carried the trial's weight for the pair, he would have strapped the heaviness on his back and carried on; unfortunately, it was impossible. After the carnage the beefy ex-military sergeant had seen in the courtroom, it was not a mystery why some families decided not to cooperate. Howard provided the Hendersons with a polite and professional smile from across the waiting room, followed by a quick wink.

Linda straightened Tommy's navy tie and then tucked his white dress shirt into his oversized pants, which would have been around his ankles if it were not for the belt his mother had found early that morning. His thirteen-inch shirt fit loosely around his twelve-inch neck, his tie hanging in scarecrow likeness. Even without his oversized clothes, Tommy looked younger than his age, habitually one of the smaller boys in his class. Still, Linda felt he looked handsome and, more importantly, believable, which was the whole point.

Linda wasn't sure that she wanted Tommy testifying any further despite his believability; she knew the process was very difficult for him – it was for her – but now that the trial had started, the comforting option to change her mind and not cooperate was all but closed. Theoretically, she could immediately halt this process and save her child from further pain; it was her sole decision to make. Surely, that is what a good mother would do? She could march over to Jonathon Sussman and announce that Tommy would not testify and there was nothing he could do about it. And, she would be correct because no Crown Attorney would force a ten-year-old boy to testify. What could he do? Throw him in jail? No, of course not; her son would do as she directed without legal consequence.

But Linda decided against stopping the process. Crown Attorney Jonathon Sussman had been convincing when explaining how important it was to obtain a conviction.

"Hiller will do this again!" he warned her emphatically, eyes wide open, hands extended. "We all have a duty to stop him," he pleaded with her, prompting Linda to consider Tommy's friend, George Gerontonis, whom she had learned Hiller had violated, from her son.

"I promise everything will work out," Sussman repeated

each time she raised her doubts.

Who was she to disagree with him? And besides, it was too late to stop all of this anyway, she rationalized after weighing everything in her hazy mind. She recalled the advice her father provided to her at age twelve, shortly before he died of liver failure after years of alcoholism.

"When a snowball starts rolling down a mountain, stop it at the top, not at the bottom after it has gained too much momentum and size," he said to her. Linda and Tommy were at the bottom of the mountain in this process and that snowball was huge; she didn't have the strength to slow it down.

And, what if another child was hurt because they didn't have courage? How many George Gerontonises were there out there, or could be out there in the future?

"They," she said to herself, ashamed that she included herself when Tommy was shouldering the majority of this damn trial. After all, it was he who had to testify. "Damn it," she said quietly under her breath.

Linda also had to consider Tommy's civil lawsuit against the Middlesex Board of Education. She had already met with Max Nailer, a personal injury lawyer whose television ads bombarded the wee hours of the morning and whose billboard ads could be seen all over the city.

"You need a lawyer who is tough as nails." She loved his slogan. During one of her regular bouts of insomnia in the early morning hours, she watched his television commercial eight times. Max stood there, all six feet, six inches of him, with his expensive suit and Rolex watch on full display, flashing those perfect teeth and literally hammering a nail into a piece of wood while green dollar signs floated around him on the screen.

"We will hammer the insurance company into submission!" he yelled bombastically, as he pulled out a gold-coloured nail and started hammering away.

"Who the hell is he advertising to at 4:00 am?" she said to herself, stretched out on the couch, failing to appreciate the irony when she picked up the phone a few hours later and called the 800 number.

After meeting with Nailer two days later, she discovered that he was not that tough – certainly not as tough as nails – and had never even conducted a trial. After a few minutes of small talk, smiles and empathetic overtures by Nailer, he explained from behind his $3,000 gleaming mahogany desk that he referred everyone who called his firm to hard-core experienced trial lawyers who had decades of experience, all in return for a handsome referral fee.

Linda could overlook his fake tan, perfectly coiffed hair and smiles over substance, but she was not pleased with spending cab money to and from his office only to be told that she had to meet with another lawyer.

Linda finally met with Anthony Kilmer, a real lawyer who agreed to take on Tommy's case; however, he would wait for her to give him written direction before personally serving legal papers on Hiller and the Board.

Kilmer was emphatic that a criminal conviction would force the Board of Education to settle a civil suit; he estimated Tommy's entitlement to pain and suffering damages as significant. Linda knew that the failure to secure a criminal conviction, which would occur if Tommy did not testify, meant that the Board of Education would not likely settle a civil suit; Tommy had to continue his testimony, she concluded.

"Come on honey," said Linda, grabbing his trembling hand and heading towards Courtroom #2D.

Disappointment grew across Tommy's face, unsettled that he was returning to the lion's den. The two of them could have easily turned around and made a beeline to the down escalator, always compliant, Tommy remained quiet.

Tommy didn't want to be anywhere near the courthouse, much less enter Courtroom #2 again. While he found the Lady Justice statue in front of the London Courthouse interesting – the fourteen-foot-bronze depiction of a blindfolded woman with a scale in one hand and a sword in the other hand – the court process was intimidating; he felt like hiding.

Had it not been for his own circumstances that brought him there, he would have enjoyed exploring the exceptional courthouse building, with its numerous gargoyles, plaques and portraits of old people, who must have been very important. His preference was to escape the drama, return to his impoverished apartment and continue his quest to reach level three on his favourite video game, Killer Comet.

Tommy found the turn-of-the-century courthouse scary, not because of its grand staircases, towering ceilings, ornate fixtures, intricate patterns and mahogany mouldings, but because everyone walked around with stern-looking faces; not one person wanted to be there.

The morning began unpleasantly. After he had finished fawning over Lady Justice, Tommy and Linda entered the courthouse at 9:00 am, well before 10:00 am, when court was to start. Two security officers asked them to empty their pockets and enter through the metal detector, a reasonable request, but his mother objected on his behalf.

"He's only ten years old! He's just a little kid!" she exclaimed angrily, an overreaction brought on by the stress of the upcoming trial. Linda had barely eaten in weeks, surviving on a steady diet of coffee and cigarettes; and with the combined lack of sleep, she was mentally fragile.

A couple minutes of bickering between Linda and the two burly security officers ensued, the most excitement the guards had been exposed to in a while and they weren't about to back down.

"Come on, lady," growled an elderly man in line, who was leaning on his cane.

Linda ignored the man, which was surprising, and was in the middle of telling the guards that she wanted to speak to their supervisor, when a bored-looking police officer strolled over and threatened to arrest her.

"Try it," she shot back, taking an aggressive step toward the man twice her size, a move that Tommy thought would result in handcuffs being secured on Linda's tiny wrists.

The officer, now realizing Linda's acute distress and

exhibiting some good judgment, calmed her down, performed a cursory pat-down search of Tommy and let him through without emptying his pockets in breach of security protocol.

The pair quickly made their way to the escalators; Linda stopped Tommy from running up the down escalator.

"We're late. Let's go!" she said irritably, and was about to say more, but reminded herself that it was wise not to scold her son, who needed to be at his best today.

After a few minutes of wandering around the second floor, they found room 201, where Jonathon Sussman had told Linda to meet him by 9:30 am and no later. Linda struggled with punctuality; she was pleased they were only a few minutes late while pushing themselves through the crowd, the clacking of her high heels on the hardwood floor barely audible over the many lively discussions in the hallway. The many people surprised her.

"Business must be good," she uttered with a wry laugh.

"What?" replied Tommy quizzically, not understanding his mother's sense of humour.

"Nothing," she answered abruptly while waving aside her own joke with her right hand.

Tommy looked at the door, "Office of the Crown Attorney."

"What's a Crown Attorney?" asked Tommy.

"That's Mr. Sussman," she replied.

They entered the Crown Attorney's office, or the "bunker" as the staff affectionately referred to it, busy with several lawyers and their assistants hectically preparing for court that morning. Some talked on the phone; others removed faxes, and the rest animatedly conversed with each other. Tommy noticed they all had one commonality - none of them smiled.

Jonathon Sussman had been waiting for them. He stood up from behind his desk, waved them over and extended his hand to both of the Hendersons; he offered a slight smile, a gesture that Tommy appreciated. The Assistant Crown Attorney bent down to eye level and squeezed Tommy's hand gently, unlike the normally strong squeeze from adults.

Sussman's office was typical for a busy lawyer with files piled high in the corners; his undergraduate and law degrees were framed and prominently displayed on the wall beside a photograph of the Supreme Court of Canada building in Ottawa. On another wall, The Canadian Charter of Rights and Freedoms hung beside Sussman's Gold Medal from Osgoode Law School, awarded to the graduating student with the highest cumulative average over all three years.

It wasn't typical for Gold Medalists from Canadian law schools to end up as a Crown Attorney, usually opting for more lucrative positions at high-powered law firms that could offer huge salaries, perks and prestige.

Sussman's route to law school was atypical, growing up in foster care after being removed from his parents' custody at the tender age of six. His father, Henry Sussman – brilliant but dishonest – received a twelve-year prison sentence for his participation in an elaborate multi-million-dollar real-estate fraud. A psychiatrist testified at his trial that Henry Sussman suffered from a high-functioning borderline personality disorder.

Tragically, Jonathon Sussman's mother had a nervous breakdown after her husband's arrest; her already-present drug dependency spiralled downward, culminating in a heroin overdose eight months later. She died at age twenty-eight.

Despite his less-than-optimal childhood, Sussman excelled academically; and upon graduation from high school, he wanted to become a criminal prosecutor. He was brilliant, usually at the top of his class academically; ironically, he inherited his intellectual prowess from his peculiar father.

After greeting the pair, Sussman took Tommy into a small meeting room, furnished only with a small desk and two chairs. Like the last time when they had met for three hours, the two met alone so that Linda had no input in what he told Sussman; the Assistant Crown Attorney wanted him to express everything in his own words, without influence. Tommy recognized that Sussman's smile had disappeared, tension now filling the man's face.

Trials are akin to game days in professional sports; lawyers develop strategies in preparation for game day, when they have to perform. Sleepless nights, nervousness and adrenaline rushes are usual. Trepidation about the unknown twists and turns that inevitably occur in a trial is the norm; the surprising answers that a witness gives, or the unexpected rulings from a judge do not allow for a moment of relaxation.

No windows existed in the interview room; it would have been cramped if Sussman had allowed Linda in with him, but Tommy still wished she was present. Sussman explained court procedures – such as taking an oath and calling the judge, "Your Honour." Then, he reviewed the questions that he would be asking his young witness later that morning, but not with the same detail as the last time they met.

"These are the same questions we went over last time," Sussman emphasized. "There is nothing new. This is just to refresh your memory."

Tommy was not sure he understood what refresh meant, but nodded anyway. The boy was fairly confident he knew his testimony; he and his mother had reviewed his anticipated testimony so frequently that he even dreamt about the answers. He thought he knew what to say; no, he absolutely knew what to say, convincing himself. After finishing with Tommy, Sussman had bailiff King escort him to a waiting room, adjacent to the courtroom, where he was to remain until it was time to testify. King observed Tommy's nervousness as they walked, a normal emotion in his experience.

"It will be fine, kid. Relax and answer the questions truthfully. That's all there is to it," he said encouragingly with a smile. "My name is Howard but you can call me Howie. If you need something, ask and I will do all I can, okay?"

"Okay," replied Tommy, who appreciated Howard's efforts to comfort him. Still, the march to the guillotine to have his head removed was unsettling. He imagined his head rolling down the escalator and hitting that old man on the way down, knocking the cane right out of his hand.

Court clerk, Muriel Lawson, had her homemade cookies and juice waiting for Tommy when he arrived at the waiting room, a thoughtful gesture for child witnesses testifying in these delicate cases; she knew it would be an emotional day. Contract disputes, wrongful dismissal claims, estate litigation and even family law trials were all preferable to observe over sexual assault trials. She wouldn't miss these highly-charged trials after she retired in six months.

The tiny interview room surprised Tommy; it was smaller than the interview room. The six-by-six-foot room had one chair and an end table just wide enough for a plate of Muriel's cookies. The institutional grey-coloured walls highlighted the complete lack of artwork or decoration in the room. Tommy stood in the middle and stretched out his arms, attempting to touch both sides of the room at the same time, but came up slightly short.

"Have a seat, Tommy; I will come and get you when it's time," said Howard. "And have a cookie or two; they are delicious!" he proclaimed, grinning ear to ear. "If any are left at day's end, they're mine," he declared with a chuckle while rubbing his rather large belly.

After Howard left, Tommy sat down, picked up a cookie and took a bite, realizing that the bailiff was correct. These cookies are tasty, he said to himself, wiping a crumb from his mouth. Chocolate chip was his favourite, too; but his stomach was churning and he didn't feel hungry, so he took one bite and put the cookie back down on the plate.

Tommy stared at the walls; there was nothing else to do except think and he was in no mood for that. He was done with thinking, having thought enough for a lifetime in his estimation; but despite his self-restricting proclamation, one inescapable thought repeatedly interloped into his mind - this must be exactly like being in jail; nothing to do but stare at the walls in a miniature-sized room. He conceded that Muriel's delicious chocolate chip cookies would not exist in jail.

Tommy mused: how would Robert Hiller manage jail, staring at the wall for years and years, without a cookie in sight?

Linda took a seat on the courtroom's back-row bench, preparing herself for the commencement of her son's testimony. Sussman told her Tommy was not permitted in the courtroom, except to testify, and that her son would be waiting in a comfortable room with homemade cookies.

Linda, concerned about her son's isolation, hoped he didn't feel like a criminal behind bars. She scanned the room. It was her first time in a courtroom; she was surprised at the solemnness, even when court was not in session. People talked in hush tones, a gesture of deep respect for the important function taking place within those four walls.

Linda dressed conservatively for court, choosing a knee-length white dress with a light pink floral pattern that she bought third-hand at the Goodwill Thrift Store for five dollars. She wore two tiny pearl earrings, a pendant that her mother purchased for her at age fourteen, and a thick, three-centimeter, black velvet bracelet that she always wore on her left wrist, unless she was showering.

To celebrate her fourteenth birthday, Linda and her mother, Barbara, visited Stratford, Ontario, attending an afternoon production of *The Sound of Music*, an indulgence the family's limited resources did not allow for. It had been two years since her father's death and without his income, or life insurance, Barbara and her daughter were barely surviving financially; their last-minute trip to Stratford surprised Linda.

Despite modest means, Barbara and her ebullient personality had a way of keeping their lives rich with tradition, celebration and laughter, even after the death of her husband, which was extremely difficult for them both. Even at her lowest, Barbara ensured that she kept it together, maintaining her appearance; without exception, she would shower, blow-dry her hair, style it to perfection, apply her make-up, and then put on her finest clothes, despite having nowhere to go. It wasn't her presentation to the world that mattered to her. Rather, she needed her daughter to know that her mother wasn't letting go; if her daughter didn't think she could take care of herself, how could she believe her mother could care for her? Barbara frequently advised her daughter, "that joy doesn't have a price tag on it but it is the most valuable commodity on Earth; and if you focus on it, you can be the richest person in the world without spending a dollar."

After the glorious musical concluded in marvellous fashion, the two strolled Stratford's main street, window shopping and singing Do-Re-Mi over and over again, intermixed with belly-aching laughter and hugs. The bustling sidewalks and patios screamed with excitement as the locals and tourists gladly co-existed on the beautiful Saturday afternoon.

Linda gazed down at Lake Victoria, dreams behind her eyes, watching a gaggle of geese land on the water with the same perfection and grace as Cynthia Dale's dancing from the stage an hour ago. Her joy hadn't reached that level since her father died; the dark clouds briefly lifted, allowing her to feel alive again. Her mother's smile, and watching her skip down the street to Do-Re-Mi, resulted in the perfect birthday gift.

"Before we head back, I have one more gift for you," said Barbara, grabbing her daughter's arm and pulling her into the Black Swan House, an expensive boutique shop on the corner of Ontario Street and Romeo Street.

"Pick anything you want," she directed her daughter.

Linda took an hour, touching every item in the boutique, agonizing over her choice; she decided upon a beautiful, silver pendant in the shape of a swan with a detailed inlay.

During the hour-long drive home, mother and daughter sang Do-Re-Mi and giggled while Linda rubbed the swan with her fingers. Lively discussion filled the time, both agreeing the exhilarating afternoon allowed them to float off to a beautiful alternate reality for a few hours.

Linda, intoxicated with excitement, couldn't shake the performers from her thoughts, their endless energy escaping through their eyes and spraying onto the audience, drenching everyone with a delightful shower. Pendant in hand, she felt like a star; Linda decided unequivocally that someday she would sing and dance on the Stratford stage, calming the enthusiastic crowds who gave her one more standing ovation. She could think of nothing grander to do with her life.

As they pulled into their driveway, Linda begged her mother to sign her up for dance lessons, her path now certain; she promised her mother that she would do anything to start those lessons.

"We'll discuss it tomorrow," replied Barbara without looking at her daughter, knowing the answer was no. She didn't have the heart to ruin her daughter's perfect day, to reach in and rip that excitement out of her soul – to take the fire burning inside her and douse it with the horrible news. No, she would wait until the following morning to tell her daughter that she was diagnosed two days earlier with an aggressive and malignant form of ovarian cancer; the disease left her daughter an orphan three months later.

After her mother's death, Linda had no option but to relocate thirty kilometres away in Brantford to reside with her elderly great aunt, Florence, a responsible woman who kept a tidy household. Florence was not known to show her emotions; stoic was an apt descriptor for this woman of the depression who discarded nothing, her basement stacked to the ceiling with boxes of ripped wrapping paper, cardboard, broken coffee mugs and used stamps; she was unable to shed the thrifty constitution that had served her well.

When Linda first arrived and extended her arms for a hug, Florence turned her back and mumbled something about preparing dinner. It was a safe environment where Linda's physical needs were well taken care of but there was no love or affection within the four walls. She lived comfortably in her aunt's house, but it was not a home.

Sitting at the back of the courtroom, Linda lightly stroked her pendant, pensive reflection bringing on the habit. Her left hand instinctively touched the top of her head, feeling her hair, which was tightly pulled back and placed into a ponytail; the style managed her normally wild locks best. She understood that her presentation would have no affect on the outcome of the trial, but Linda felt better making an effort.

A sizable oil painting of Queen Elizabeth was centred on the wall behind the judge's bench, flanked by the Canadian and British flags. The authentic mahogany courtroom walls with their rich hues and undertones constituted a measurable upgrade from Linda's apartment.

Another clerk entered the courtroom with water jugs, placing one beside the judge's chair, one near the witness stand, and one on each of the lawyer's tables. Nearing retirement, like Muriel, she had placed those jugs in the same spots too often to count; her zombie-like stare betrayed any attempt to hide her boredom.

Muriel tested each of the microphones, walking to each one and tapping, "Testing."

When Muriel and Linda's eyes met, the clerk offered a quick smile and a wink, which was quickly reciprocated by Linda; the nervous mother appreciated the modest gesture.

Muriel had children too, and was sympathetic to how the woman in the back row must be feeling; any parent would be devastated. The clerk thought of Tommy; hopefully, the cute boy was munching on the homemade cookies that she had prepared especially for him.

Although only twenty-six, Linda she felt much older; the death of her parents, becoming pregnant at age fifteen, and an unhealthy teenage relationship provided the foundation for premature aging. Life had shaken Linda's hand, cruelty inconspicuously tucked in its palm.

After the death of her mother, Linda craved attention – anything to fill the crater left after her life exploded into a million pieces. Tommy's father filled that hole for a short period; a lonely and parentless girl will do almost anything to be loved.

Although never regretting having Tommy, becoming a young mother had been difficult, emotionally and financially. The boy's father, Jeremy, a year older than Linda, provided no emotional or financial support; he was a boy himself. The relationship deteriorated quickly when Jeremy decided fatherhood was inconvenient, leaving Linda to raise their son alone and rely solely on Florence; her aunt was not pleased with the addition of another Henderson under her roof, especially such a noisy one.

Linda constantly pursued child support over the next decade, but Jeremy's part-time minimum-wage job while he completed high school amounted to insignificant support; and, once he graduated, the man purposefully worked cash jobs to hide his true income. Linda lost all contact when he moved to Alberta and disappeared.

When Linda was seventeen, Florence died; her great aunt's children, imitating vultures, swooped in and picked that carcass of a house clean, scooping jewelry or anything of value before Florence's body was buried.

Her great aunt's two children inherited the entirety of her estate and wanted the house sold immediately; vacations, waterfront cottages and Las Vegas trips landed behind the heirs' eyes. They demanded that Linda and Tommy vacate within thirty days.

Although explained with a smidgeon more tact, the children explained that Linda had mooched off their mother for long enough – she was fortunate to have stayed for as long as she did; Linda was not their problem.

Those events kicked off an existence of relying on welfare, food banks and sub-standard social housing apartments with leaky pipes and the occasional cockroach. Linda focused on ensuring that Tommy had enough to eat and paying her modest bills each month, although bill collectors were constantly at her door. Occasional part-time jobs – waitressing at local pubs or cashiering at Walmart – never lasted long, her constant tardiness always having the same outcome. It was too difficult to climb out of bed.

Linda had neither the energy nor the inclination to date; any relationship she had was casual, never particularly rewarding, and always fleeting. Depression became an insidious and constant companion, holding her in a perpetual bear hug until she couldn't breathe. Her condition improved with medication since her suicide attempt on her twenty-fourth birthday, pushed to that unimaginable desperate act as she sat alone in her living room. Besides her son, nobody gave a damn that it was her birthday, the realization squeezing the last ounce of hope from within. Only the fortuity of Tommy waking in the middle of the night to get a glass of water, finding his mother, and calling 911 kept Linda from completely bleeding out from her left wrist.

Linda attempted to escape the grasp of her dire circumstances; however, her companion, settled deeply in the recesses of her mind, prevented her from reaching out and grabbing life preservers that floated by. She declined social invitations, preferring to remain in her apartment, having meager energy for life. Frequent moves, because of eviction and evading unpaid debts, required Tommy to frequently change schools; the family's transiency added to their unsettled existence.

Tommy knew his mother was not well - the pills, the alcohol and the muffled crying late at night. When he heard her sob, he tiptoed into her room, crawled into her bed and gave her a hug, "Everything will be okay, Mom.

Tommy had no reason to believe it would be, okay; Linda's suicide attempt, which resulted in a two-month foster-care stay for the impressionable boy, siphoned the youngster's remaining optimism.

While Linda monitored the courtroom, Robert Hiller entered the courtroom with his lawyer, Lester Mobey. She recognized Hiller's distinctive deep voice; she did not turn around or acknowledge the two men as they walked by. Her hands trembled watching them walk in conversation as they passed her until they reached the defendant's counsel table. Mobey put his briefcase down and hooked his cane on the back of his chair.

Mobey looked relaxed and confident in his black court robe, the required attire for barristers in the Superior Court of Ontario, but Hiller was fidgety and speaking quickly to his lawyer. Hiller, dressed in a navy-blue suit, looked around the courtroom and waved at his father, who he found sitting about ten feet to Linda's right. The disgraced teacher had maintained his innocence of the charges levelled against him; his father, Raymond, supported him unconditionally through this difficult time, which was typical for most of Mobey's clients. Raymond had shed twenty pounds since his son's arrest; the father worried incessantly, never having imagined that his retirement years would be this stressful. He knew Linda Henderson was to his left but he wouldn't look at her, preferring to focus on the front of the courtroom.

Sussman walked in two minutes later wearing his black court gown, a briefcase in hand; he had his game face on but comfortingly touched Linda on her shoulder while passing her on his way to the table reserved for the Crown.

Both lawyers began shuffling papers, positioning and re-positioning their binders and readying themselves for battle – trying to control their pre-game jitters.

There were nine observers in the courtroom: Linda, Raymond, two local reporters, who were busy scribbling notes, and five others whom Linda did not recognize. The courts were open to the public; rather than walk the mall, perhaps those five decided to take in a criminal trial for some variety, mused Linda.

Muriel stood up. "All rise," she announced, prompting all in attendance to stand.

A side door opened; Howard King walked in, followed by Judge Handy. Handy, wearing his own black robe with a red sash over his right shoulder, climbed the few stairs to a raised platform and bowed, which was reciprocated by everyone in the courtroom.

"In the matter of Her Majesty the Queen and Robert Hiller, the Honourable Judge Handy of the Superior Court of Justice presiding," declared Muriel.

Handy – older and distinguished with silver hair meticulously slicked back and reading glasses on the bridge of his nose – presented himself with confidence and authority. The tall man had seen it all through his green eyes, surmised

Linda.

"Bailiff, please call in the jury," directed Judge Handy.

Ten seconds later, Howard returned with twelve of Robert Hiller's peers, who had been given the solemn duty of deciding his fate.

"Please call your first witness, Mr. Sussman," ordered Judge Handy.

Jonathon Sussman, the twenty-seven-year-old Assistant Crown Attorney, was an impressive lawyer who carried himself with self-assurance. Although he was confident prosecuting Robert Hiller, this was the first sexual assault case, and only his tenth case since becoming a lawyer.

Sussman, considered a rising star by the Ministry of the Attorney General, was ambitious; his employer had high expectations for the novice, a student who had been accepted to Osgoode Law School in Toronto on a full academic scholarship. At university, he had taken a leadership role in many clubs: social activist committee, President of the Law Review magazine, organizer of the annual Christmas food drive, board member of the LGTBQ Association and Chair of the Criminal Law Association.

Sussman's athletic six-foot frame and handsome looks completed the package for the man who was equally at ease on a baseball diamond as he was in a courtroom.

When the matter of *Regina v. Hiller* was assigned to him, his boss, Crown Attorney Roger Tillman, entered his office and slapped the Crown file on his desk, "Sorry for the interruption; you're ready to prosecute crimes more serious than petty thefts and forged cheques."

"Sounds good. What do you have in mind?" replied Sussman, excited to be given more responsibility; his eyes opened wide in anticipation.

"Regina v. Hiller," explained Tillman; "Sexual assault by a teacher against one of his students. This was Ken Steele's matter but he broke his leg skiing yesterday and we're scrambling to cover his cases."

Tillman explained that the brief was complete with the

witness statements, police notes and investigation summaries, "Classic sexual grooming of a child."

Sussman understood that sexual predators often befriended vulnerable children; step by step, the offender gained their victim's confidence, abusing them once they were comfortable the child would remain silent. Usually, by the time the abuse started, the child viewed the predator as someone to protect.

"Lester Mobey is the defence lawyer for Hiller," explained Tillman.

Mobey had an impressive record in the courtroom; the forty-year-defence lawyer resembled Winston Churchill, bald with a paunch at the waist – he had not been physically able to exercise since his wedding day four decades earlier. His intellectual brilliance was often obscured by his rumpled exterior and his peculiar habit of riding an adult-sized tricycle fitted with a side-saddle for his legal files. Mobey had neither owned a car nor had a driver's licence in forty years – it was odd, watching him pedal his tricycle to court in a suit with his wonky leg in the middle of a snowstorm.

Mobey's flair for the irreverent had placed him in hot water with several judges; although he had mellowed over the years, three things riled him: bullshit, hypocrisy and injustice. He had difficulty keeping his mouth shut when faced with any of them.

Those who had faced him in the courtroom quickly learned not to underestimate Lester Mobey, earning himself the reputation of a top-notch litigator. Now in the twilight of his career, he only took on serious and high-profile cases.

Unlike Sussman, Mobey had done it all and seen it all in a courtroom; experience did mean something. Even after forty years, it still amazed him that a trial's outcome could be determined by only one document, one word, or the way a witness emphasized an adjective when testifying.

He took his role of defending clients with a silent ferociousness and an unwavering commitment; the responsibility to keep a client out of jail was immeasurable –

the loss of freedom and liberty traumatically damaging the soul and mind. Unless you have gone through it, you truly do not understand it.

Hiller's case would be his last. He was tired of mucking it out in the legal trenches, retirement behind his eyes; however, his client would receive his best.

Although the allegations against Hiller were serious, it was not the case Mobey would have chosen for his last except for his connection to Hiller's father, Raymond. The pair had grown up together; when his old friend called in a panic after his son had been arrested, Mobey advised him to come over immediately.

Raymond rushed to his friend's office, inconveniently sandwiched between a pawn shop and tattoo parlour in the seedier section of east London, Ontario, pleading for help. He was met in the small lobby by Mobey, who walked towards him haltingly, his noticeable limp slowing him down. A cane in his left hand steadied the aging lawyer while the two old friends shook hands and then embraced. Raymond was appreciative of having someone trustworthy to reach out to in this challenging time, although the knot in the pit of his stomach remained.

"It's been a long time, Raymond," greeted his friend.

"It has been, Mato. I wish I was seeing you again under different circumstances."

Mato. It was a nickname that caught Mobey off guard. Only two people ever called him Mato; hearing that name sent adrenaline rushing through his body – a bullet from his past whizzed by his head. Mobey, a voracious reader, was a fan of *Kill the Dead*, a Richard Kadrey novel; a line from the book remained with him – *Memories are bullets. Some whiz by and only spook you. Others tear you open and leave you in pieces.*

Under other circumstances, the defence lawyer would have pulled out a bottle of Scotch and called it a day, but he knew he had work to do.

"Shit, Mato, I know how successful you are. Why don't you use some of that cash on a little more expensive real estate?" exclaimed Raymond, slapping his friend on the back with a laugh, feigning calmness.

"Better to use my dough for experts to get the innocent off bogus charges, you old fool," replied Mobey, smiling.

The tone quickly became serious as the two men sat down; Raymond explained the circumstances surrounding his son's arrest and insisted that his son was innocent.

"Robert would never do anything like that!" declared Raymond. "I've never been so sure of anything in my life," he said passionately, pounding the table with his hand. "That kid is a damn liar."

The two talked for ninety minutes; Mobey would not turn his old friend away, but he didn't have the heart to tell his friend, at least not today, that Raymond should be prepared to consider that his son had a darker side. Mobey knew that a client's explanation did not always align with the actual evidence; the lawyer had confidence there was more to learn about the accusations against Robert Hiller. All in time, he mused.

Where it concerned grand proclamations of innocence, Mobey had become one cynical son of a bitch; while he was always a zealous advocate for his clients, guilty or not, he was not a fool either. He had hundreds of former clients who had professed their innocence, and were now rightfully looking through bars from the inside of a cell. But, and it was huge 'but,' not everyone was guilty; Mobey never lost sight of that fact, his mind racing as Raymond thanked him and left his office. More importantly, Mobey only had to convince a jury that there was reasonable doubt that Hiller had committed this crime, not that he was innocent – he never allowed a jury to forget the fundamental distinction.

Mobey's last case would not be high-profile with extensive media attention. Rather, it would be one done as a favour to an old friend; he was content with the decision, thinking it apropos.

After Raymond left, he immediately drove to the London jail and met Robert Hiller in the basement cells. Hiller retained him after promising to provide a ten-thousand-dollar retainer payment within the following two weeks; his new client was not wealthy but a fifteen-year-teaching career allowed for modest savings.

Mobey secured Hiller's release the following day on bail with strict conditions, including the requirement to live with his father, who agreed to be a surety; but it had been a rough night in the cell for Hiller. Two police officers, who Mobey knew well, pulled him aside as he left the station and told him that his client had sobbed all night. The cell walls had a way of moving in and crushing a man – the chirping from the seasoned cons unrelenting.

Six weeks later, Mobey reviewed the Crown disclosure – all the evidence that had been gathered by the police: investigative notes, records, witness statements and photos; Mobey meticulously scoured every document, searching for anything that might create reasonable doubt in the jury's mind.

Occasionally, the Crown did not disclose important evidence that would have helped to exonerate his client; this unethical practice was becoming rare, fortunately. He didn't know anything about Jonathon Sussman – had never heard of him; there was no reason to suspect he would act unethically, but he was being paid to appreciate the possibility.

Mobey didn't care if his client committed the crime; he provided his best effort regardless. Hiller strenuously professed his innocence; but after several interviews with Hiller and a thorough review of the disclosure, Mobey concluded that his client was probably guilty. The lawyer told his client that he believed in his innocence, a lie that the accused wanted to hear.

It was his responsibility, professionally and ethically to vigorously cross-examine witnesses, even if they were children. While some considered his approach distasteful, he viewed his sometimes aggressive and fierce approach as his unwavering obligation to his client.

"I'm not here to win a popularity contest, Mother," he gently explained at the last family gathering, flatly refusing to allow anyone's perception of his role to influence his approach.

Mobey dedicated nine hours on a Saturday, reviewing disclosure; some areas might prove fruitful in the cross-examination of Tommy Henderson, he concluded; generally, trials were not won by the "gotcha" moments on television. Winning a trial required casting doubt on witness testimony – if a jury concluded someone was lying, that was great; but, it was enough if the jury questioned the reliability of the testimony. Was the memory faulty? Had the witness made a previous inconsistent statement to their courtroom testimony? Mobey looked for anything to raise questions in the jurors' minds.

An entry on page 672 of the disclosure caused Mobey's eyes to open wider; he raised his eyebrows and stroked his chin.

"Bingo," he said to himself. "That's it. That's what I'm looking for," he said softly, even though he was alone. He leaned back in his chair, crossed his arms and considered his find; it may be reasonable doubt, he speculated, but it will depend on what young Tommy Henderson says at the trial. Indeed, what will the boy say? Mobey snapped his briefcase shut and called it a day.

CHAPTER THREE

The Tower of Brotherhood

Linda shifted on the hard wooden bench, seating that was not designed for courtroom comfort. Her son would be the first witness; she was nervous, occupying her time by scanning the courtroom and repeatedly rubbing her silver swan from the Black Swan Boutique.

Linda's mind drifted to how Robert Hiller came into Tommy's life – how this entire process began. Hiller was Tommy's grade-four teacher at Middlesex Elementary School in London; the man paid special attention to the boy when he transferred from Walnut St. Elementary School in Simcoe. As a single parent, Linda was appreciative of positive male role models in her son's life; Hiller's attempt to make Tommy welcome was admirable.

Tommy had moved schools three times in three years, difficult changes given the shy boy did not easily make new friends; he warmed to Robert Hiller's efforts to make him feel comfortable. The two developed a positive relationship.

In the Spring of grade four, Hiller invited Tommy for a weekend visit at his cabin along with two other classmates. Tommy was eager to go. Hiller explained to Linda that he had no children of his own and that he enjoyed taking children without fathers in their lives to his cabin occasionally. It was his version of a Big Brother program.

Respecting her gut feeling, Linda thanked Hiller for his generous offer but declined on behalf of Tommy, reluctant at the arrangement, but suggesting that a future visit was possible.

However, over the next two days, Tommy begged and pleaded with his mother to allow him to attend, "Come on, Mom. Some of my classmates, who have already gone, bragged about how much fun they had. I'll make new friends," he implored, thrusting a guilt trip on her. Unbeknownst to him, he had gone right for the jugular of her self-condemnation;

Linda knew the multiple school moves had been difficult for her son – and were her fault.

Tommy desperately wanted to attend; rumours of children driving a car on Hiller's ten-acre property, shooting pistols and staying up after midnight were plentiful, details that he did not offer his mother, for good reason. She would not approve.

"Some of the guys might like me if I go, Mom!" he blurted out.

Linda did not want to disappoint her son; it was the first time Tommy genuinely appeared excited since transferring to his new school.

"Okay, you can go," she relented, rationalizing that she was initially overly cautious. After all, the other parents had no issue with their children attending Hiller's cabin.

The following evening, Friday, Linda drove Tommy to Hiller's cabin, hoping her twelve-year-old uninsured car with an odometer reading of nearly three-hundred-thousand kilometres would survive the trip. After a fifteen-minute drive, Linda turned off Highway #2 onto a long meandering dirt road abutted by dense forest on each side. Tommy stared out the window. His back straightened. His eyes lit up, imagining himself running through the forest, shooting paint guns, playing tag and skipping rocks on the wide creek that ran through the property. Would Mr. Hiller allow him to drive his car? Maybe shoot a real gun?

Linda shoved her doubts down deep, convincing herself that this would be a fantastic experience for Tommy. When she picked him up Sunday night, he would be smiling ear to ear and gushing about his newfound friends. It broke her heart to see him holed up in his room, alone, while the laughter of the neighborhood children playing outside echoed through their apartment.

"Look, Mom!" yelled Tommy, pointing to a cabin perched on a hillside at the end of the lane. Excitement hopped on his back when he caught sight of the charming log cabin that had two windows framing a redwood front door. Smoke wafted out of the chimney into a cloudless, blue sky – pushed eastwardly on account of Lake Huron winds. A freshly stained Maple front deck, twenty-by-twenty for invited guests; a propane barbeque, picnic table and several deck chairs completed the ensemble. A cord of cut hardwood immaculately stacked on the south side of the deck, overlooked a deep ravine. Several bicycles and a mini-bike lay against the north side of the cabin.

A carefully manicured acre surrounded the cabin, in contrast to the rustic and forested lying further out. At the ravine's bottom, a swimming pond equipped with a floating dock flanked a sandy volleyball court. Linda and Tommy both watched as a boy ran, jumped off the dock and performed a cannonball maneuver, creating a huge splash in the pond. They looked at each other and smiled.

Linda brought her car, clunking with each revolution of her tires, to a stop at the base of the six stairs that lead to the deck and front door. Tommy stepped on several empty cigarette packages on the car's floor and hopped out with his backpack before Linda had time to grab her driver's-side door handle.

Hiller pushed open the cabin door and enthusiastically waved at the pair. "Hello," he bellowed, greeting them with a wide smile.

Tommy, accustomed to seeing Hiller in class with ironed slacks and a button-up shirt, considered it strange to see him in casual attire of sunglasses and Bermuda shorts; his t-shirt didn't hide his extended stomach quite as well as his regular attire. As the screen door slammed behind him, Hiller removed his Detroit Tigers baseball cap and offered his right hand to Tommy.

"Thanks for coming!" he said enthusiastically. "Thank you too, Linda. I promise he will have a terrific time!" exclaimed Hiller, paired with another smile.

"Hi, Mr. Hiller," responded Tommy while shaking his hand.

Hiller responded with a strong handshake. "Hi, buddy.

I'm so glad you arrived! Listen, when you're here, call me Robert. At the cabin, I'm not your teacher; we're just friends."

Tommy nodded; that is cool, he thought, knowing his weekend would be great.

Robert turned his attention to Linda. "Thanks again. I hope he's excited to be here."

"Of course, it's all that he's been talking about," she responded, feeling relieved.

Robert was quite attractive, in Linda's opinion. Yes, Father Time had affected Robert, as it had with most men in their forties – a receding hairline and a slight paunch; but he was tall, maybe six feet with bright blue, penetrating eyes. Despite the expanding waistline, his athletic past was clear; broad shoulders and strong arms provided proof.

Linda surprised herself as she eyeballed Hiller, finding herself attracted to the man, partially fueled because he had taken her son under his wing.

Chris Jackson and George Gerontonis, two of Tommy's classmates, appeared, running from the rear of the cabin.

"Hi, Tommy," said George.

"Hi, guys," replied Tommy, sensing that they both welcomed his arrival.

George was the biggest kid in his class, tall and stocky. With jet black hair and Greek heritage, he brought the best lunches to school, prepared by a mother who loved to cook. George could be a bit of a bully; but he portrayed his jokester side usually. His father died in a work-related accident a year earlier, a deadly mishap involving electricity; Tommy overheard Mr. Hiller telling another teacher that George was having a rough time.

Linda bent over and kissed Tommy on the cheek. "Have a good weekend, honey."

Linda drove away, looking in her rear mirror, but her son was already out of sight, off to explore Hiller's wonderland.

During his first weekend at the cabin, Tommy enjoyed himself; his classmates embraced him, which had him wondering why they didn't behave the same way towards him at school.

Tommy considered Chris cool, a kid with bright curly red hair, like his own, but he was at least four inches taller. Despite his athleticism, Chris wasn't popular at school, carrying a shy and awkward disposition.

The legendary rumoured activities were accurate, the first weekend filled with driving Hiller's jeep around the property. Because the boys could not reach the pedals, they sat on Hiller's lap; he controlled the pedals while the children steered the vehicle. Tommy felt like an adult, steering the car, not an insecure boy searching for his place.

Hiller did not become upset when he nearly hit a tree; his teacher laughed, directing him to be careful. Tommy pondered having a father permanently in his life. Where was his father, a man he had no contact with?

Target practice occurred on Saturday afternoon – the thrill of the weekend. Hiller exited the cabin with binoculars slung over his shoulder and a black case that he placed on the picnic table. With a click, the top popped open to reveal three guns secured in individual sleeves, side by side, their handles facing out.

"Listen, boys," said Hiller, suddenly becoming serious, and removing his ball cap. He fixed his eyes down at the boys, pausing to ensure he had their full attention, because it took a moment to draw their attention from the trio of handguns.

"Guns can be dangerous; your parents may not approve. So, I'm willing to allow practice shooting, but with one condition. We have to promise each other that this will be our secret. You can't mention this to anyone, including your parents."

Hiller took a quick look down the ravine at the targets and then returned his attention to his visitors.

"I guarantee that if your parents find out, you will not be permitted back here. I will only do this with students that I trust and who trust me."

The three boys hurriedly nodded their heads in agreement without a hint of reservation.

Now that the pact was in place, Hiller reached down and pulled out a black Glock 17 semi-automatic pistol, leaving the Beretta 92 FS and Colt M1911 in their sleeves. The boys had never seen a gun in person before; they were surprised by how menacing the hand-held killing machine looked up closely. Hiller pointed to the bottom of the ravine alerting the boys to several targets – a few tin cans, a traditional multi-ringed target with a red bullseye, and a stand-up mannequin dressed in camouflage army fatigues tied to a tree. Hiller methodically showed the boys how to unload and load the gun clip, and how to activate the safety, and then discussed some general safety tips, such as not pointing a gun at anyone. The boys listened intently and wide-eyed while Hiller illustrated how to properly shoot a pistol.

"First, hold the gun firmly in your right hand," explained Hiller as he extended his right arm at the targets. "Then, align your target with the gun sight. And then, place the centre of the pad of your trigger finger on the trigger; then slowly squeeze the trigger smoothly keeping the gun and your entire body completely still." Bang! Bang! Bang!

He knew the shots were coming, but the noise was strikingly louder than Tommy expected, startling but exhilarating; it sounded like a baseball bat smashing against a metal garbage can three times, echoing through the ravine; smoke slowly wafted away from the deck. Shells flew from the Glock, bouncing around on the deck, sounding like dropped coins – only better.

Tommy, George and Chris stared at each, awe stalking them from head to toe.

"How cool was that," uttered George, eyes turned downward, following the last shell as it rolled off the deck.

Hiller motioned at Tommy to grab the Glock; he did as instructed, but with some trepidation. Tommy raised the pistol, aiming at the mannequin forty yards out; his trembling hand fought to keep the one-and-a-half-pound gun steady until he finally fired a shot. Bang! Tommy gently squeezed the trigger, sending a bullet out the barrel and into the ravine where it glanced off a tree, three feet above the mannequin's head, which drew a chorus of "wows" from George and Chris, binoculars at their eyes.

"Well done, Tommy!" shouted Hiller, patting him on the back.

Tommy felt an unexplainable power when he fired the gun, something never felt before in his pint-size body; he felt like a man – it was intoxicating.

"How did that feel?" asked Hiller, who appeared as excited as Tommy.

"It was amazing! So amazing!" replied Tommy, an understatement.

He and Hiller looked at each other; instantly they bonded, a connection unfamiliar to the boy.

Tommy squeezed the trigger ten more times with rhapsody, euphoria filling his body.

Tommy understood the need to keep the shooting secret; if his mother saw him surrounded by all those empty bullet shells, she would yank him off that property so fast his head would surely spin. He need not dare risk spoiling all this fun; Tommy paused to consider when he had had this much. The answer was obvious, never.

For meals, Hiller, Tommy and his classmates sat around a fire and cooked wieners on the end of sharpened sticks. Hiller told stories about his army experiences, enthralling and scaring the boys. The boys laughed and laughed, sometimes to tears, when Hiller told off-coloured jokes. They all agreed: what happened at the cabin, stayed at the cabin.

Hiller's cabin was small, about 900 square feet, but tidy and organized with masculine furnishings including a dozen, or so, framed photographs with him and his war buddies dressed in combat gear holding machine guns. To Tommy, the photos appeared to be taken in far-away lands. Hiller told the boys that he trusted the men on the wall with his life, and they with his; when they made a promise to each other, it was always kept.

"Real men keep their promises, no matter what,"

explained Hiller, with emphasis; he became serious again, looking each of them in the eye. All three slowly nodded back in agreement.

The rustic cabin boasted thick exposed beams and pine walls; furnishings included wicker furniture and an Amish-made oak kitchen table. A combined living room/kitchen, three-piece bathroom and one large bedroom completed the living area.

Tommy loved the indoor activities too: a Coke-themed beer fridge full of pop, pinball machine, Nerf basketball net, dartboard and foosball table ensured boredom never set in.

Hiller provided simple toileting instructions, "If it's brown, flush it down. If it's wet, off the deck," he directed the boys with his robust laugh, directing them to pee off the southeast corner of the deck under the kitchen window to save well water.

"Always in the same spot, boys. I'll keep the porch light on at night to make sure you don't piss on your feet!"

"That's gross," said George, pretending to shake his leg as if he had just peed on himself.

What a great dad Mr. Hiller would make; Tommy's stomach hurt by the time he hit the sheets Saturday night from laughing so hard.

On the first night of his visit, as night settled in and the boys took a break between watching movies, Tommy walked over to Hiller at the kitchen table.

"Robert, how come you don't have any children?"

Hiller slowly looked up from his magazine and smiled softly.

"Well, Tommy, I was married once but I didn't have children. But I love children, which is why I became a teacher." After removing his glasses, Hiller continued, "I'm not sure I'll ever have children at this stage of my life; that's why I love having you boys to my cabin."

On the second evening, approaching midnight, Tommy noticed that Hiller was acting differently, slurring his speech; an almost-empty bottle of wine opened after dinner sat empty on the kitchen table. He had often seen the same behaviour in his mother. Hiller was laughing and talkative, which didn't bother Tommy, but he had witnessed such lively disposition morph into darker moods.

Hiller poured the last two ounces into a cup, held it out, and offered it to Tommy. Tommy stared at Hiller, frozen, confused and unsure how to respond. Finally, the boy shook his head, no, and walked back to the couch to sit with his friends.

It was dark by 9:00 pm each night. Hiller reminded the boys that the outside light would be kept on all night so they wouldn't fall off the deck, "I don't want to have to fish you out of the wet grass."

At 10:30 pm on the second night, Tommy did have to go pee after dark.

"I'm going to take a leak," he announced to Hiller and the boys who were watching an Arnold Schwarzenegger movie, *Predator*. Hiller made each of the boys promise that if he let them watch the rated "R" movie, they would never tell a soul; they all agreed without hesitation.

"Okay, Tommy, I'll pause the movie," replied Hiller. "Go take a leak and I'll do a few more dishes."

Tommy opened the screen door, crossed the deck in his pyjamas and absorbed the beautiful warm night; the moonlight reflected off the pond at the bottom of the ravine. He took a deep breath, stretched his arms and took a few seconds to enjoy the chirping crickets that surrounded him; they created a constant chorus of music.

Tommy felt the light comfortable breeze on his face as he stepped to the edge of the deck and looked down. It was off-putting, to observe the residue from the urine glistening off the tall grass below. He pulled down his pyjama bottoms and took out his penis to urinate. At age nine, he did not have one hair down below, his bare pre-pubescent genitals now exposed to the crickets and creatures in the ravine; the deck light shone down directly on Tommy as if he was the star of the show.

After emptying his bladder, he sheltered his penis behind

his pyjama bottoms, but something caught Tommy's eye to his left. He quickly looked over his shoulder and saw Hiller staring out the kitchen at him. Their eyes met; Hiller immediately looked down into the sink and fumbled with something.

Tommy felt embarrassed, similar to when he accidentally walked in on his naked mother, but this felt different. Maybe, it was because it was he who was naked this time. A greater level of privacy was possible on the other side of the deck, away from the window, thought Tommy; if he got a chance, he would mention it to Robert.

In the lone bedroom, Hiller had pushed three mattresses together on the floor, resulting in a huge bed, wider than a king-size bed. Tommy asked his host why the beds were pushed together.

"Because the room is small; I want as much sleeping space as possible for the children that I invite to the cabin," he replied. "I can get four of us in this bed."

That made sense, reasoned Tommy.

The following morning George and Tommy sat on the bed, their legs crossed, while Hiller and Chris cooked breakfast in the kitchen.

"Tommy," George whispered, "I want to tell you something."

"What?" Tommy replied quietly, appreciating that it was something important.

"Last night, in bed, Robert put his hands down my pyjamas and touched my balls," he explained.

"What?" replied Tommy. "What do you mean?"

"He put my balls in his hand and kind of rubbed them. I pretended to stay asleep. Don't tell anybody, okay?" asked George.

Tommy nodded mutely, attempting to process what he had heard; he wasn't sure what it meant.

"Promise?" asked George, who extended his hand toward his friend in the form of a fist, with his thumb facing up.

Tommy had an important decision to make. Over a roaring fire, Hiller taught the boys the secret handshake that he and his war buddies used, a modification of the tower of fists game, where each successive participant puts a fist on top of the other, until everyone had a fist on the tower. Hiller asked the boys if they wanted to adopt that secret handshake between the four of them, but warned them it was not a decision to make lightly.

He made them pull their sticks out of the fire and stop roasting their marshmallows to ensure he had their attention.

"Once you agree to be bound by the secret handshake, you are now a brother, obligated to protect your brother no matter what circumstance," he explained. Hiller talked about his war buddies with reverence and how having them as his brothers were the most important relationships that he had ever had; they were more important than even his parents.

"Do you know what it's like to know that your brothers are always there to protect you? said Hiller passionately to his young guests.

Tommy did not know what it was like; but it sounded wonderful, similar to the connection he made with Robert after squeezing those rounds out of the Glock – perhaps ten times more powerful.

Hiller, who had the boys completely captivated, went on, "If you did something wrong here at this cabin, once we're brothers, I would never tell your parents because that would violate the brother code."

The three boys looked at each other. It was an easy decision to make without any discussion. George put out his fist, followed by Chris, then Tommy, and finally Hiller put his on top to complete the tower – creating the brotherhood.

So, as they sat there and George put his fist out, Tommy knew exactly the type of promise he was being asked to keep; and with the smack of his fist down on George's, the code was in full effect, consummated by the tower of brotherhood.

Tommy became a regular at Hiller's cabin, attending every other weekend throughout the spring and the summer, the boys and Hiller stacking their fists to create the tower of brotherhood at the beginning and end of each visit. His mother thought her son had been reborn, even as she deteriorated. Any threat from Tommy's mother to forbid him from visiting Hiller's cabin resulted in an immediate correction in his behaviour; Linda referred to it as the Hiller effect, her new secret parenting weapon.

Abruptly though, in the beginning of August, a few weeks before the start of Tommy's grade-five year, Linda forbade her son to attend the cabin. She put an immediate stop to the visits; Tommy would never see the cabin again but it was unclear what would become of the tower of brotherhood.

CHAPTER FOUR

Game Day

Linda felt a poke in her side. Howard King saw that she was daydreaming, or perhaps nodding off; but it was clear that she was not aware that her son had just taken the witness stand, so he wandered over to subtly alert her.

"Thank you," she silently mouthed to Howard.

It was true. She did not see the bailiff escort him in after slipping into a trance-like daze, ruminating about Hiller's cabin.

The court permitted Tommy to testify from behind a white screen, protecting him from having to look directly at Robert Hiller while testifying so he would not feel intimidated. It resembled a film projector screen to Tommy, placed between him and Hiller, but allowing him to see the judge, jury and Sussman.

Mobey had little faith that his client was not severely prejudiced by the use of the screen – that the boogie man had to be hidden from Tommy Henderson. What juror would not be affected by that? But nothing could be done – the law permitted its usage.

Sussman encouraged Tommy to relax when testifying; to assist him, he would not have to look at Robert Hiller. But Tommy was not relaxed; he was scared. Robert Hiller was steps from him – a shield did not change that uncomfortable reality. Besides, he could feel Robert Hiller's eyes piercing through that flimsy screen, the man seething over Tommy's audacity to violate the brotherhood code – breaking the promise to never hurt a brother. Tommy could hear the crackling of the campfire as Robert's huge hand came down on his to create the tower of brotherhood with George and Chris.

When Tommy climbed the two steps to the witness stand beside Judge Handy, he was convinced that Robert would pounce on him from behind the screen and that would be the end of poor old Tommy Henderson. And, he deserved it for breaking his promise – for betraying the code.

Once on the stand, he wondered if Robert Hiller could see all twelve members of the jury as well as he could, seven women and five men. With every eye in the courtroom on him, Tommy was the star of the show, clearly the main event. The spotlight of the fluorescent lights was bright; he wondered if he might melt under the heat.

Tommy was not present when the jury was picked. Sussman and Mobey were each given twelve peremptory challenges or twelve chances to exclude a potential juror without having to give any reason at all. Those challenges were similar to a veto, an opportunity to exclude someone as a juror, even if the other side felt the person was acceptable as a juror. So, Sussman and Mobey had to be very careful when evaluating whether each potential juror was likely to be helpful or hurtful, a difficult and subjective determination.

Jurors could also be excluded for cause if they showed a bias or had any connection to the case, which did not affect the number of peremptory challenges each lawyer had available to them. One juror was excused for cause because of her connection to Hiller. Her adult son had been a student of Hiller's many years ago and she considered him an excellent teacher.

Sussman used three of his peremptory challenges, waffling on using his fourth but deciding against it; Mobey used all twelve of his.

Tommy's morning testimony proceeded smoothly. Because it was the Crown that had brought its case against Hiller, the Crown was required to call and question its witnesses first. Sussman asked him all of his questions during the first morning of the trial; Tommy thought that he testified exactly as he and his mother had reviewed, even with his nervousness.

Sussman asked the young witness short and straightforward questions in his examination-in-chief, a more difficult process than it looked because none of the questions could be leading. Mobey objected a few times on this basis, but Sussman believed no damage was done to the Crown's case.

Sussman explained to Tommy, in preparation for trial that morning, that a leading question suggested the answer. Tommy was not entirely sure what that meant, so Sussman gave him an example.

"If I asked you, 'what colour was the car', that is not a leading question, but if I said to you, 'the car was blue wasn't it,' that would be a leading question."

A good example, thought Tommy, now understanding the concept.

During Sussman's examination-in-chief, he did an excellent job of putting Tommy at ease, asking questions slowly, using simple words, and giving his young witness ample time to think about the answers to his questions. The Assistant Crown Attorney smiled and repeated his questions when Tommy did not understand or appeared confused.

Linda listened to her son for two hours; he repeated and testified to almost everything that she had just recalled while daydreaming at the back of the courtroom. Sussman methodically brought Tommy through his testimony and told the jurors about Robert Hiller's cabin and their activities, including those he was sworn to secrecy by the brother code. The courtroom remained hushed when he described urinating off the deck, Hiller's lurking at the kitchen window, the offering of alcohol, the big cozy bed; and, of course, the tower of brotherhood.

While testifying, Tommy witnessed Mobey furiously making notes; what could he be writing down, he wondered?

He testified that on the second weekend he visited Hiller's cabin, Hiller began sleeping beside him in the big bed, the four of them uncomfortably squished together. Hiller then started fondling Tommy's privates during the night; he heard Hiller groaning while this was going on, confused as to what it meant.

Tommy testified that Hiller told him that they had an

extra-close relationship and that what they were doing was okay because they were special friends. Eventually, Hiller told him that he loved him and would do anything for him. He warned him that both of them would get into serious trouble if he talked; his mother might be jailed.

This was the reason he never told his mother about the touching at first. He didn't know that this type of touching was wrong; it was not until August that he realized it was improper and told his mother.

He went on to tell the court that the abuse escalated to where Hiller was having him kiss Hiller's private parts on each visit to the cabin, sometimes more than once.

"I wondered why he peed in my mouth each time," testified Tommy, his voice quivering.

The already quiet courtroom came to a complete hush. Linda heard the clock tick on the wall as it moved to the next minute. An icy cruelness blew out into the courtroom from Tommy's mouth, freezing everyone. The jurors' eyes dipped down away from Tommy's face, afraid to peer into the soul of a boy subjected to such unimaginable acts. To Mobey's chagrin, some of the jury members cupped their hands over their mouths.

Sussman purposefully delayed asking his next question, content to let Tommy's testimony penetrate as deep as possible. Muriel fought back tears, knowing it would unprofessional to show, or worse, grounds for a mistrial; but she was also a mother.

Mobey considered standing up and asking the judge to have Sussman move things along, but thought better of it, afraid of looking callous in front of the jurors.

Tommy testified how Mr. Hiller routinely found an excuse to get him away from the other boys and into the woods. Then, he explained how his visits ended.

"At the beginning of August, I told my mother about the touching; she cried as I had never heard her cry before. She said I could not go back to Mr. Hiller's cabin."

Tommy paused for another moment before continuing.

"Then the police came to see me soon and I told them everything."

The jurors looked on intently. Mobey was not pleased to see juror number five wiping a tear from her eye, perhaps an unequivocal sign that she believed absolutely every word of Tommy Henderson's testimony. He was sure that every last person in the courtroom believed the boy; hell, even Lester believed him.

Linda wiped tears from her face while rubbing her pendant; surrealness enveloped her.

Following the strict instructions given to him by Mobey, Hiller did not look at the jurors during Tommy's testimony and simply stared straight ahead with a poker face. Mobey explained to him that jurors unfavourably viewed defendants who shook their heads or appeared frustrated.

"You will appear less credible," explained his lawyer.

If Hiller did not testify on his own behalf – an important step that remained to be decided – Hiller's only influence on the jury would be his demeanor while sitting in court. Hiller sat, stone-faced – exactly as instructed – praying his lawyer had four aces up his sleeve because the boy had just dealt him no face cards, not even a pair, with his powerful words.

Mobey was concerned too; Sussman had effectively drawn out Tommy's testimony clearly and coherently for the jury, a difficult task with a nervous child. More importantly, Tommy appeared believable.

But this was a criminal court; it was all about reasonable doubt. Mobey had been in this position frequently before; it didn't matter how solid a witness looked after the Crown was done its questioning in examination-in-chief. Was it solid after defence counsel's cross-examination? That was the only question that mattered. Mobey had turned fantastic-appearing witnesses into stuttering fools after he was done with them – easier to accomplish with a child. His opportunity to earn his legal fees would come after the lunch recess.

Despite his experience in the courtroom, Mobey still felt butterflies in his stomach anticipating the cross-examination of a key witness. He completed hours of preparation so that he could execute flawlessly; the casual observer had no idea that his smooth and confident demeanor resulted from meticulous planning.

The stakes were high if Mobey didn't perform well; some clients lost their reputations, others went to jail, families split up, and lives were destroyed.

During the lunch recess, Mobey remained in the courtroom to prepare for his cross-examination, munching on a granola bar that he had placed in his gown pocket a few weeks earlier. He was as alert, as focused as a starving hawk soaring overhead and looking for prey below, not missing the slightest movement. For example, when Howard King summoned everyone back into the courtroom after the recess, he noticed Tommy's pants were no longer dragging on the floor and Linda Henderson had a tissue pressed up against her finger.

Mobey prided himself on not being a long-winded lawyer and asking witnesses question after question just for sake of asking – there must be a specific reason to ask. Quality over quantity was his mantra; it was clear when a lawyer did not have an effective plan heading into their cross-examination.

Tommy took his position back on the witness stand, once again shielded from Hiller's view.

Judge Handy addressed Tommy, "Do you understand you still have to tell the truth and only the truth? This is very important."

"Yes," he replied faintly.

"Okay, and it is important that you speak loudly so everyone can hear you. Can you do that?"

"Yes", replied Tommy, slightly louder.

Judge Handy looked directly at Mobey. "Please proceed."

The lawyer rose to his feet, walked to the podium and placed his notes down, adjusted his reading glasses and looked directly at Tommy.

"Do you understand the difference between a lie and the truth?" asked Mobey.

"Yes," replied Tommy, nodding.

"And do you promise to always answer my questions truthfully?" asked Mobey.

"Yes, sir."

Cross-examining children on sexual abuse allegations was difficult strategically. Mobey intended to undermine the credibility of the child's testimony, even if it was true. The truth did not matter; jurors never knew the truth with certainty. Rather, jurors could only interpret evidence and make educated determinations. Only Tommy Henderson and Robert Hiller knew the truth; and one of them was lying.

Mobey walked on a high wire, trying to be aggressive with a child witness, but not crossing over the line to badgering; crossing the line brought an objection from the Crown Attorney and a rebuke from the judge. More importantly, it could result in the jury becoming sympathetic to the child.

Judges understood a defence lawyer's need to test a child's evidence – to put the child under pressure to see if the child's memory was accurate, or if the story changed. It did not follow that jurors understood; if jurors disliked the defence lawyer because of a perceived unwarranted attack on the witness, that sentiment may transfer to his client.

"Is it okay if I call you Tommy?"

"Yes," replied the young witness faintly.

"I know that you understand that it is very important that you provide the court with as accurate answers as possible," said Mobey in a gentle voice. "If I ask you a question and you do not understand the question, please do not answer," instructed Mobey. "Instead, tell me that you do not understand the question and I will ask the question in a different way until you do understand. Can we agree on that?" he asked, still using his gentle voice.

"Yes, I understand," replied Tommy.

"How many times did you attend Mr. Hiller's cabin?"

"About twelve times," replied Tommy.

Mobey continued with routine questions for an hour, trying to lull Tommy into a comfort zone. The answers to these questions were uncontroversial, but the lawyer wanted to fill in gaps from his morning testimony; leaving no wiggle room when the more crucial questions came later was essential. Boxing the witness in was key.

By the time the afternoon court recess had arrived, Mobey felt he had pinned Tommy down on his story and hoped that the real fireworks would start after the break when he arrived at his "bingo" moment.

Did Sussman see what he saw in the disclosure? If so, why did he not try to address it in his examination-in-chief of Tommy? If your witness had to deal with evidence that was not favourable, it was better to come out during examination-in-chief; get it in front of the jury on your terms. Allowing it to leak out in cross-examination was risky – appearing as though the witness was attempting to hide the testimony.

Mobey hoped to score big points after the recess.

CHAPTER FIVE

The Right on Arrest

On the third last Monday in August before Tommy's grade five school year was to begin, Linda called the Middlesex Board of Education at 11:30 am, demanding an appointment with the Superintendent of Education.

When the secretary attempted to sluff her off to the following week, Linda blurted out, "child abuse is not a matter to be put off to next week." The secretary put her on hold; a few minutes later she returned to the line offering an appointment for 2:30 pm that day.

That afternoon, Linda bussed her way to 635 Dundas St. in London. Her car wouldn't start; with no money to repair it, and a nearly empty bank account, the bus was her most economical option.

Linda met with Superintendent Frank Rose at 2:30 pm on the 7th floor of the Board offices as scheduled, less than four hours after she called. Rose, tall and lanky with tiny spectacles on the bridge of his nose greeted her with a forced half-smile. He had rearranged two important meetings to see her; the school board took allegations against teachers seriously, especially this variety.

The superintendent presented as friendly but stressed – blinking quickly and fidgety; the man knew has was not about to receive good news.

"Ms. Henderson, very nice to meet you. Please sit down," he offered, pointing to an institutional-like chair with a metal frame and no cushion. As she sat down, Rose took out a pen and pad of paper from his desk.

"Are you okay, Ms. Henderson?" asked Rose, thinking that she did not look well; dark circles under her eyes and thinness bordering on malnourishment suggested sickness. Her ghostly-white complexion and beads of sweat on her forehead added to his suspicions.

"Thank you for seeing me," replied Linda, ignoring the

question. "Do you know what Robert Hiller has been doing to my child? He has been diddling my boy, playing with his crotch and worse!" she exclaimed. Linda continued for fifteen minutes, explaining the entire story, while Rose took notes.

"Ms. Henderson, have you contacted the police?" asked Rose.

"I haven't yet. He just told me last night; I was so upset I wanted to get down here and tell you about it," she replied. "You're lucky that my first call wasn't to a lawyer. He's been diddling George Gerontonis, too."

"Please tell me what you know about George," he requested, shaking his head, eyes down in frustration; this was the last thing he needed to be dealing with today.

Linda knew little, but offered what her son told her - that George told Tommy that Hiller was fondling him at night in the big bed.

Rose made a few more notes and peeked up at her, sighing, "I'm sorry to meet you under these circumstances, Ms. Henderson. I'm sure you're very upset."

"You're damn right I'm upset!" she retorted, raising her voice; her eyes pushed out of their sockets. "I trusted that man and the school with my son!"

"Please calm down, Ma'am. I appreciate how difficult this is, but please don't yell," he asked. "I'm here to help." He sighed again and crossed his arms, absorbing the information.

Linda settled herself. "So, what's the next step? Will I hear from your lawyers?"

"My first step is to call the police," replied Rose. "I'm sure the police will want to speak to you and Tommy."

"That's fine," muttered Linda. "But, if you want to deal with this fairly and compensate him for this, maybe we can resolve this. I would understand if you didn't want to make a big spectacle of this and involve the police. I don't want to put my son through anything more than is necessary," she stressed. "All of the attention won't be good for anyone, especially my son."

"Ms. Henderson, the Education Act requires me, by law,

to report any allegations of abuse to the police. I don't have a choice. Otherwise, I will be breaking the law," he explained.

"I didn't realize that," replied Linda. "Very well."

Rose put down his pen. "As for any civil remedy, I suggest you seek counsel to address this. The school board has a process to deal with these situations; an investigation will be completed. Typically, we wait for the results of the police investigation before addressing any possible damages. It's premature to know what position the school board might take."

Rose walked Linda to the main lobby, said goodbye, and returned to his office to call the police.

Linda's heart was still racing as she stepped off the bus, a block from her apartment. Tears trickled down her face; how much one person can take? She reflected back on her twenty-fourth birthday – scared she was closing in on that low point again.

Rose was correct. Linda had barely put her purse on the kitchen table when the police called, confirming that an officer would be over in two hours.

Detective Lenny White arrived on time; he took statements from Tommy and Linda, offering his sympathies and promising he would do everything he could to ensure Hiller went to jail. White explained that he would interview Hiller, if the teacher allowed it; but the man would be arrested today if he could find him. The detective shook Linda's hand and said he would be in contact to update her.

The veteran police officer had long ago lost the fit physique that he had entered the police academy with forty-one years earlier. His zest for the job had faded over the last few years – gone if he was truthful with himself. White had only had one month to go before retirement; the man didn't have the stamina or enthusiasm to follow up on leads as he used to. He explained it to his wife this way: he had seen too much of everything - too many tragedies, too many people hurt, too many murders and too many abused kids. The officer was a good cop, but the job had taken its toll.

The stereotypical child abuser was a fantasy – they

didn't patrol washrooms or give you the creeps; they were your neighbours, bosses, husbands, uncles and priests. Hell, they were even police officers. They coached your children's baseball and hockey teams. The abusers stood in plain sight, relying on popularity and stellar reputations to cloak their dark, shameful secrets. White stopped listening decades ago to the "he wouldn't do such a terrible thing," or "he's such a nice guy," or "but he does so much for the community" responses when an individual refused to believe someone accused of abusing children was capable of it.

So, when the detective knocked on Robert Hiller's cabin door later that afternoon and Hiller invited him in, it was not surprising that he found Hiller to be charming and personable. But his charisma did not persuade White that he didn't abuse Tommy Henderson.

Hiller invited White to sit down at the kitchen table. The two of them took chairs at the oak table; White pulled out his notebook. While the detective cranked his neck side to side to scan the cabin, a puzzled look came over Hiller's face as if to say "why are you here?"

"Do you live here alone, Robert?"

"I do," replied Hiller.

"Got a lot of toys in here for a grown man, don't you?" remarked White with a hint of attitude.

"Detective White, perhaps you should tell me why you are here," retorted Hiller, trying to remain calm but irritated with White's change in tone.

"Do you know Tommy Henderson?" asked White.

"Yeah, is everything okay?" he replied, an eyebrow cocked.

White stared at Hiller intently with a furrowed brow. "Not really, no. He slept over here frequently, didn't he?"

"Yes, Tommy and several other boys. What exactly is going on here, detective?" demanded Hiller firmly, his hospitable disposition dissipating quickly.

"I just met with Tommy Henderson and he tells me you have been a very naughty man," replied White, his tone unmistakably accusatory.

"I have absolutely no idea what you're talking about," stated Hiller, now outwardly frustrated, shaking his head and placing his hands palms up.

"Do you mind if I take a look around, Mr. Hiller?" asked White, failing to wait for an answer. Instead, he jumped up, walked to the bedroom door and peaked in.

"Actually, I do mind!" exclaimed Hiller. "Please leave, immediately!" ordered Hiller, nearly yelling.

"That's quite the bed, Hiller," said White sarcastically. "I've never seen such a set-up; it must get real cozy in there at night with you and the boys."

"Get out of here now!" hollered Hiller, his face beet red. "This is all bullshit! I don't know what the hell you're talking about."

White ignored him, took a few steps to a shelf full of movies and mockingly scanned through them.

"A lot of inappropriate movies for kids here, too, Hiller. Did you get permission from the parents before you let the kids watch them, you pervert?"

"Get the fuck out of my house now!" screeched Hiller, now raging at the audacity.

White wasn't done pushing his host's buttons; he walked to the kitchen window and looked out. "I can't imagine how many little dicks you've seen over the years looking out this window. Tell me, is the view better in the day, or do you prefer the more romantic porch light on when you get yourself off?" exclaimed White, oozing contempt.

"Get out now, or I'm calling your supervisor," threatened Hiller.

"Oh, I'm leaving, but you're coming with me. Turn the fuck around and place your hands behind your back you son of a bitch," ordered White.

"You've got to be kidding. What's going on here?" asked Hiller, his tone transitioning from anger to desperation as the gravity of his predicament set in.

White flipped him around and secured handcuffs on him,

tight enough that Hiller flinched with pain.

"They're too tight," said Hiller, grimacing.

"I know," replied White. "Robert Hiller, you are under arrest for the sexual assault of Thomas Theodore Henderson. You have the right to remain silent; anything you say can and will be used against you. You have the right to consult with a lawyer."

As White read him his rights, Hiller's father, Raymond, walked through the front door, a rippled forehead confirming his confusion at the handcuffs on his son's hands.

"What in the almighty God is going on, Robert?" asked his father, startled at the spectacle. "What did you do?"

White trotted Hiller out the front door to his unmarked police car. He did not provide the detainee time to grab anything, even his wallet, shoving him into the back seat; before closing the car door he leaned in and smirked, "I hope the boys in the cells don't find out why you're in the can tonight."

"I will call a lawyer," yelled Raymond from the front door as White pulled away. "And don't say a thing!" The startled father ran back into the cabin, picked up the phone and called Lester Mobey, hoping his old friend could help his son.

Later that day, armed with a warrant, three members of the Middlesex Police Department attended Hiller's cabin to search the premises and to take photos. Officers photographed the deck, the grassy area where the children urinated, the "big" bed and the kitchen window looking out over the deck. Photographs of the child-friendly games and activities were taken; they took samples of the grass and soil to test and confirm the presence of urine. The black case with three guns was confiscated and placed in the trunk of a police cruiser.

CHAPTER SIX

The Art of the Cross

Once everyone had taken their seats in the courtroom after the completion of the afternoon recess, Judge Handy entered the courtroom. Tommy resumed his position on the witness stand.

Mobey stood at the podium and looked at the young witness.

"What grade are you in?" asked Mobey.

"I'm in grade five now, but I was in grade four when I started going to Mr. Hiller's cabin," explained the nervous boy.

"Okay, so you know about measurements, Tommy, right?"

"Yes, sure I do."

"So, you understand how long an inch is?" asked Mobey.

"Yes," replied Tommy.

"Please show me with your thumb and finger how big an inch is," directed Mobey.

Tommy held up his hand and put his thumb and index finger about an inch apart.

"Great. I would say that is exactly right," remarked Mobey. "Your Honour, may the record show that Tommy Henderson has made a gesture with his right-hand thumb and pointer finger of approximately one inch?"

Sussman stood up. "Objection, Your Honour. Without measuring, I'm not sure it's fair to say."

Judge Handy interrupted him, "Please sit down, Mr. Sussman. It looked like about an inch to me. The record shall show that Tommy Henderson has made a gesture with his thumb and pointer finger approximating one inch."

There was a time to object and a time not to object, thought Sussman who felt somewhat embarrassed by his objection.

"Now, you testified earlier this morning that you "kissed" Robert Hiller's penis on several occasions, right?" he asked.

"Right," responded Tommy.

"And you testified that this happened on over ten occasions, correct?"

"Yes," replied Tommy.

"And these times when you kissed his penis, it happened sometimes in the daylight?" asked Mobey, knowing the answer from the disclosure.

"Yes," Tommy replied.

"About half the time, right Tommy?"

"Yes, sir."

"Please tell the court how big Robert Hiller's penis is," asked Hiller.

Tommy paused – did not answer for thirty seconds, "What do you mean?"

"How many inches long is it?" Mobey demanded, raising his voice just enough to ramp up the pressure.

Tommy's thoughtful look turned quizzical, his eyes fixed at his feet; he didn't answer. Then, he looked out at his mother.

"You don't know, do you?" pushed Mobey.

Tommy was still thinking, the wheels grinding slowly – his pensive look obvious.

Sussman stood up, "Your Honour, badgering the witness."

"Not in the slightest, Mr. Sussman," replied Judge Handy.

Mobey went on, "You know how long an inch is but you can't say how big his penis is; that is what you are telling the court," asserted Mobey, again ratcheting up his tone, the gentle and straightforward questioning from Sussman's morning examination-in-chief gone.

"It's just difficult to say for sure," Tommy managed to squeak out, briefly looking up before dropping his head again.

"You can't estimate its length because you have never

seen Robert Hiller's penis, have you?" accused Mobey.

"I have. I have. It's just difficult," said Tommy, still searching for an answer.

"Let's move on then, if you can't answer the question," announced Mobey.

Sussman stood to his feet, "Objection, Your Honour. He didn't say that he couldn't answer the question."

"But he didn't answer it, Mr. Sussman," said Judge Handy.

Judge Handy looked at Tommy. "Can you answer the question?"

"No, sir," he responded.

Sussman sat down, irritated with himself. Damn it, why didn't I leave it alone.

Mobey refused to take the pressure off. "You testified that nobody ever saw you or caught you doing any of these acts with Mr. Hiller, correct?"

"Yes, correct," replied Tommy, searching for his mother's support at the back of the room.

"Keep yourself focused on Mr. Mobey's questions please," directed Judge Handy.

Tommy's face became red, flustered by his uncomfortable circumstance; he was sure the heat had been turned up in the room.

"Nobody saw it because none of it happened, isn't that the truth?" pressured Mobey. "Tell the truth!"

"It did happen! It really did! Why are you doing this?" asked Tommy, his voice cracking.

Mobey paused. He didn't want Tommy breaking down or Sussman requesting a recess.

"Do you want a tissue?" asked Mobey, momentarily taking his foot off the gas.

"No," replied Tommy, who was looking at the floor.

"You have to speak up, okay," requested the judge, staring down at the boy.

"Okay," Tommy responded, but no louder.

Linda wanted to rush to her son and immediately stop

this. She shouldn't have listened to Sussman.

"Tommy, when was it that you first knew that the alleged sexual touching on the part of Mr. Hiller was inappropriate?" asked Mobey.

All of these questions were hard now, thought Tommy, wishing that Mr. Sussman would ask the questions again.

"I guess when I told my mom that Mr. Hiller was touching me and he was making me touch him. That was when she told me it was inappropriate," he answered, with barely any confidence, his voice trailing off at the end of his sentence.

"What do you mean you guess?" pushed Mobey. "I don't want you to guess, Tommy. When was it that you first knew that these so-called inappropriate activities were, in fact, inappropriate?"

Tommy paused again, his mind swirling; he wanted to run away but knew he couldn't. The small waiting room with Muriel's chocolate chip cookies looked attractive to him at the moment; even if it felt like a jail, it was preferable to this. At least he would be alone and out of the spotlight.

"Answer the question, Tommy," ordered Judge Handy firmly, but with a measured tone.

"It was in August, when I told my mom about the touching," said Tommy. "I'm absolutely sure of it."

"So, you're sure that was the first time?" pressed Mobey.

"Yes," replied Tommy.

"No doubt at all?"

"No doubt," the boy answered.

Sussman wondered where Mobey was going with this; he didn't have a good feeling, but there was nothing he could do about it anyway.

"Tommy, I'm going to show you a document," said Mobey. "It's a school record from your school dated May 13, 2003."

He handed a copy of the document that was contained within the disclosure records to Sussman.

"Your Honour, if it pleases the court, I wish to make this

document Exhibit 6."

"Yes, Mr. Mobey," replied Judge Handy. Mobey passed a copy to Muriel, who handed it to the judge.

"Tommy, you attended Middlesex Elementary School in May of 2003, correct?"

"Yes, sir."

"And did you miss any school days in May," asked Mobey.

"I don't think so."

"Do you have any reason to believe you missed any days in May, Tommy?"

"No," replied the boy, again looking out to his mother for help. He knew another difficult question was on its way. His eyes glanced at the door he had entered through, wondering the consequences of stepping off the stand and out of the courtroom; he could race down the escalator, run out of the courthouse past Lady Justice and never came back. Would Howie chase him, slap those handcuffs on him, and drag him back under the spotlight? Howie would likely order him to now call him Mr. King because only his friends called him Howie. Muriel would regret making those delicious chocolate chip cookies for the scared brat who let them all down.

"Tommy, I'm showing you Exhibit 6," he said, placing it in front of his face. Mobey looked at Tommy, "What is the title of the document?"

"Safe Choices Certification," came the reply after a few seconds.

"And what is the date on the document?"

"May 13, 2003," replied Tommy.

"And there is a name handwritten at the bottom. That's your name, correct?" asked Mobey.

"Yes."

"And you received this for taking the Safe Choices Program at school, isn't that true, Tommy?"

"Yes."

"What was this program for?"

Tommy hesitated. Eureka! He suddenly realized what

Mobey was up to – and it wasn't good.

"It was a program about sexual abuse," the boy responded.

"You will agree with me, Tommy, that it was a program that went over in detail what is appropriate touching and what is inappropriate touching?"

Silence ensued for a few seconds.

"Tommy?" said Mobey. "I need an answer," he demanded.

"Yes," admitted Tommy. "Yes, it was."

"And you will agree with me that a teacher touching your penis, or you touching a teacher's penis is inappropriate sexual touching?" asked Mobey.

"Yes, it is, sir."

"And you were taught that in May of 2003, correct?" asked Mobey.

"Yes."

"And May of 2003 is three months before August of 2003, isn't it?"

"Yes, but." Tommy's voice trailed off; he wasn't sure what to say. He knew his answer wouldn't look good.

Tommy looked to the back of the court and shouted, "Mom!"

Judge Handy looked at him and said sternly, "You may only answer Mr. Mobey's questions."

The judge's rebuke only heightened his anxiety. How could he get himself off the witness stand as quickly as possible? It was the only question that now mattered to Tommy.

Mobey did not allow Tommy any time to compose himself. "You were lying when you said you first became aware that the alleged touching was inappropriate in August of 2003, weren't you?" he asked indignantly.

"No, no, I wasn't," he replied. "It's not like that."

"Well tell me what it's like then," demanded Mobey, feigning exasperation, shooting a look of incredulity at Tommy.

Judge Handy monitored the exchange; he would give defence counsel some leeway on testing the boy's evidence but would not allow intimidation – the precipice neared.

Tommy remained quiet for several more seconds, his mind overwhelmed.

"I guess I'm not sure," he replied.

"Did you or did you not know in May that the sexual acts you allege were wrong and inappropriate?"

Tommy didn't answer. He definitely did not remember going over this question with either his mother or Mr. Sussman. How was he to answer?

"Please answer the question," directed Judge Handy.

"I guess I did know," he replied.

"I don't want you to guess, Tommy. Did you know or didn't you know in May?"

"Objection, Your Honour," said Sussman, standing to address the court.

Before he could explain his objection, Judge Handy responded quickly, "No, he's not badgering the witness, Mr. Sussman. Tommy, answer the question."

"I did know," Tommy blurted out, exasperated, wanting it all to end.

"So, when you told the court that you only knew in August, that was incorrect, wasn't it?" pushed Mobey.

"Yes," he admitted.

Sussman felt helpless. He had no power to stop this slow-motion train wreck.

"And, in fact, you lied to this court when you testified that you only knew in August, didn't you?"

Again, Tommy paused. He didn't think he lied. Well, maybe he did. He wasn't sure. Maybe he did? He was so confused now.

"I don't think I did."

"You don't think, Tommy? You don't know what a lie is?" asked Mobey, smelling blood in the water; it was time for the shark to circle the little fish.

"I do know, yes. I do know what a lie is," replied

Tommy. What else could he say, he wondered?

"So, when you told the court that you only knew in August, it was a lie, wasn't it?

"Well...I knew it was incorrect."

"If you knew it was incorrect, then you knew it was a lie, right, Tommy?"

The young witness stood there, frozen. How was he to argue with that logic? Mobey was content to let the boy sit there in silence and let the jury take it all in. Accule comme un rat. The boy was cornered like a rat, mused Mobey. How would Tommy Henderson answer? Mobey felt sorry for the boy, observing the inexperienced swimmer treading water in rough seas, but this was his job – he couldn't be soft.

"Answer the question, Tommy, "ordered Judge Handy after giving him enough time to consider his answer.

Tommy didn't know how to fix this; he certainly did not want to admit to telling a lie in court. He heard about perjury – you could go to jail for lying in court – which would give Howie another reason to slap those handcuffs on him and lead him right out of that courtroom to a real jail cell, one with bars and no tasty chocolate chip cookies. He wanted this to be over.

"Well, I did know it was incorrect. I'm not sure that is a lie, but it could be. What I mean is, I didn't mean to lie. It was an accident. I'm sorry I lied." Tommy stammered his way through an answer; inescapably, he admitted to lying under oath to the jury.

Bingo! For Mobey, the answer was better than having your final number called for a full-card jackpot. Mobey paused. He wanted that answer to sink in with the jury. Did I just hear that answer correctly, he wondered? He knew that he did – an unbelievable admission. Is that how the jury would see it? What conclusions would they draw from it? The defence lawyer didn't want to ask one more question; he would not provide Tommy Henderson with an opportunity to wiggle out of that answer. It was a powerful ending to his cross-examination, an answer with a stench that Mobey was content to let linger in the stale air of the courtroom for as long as possible.

"Those are all my questions for this witness, Your Honour," announced Mobey.

"Thank you," replied the judge.

"Mr. Sussman, do you have any questions on re-examination of this witness?" queried the judge. Civil procedure rules provided Sussman with an opportunity to ask Tommy follow-up questions on new issues raised in Mobey's cross-examination. The prosecutor quickly considered whether asking further questions would be helpful, or detrimental, similar to the ill-advised objections from earlier in the day.

Sussman stood up. "No re-examination, Your Honour."

"Very well, then," said Judge Handy.

"Tommy, thank you. Please step down," directed the judge.

Tommy found his mother at the back; Linda waived at her shaken son, blowing him a kiss. Judge Handy raised his eyebrows, in obvious disapproval of this exchange in front of the jury, but said nothing. Howard King assisted the boy from the witness stand, escorting him through a back door, behind the jury. Relief fell on Tommy when Howie didn't slap handcuffs on him.

Mobey slowly returned to his counsel's table and took his chair beside Hiller. Tension permeated the courtroom, thicker than a Sleepy Hollow fog. Everyone recognized that Mobey had just scored big points for his client – not necessarily a knockout punch – but this wasn't boxing; he only had to raise a reasonable doubt.

Mobey was shocked that Sussman didn't accept the opportunity to re-examine Tommy Henderson. Surely Sussman could have undone some of the damage. Maybe Tommy just didn't think to look at the size of Hiller's penis? Maybe his eyes were closed? Maybe he was too traumatized to remember? Maybe he knew that the touching was inappropriate, but was too embarrassed to tell his mother earlier? There were dozens of plausible explanations; but

Sussman had a significant problem now, because he didn't take advantage of the opportunity to undo the damage. A rookie mistake, concluded Mobey.

Sussman maintained a brave and confident face in front of the jury, knowing the outcome of this trial was now in doubt. Inside, he was screaming at himself; he had neither anticipated Mobey's questions, nor prepared Tommy sufficiently.

Both lawyers studied the jurors' faces, but came to no conclusions. What were they thinking?

"Mr. Sussman, will you be calling any further witnesses?" asked Judge Handy.

Sussman did not need to call the police officers who had photographed Hiller's cabin and the experts who had analyzed the soils samples because he and Mobey had arrived at an agreed statement of facts; a detailed brief had been filed with the judge on consent, which included photographs of Hiller's cabin and the lawyer's agreement when they were taken and what they depicted. Additionally, the soil sample results were agreed to and included in the brief.

Judge Handy accepted the 121-page brief as Exhibit #7, twelve copies provided to the jury. Both lawyers had different motivations for coming to this agreement, rather than having witnesses testify. For Sussman, he did not now have to prepare for these witnesses and worry about proving the chain of custody of the physical evidence. Also, Mobey would not be able to argue that the photographs somehow distorted the accuracy of the photos because of the camera's angle, or the type of lens used. In a digital world, defence counsel employed this common technique.

Mobey's reasons were simple: He believed it was unlikely that he would be able to attack the authenticity of the photographs and samples because they were accurate. Hiller admitted to him that everything in the brief was accurate. Mobey preferred that the jurors read a report, rather than have two or three days of repetitive emotional police officer testimony reach the jurors' ears. The impact would be reduced if the evidence was presented in written form.

Sussman considered calling Linda Henderson as a witness; however, she could not provide eye-witness testimony. He was not satisfied that she could offer any evidence of significance to prove Hiller's guilt. Besides, Mobey would have his way with Linda Henderson, a woman with drug and alcohol dependency paired with serious mental health problems. He was confident that Mobey would call several witnesses – her therapists, social-service workers and previous landlords who would cast doubt on the reliability of her testimony. She might make the Crown's case worse.

George Gerontonis was not on Sussman's radar as a possible witness. As such, Sussman had no further witnesses to call and rested his case.

"No, Your Honour. The Crown rests its case."

"Mr. Mobey, will you be calling any witnesses?" asked Judge Sussman.

"Your Honour, may I have a recess to seek instructions from my client," responded Mobey.

"Of course. That is entirely reasonable."

The clock read 4:14 pm. The judge addressed the entire courtroom, "We will adjourn until 10:00 am tomorrow morning, to hear from defence witnesses or to listen to final arguments from counsel."

"All rise," announced Muriel.

And with that, Justice Handy stepped down from the bench and out of the courtroom.

Linda quickly exited the courtroom's back door of the courtroom, racing to an adjacent hallway to find her son. She couldn't believe that the trial was heading in this direction, her confidence low after Mobey made Tommy appear to be a pint-sized liar in front of the jury.

Linda found Tommy, standing with Howard; the two rushed into each other's arms and embraced.

"I'm sorry, Mom," he said, tears streaming down his face. He tucked his head under her arm to shield himself from the world.

"No need to be sorry, sweetie. It's okay," she said, holding him tightly. Tommy could smell liquor on her breath. His already-slumped shoulders drooped further in disappointment. Not again. Please, not again.

"We didn't go over those questions that lawyer asked me, Mom," sobbed Tommy, pleading for understanding.

"I know. We sure didn't," she readily agreed. "Mr. Sussman should have gone over them with you," she said, irritated, fire in her eyes.

Mobey met with Hiller, privately, after court. Hiller remained extremely nervous, but he knew that his lawyer had scored some points on his behalf; was it enough to tilt the jury in his favour? He had a crucial decision to make, perhaps the most important decision of his life; his freedom was at stake.

Mobey and Hiller huddled for an hour, discussing whether he should testify the following day. Hiller said he preferred to testify; he wanted to look at each juror and tell them that he was innocent – that he would never hurt a child. Mobey was clear; it was Hiller's sole decision, but in his experience, those that testified often regretted doing so. The accused understood his lawyer's concern after observing him dismantle Tommy Henderson in cross-examination. Yes, a child may be easier to fluster, but who knew what Sussman could accomplish. Was the trial about the truth? Or, did the outcome depend on who had the better lawyer?

Hiller asked his lawyer for his opinion; how should he proceed? Mobey thought carefully – his recommendation carried significant weight, a heavy burden for the veteran counsel. Clients always wanted a strong recommendation, to be nudged in a certain direction. If Hiller was convicted and he didn't testify, the defendant would agonize over his decision forever.

"We may have established reasonable doubt right now, Robert," suggested Mobey. "You may be acquitted based on where we are now in the trial. If you testify, you may enhance your position or you may hurt your position. The question is, do you want to take a chance testifying when you are in a fairly good position?"

"I want your opinion, Lester."

"It's totally up to you; however, I don't recommend that you testify." Mobey was always frank with his clients and he would be with Hiller, as well, if needed. He was not paid to be a cheerleader; if candour served his client's interest, he would be honest.

Mobey was concerned about several areas where Sussman would force his client to explain himself. Why did Hiller have boys to his cabin almost every weekend of the summer? This wasn't normal, healthy adult behavior, at least as Mobey understood it. Why did he have one extended bed which permitted no separation between him, an adult, and children? Why did he arrange to have children urinate off the deck, rather than in the toilet; and why would he have them piss in front of a window? The facts were unseemly at best, and extremely incriminating of the serious charges Hiller faced at its worst.

Sussman would have Hiller on the stand for hours – maybe days – asking question after question, permanently hammering these incriminating facts into their minds. That is what Mobey would do if he was in Sussman's position. It was inconceivable his client could convincingly explain these circumstances away as being innocent.

"Okay, Lester. I will follow your advice," a decision that did not now require his lawyer to brutally lay bare why he made his recommendation.

It was Mobey's experience that his innocent clients usually wanted to testify, regardless of his recommendation. However, exceptions occurred; the practical ones, even if innocent, could accept when the facts did not support them. The guilty ones, despite their professions of innocence, were less inclined to testify – worried about being tripped up in their own lies.

At 10:00 am the next morning, after Mobey advised the court that he would not be calling any witnesses, both lawyers made passionate and persuasive submissions to the jury, a process that took about six hours.

Although Linda wasn't convinced Sussman totally undid the previous day's damage with his argument to the jury, some positivism crept in; she felt better than at the end of court the previous day.

The Assistant Crown Attorney's argument to the jury essentially asked them to consider whether Tommy Henderson had any motivation to lie, highlighting the incriminating facts, such as the big bed and having the children urinate off the deck in front of the kitchen window. He focused on all of the areas that Mobey didn't want his client to have to answer on the stand.

Sussman summed up, "Ladies and Gentlemen, when you are deliberating, please consider that Tommy Henderson is ten years old. He provided consistent and credible testimony about the abuse he suffered at the hands of Robert Hiller. He has been truthful. Ask yourself this - what motivation does he have to lie to you? What evidence is there that he has an alternative motive? There is none, ladies and gentlemen. Tommy Henderson testified to multiple and repeated sexual assaults. Robert Hiller spent an inordinate amount of time, alone, with prepubescent boys at his cabin. He slept in the same bed with them. He arranged to have them urinate with their exposed genitals in full sight of him. Those are damning facts, ladies and gentlemen; they are consistent with someone who was grooming young boys for his own sexual pleasure. I urge you to return a guilty verdict on all counts. Thank you."

Sussman was handcuffed dealing with the sexual assault course that Tommy took in May. Because he failed to re-examine Tommy, he decided not to address it in his closing. Tommy's testimony on this subject would have to stand bare. He couldn't advise the jury that he screwed up and that he should have asked Tommy Henderson some more questions regarding the issue. That was not how it worked.

Sussman was not permitted to make any reference to the fact that Hiller did not testify on his own behalf; it was his constitutional right. Judge Handy would later advise the jury of this very important principle in criminal law.

Mobey was pleased to have the last word with the jury. Predictably, in his final argument, he hammered away at Tommy's admission of lying, during his testimony. He summed up his argument, emphasizing this point.

"Ladies and gentlemen, the Crown has brought this prosecution against Robert Hiller. The burden rests entirely with the Crown and the Crown alone. Robert Hiller has no obligation to call witnesses or to lead any evidence or to testify; you are not permitted to hold that against Mr. Hiller, in any way. Tommy Henderson is lying to you about being sexually assaulted. Mr. Sussman argued that Tommy Henderson has no motivation to lie. It is not Mr. Hiller's legal obligation to provide you with the reasons why he lied. That would be an impossible burden. I will provide you with an analogy. What if, out of the blue, someone accused you of selling them cocaine but you were completely innocent? And then, what if you were in court and the accuser's story did not add up? And then, the accuser admitted to lying to the jury. Would you think it was fair for you to have to prove why your accuser was lying? Of course not! And that is the exact position Robert Hiller is in today. It is unfair for him to have to prove why Tommy Henderson is lying."

Mobey let that sit in with the jury and finished up his summation.

"We already know that Tommy Henderson lied to you. He was under oath and apologized for lying. Do you know why he lied? No, it is speculative, but he lied. I can't emphasize this enough. His testimony is neither trustworthy nor credible. Other than Tommy Henderson's dubious testimony, what other evidence is there of a crime? Absolutely nothing. There is a doubt of Mr. Hiller's guilt and that doubt is reasonable."

After Mobey finished, Judge Handy addressed the jury, explaining that regardless of their personal opinions, their solemn duty required that they follow the law as instructed.

"The Defendant, Robert Hiller, has pleaded not guilty.

The burden of proof on the Crown is to prove beyond a reasonable doubt that the Defendant is guilty of the crimes charged. This burden is absolute and never shifts to the Defendant.

"The Defendant has no burden to call any witness or provide any evidence in a criminal trial. The Defendant has elected not to testify, which is his right. Under no circumstances does the law permit you, the jurors, to make any inference of guilt from the fact that the Defendant did not testify.

"Importantly, the Defendant is presumed to be innocent of the charges laid against him. As such, while deliberating, you must presume the Defendant to be innocent until, and only if, you are satisfied that the Crown has proven the Defendant guilty beyond a reasonable doubt.

"A reasonable doubt is one that is based upon common sense. It is a doubt that a reasonable person has after carefully considering the evidence presented in this trial. A reasonable doubt is not a speculation or a whimsical doubt. It is a doubt which would cause a reasonable person to question the guilt of the Defendant. You will now be excused to the jury room to begin your deliberations."

And with that, each of the twelve jurors rose and left for the jury room to decide the fate of Robert Hiller.

After Judge Handy left the courtroom, the two lawyers also shook hands.

"Well done, Lester," said Sussman.

"And you, Jonathon," replied Mobey, although he only half meant it.

Outside of the courtroom, Sussman approached Tommy at his mother's side. He placed his hand on his head and gently tussled his red hair. "You did great, buddy," he said.

"I'm very proud of you."

Sussman looked at Linda. "Can I speak to you privately for a moment?" he asked, motioning her to the side. The smell of alcohol was unmistakable.

"Listen, you know that I believe everything that Tommy

said, but..."

Linda cut him off. "I know, Mr. Sussman. I know about reasonable doubt; I saw what happened in there yesterday," she said, perturbed. "This is exactly what I was concerned about," her voice becoming louder. "I guess you believe there won't be a conviction?" she asked, her irritancy made clear with a scrunched face and clenched hands.

"I don't know," he replied. "I'm sorry." He looked at her, solemnly. "As you can see, the system is not a perfect one."

"No kidding," she retorted. "I like you, Jonathon, but I guess you're not that perfect either because you're responsible also," she accused. "You are in charge here aren't you, damn it?" she yelled. "You are in charge, aren't you?" she asked again, the alcohol fueling her attack. Everyone in the vicinity watched Sussman's beratement unfold, including Mobey and Hiller who stood fifty feet away.

Linda could not hold it in any longer. Her tear glands released a waterfall that put Niagara Falls to shame, overwhelmed not just by the day, but by the last year; the entire drawn-out legal process that had pushed her to a breaking point.

Tommy gazed up at his mother, the guilt of performing poorly in court crushing him. He recalled her twenty-fourth birthday, the similar signs undeniable.

"I'm so sorry. I am. But we haven't lost yet," said Sussman in a hushed tone, embarrassed by the spectacle that he had not anticipated. "It's just unclear, now. That's all I can say," he said, dejectedly. Sussman did not advise Linda that he did his best because he hadn't. Did he prepare Tommy enough? Maybe he should have done more? He would only know the answers to those questions after the verdict was returned by the jury.

It was a restless night for both lawyers. A conviction would result in a prison sentence for Mobey's client accompanied by ridicule and shame. For Sussman, although trite, it was about justice; he had also made a promise to Linda when he encouraged Tommy to testify. The prosecutor promised them that everything would be okay; that was in doubt now. Nobody gave a shit about his gold medal from Osgoode, chastising himself. He may have just dropped the ball and allowed a dangerous predator to walk free. How would he forgive himself? The next child's emotional scars would fill his conscience if Hiller got away with it.

Lester felt that he had performed well. No matter the final outcome, he did his best; he harboured no regrets. His client had a fighting chance, despite odds that did not favour him.

Except for listening to the verdict in Hiller's trial and the remote possibility of appealing a decision, Mobey had completed his final trial, his last act as a barrister and solicitor. He celebrated his retirement that night, sitting alone in his living room in front of a roaring fire, as he was prone to do. There would be no gathering with his fellow lawyers and friends at the local pub, full of well wishes, over-the-top toasts and slaps on the back congratulating him for a storied career. Instead, he invited an old companion that had not joined him for decades – a bottle of scotch – an unceremonious reunion.

The avid military history buff read the words of the Greek historian, Diodorus Siculus, describing how the undermanned Spartans used the cover of night to overwhelm the Persians. Although he probably knew it all along, Mobey came to an inescapable conclusion - that brilliant brain of ours had a flaw comparable to that suspect heel of the great Greek warrior, Achilles.

Mobey reclined in his chair, with nobody to call, and poured his second shot of Johnny Walker Black, reflecting on Robert Hiller and the day's proceedings. Was his client thinking of him at this moment? Probably not. As the liquor took hold, he drowned himself in hazy speculation, cursing at Linda Henderson. What mother would have allowed their boy to attend Robert Hiller's cabin? What the fuck was she thinking?

His recommendation to Hiller not to testify weighed on

him. Despite the law and the clear instruction from Judge Handy, he knew it was impossible for the jury to completely disregard the fact that Robert did not testify. Jurors are human beings, not robots.

Mobey poured his last drink and watched the whisky drizzle down over the ice cubes. Four drinks, each with double shots, was excessive for a man who had not touched alcohol in about thirty-five years; he wasn't strong enough tonight. "Mato," he said out loud. "Mato," he repeated louder. Why did Raymond have to call him that? The name had been suffocating him ever since he reunited with his friend.

Once the jurors settled themselves in the jury room after Judge Handy's instruction, deliberations began. The men and women sat under two flickering fluorescent lights. The room, stark and bare, contained only twelve chairs and an extended board-room table that required refinishing.

It became evident early, that the jurors would have difficulty arriving at an immediate and unanimous decision. During the first couple of hours of deliberations, as discussions progressed, the possibility of a hung jury was real, given the lack of consent and diverse opinions.

Mobey had participated in thirty-eight jury trials over his career, which made him somewhat of an expert on the matter of jury psychology. For the first twenty years of his career, he read many of the leading books on the subject and attended seminars that presented cutting-edge research on how juries deliberate. He even published a few articles himself on the subject. Two decades in, he concluded that there were two overriding conditions that determined how a jury member would decide a case, both of which made it difficult to predict jury decisions.

First: jury members filter everything based on their own experiences and biases developed during their own lives. The second: is how easily a juror is influenced by fellow jurors. Certain jury members become fixed into a position and won't budge, whereas others are more easily moved from their original position. One or two dominant jurors can influence and even change the rest of the members' positions.

Mobey frequently thought of his late uncle, Franklin, as intellectual, but hard headed. Family debates at family gatherings in his youth fostered his love for debate. He could count on two things at every get-together: his great-aunt would serve a god-awful-tasting tomato aspic and Franklin wouldn't change his mind on any issue, regardless of the arguments and different perspectives around the dinner table. If such a dogged refusal to change one's position was based on sound principled analysis, then Franklin's persistence was to be admired. Mobey referred to this as good stubbornness.

However, after years of observing Uncle Franklin, Mobey discerned that he had the bad stubbornness, a stubbornness borne out of low confidence, or perhaps low self-esteem, with a view that changing one's mind was somehow a personal failure rather than an intellectual awakening.

Mobey's goal in court was to have his client acquitted; often, the ideal juror for that purpose carried the bad stubbornness.

CHAPTER SEVEN

The Law of Averages

Once the jury in *R. v. Hiller* commenced deliberation, Stephanie Rogers, a middle-aged mother of two young children, began the discussion. The daycare provider thought it was impossible that Tommy Henderson would fabricate such a story – she agreed with Sussman.

"There is no way on Earth that my children, especially at Tommy Henderson's age, could ever have come up with such an elaborate tale unless it was true," she said. "I can't believe for one minute that he made up that story. Why would he lie?"

Paulette Jenkins, a twenty-two-year-old receptionist agreed with Rogers. "I just don't see him making it up," she remarked. "I agree with Mr. Sussman too, and it's not because he's such a good-looking guy," she said, smiling.

Roger Duncan, a quiet but confident retired school teacher, spoke next, "I understand both your views; but it troubles me that Tommy provided inconsistent testimony about his understanding of sexual abuse. I'm having some difficulty getting around that."

"Well, it bothers me that Robert Hiller did not take the stand," expressed Henry James, juror number eleven. "If a child accused you of those terrible crimes, why wouldn't you take the stand and deny it. It doesn't make sense."

The jury foreman, Carl Flemming, patiently listened. Before speaking, he wanted to hear from all the jurors, but decided to respond to James' comment, "It is necessary that we follow Judge Handy's instructions. We cannot draw any conclusion from the fact that Robert Hiller did not testify," he implored.

"Easier said than done," replied Duncan. "Wouldn't you want to get up there and tell a jury that you are innocent, in a situation like this?"

"It doesn't matter what I would do," explained Flemming. "If we don't follow the judge's instructions, we aren't fulfilling our obligation to the justice system; we would also be letting Tommy Henderson and Robert Hiller down!" he argued emphatically. "We must follow the law. And, I know you were kidding Paulette, but we can't care about anyone's personality or how good looking someone is."

"Who else hasn't spoken yet that would like to?" asked Flemming.

Amy Lightfoot spoke up, "The test is beyond a reasonable doubt; that's what the judge told us. Even if I believe Hiller likely did it, that's not the test," she explained. "I absolutely have doubts. Are my doubts reasonable? I don't know. She was accustomed to dealing with many opinions and personalities in her middle-manager role.

"All I know is that a man's life is in our hands," said juror number ten, Walter Jewel. "This man is going to jail if we find him guilty; his life will be destroyed. We owe it to him not to jump to a conclusion, to carefully review the evidence and apply the law as we were instructed," he stated unequivocally.

The other eleven jurors nodded their heads in agreement with Jewel's statement.

"This is a difficult decision that we have to make," said Flemming. "The fact we have all these opinions and issues to discuss proves it. I agree, we're in no rush to make our decision."

The twelve remained quiet for a few minutes in pensive reflection; the weight of their responsibility set in – no middle ground existed – Robert Hiller would be set free, or, he was headed to prison for an extended period. What if they set him free in error? What about the next child? They all understood pedophiles often abused multiple victims.

"Let's remind ourselves that the Crown has the burden of proving guilt," explained Flemming. "I haven't made up my mind yet, but the Crown has to prove guilt beyond a reasonable doubt; Robert Hiller does not have to prove his innocence," he reminded his fellow jurors. "Lester Mobey's argument that it is not our responsibility to determine why

Tommy Henderson may be lying had a strong impression on me. Although, I don't think it's wrong to ask ourselves why he might lie. In fact, I think it's our responsibility to ask the question."

"But, why would that little kid lie about something like that? asked Jewel.

"I understood Mr. Mobey's point to be that if we can't come up with a reason, it does not necessarily follow that Tommy Henderson must be telling the truth," explained Flemming. "Does everyone agree with that proposition?"

Before giving anyone time to answer, juror number eight, Samuel Franks spoke for the first time, "The kid might not be lying. It could be the kid has misidentified Hiller. Maybe Hiller's twin brother was also at the cabin, or someone that looks like him."

"Or, maybe the kid is psychotic, or he is an alien," scoffed Stephanie Rogers. "There's absolutely no evidence of those propositions."

"Our doubt has to be reasonable; there must be some evidence to base a decision on. I agree with that," said Flemming.

The jury was an hour into deliberations when juror number nine, Perry Fields, joined the debate. The mathematician and university professor had been listening intently to the opinions in the jury room, but only now decided to participate.

"Has anyone ever heard of the Law of large numbers?" asked Fields, not expecting an answer. "According to the law, the average of the results obtained from a large number of clinical trials should be close to the expected value and will tend to become closer to the expected value as more trials are performed."

Every other juror shook their head in confusion, quizzical looks on their faces.

"I'm not following you," said Paulette Jenkins. "I'm not sure anyone has."

Fields pulled a quarter out of his pocket. "Let's say I

flipped a coin. What are your chances of getting heads?"

"Fifty percent," replied Jenkins.

"And what are the chances of tails coming up?" asked Fields.

"Fifty percent, of course", said Jenkins, chuckling.

Fields proceeded to flip the coin ten times on the jury table, with all the jurors huddled around, observing the spontaneous experiment. Flemming took a pad of paper and kept a tally of the outcome.

"Seven heads and three tails," he announced, to a mixture of laughter and smiling.

"That's why I always choose heads!" laughed Walter Jewel.

"Okay, what's your point, Perry?" asked Flemming.

"If I flipped this coin one million times, the outcome still won't be exactly fifty percent for each of the two possibilities, but it will be significantly closer than the 70-30 split we just witnessed," explained Perry. "Whether I flip this coin ten times, or one million times, Paulette's answer of fifty percent would have been wrong."

Perry Fields scanned the faces of fellow jurors; it was evident that some of them understood his point while others struggled to comprehend it.

"Let me give you another example," offered Fields. Let's say this jury was tasked with deciding, beyond a reasonable doubt, whether Robert Hiller developed Guillain-Barre Syndrome, an autoimmune syndrome, because he had the flu shot. Let's say there is a one-in-a-thousand chance of developing Guillain-Barre Syndrome if you took the flu shot, and a one-in-ten-thousand chance of developing it even if you didn't take the flu shot – odds that are quite accurate."

The professor, now in his teaching comfort zone, had captured the jury room, all eyes fixed on him as he attempted to make his point.

"If a woman was given the flu shot and then developed Guillain-Barre Syndrome two days later, is it more likely that she developed it because she had the flu shot – or, is it more likely she would have developed it, anyway, even if she had not received the flu shot?"

"Because of the flu shot," replied Flemming. "The close temporal connection between taking the flu shot and developing the illness would bring you to that conclusion."

"Sound reasoning," agreed Fields, looking around the table at each of the jurors. "But statistically, there will be a number of people who took the flu shot and were just about to develop the illness, anyway. That's what you call a coincidence; and, it's a statistical certainty there will be many coincidences. If juries always came to the conclusion that the illness was caused because of the flu shot because it developed shortly after taking the flu shot, the conclusion would have to be wrong, sometimes."

The jurors remained quiet, absorbing Field's second example, most of them nodding their heads confirming that they understood.

"What if, on the occasions when the jury was wrong, a man went to jail for five years because of the incorrect conclusion?" Fields raised his eyebrows to the group.

"What are you saying, Perry?" asked Flemming.

Fields went on to discuss English scholar William Blackstone's often repeated principle that it's better that ten-guilty men go free than one innocent man be convicted.

"I'm saying that even if the odds point to guilt, Hiller could be innocent based on the principles of my two examples. Now, combine that with Tommy Henderson's admission that he lied to us – it creates a reasonable doubt in my mind. I'm not prepared to speculate on the boy's motivation. Maybe it was an honest mistake. Maybe he was confused. But, maybe not. I'm not prepared to send a man to jail when I have this doubt."

The jury continued to deliberate. Sussman's failure to re-examine Tommy after Mobey's cross-examination troubled the jurors. Why didn't he? The question remained at the forefront of their discussions. What were they missing?

Tommy Henderson devoted an entire day to learning the

difference between good touching and bad touching. How could he not understand the touching over the summer was abusive before he told his mother in August? Legitimate reasons could exist for the delay in reporting the abuse right away – but that was entirely different than knowing Hiller's actions constituted abuse. When given the chance, Sussman did not assist in clarifying the answers to these questions, which was not Robert Hiller's failure.

The jurors took two further hours that day and four the next, reviewing and rehashing the evidence. One very influential voice existed in the room – Perry Fields.

Finally, at 1:40 pm, a day removed from final submissions, the jury foreperson notified the court clerk that the jury had reached a verdict; Muriel summoned the lawyers to the courthouse.

At 3:20 pm, Judge Handy sat himself down behind the bench and asked Howard King to bring the jury in, the bailiff returning in thirty seconds with the jurors in single-file formation behind him.

Upon their entry, some of them looked at Hiller squarely in the eyes, a sign that Mobey considered positive, although the observation was not determinative of the jury's finding. Sussman also witnessed the eye contact; his heart slightly sank, but he did not want to construe too much into the unscientific conclusion.

"Have you reached a verdict, Mr. Foreperson?" asked Judge Handy.

"Yes, we have, Your Honour," replied Flemming.

"Is the verdict unanimous?"

"It is, Your Honour."

"On the first count of sexual assault in the first degree, how do you find?" asked the Judge.

"Not guilty," announced Flemming.

Linda gasped, followed by extensive murmuring in the courtroom. She lowered her head, commenced rubbing her pendant and covered her mouth with her hand.

Judge Handy verged on admonishing the courtroom;

however quiet returned swiftly, so he didn't bother.

"On count two of sexual assault in the first degree, how do you find?"

"Not guilty."

Jury foreman Flemming went ahead and pronounced Robert Hiller not guilty on all counts.

Hiller stood, hugged Mobey and released a deep sigh, the tension dissipating from his body as his nightmare came to an end.

The Assistant Crown Attorney's shoulders slumped. Damn it. Damn it. He knew that verdict was coming.

"Members of the jury, the court expressed its gratitude for your service," offered Judge Handy. "Bailiff, you may excuse the jury."

Stoned-faced, each of the twelve jurors left the courtroom, their duty now complete.

Sussman was not used to failure. He had lost cases before; sometimes, when the evidence was in, a not guilty verdict was reasonable. This case was different. The system had let the boy down; the "gold medalist" wonder boy had let him down – it stung.

Linda left the court without waiting to talk to Sussman, which he was grateful for – he didn't know what to say to her anyway.

The prosecutor had no reason to have any further contact with Linda Henderson. Their relationship abruptly ended once the judgment was rendered, which was understandable. Still, the ending felt strange. After an intense year, of listening to the fears and woes of the Henderson family and fostering mutual trust, their connection went beyond the mere professional; this is how he viewed it. But circumstance created their relationship – not friendship – and those circumstances had finished. He truly believed he would never see the Hendersons again.

CHAPTER EIGHT

Karma

Surprisingly, three months after the trial, fate intervened; Jonathon Sussman found himself knocking on Linda Henderson's apartment door.

Linda struggled mightily since the verdict, although she had grappled with her emotions for the last decade of her life. While faring better than his mother, gauging Tommy's mental state was difficult. His mother extended modest efforts to talk with him, attempting to discern what turmoil swirled within him, but Tommy refused to engage – retreating to the confines of his room.

When Linda opened her apartment door to find Jonathon standing at the threshold in jeans and a casual button-up denim shirt, she jumped. Without his eyeglasses and perfectly pressed suit, he appeared much younger – almost boyish.

"Hi Linda," he greeted her, barely smiling. "May I come in? I need to speak with you."

"Of course. Come in," she replied, somewhat reluctantly given the unkempt state of her apartment. She directed him to the kitchen table, having already concluded the drop-in visit went beyond social. The coldness in his blue eyes spoke clearly.

"I've made coffee; it's instant. Would you like some?" she asked.

"Yes, thank you," replied her visitor.

Tommy had been laying in his room when Sussman arrived, playing Killer Comet. His mother had purchased a small, garage-sale television; Tommy devoted hours playing video games in the confines of his only sanctuary. Otherwise, he stared at the posters of his favourite professional athletes, taped on his bedroom walls – dreaming that someday he would become a famous athlete, like Sidney Crosby or Miguel Cabrera. Those dreams transported him to another place, a respite where everyone admired him. He signed autographs for cheering fans who thanked him for his generosity, when he had so many other important things to do and places to go.

Tommy had been daydreaming extensively lately – his therapists explained that he dreamed far too often; apparently, it was not healthy. Tommy reasoned they had it all wrong. Dreaming meant that he had hope – hope for a better future and life; he needed hope. His psychologist had a bizarre name for his daydreaming – short-term detachment, which sounded awfully negative. Apparently, Tommy Henderson was avoiding his past trauma; but Tommy wasn't convinced that detaching was terrible. He had his reasons. After all, telling a kid not to dream was like telling a bird not to fly.

When Tommy heard voices in the kitchen, he hopped off his bed and crept to his slightly ajar bedroom door. Crouching down, he placed his ear to the crack, recognizing Sussman's voice. Small talk ensued before the lawyer's tone turned serious.

"Listen, Linda, there is something I need to tell you; I wanted you to hear it from me, first," he said.

"Okay," she replied, curiously, dread climbing aboard.

"Robert Hiller is dead," he said, his tone too matter-of-fact for the grenade he lobbed at his host, the projectile having the capability of tearing her into a million tiny pieces.

Linda's jaw dropped. "What happened?" she asked, the concern obvious on her face.

"He hung himself last night at his cabin; the suicide note he left stated that he couldn't take it anymore, or words to that effect," explained Sussman. "I didn't want either of you hearing it on the news or from some other source."

The news stunned Linda, her body accelerating towards shock at lightning speed. She pulled her elbows off the table, grabbed at her pendant and started rubbing it vigorously with her index finger. She slumped back into her chair, not believing what she just heard.

"I feel weak, Jonathon. I might be sick," she said as she put her head into her hands.

Silence followed – Linda battling to compose herself;

the mismatched fight had predictable results.

"Perhaps it's rough justice for what he did to Tommy. I don't know," he said, more as a question than a statement. "It's boorish of me to think that way, but at least he can't harm any more children." Sussman searched for relief in the mother's eyes – the monster now disposed of; he wasn't sure what he found. Perhaps the prospect of relief belonged in fairy tales with such matters.

Tommy listened intently to the kitchen conversation; he couldn't believe it, the news incomprehensible. His chest pounded louder with every word escaping the lawyer's mouth; it became deafening, causing him to look down to make sure his heart had not escaped the confines of his body. The boy jumped back onto his bed in response to Hiller's suicide, sobbing face-first into his pillow to muffle his whimpering.

How could anyone be happy that someone killed himself? How could Jonathon Sussman think like that, the young boy's face buried deeply.

Detach Tommy, he ordered himself. Please detach. He tried but he couldn't, the vision of Robert Hiller hanging from the cabin taking control, bullying him to focus on his former teacher's lifeless body dangling from the rafters.

More than one way existed to detach yourself from reality, thought Tommy; Robert Hiller found it – a permanent way. Dreaming must not have worked well for him, either. The young boy lifted his chin and scanned his bedroom ceiling, knowing that no beams existed; he checked anyway. Tommy didn't believe he had the courage to go through with it – his mother's messy and failed attempt on his mind – and how she wore that black velvet bracelet on her left wrist to hide that nasty two-inch scar. Surely, an easier way existed. Maybe he could drift away on a cloud, falling into a forever blissful sleep?

Linda rose from the kitchen table and thanked Jonathon for coming; she began walking towards the door, signalling that their visit had ended. Jonathon was about to ask about Tommy's well-being, but instead, accepted the unambiguous cue and got up himself. He was not inclined to have an extended conversation. Sticking his head in the sand about Tommy served a purpose; he didn't have the strength today.

Sussman grabbed the doorknob, slightly opened the door and turned back.

"Take care, Linda," he said solemnly, scanning the drab apartment and the grey walls that had not been painted in twenty years. Where were the photos, artwork, or anything that demonstrated that the apartment was a home? He didn't want the answer to that question either.

A week's worth of piled dishes in the sink, several empty pizza boxes stacked beside the overflowing garbage can and several empty beer cases had Sussman considering whether he had a legal obligation to contact child protection services; however, he didn't have the appetite to make that telephone call, at least not today.

"Linda, you and Tommy have been through a lot," said Sussman. "Can I put you in touch with Victim Services or arrange for some counselling? It's important."

"I appreciate the offer, but we are dealing with it," replied Linda, her dark circles and feather weight contradicting her response. "Listen, Jonathon, the things I said after the trial – I was out of line. I'm really sorry. The stress of the trial got to me. I hope you understand."

"No apology required, Linda. You weren't entirely wrong with your criticism," he admitted. "All the best," he said, shutting the door behind him.

Four days later, Robert Hiller's funeral was held at St. Allouette's Presbyterian Church on Nowak Street in London. A dreary, grey sky served as a backdrop against the church's roof, gargoyles and steeple for those making their way up the sixteen stairs to the front door, umbrellas activated to protect against the steady drizzle. For the spiritual, the bleakness of the weather served as a sign from God that reflected the solemnness of the occasion. For the agnostics and atheists, it was simply apropos.

Exactly twenty-five people attended the funeral, a scant

figure that included Lester Mobey, who made the mental tally, sitting at the back. Maybe he shouldn't have been surprised at the poor turnout, but he was – or perhaps it was only disappointment. Maybe the rain contributed to the modest tally, either a misguided assumption, or a damning commentary on Hiller's friends and acquaintances who wouldn't brave a few raindrops to pay their last respects.

Raymond expected hundreds to attend, asking the church staff to add another fifty chairs in addition to the regular seating capacity. The popular teacher had thousands of former students, friends and colleagues who would need to line up in the street waiting to pay their respects – Raymond's assumption missed the mark. The low turnout was so incomprehensible that Raymond double-checked the funeral notices to make sure the wrong address or date was not inadvertently placed. Where were his close friends from the Rotary, Kiwanis and curling clubs?

Mobey had found an empty seat at the back of the room, which was not difficult given the sparse attendance. He put his coat on the empty chair to his left and his black fedora on the empty chair to his right, attempting to create the appearance of a more crowded room; the pathetic attempt felt short.

People say that you can tell how many lives you've touched in your life by how many people come to your funeral. Surely, Hiller's number exceeds twenty-five. Damn, he said to himself. Twenty-five goddamn people.

Even those adept at avoiding any thought of their own mortality, the mental dodging of the uncomfortable subject was nearly impossible at a funeral. Mobey scanned the room, wondering how many would show up to his own funeral, remembering the paltry number, zero, who had attended his retirement party. Twenty-five might be shooting high, determined Mobey. His parents had died years ago and although married once, long ago, he never remarried; he had no children. Other than Raymond, who would mourn his death? Shit, he hated funerals.

Mobey had just exhausted every ounce of his skill and determination to keep Hiller out of a jail – to keep his client out of a dastardly prison cell so he could maintain his status as a free citizen. The irony that the man preferred the end of a noose a few months later was inescapable.

Hiller trusted his life to Mobey, their solicitor/client relationship intense. Yet, the two had not spoken since the jury rendered its verdict. A gulf existed between who was a friend and who was an acquaintance. Whereas a friend would drop the phone, in shock, if told that you committed suicide, acquaintances would spend a moment acknowledging the tragedy, but continue on with their busy lives. Hiller was nothing more than an acquaintance.

Being a workaholic for forty years cramps your social life – it cramps all facets of your life. John Lennon had it right, *Life is what happens to you while you're busy making other plans*.

Hiller remained a pariah in death; lying in a casket changed nothing.

The service commenced with some introductory welcoming words from the minister, followed by the requisite prayers. Hiller's thirteen-year-old niece, followed with a poem, her trembling hands making it difficult to hold the paper she was reading from still. She described her uncle as wonderful, a man that never forgot her birthday and taught her to ride a bike.

Raymond stepped to the podium to deliver the eulogy, moving slowly with a hunched back, the weight of the world too heavy for that body.

In *Life of Pi*, one of Mobey's favourite books, the protagonist, Piscine Molitor, aimlessly drifts on a raft in the Indian Ocean, a Bengal tiger his only companion. As starvation took hold, Piscine laments that "hunger changes everything you thought you knew about yourself." With great regret and anguish, the vegetarian violates his deeply religious principles by killing fish to keep both him and his accidental tiger passenger alive.

In Mobey's view, Piscine had it right, but only partially. It is desperation that changes everything you thought you knew about yourself – and can cause you to violate your principles in ways you never could have imagined.

Raymond was sixty-seven-years old and a widower of thirteen years. His wife, Robert's mother, died from breast cancer, a difficult experience that brought him and his son closer while leaning on each other.

Raymond, his eyes red from crying, had aged ten years since he rushed to Mobey's office, his hair whiter and thinner now – his waist shrunken by two inches. He presented unkempt, a departure for a man who cared about appearances.

Raymond looked out over the gathering and began, "It's never easy to bury a child; it's the hardest thing I've ever done. To know that your child was in that much pain – was that desperate and couldn't come to me…" His voice cracked and then choked to a halt.

After a few seconds, Raymond continued, "is my biggest failure in life. I'm grateful that my late wife is not here today; it would've been too much. Robert was born forty-two years ago. I remember it like it was yesterday."

Raymond paused, took a drink of water and went on, "I have many great memories. Two summers ago, we spent a week canoeing in Algonquin Park. We talked for seven days straight, discussing everything while we took in all the majestic landscape.

"Robert told me things that I didn't know about him: his dreams, his fears, how passionate he was about teaching and that he had applied to earn his Master of Education degree on a part-time basis. The two of us were portaging in this particularly difficult area; Robert laughed at himself, explaining that he tackled the New York Times crossword every day, but it was challenging and he considered himself somewhat inept. Robert said to me, 'Dad, do you know what the most common answer is for a middle name clue in the New York Times crossword? It's Lee.' It was trivial, but it was part of who he was and it was a privilege to learn of it. Better late than never, as they say.

"On the fifth day of our trip as we gently paddled past a beaver dam, out of the blue, Robert told me that he loved me; I'm not sure why he said it, then and there. I didn't say 'I love you' back; it's my biggest regret. If I could bring back one moment, it would be that one."

Raymond looked upwards towards the sky, "Today Robert, I want you to know how much I love you."

Mobey doubted that a single person in attendance didn't know that Robert was charged with sexually assaulting Tommy Henderson, the proverbial elephant in the room. They didn't know that Robert's acquittal didn't end his year-long nightmare – not at all.

Naturally, relief came with his acquittal. He had been suspended from teaching for over a year and was excited to return to his old life and normalcy. Although it was not one with bars, he had been locked in prison since his arrest; with the end of the trial, the shackles were finally coming off – or so he believed. However, the stench remained; even when you clean dog shit off your shoe, the odour lingers.

Hiller's school board refused to reinstate him. His principal explained that he had received at least a dozen calls from parents requesting that their children not be placed in Robert Hiller's class, acquittal or not. The sentiment was clear - Hiller had a good lawyer, who got him off on a technicality.

As one parent put it to the principal, "I don't care if there is a half-percent chance that he did it, my son is not going into a classroom taught by Robert Hiller."

The board decided that it would conduct its own investigation, the length of time required to complete the process undetermined. Hiller's union representative warned him that the inquiry would be dragged out forever – the board did not want him back.

Robert's ex-wife, Catherine, sat in the back-row, sobbing quietly. Robert's ex-girlfriend, Leanne Shine, also sat in the back row, weeping uncontrollably. Under different circumstances, Raymond would have chuckled at the two of them, wailing away, but the occasion prevented him from enjoying that moment.

Leanne and Robert started dating shortly before Hiller was charged. Initially, she remained supportive after his arrest, but the stress on the relationship became overwhelming as the months passed. She was confident that Robert Hiller was not capable of hurting a child in that way; she knew him. They were lovers, after all. It was impossible to hide that sort of evil.

Her friends constantly asked her how she could be with a man who might be responsible for such disgusting acts. Co-workers tossed her the odd snide remark about dating a pedophile. She believed in Hiller's innocence and in the "innocent until proven guilty" principle but eventually, the stress and aggravation became too much. The principle was a noble one, but a farce in the court of public opinion. Despite Robert's pleading and begging, she ended it. Even as the tears streamed down his face, and knowing his supporters had dwindled to single digits, she was resolute in her decision.

The break-up was devastating to Hiller – one further cascading effect of his arrest.

As Leanne listened to the eulogy, she knew that she played a role in pushing her former lover to sling that rope over that beam – the admission was too much for her soul to absorb.

Two weeks after his acquittal, Hiller attended his school to pick up some papers that he was asked to sign by the principal. He finally felt comfortable showing his face in the school, fresh off his court victory, but when he returned to the parking lot, he found his car covered in raw eggs. A note tucked under his windshield wiper read, S*tay away from our kids, molester*!

Naively, Robert believed his friends would start calling him after his acquittal. He knew exactly what they would say, "Congratulations, Robert. I'm sorry I haven't called, but I always knew that you got a raw deal. Let's grab a beer Friday night and shoot the shit." But no calls came – and his went unreturned.

"Thank you for coming today," said Raymond; and with that, he stepped down to end the service, only to collapse into the arms of the minister. His body, exhausted from the grief, heaved in and out as he cried into the minister's shoulder.

Hiller, stuck in limbo, had no idea if he could ever teach again. The social shunning became unbearable. He wasn't even sure that his own father believed in his innocence one hundred percent, although Raymond never wavered with his support. Still, the way that his father looked at him changed.

Hiller spent most of his savings on Mobey, but that was the least of his problems. At least Mobey earned his money.

In the end, it was too much for Hiller, his life turned into a nightmare, becoming persona non grata everywhere that was important to him. From the day of his arrest, when he cried himself to sleep in the cold and dark jail cell, to an old friend who crossed the street earlier in the day with her children to avoid talking to Hiller, there had not been one day of peace.

So, with the consumption of a bottle of Jack Daniels and a handful of sleeping pills, prescribed for his anxiety and depression, Hiller had just enough will to sling a rope over that beam and hang himself.

CHAPTER NINE

What are the Odds?

Professor Smyth stood at the front of the classroom staring at the eighty-six University of Toronto second-year students who took her sociology class, *Groups and Organizations*. It was her last class before the final exam, delivering a lecture and summarizing the important points from the year's material.

Twenty-year-old Lester Mobey sat in the front row, listening intently and chuckling to himself about the circumstances that brought him into Sociology 101. Nevertheless, he had genuine interest in the course; he desired to be a lawyer someday and believed that the course would be relevant.

While completing his university undergraduate degree in the Honours Military History program at the University of Toronto, Mobey decided between his first and second year he would pursue a law degree after completing his undergraduate degree. Entrance into law school was highly competitive, with thousands applying for a couple hundred sought-after spots in any particular law school. Admittedly, young Mobey carried a dose of pretension with him during university – explaining to whoever would listen that he was in the Honours History program, when saying history would suffice. But he took his high-brow mentality to a new level in his second year, advising everyone that he was in pre-law, when no such program existed; he had neither applied nor been accepted to law school yet.

Because excellent undergraduate marks would play an important role in successful admission to law school, Mobey started searching for "bird" courses that would inflate his grade-point average.

While at a dorm party, Mobey was pontificating about the importance of lawyering and explaining his pre-law strategy to a bunch of sorority sisters, when he put his foot squarely in his mouth. He announced to a full room that he was considering taking sociology or anthropology as his bird course, a statement that irked Joan Cullen, who was in the midst of a double major in sociology and anthropology.

"Do you even know the difference between anthropology and sociology?" she asked him, indignantly – her dagger of a glare fixed on him with one hand on her hip, waiting for an answer. Five of Joan's friends stood beside her in solidarity, waiting for the ass in front of them to answer. The women had already wondered how many times the pompous jerk could say pre-law in one conversation before his latter incendiary comment set Joan off.

Lester was taken aback. He didn't know the difference, exactly, and blushed with embarrassment while searching for a response; he could think of nothing to say – no witty comeback to illustrate his exceptional intellect.

As Mobey's face turned a brilliant shade of red, Joan showed no mercy, "You look like a bloody tomato! What do you have to say for yourself?" she demanded.

Mobey stood there, squirming under the spotlight. He looked to his friend and roommate, Raymond Hiller, to save him from the awkward situation but the cavalry did not arrive.

"You do resemble a tomato, something between the shade of a beefsteak and cherry tomato," said Raymond, who could not resist piling on, laughing at his own joke.

To Mobey's surprise and relief, all five of the women joined Raymond in laughter, reducing the tension.

"I'm sorry!" squeaked Mobey, staring at Joan, his eyes asking for forgiveness.

Mobey eventually learned the difference between anthropology and sociology when Joan explained it to him on their first date. He even took a couple of courses, including *Groups and Organizations* with Joan, which were not "bird" courses, but quite challenging.

Lester and Joan engaged in debate for hours about what it meant to be human and the influence of groups on individual behaviour. They agreed the formation of groups was essential in what it meant to be human.

Most nicknames are ephemeral, but some stick – even if ridiculous. Mobey detested being called Tomato for the rest of his university career – he was a serious fellow; he begged Joan to call him something else.

"Call me Big Lester, Big Mobey or Mobes. I don't care, but please, anything but Tomato," he pleaded, but to no avail.

By the time he arrived at law school, only Raymond and Joan referred to him as Tomato – the nickname morphing to Mato by then.

Mobey married Joan in the summer following his graduation from law school; when offering her vows in front of the Justice of the Peace at City Hall, she promised to take Lester "Tomato" Mobey as her lawfully wedded husband.

Raymond and Joan's best friend, Lydia, smirked, knowing the groom hated his nickname, but they were mistaken on that special day.

As Mobey stared lovingly into Joan's eyes, he understood true love. In that moment, he absolutely loved the nickname, Tomato; he looked forward to his wife calling him Tomato for the rest of his life.

Tragically, the number of people who referred to Mobey as Mato was reduced to one, when Joan died in a terrible automobile accident that very night on the way home from celebrating their wedding. Whether it was because of Mobey's ill-advised final glass of wine, or his lack of sleep, when the groom dozed off and failed to navigate a bend on Highway 8, everything changed in his life, forever.

His new Honda, purchased two days previously, skidded off the road and struck a tree on the passenger side, the sound of twisting metal and shattering glass piercing the silence of the night. When the automobile came to a rest, eerie silence ensued lasting twenty seconds while their bodies released a wave of endorphins to block the pain signals, momentarily fooling the brain as to the trauma that had occurred.

Mobey, blood trickling into his eyes, looked over at Joan in her seat, secured by her seatbelt. As those endorphins flooded her body, she looked at him and mouthed the words, "I think I'm all right," fooled by the lack of pain and unaware of the reality. After a minute, she began to groan in agony. Mobey, suffering a shattered left tibia, fibula and hip, cried out in pain.

The two lovers kept their eyes on each other. As the catastrophic internal hemorrhaging within Joan's body gradually stripped her vital organs of oxygen, Joan squeaked her final words, "I'm sorry," before closing her eyes and dying.

Mobey wasn't sure if Joan heard him tell her that it was he who was sorry, before she died. He yelled through tears and writhing for the next ten minutes, pleading for his wife of seven hours to wake up, until he had no choice but to accept the tragic truth. Joan's face had lost all colour; she was not breathing – she was gone.

Mobey couldn't attend his wife's funeral, stuck in the hospital and unable to move after fourteen hours of surgery; six plates and twenty-eight screws had been inserted into his left leg and hip.

Mobey's feet remained stuck in quicksand for years dealing with loss and guilt, before he finally broke free, although he never completely healed, emotionally – some punctures will sink even the most seaworthy vessel. He delayed writing his law licensing exams for two years while attempting to gain balance and pick himself up.

After convalescing in the hospital, he quit his job and then became homeless when he was evicted from the one-bedroom apartment that he and Joan were to share. The landlord was sympathetic, but as the rent arrears accumulated, he had no choice but to force Mobey out. Mobey didn't inform his parents of his eviction, not feeling worthy of anyone's assistance, and certainly not of happiness – a self-imposed penalty that he would accept for the rest of his life. It was the reason that he never remarried.

After his eviction, his parents found him on a steamy grate; they gathered him and his cane before returning home to nurse his broken bones and psyche back to health.

Mobey regularly woke up in the middle of the night, screaming after a brutal night of nightmares, attempting to repel the demons that attacked while he slept. Often, he would simply lay in bed, staring at the ceiling, afraid to go back to sleep.

Nobody understood that anytime someone said "I'm sorry," or when he saw an automobile, the memory of his wife's closing eyes visited – a bullet that tore into him and left him in pieces.

He did not have the will to fight his automobile insurer when he was advised that his car could be repaired for less than its value; it should have been written off. When he retrieved the car after repairs, it appeared new on the outside; but after a few weeks of driving it, clunky sounds commenced, the acceleration was not as smooth and it shimmied when he reached highway speeds – the auto would never be the same.

A few weeks later, Mobey sold his Honda at a loss, not having the will to keep looking over at that empty passenger seat. He also made the decision to give up his driver's license. Mobey never drove again; eventually, he purchased a bicycle for transportation, and subsequently an adult-sized tricycle.

But that bicycle purchase only occurred after he reached rock bottom and attended Alcoholics Anonymous. His parents arranged treatment with a psychologist. His recovery was arduous – full of ups and downs – but Mobey slowly crawled out of his hole and finally took his bar exams and began to practice criminal law.

Mobey began his own criminal defence practice, devoting everything to his craft, practicing by day, reading by night. He attended court to observe the trials of well-respected lawyers in the community, learning how the best performed in a courtroom. His immersion into lawyering and his practice was a distraction that he sorely needed, not realizing at the time that it would become a forty-year distraction.

Like other professions, lawyers love to congregate. Of course, a legitimate professional development component exists to these gatherings – an opportunity for lawyers to gather and discuss trends, current jurisprudence and their role in maintaining the rule of law in a civilized society. Throughout the beginning of his career, Mobey attended these professional development days with passion, but as the years passed, his motivation waned.

In 1992, Mobey attended his final seminar, *Psychology of the Juror and What is Reasonable Doubt Anyway?* By this time, Mobey had participated in many jury trials, the lawyer fascinated with how juries deliberate. Under Canadian law, the twelve random jurors who decide your fate, are not permitted to discuss how or why they came to a certain conclusion. It was a significant departure from American law, which allows jurors to discuss their deliberations and verdict rationales. Because of this peculiarity, other than a judge's jury instructions, no oversight or understanding of how a jury deliberated existed in Canada. The inner workings of jury deliberations were mysterious at best – a star chamber at worst.

Mobey appreciated that most citizens did not understand that two different juries, presented with the same facts, could easily come to different conclusions. The randomness of an outcome should be unsettling, or even terrifying, for an accused.

One of the more interesting topics at Mobey's last professional development day was that of reasonable doubt. The idea of reasonable doubt is theoretically easy to comprehend, but difficult to apply in reality. The line between what is reasonable doubt and what is unreasonable doubt is fraught with complexities, the issue extensively debated by legal scholars and practitioners.

One of the more interesting professors at the seminar staunchly advocated for the abolishment of juries. He argued, before the crowd of lawyers, that judges were better equipped to deal with complex laws and issues of causation. Jurors did not have the skills to properly and effectively deal with the weighing of evidence and were unduly influenced by other juror members. The professor's argument wasn't novel, and some support existed in the room for his view.

But the other theory he pushed at the seminar was somewhat novel: He believed that reasonable doubt was being applied improperly and that innocent defendants were being improperly convicted. The professor had limited support in the room for his theory; the man became standoffish and refused to acknowledge others' arguments. His fellow panel members became exasperated by his obstinate and uncooperative attitude. Even when it was explained to him that the Supreme Court of Canada had already rejected probability theory and the law of large numbers argument regarding the reasonable doubt issue, he did not relent.

But Perry Fields, the math professor who had long ago taken an interest in statistical analysis and the outcome of jury trials, doubled down on his position. He argued that the Supreme Court had it wrong, exhibiting that "bad stubbornness" that Mobey's uncle had shown around the dinner table. Fields face became red with anger once he realized he had no support from his fellow panel members – a face that resembled a tomato, thought Mobey, ducking the bullet that whizzed by his head.

When Mobey saw Perry Fields in the jury pool decades later at Hiller's trial, he had no idea that the professor had retired five years earlier and subsequently moved to London to live with his frail mother. Mobey easily picked the man out; Perry Fields sat in a wheelchair, as he had many years ago at the seminar. His pumpkin-shaped face, full of wild and straggly hair remained. Despite being born in Canada, he had a hint of a Louisiana accent courtesy of parents who had grown up in America – his southern drawl standing out from the other potential jurors.

Before he and Sussman started picking the jury, Mobey quickly considered if anything excluded Fields as a juror: police officer, lawyer, bankruptcy trustee, or employee of the Ministry of the Attorney General. None of those exceptions applied and he concluded Fields could sit on the jury. Would

Fields push that Law of large numbers routine on fellow jurors if he was on the jury? Did he harbour the same opinions about innocent people being convicted using probability theory? Would he exhibit the "bad stubbornness" if on the jury?

When Fields was not one of the first twenty potential jurors picked from names drawn out of a box, Mobey was disappointed. As the first twenty sat down to be considered, Mobey had a decision to make. Each lawyer had twelve peremptory challenges, which could be used to exclude a juror without any cause. Mobey wasn't guaranteed that Sussman would use any of his challenges on the first twenty. Mobey could guarantee a second round of potential jurors was called if he used all of his twelve challenges but that would only leave four more jurors to pick if Sussman didn't use any. And, Fields still might not get picked as a potential juror in the second round because they might not reach him. And of course, Sussman could always challenge Fields anyway, although Mobey believed that was unlikely. The risk of using all of his challenges, in an attempt to get to Perry Fields, was passing on some satisfactory jurors.

Mobey took Hiller aside to explain the situation and obtain instructions.

By the time the two lawyers moved through the first twenty potential jurors, eleven of the twelve jurors were picked. Sussman used three challenges and Mobey used five. One juror, luckily for Hiller, was excused for cause, a parent whose child was taught by Hiller and had a bias. One juror remained to be picked and Mobey had seven peremptory challenges left; it was unlikely that Perry Fields would be serving on Hiller's jury.

As the court clerk picked out the next twenty names, amazingly, Fields was the eighth name chosen. Simple math meant that if Mobey used all of his challenges, they would reach Fields, but the optics of what he was about to do would understandably raise eyebrows.

The first potential juror was presented to both lawyers.

"Acceptable," said Sussman.

"Challenge," announced Mobey.

The next potential juror was presented, the process repeated.

"Acceptable," said Sussman.

"Challenge, Your Honour," announced Mobey.

The Assistant Crown Attorney barely raised his antenna.

The third juror was presented.

"Acceptable," said Sussman.

"Challenge," said Mobey.

Sussman became suspicious. There were no obvious reasons for Mobey to challenge the last three potential jurors, so he looked down the list of potential jurors and wondered what he was up to.

The fourth juror was presented, and the same answers repeated.

"Acceptable," said Sussman.

"Challenge, Your Honour," announced Mobey.

Judge Handy looked up from his papers. Four challenges in a row, the judge mused. What the hell was going on?

The fifth juror was presented and two familiar answers followed.

"Acceptable to the Crown."

"Challenge, Your Honour," announced Mobey.

The process repeated itself exactly for the sixth and seventh jurors.

"Mr. Mobey, the court advises you that you have exhausted your twelve peremptory challenges," announced Judge Handy.

The eighth potential juror, Perry Fields, presented himself.

Sussman's mind raced. What was Mobey up to? Seven challenges in a row were unprecedented. It was now obvious to him that he wanted Perry Fields on the jury. But why? Maybe, I should just challenge Mr. Fields, considered Sussman? However, he had a problem, partly perception and partly real. The Crown accepted those first seven potential jurors in a row; the eighth sat in a wheelchair. He wanted to challenge Mr. Fields, for no other reason than Mobey wanted him on the jury – but Sussman needed to be liked by the other jurors; he knew he would appear like a bloody heel, or worse, discriminatory, if he challenged Fields. In high-stakes jury trials, both lawyers needed every advantage. He couldn't risk commencing the trial having the jurors viewing him unfavourably.

Sussman contemplated further. Maybe Mobey was pulling the bait and switch routine? Perhaps he wanted him to believe that he desired Fields, when really it was the ninth that he wanted, hoping that he would use a challenge on Fields? That would be classic Lester Mobey.

Mr. Sussman?" said Judge Handy, looking for the Crown's position.

"Acceptable, Your Honour," replied the Assistant Crown Attorney confidently, flashing Mobey a quick smile, pleased that he had just outmaneuvered the wily veteran.

CHAPTER TEN

Alex

"Tommy, you have PTSD, Post Traumatic Stress Disorder," explained his psychologist. "Your abuse was a very scary experience for you." The psychologist explained to him that PTSD was a fancy name given when someone is shocked by a scary event and then thinks about that event frequently, has nightmares and becomes anxious because of it.

"Do you understand, Tommy?"

He nodded; his nightmares were awful – nightly occurrences causing him to wake up screaming in terror. Tommy's deepest fears came over the wall as he slept; he struggled mightily to repel them back down the wall, the battles bloody.

Occasionally, after waking up, he crawled into bed with his mother; but usually, he simply lay on his back and stared at the ceiling, afraid to sleep. After hours of concentrating on the ceiling, he became convinced the meandering crack in the plaster above that traversed from one side of the room to the other resembled the Nile River, the 6,650 km wonder that he had learned of in geography class.

Tommy came to believe that he was born with a stubborn brain; it repeatedly thought about the same thing. His psychologist referred to it as "ruminating."

Tired and uneasy most of the time, Tommy entertained a permanent solution to quiet his mind – it had to be a less painful and certainly less messy.

His counsellors had fine intentions, but no improvement followed after a year of therapy. Even Tommy understood that he had to freely discuss his problems for counselling to be effective – but he couldn't; that was part of the problem, he determined.

Tommy invented a game of distraction; lying in bed with closed eyes, he attempted to list and spell the drugs exactly as lined up on his desk: Paxil, Cymbalta, Xanax, Ativan,

Wellbutrin, Effexor and a few others, most of which had been discontinued for lack of effectiveness. After sixteen attempts, he accomplished the task with perfection, even if it was a miserable one.

The several years following the trial did not proceed well for Tommy or Linda. Initially, brief pockets of joy appeared, similar the sun peeking out through the skies for a few minutes during an all-day drizzle; but the good times became scarce, overwhelmed by the grey clouds and dark secrets that enveloped their lives.

Tommy's relationship with his mother soured as he aged, his resentment towards her gaining momentum, fueled by her emotional unavailability and his comprehension of her significant parental shortcomings. He was too young to be the more responsible and stable of the two. His shoulders slumped each time he opened the fridge door to find nothing but Zinfandel or a case of beer. He envied his classmates whose mothers dropped them at school, handing them a lunch accompanied by fully attentive eyes. Why did Tommy Henderson lose the lottery of good luck?

Did his mother have any idea of his torment? He blamed her for every agonizing night that he stared up at the ceiling, wondering when the pain would end – readying himself for his demons' nightly advance.

After the trial, more so after Jonathon Sussman's visit, Tommy and Linda ceased talking – not literally – but in the substantive sense, although the apartment was quieter. No discussion of the trial or Sussman's visit occurred, the topics non grata.

Linda vowed to keep Sussman's unannounced visit from her son, unaware of Tommy's eavesdropping – a dubious parental decision if she concluded his teacher's suicide would remain a secret from the boy. Her choice, unclear as to whose interest it was made, had become moot.

Linda's mental health, which had been unstable for years, deteriorated quickly. Tommy's descension into depression compounded his PTSD symptoms, his mother having no capacity to respond to her son's needs. Some events existed that a mother couldn't face.

Tommy had always been a bright child, an "A" student with the odd "B" dotting his report cards. He loved to read, his teachers complimentary towards his comprehension abilities, his home environment tempering the intellectual and precocious child.

Before Hiller's arrest, Linda regularly grabbed used books at garage sales; Tommy read daily for hours; however, the routine abruptly stopped. Tommy lost his enthusiasm for school and reading, the decline commencing with the bullying that followed Hiller's charges becoming public.

"Hey, Tommy, did you get diddled today?" yelled kids in the schoolyard, cruel laughter ensuing. Shockingly, the hurled insults originated from beyond the dim-witted to those he considered friends. Cruelty could be found in the hearts of anyone, a depressing lesson learned far too young; it would have been an appropriate time to question humanity had he understood the concept.

Ironically, a court order banning the media from reporting Tommy's name after Hiller's arrest was ineffective; the boy likened it to a strainer catching water. It was not the first occasion that adults had disappointed him. After Hiller's teaching suspension, Tommy's involvement became the worst-kept secret at school, everyone aware of Hiller's affinity for fresh-faced boys at his cabin.

At age twelve, Tommy met Alex for the first time, an introduction that arrived at an opportune time in his view. Alex was unique, able to reach out and instantly pull you in, allowing you to forget your problems; a warm blanket was thrown around Tommy during the coldest of times. After their first hour together, Tommy had the capacity to smile and laugh, the ability to look out at the world through a different lens. With their first encounter complete, Tommy focused on the next, a testament to Alex's profound impact during these difficult times.

Tommy was tired of the dry mouth, constipation, and

drowsiness brought on by his medications caused by his ineffective medication; he had tired of feeling like crap, ditching the pills lined up along his bedroom desk.

He now looked forward to hanging out with Alex, something new in his stale life. Alex never disappointed Tommy, bringing the best out of him – producing laughter until his stomach hurt. The two quickly became inseparable, a relationship that permitted young Tommy to escape the chaos and turmoil that had enveloped him, even if ephemerally. Tommy felt good in Alex's presence. How many people in his life did that? Alex did more for him than any of his counsellors or doctors.

Unfortunately, his visits remained occasional; it wasn't practical to get together frequently, although he often schemed about upping their time together. Maybe, someday they could visit all the time?

Even to the untrained eye, Tommy's modelling of his mother's behaviour was obvious. When he was fourteen years old and in the ninth grade, he was missing school regularly, usually because he was hanging out with Alex. Thankfully, Tommy could hang with Alex more than he appreciated, because Linda provided no effective oversight; however, he did keep Alex a secret from his mother, knowing that she would not approve.

Alex was somewhat complicated and misunderstood, a bit of a social pariah at times; but Alex was good to Tommy – they understood each other. It became his most important relationship, never wanting to have to choose between Alex and his mother.

Two years into his relationship with Alex, the once close mother and son became divided by the hand of Linda's addiction and Tommy's focus on Alex. Tommy, once a dreamer, lost any visions of overtime goals, or the excitement of the future – Alex his only solace.

At age fifteen, Tommy finally stopped keeping Alex a secret from his mother; his mother barely reacted to the discovery, mumbling words about being careful. She did not step in.

A few drop-in visits by child protection workers occurred, a consequence of concerned calls from Tommy's school, but Linda managed enough action to keep them at bay. Besides, the agency wouldn't remove a fifteen-year-old from his home; fault did not lie with the mother, whose son suffered abuse by a teacher.

As Tommy's school attendance became sporadic, the school stopped calling, realizing no change in behaviour would follow. He became a "D" student and failed a few classes, a first for the bright child. The regular praise that he normally received from his teachers was replaced by hushed discussions and shaking heads between teachers while they expressed their sympathy for the terrible acts that one of their own had inflicted on Tommy Henderson.

"He had such promise," lamented his scienced teacher, eyes to the floor.

One Friday evening, a few days after his sixteenth birthday, Tommy relaxed in his bed, stolen headphones on his ears, listening to a popular rap artist while staring at the ceiling. He did not give the Nile River any thought, his mind consumed with his buddies and the upcoming night of debauchery. Alex would be there, as usual.

In sync with the pounding of the music in his ears, he watched a moth flutter aimlessly around his room – up, down, side to side – repeatedly bumping into the window. It was the most innocent of human life, he figured, a life that surely had never hurt a soul. Where was it going? It was attempting escape; where to? Tommy understood the desire – to get the hell out of that apartment.

He watched the moth continue to bounce around, feeling empathy for the insect fruitlessly attempting to escape through his impenetrable bedroom walls. Tommy rooted for the moth as it made its way back towards his bedroom door, where surely it had first entered. Freedom became imminent, requiring a flight path six inches lower to navigate under the top of the door frame.

Fate intervened, thwarting the great escape; the moth flew up into the corner of the room directly into the silky strings of a spider web. Now stuck, the moth frantically flapped its diminutive and fragile wings, unaware that freedom was beyond possible.

Tommy admired the moth as it continued to flap for five minutes, never accepting the outcome while the spider steadily made its way across the web towards its prey. Yes, sir, that moth was a fighter. However, the inevitable occurred. Because of exhaustion or acceptance, the wings came to a swift halt – all will for combat extinguished.

Innocence didn't protect that poor bastard, thought Tommy, who turned over on his side away from his door, not having the heart to watch the spider enjoy his meal.

Tommy rested for several minutes. Suddenly, his face became flush, the outrage with himself gathering momentum. Why didn't he get up, take a few steps and cut that helpless moth from the web before he became dinner? It would have been easy. He could have carefully cupped that moth in his hands, saved it from its death sentence and released it to a blissful life. Instead, consumed with his own thoughts, he let that courageous moth die a horrible, lonely death. How could he be so selfish? Tommy didn't have the heart to go out that evening. Instead, he turned the volume from level five to eight and cried himself to sleep.

The following morning, Tommy awoke at 7:00 am, several hours earlier than he normally raised from his usually hazy Saturday morning slumber. The warm and comforting first rays of the day's sunshine penetrated his window and landed on his face. A background mix of chirping, whining and gurgling emanated from two tree swallows in the throes of a mating ritual a few feet outside his room. Tommy stared at the ceiling as he had a thousand times before.

Tommy's eyes found the spider; no evidence remained of the moth and the drama that had played out the night before. Maybe he turned over too soon last night? Maybe that helpless creature had simply paused to rest, gaining strength for one, last, furious storm of flapping to heroically free himself off that web? It was possible – the greatest of escapes. That was how it happened, a conclusion that elevated his spirits a tad.

Tommy hadn't had such a clear mind for some time; the fog had lifted, even if momentarily. He sat on his bed for an hour in pensive reflection, struggling, before pushing himself off his bed and making his way to his window.

The two swallows remained in dance, flitting and singing without a care in the world. Tommy could not differentiate between the male and female, their royal blue upper bodies and cream-coloured bottoms appearing identical. He imagined himself a bird, flying from tree to tree all day, being free his only purpose; it was fanciful but many impossible dreams come true, he figured. Singing and dancing; he mused of his mother's abandoned goal, a consequence of life imposing its own agenda.

Tommy closed his eyes and envisaged himself soaring with spread wings, looking down with sympathy at the humans carrying miserable expressions on their faces. Oh, how he wanted a bird's life – no Robert Hiller – and no Howard King forcing him into a tiny room; an adult could not let him down a hundred feet in the air.

One of the swallows landed on the window sill, cocked its head and stared at Tommy before commencing an elaborate song. Was the bird looking at him – or at its reflection in the glass? It did not matter. Tommy gently tapped on the window, acknowledging and thanking the swallow for its presence.

The teenager turned and walked to his closet. He grabbed two duffle bags and began packing, appreciating that he was about to leave with almost nothing. After jamming them full, Tommy took two steps to his sock drawer; his right hand fished around the bottom until he found what he was looking for. Surprised that it remained after all these years, he snatched it and pushed it deep into his pants pocket.

Tommy had an important decision to make. What about Alex? Maybe it was time to move on and end that relationship? They remained inseparable, Alex the only constant in his life; however, a strain had developed in their connection. Alex had begun to show a different side, wanting more and more of his time. Tommy had begun to feel crowded at times, even claustrophobic.

It was apparent that Alex didn't want him to change or improve, content with the status quo. Alex would not be receptive of his plan, so perhaps now was the time to end it; Tommy could see the benefits of making a clean break right now. Alex was beginning to drag him down, like an anchor sinking to the bottom of the ocean.

Tommy mulled the difficult decision for a few minutes, concluding he couldn't turn his back on Alex. Who was he kidding, anyway? He needed Alex more now than ever. Surely, the two could work out their differences, if they both bent a little.

With each of the duffle bags slung over a shoulder, Tommy peeked into his mother's room; as expected, he found her asleep, long black disheveled hair concealing most of her face. A half glass of white wine sat on her night table, a beer can beside it. Only a slight movement in her chest confirmed life; otherwise, she appeared dead.

His dislike for her unnerved him. The hate in his heart for his mother frightened him – more than his own self-loathing.

Turning the apartment doorknob, he abruptly stopped – frozen in fear at his decision. This was crazy, he thought, pulling his now trembling hand from the doorknob, knowing it wasn't too late to retreat back into his room. He scanned a room in disarray, the bare walls no less a jail than the one Robert Hiller had narrowly escaped, six years earlier. A fly landed on an empty pizza box that lay open on the kitchen table, reminding him of the defenceless moth and its courage to fight for its life. He shuddered at the thought of staring at the Nile River one more time.

Tommy placed his hand back on the doorknob and turned it; he stepped into the hallway apprehensively, letting the door close behind him. Liberation quickly overtook him, shoving aside his doubts of leaving apartment 2B behind. It wasn't clear if the tears that trickled down his face resulted from sadness, regret, or relief; but he felt all three as he made his way down the hallway.

Tommy walked a block before arriving at the bus stop. He counted the twenty-three dollars in his wallet while waiting for the city bus to take him to the Greyhound bus terminal. He used the wait to gather himself and enjoy the warmth of the sun. The rays were soothing and somehow felt different now that he had made this important decision. Challenges lied ahead; he had taken but one step, when he needed to complete a marathon to reach his final, elusive, destination. Maybe he and that moth had something in common? Maybe the bird flying overhead and looking down on Tommy saw something more than a miserable face?

How long would it take his mother to realize that he was gone for good? He left no note and didn't even say goodbye; his parting words would have been cruelly harsh. Absurdly, compassion required that he leave in silence.

Indeed, Linda did not search for a note, not surprised at her son's clandestine exit. With waterfall force, tears followed from the broken woman. She promised to think of him every day, not realizing that fifteen long years would separate their next visit.

After Tommy's departure, Linda continued checking the box and signing the statutory declaration on her monthly government disability papers, indicating that she had a minor dependent living with her. She needed the extra three hundred dollars a month.

Tommy stepped off the Greyhound bus in downtown Stratford, Ontario, the beautiful southwestern Ontario city that Linda Henderson had visited on her fourteenth birthday. With two dollars and thirty cents remaining after purchasing his bus ticket, he walked east on Ontario Street, a late afternoon sun warming his back. Tourists congested the sidewalk, darting in and out of the quaint shops that lined the street, many carrying bags holding their purchases. Tommy passed the Black Swan

House, oblivious to his mother's excited exploration eighteen years earlier.

Tommy listened to laughter and excitement overflowing from the restaurants and cafes. Patrons at Pazzo, Fellini's and Bentley's sipped on sangria and local craft beers, the frequent sound of clanking glasses piercing the air as they wished each other good cheer. Did they take that blissful existence for granted, while beaming from behind sunglasses and ordering smoked salmon on toasted crostini bread? Tommy sure wouldn't. Whimsically, he considered approaching one of those tables, sitting down and ordering balsamic bruschetta on French bread, seasoned with the appropriate touch of peppercorn medley. Or, maybe oysters Rockefeller, garnished with butter, parsley and lemon. Alex could join him; together they would slap backs and make new friends.

But Tommy had other priorities – like finding a place to sleep that night. With the temperature dropping to twelve degrees overnight, he faced a very chilly sleep outside.

Tommy put his hand into his jean pocket and pulled out the note that he had kept in the bottom of his sock drawer for the last few years. He could barely discern the address from the faded ink.

Walking out of the downtown core and away from the bustling crowds, Tommy proceeded six blocks until he reached Front Street; he took a left and headed north towards the Avon River. After five minutes, with butterflies now bouncing around the inside of his stomach, he arrived at 102 Front Street.

Tommy stood on the sidewalk; he pulled the note out again to confirm he had arrived at the correct destination, his hand shaking. Lights and a flickering television were visible through a crack in the living room curtains. That observation and the two cars parked in the driveway raised Tommy's hope.

The Tudor-style dwelling, with its steeply pitched roof and front-facing gables reminded Tommy of the Hansel and Gretel fairy tale book that his mother read to him as a young boy. He immediately thought of Hansel and Gretel's mother, who was willing to abandon her children in the forest so that she would have enough food to feed her and her husband. Luckily, Hansel and Gretel had each other; it would have been awfully scary for either of them to leave their house on their own.

Finally, Tommy gathered the necessary courage; he headed up the cobblestone walkway to the front doorway and pushed the doorbell. Both hands now trembled, worse than accompanied his early morning departure.

After an agonizing thirty seconds, the door swung open. A puzzled Ryan Hart stood in the threshold, looking at a teenager who arrived, unannounced, with two duffle bags. Three years had passed since Tommy had seen his former grade-eight teacher. Tommy's appearance had dramatically changed, now five feet eight inches tall and one hundred and fifty pounds. Tommy barely resembled the geeky, stick-thin kid that Ryan remembered.

"Tommy?" asked Ryan, peering out onto his stoop with wonderment and a rippled forehead.

"Yes, sir," he replied, tears rolling down his face. The once-friendly face, who previously reached out to him overwhelmed him – his only lifeline. "I'm so sorry to show up like this but I had nowhere else to go."

"Come in, come in," urged Ryan, grabbing Tommy's arm and pulling him into the foyer. The soft-spoken teacher grabbed his duffle bags and escorted him into his study to talk. On the way, Ryan's subtle nod assured his wife that all was well. He politely asked her to bring water.

Ryan sat his unexpected visitor into a comfortable wing-backed chair. His fifty-year-old former teacher appeared the same, bookish with unadventurous eyeglasses attached to a silver necklace. Mr. Rogers would have been comfortable in his red sweater. The haircut was traditional, his greying hair shaved closely all around. Although not athletic, Ryan maintained a slim figure because of his healthy diet.

Ryan knew his grade-eight student was struggling at the time; the bright boy became withdrawn and lost interest. As did everyone in the school, Ryan knew of the allegations against Robert Hiller that ended in an acquittal. He suspected his home environment was unstable, even before the allegations, and became concerned about the boy's mental health. Ryan reached out to his pupil several times, attempting to engage him, but without success. On a day when Tommy appeared particularly despondent, Ryan met with him after school and handed him a paper with his telephone number and address written on it.

"Tommy," he said. "If you ever need to talk; if ever you're desperate; if ever there's an emergency, I will be someone you can count on."

It was a thoughtful gesture; Tommy appreciated the sincerity, a trait that was in limited supply in his increasingly small circle. At home, Tommy had hidden the note at the bottom of his drawer where it remained for several years. When the boy transferred to high school the next year, he never saw Ryan Hart again, until that very night, when he showed up at his front door.

The study had a wood-burning fireplace, the hypnotic flames crackling and licking at the new log placed ten minutes earlier. Tommy was content to stare at the fire the rest of the evening and lose himself, despite the cabin memories it evoked.

A steaming cup of coffee sat on Ryan's desk. Wide, reclaimed wood planks that creaked covered the floor. Photos of Ryan, his wife, and their two adult daughters dotted the wall. A perfect family, mused Tommy, looking at the smiling faces.

"I'm sorry for interrupting you, Mr. Hart."

"It's not a problem, young man. Tell me what is going on."

Ryan's wife brought in a glass of water with three ice cubes, "There you go, hon," she said quietly, smiling. Jennifer was a beautiful woman; her blue eyes came alive when she spoke. Tommy knew she loved living in that house with Ryan Hart, curling up in front of that cozy fireplace and telling each other about their fantastic days.

"Thank you," replied Tommy, appreciating the warm hospitality that he didn't deserve.

Jennifer left. Tommy explained his circumstances – although not the entire story. After an hour of discussion, Ryan left the room to consult with his wife, returning a half-hour later. Tommy had no idea of the intense conversation Ryan had with his wife. Despite being a social worker, Jennifer Hart had serious reservations about inviting a sixteen-year-old with PTSD and depression into their home.

"We don't even know him, Ryan," Jennifer reminded her husband.

Tommy remained unsure if he was about to have a chilly night, when Ryan returned to the study wearing a poker face.

"Okay, Tommy. Jennifer and I have spoken; here is our offer. On a trial basis, you can to live with us, under certain conditions." Ryan explained that he must enroll at high school and attend every class; he must attend a group two evenings a week called Choices for Change; he must obtain a part-time job as soon as he reasonably could and lastly, that he respects the Harts' home.

Tommy nodded his head in agreement. He held back the tears and resisted the urge to hug Ryan.

Ryan continued, "If you agree and can follow those conditions, then the three of us will meet in two weeks and see where we are."

"Thank you. Thank you," replied Tommy. "Yes, I can follow those rules. I can't tell you how much this means to me."

Ryan stuck out his hand and they shook.

Jennifer brought Ryan to the second-floor guest room, decorated femininely with a floral-patterned comforter and curtains; Tommy did not care. Once alone, he spread out on the comfortable bed, moving his arms and legs in and out as though he was making a snow angel. The room had penthouse quality, given the upgrade from his previous accommodations. Linda did not have cable television; Tommy grabbed the remote and turned on the forty-two-inch Sony hung on the wall. He flipped channels until he found Animal Planet, a television show that explored animals in the wild.

The host, Benjamin Hunt, wore snappy safari clothes, which included tan khaki pants, a collared short-sleeve button-up shirt, sun hat, and Ron Spomer boots. The man exhibited his passion for animals, talking with animated hands, while standing on the back of a jeep in some far-away desert. Benjamin's eyes lit up when he discussed animals and their habitats. Tommy wanted those eyes.

This particular episode dealt with mothers in the wild, who abandon their offspring. Mr. Hunt explained that snakes had absolutely no maternal instinct and left their eggs after laying them, never to return. If the mother gave birth to a live snake, the mother would simply slither off, right away, never to see its baby again. Lizards behaved similarly, explained Mr. Hunt, smiling while discussing the African Long-Tailed Lizard's less than ideal maternal strengths.

Then, he explained that pandas, who usually had twins, abandoned one to the wild, choosing the stronger one to stay with mom.

The Harp seal left her young pup after approximately twelve days, which resulted in a mortality rate nearing thirty percent given the harsh elements and lurking predators.

More examples were coming after the next commercial, but Tommy turned the television off, finding it all quite depressing. However, he remained fond of Benjamin Hunt's sparkle in his eye, even when discussing those poor abandoned babies.

Tommy looked up at the ceiling. Would they be coming over the wall tonight? God, he missed Alex. During the bus ride to Stratford, he decided to set some ground rules to better define their relationship. He meant it this time.

Those babies filled Tommy's mind as he faded off to a fourteen-hour sleep after a terribly long day.

CHAPTER ELEVEN

Who Doesn't Like Baloney?

"Duncan and I strolled on Waterloo Street, crossing the William Hutt Bridge on a glorious Stratford morning. The view to the west along the spectacular Avon River was spectacular as the currents flowed towards Shakespearean Gardens and the oldest double-arch stone bridge in Ontario."

The facilitator, Doug Knight, and five others, including Tommy, listened intently to Janice Thorton address the Choices for Change group. The aging Stratford Festival veteran had been cast in twenty-six musical productions in her career. She presented immaculately, overdressed for the church basement meeting. Classy was the best description.

Janice went on, "After our delightful observation, Duncan and I continued across the bridge until we arrived at Lakeside Drive, where I found a raised flower bed at the southwest corner of the intersection. I gave Duncan, my miniature schnauzer, the command to stop; I took a few minutes to admire the twenty beautiful daffodils that had been carefully spaced within the perfectly manicured flowerbed.

Tommy wondered where Janice was going with her story.

"As I bent down to pet my pup, I realized that one of the daffodils was noticeably smaller than the other nineteen. Perhaps, it wasn't getting enough sun or water. It looked out of place; I had the urge to pull it myself and discreetly drop it into the garbage can a few feet away, but of course, I didn't."

Two days removed from his new living arrangements, Tommy wondered the reasons for Janice's participation in the group.

"Thirty minutes later, when I arrived home, I walked up my front stairs and passed my garden on the right, a work in progress over the last several weeks. One empty spot remained, but I couldn't decide what plant would fit the best; I immediately appreciated how perfectly that undersized daffodil would complete my garden."

Janice proceeded to discuss the concept of perspective and finding your place in the world. Tommy eventually learned that Ms. Thorton had battled eating disorders; her insecurities were now at the forefront as she aged and the roles she was offered dwindled.

Bulimia was a strange condition; Tommy wasn't sure what it all meant, but extensive discussion about perfectionism and traumas that she had suffered as a child followed. He couldn't imagine throwing up all that good food after eating it. However, Janice looked unbelievably sad – that he was sure of. Unlike that daffodil, Tommy wasn't sure that Janice had found her place in this world yet; she had the eyes to prove it.

Emily Sampson spoke next. She appeared sadder than Janice, the nineteen-year-old struggling with a serious heroin addiction, her frail and emaciated figure proof of the battle that was raging within her.

"It was an amazing feeling," she said, describing the first time she injected heroin in her arm. Literally, every worry I had disappeared." But as the addiction took hold and she needed more and more of the drug to get that feeling, the physical and psychological effects were devastating. She lost forty pounds; her body ached with pain when she had no money to buy heroin. Eventually, in a fit of rage, she assaulted her boyfriend with a tennis racket, an outburst requiring two nights in jail. She still could not rid the jailhouse stench smell from her nose.

Emily was shockingly open about being raped by a stranger at age thirteen years; she never felt safe until she put that needle in her arm, replacing one set of issues with a host of others.

Earlier in the day, Tommy attended his first day of school at Central Secondary School; his experience proceeded smoothly – his anonymity providing a measure of protection. By the end of his first week, he had connected with Dillon Wortley, a fellow student who he chatted with over lunch. Fortuitously, Dillon introduced Tommy to his father, who owned a pet store in Stratford and was seeking someone to stock pet food three days a week after school.

By the time Tommy met with the Harts on the two-week anniversary of his arrival, he reported that he had not missed any school, had secured a part-time job, and had been attending Choices for Change. Tommy had ensured he remained invisible in the Hart household, preparing his lunches, staying in his room studying; occasionally, he ate with the family when invited. The Harts extended their invitation – Tommy sighed in relief.

Tommy enjoyed Stratford's beauty, his mother's often-told story about her attendance at the Stratford Festival for her fourteenth birthday, remained near his thoughts; his mother's eyes lit up when she recounted the story – Tommy clung to the memory.

Inescapably, Linda Henderson failed her son as a mother and as a protector. The separation began to clear his mind, although Robert Hiller and his secret patrolled his very being.

Tommy fell in love with Stratford's Avon River, or Lake Victoria as it was named within the city as a dedication to the Queen of England, a body of water that split the city just north of its downtown core. Its banks quickly became his favourite spot to sit and think, the river abutted with expansive parks and walking trails.

Legs crossed in repose, Tommy found Lake Victoria's beautiful and tranquil waters a fleeting antidote for the stormy waters in his soul. He smiled at the picnicking families relaxing under the century-old maple and oak trees, couples walking along the river's edge, and teenagers throwing frisbees under the sunlight. While sitting on the river's banks, he made a choice to live.

His pockets stuffed with grain, Tommy fed the numerous ducks and swans that called the lake home. With a combination of amusement and consternation, he observed the most aggressive ducks racing to the grains first, imposing their will on their weaker companions. The ducks scattered once the swans, with their cygnets in tow, swam over to feed and take their rightful place at the top of the lake hierarchy. When the sun set in the west, creating a glass-like reflection on the water, Tommy returned to the penthouse, comforted by the image.

A fierce battle raged within Tommy, the crafty and vicious invaders attacking at night possessing impossible stamina. Fortunately, Tommy came to a mutual understanding with Alex – setting specific ground rules to relieve the increasing crowding of their relationship. The wee-hour get-togethers were over – they could only meet three times a week, and Tommy's head hit the pillow by 11:00 pm to ensure he was fresh for school.

Eyebrows cocked, observers considered it strange to see a young man spend hours walking the lake's edges; but Tommy Henderson had been robbed of his youth, forced to age quickly. A genie can't be put back in a bottle. Innocence is bestowed once; when it is gone, it is gone forever.

Despite their emotional intensity, Tommy continued attending every Choices for Change meeting. Each gathering left him exhausted, the group hoisting incremental perspective on his back. But Tommy learned a far more valuable lesson – mighty and dominating; once harnessed, it changed everything. It was elusive; everyone in the group said so.

After three months in the Hart residence, Tommy began to feel comfortable in his new abode, particularly because of one incident. Prior to that event, he woke every morning wondering if it would be his last day in the house. Jennifer remained pleasant; however, he sensed her uneasiness about the stranger with a propensity to scream in the middle of the night that had arrived at her doorstep unannounced.

The incident occurred on a Monday morning and involved a baloney sandwich, an incident that brought him to tears, uncontrollable sobbing to which he had not succumbed to since the night he heard about Robert Hiller's suicide.

In his Choices for Change meetings, a popular topic was family and the meaning of family. Much discussion of the importance of non-traditional family members filled the room.

During his first three months in Stratford, the facilitator and other group members never pushed Tommy to say a word. Every meeting, he was invited to speak; the youngest attendee respectfully declined each time. Other than introducing himself at the first meeting and offering the customary pleasantries at the beginning and ending of each gathering, Tommy simply listened. Nobody knew his reasons for sitting in that chair.

Six months into those meetings, Tommy raised every eyebrow when he asked to say a few words; he wished to share a story about a baloney sandwich with the group.

Slowly, Tommy detailed his journey, culminating with his arrival at the Hart household where he attempted to remain invisible, staying in his room and purchasing his groceries with his part-time job earnings. His second-hand purchase of a mini-fridge, tucked in the corner of the penthouse, ensured he didn't intrude upon the Hart's fridge space. Tommy cooked his meals in his room with a toaster oven, carried under his arm from a garage sale.

"I'm amazed how many different meals you could make in a toaster oven," he explained, the group laughing in response, bringing a smile to the teenager's face. It had been years since he had caused anyone to laugh – it felt good; a warmth washed over him.

"My favourite is the quesadilla – good for any meal – and versatile; all the ingredients are easily kept in my fridge. I've now eaten one hundred and eighty-two quesadillas, which I'm sure is some kind of record," he bragged, creating a second round of chuckling.

Tommy stared at the group members, uncomfortable with every gaze cast upon him; still, their unspoken support pushed him to continue. The facilitator fixed his eyes on the boy, his torso bent forward from in his chair, elbows on his knees and hands clasped together. The man wanted to hear more, and that meant something.

Tommy cleared his throat and explained how he showered and cleaned his dishes when the Harts were not home, guaranteeing that he never inconvenienced them. Privately, the Harts laughed, joking with each other that a ghost patrolled their house; small items mysteriously moved around the house but nobody was there to move them.

Three months after his move to Stratford, Tommy finished up a Saturday morning breakfast quesadilla, when Ryan Hart knocked on his bedroom door. With a warm smile, he invited his guest to join the Harts on an organized city walking tour that morning. Concerned about jeopardizing his fragile existence, Tommy was hesitant, but Ryan became insistent, waving an extra ticket in his hand. With reluctance, he agreed to go.

A group of thirty gathered in front of Bentley's Inn on Ontario Street, some of whom had spent the previous night in the inn's second-floor rooms.

The group strolled west, walking two short blocks to its first stop, Shakespearean Gardens, located beside the Huron Perth Courthouse and, ironically, at the foot of the Stratford Jail. An interesting gentleman by the name of Rodney McKinnon, President of the Stratford Heritage Committee, led the group and bragged, inoffensively, that he knew everything about Stratford and its history. He explained that "he ate, slept and breathed Stratford", a city that he described as Canada's best-kept secret. Many referred to Mr. McKinnon as Chuck, including Ryan Hart.

Unbeknownst to Tommy, Rodney received his nickname, Chuck, as a baby when inflicted with a terrible case of colic; Rodney vomited frequently, or, as his parents described it, up-chucked, when he cried. Affectionately, they began calling him up-chuck; over the years it became shortened to Chuck. The name stuck.

An encyclopedia of facts about Stratford, Chuck explained that Shakespearean Gardens was his first and favourite stop on the tour. The original roses in its gardens were a gift from Queen Mary. In 1937, several oak trees from the grounds of Windsor Castle, in England, were replanted in Stratford; the only one to survive stood in front of the Perth

County Courthouse. Tommy looked up at the towering and majestic tree in wonderment, just as he had six years earlier at the Lady Justice statue in front of the London courthouse.

Chuck's eyes lit up with excitement as he explained that the oak tree had survived winds of over 100 km per hour on eighteen occasions since it was planted. Tommy wondered how the mature tree, one hundred feet high with a trunk measuring nine feet in circumference, survived so many repeated assaults on its very existence. What did this magnificent oak have that the others didn't? It had been uprooted, crossed the Atlantic to North America, and replanted; it grew to its full potential, strong and mighty, while its boat mates succumbed to their environment.

Chuck moved the group deeper, boasting about the beautiful gardens with the passion of a proud father.

"This is the hidden gem of Stratford. Peaceful, tranquil and calm. All day, you'll find people in the gardens meditating, practicing Tai Chi or simply relaxing under the pergola. Others love wandering the gardens, taking in its flora and admiring the almost sixty varieties of flowers, herbs and shrubs."

Tommy sat down on an iron bench facing the Avon River and watched the water easily glide over the few rocks that pierced the surface of the water. With a deep breath, he took in the fragrance of roses, enjoying the experience to its fullest.

The group continued on, viewing several other landmarks including the Stratford Cenotaph, St. James Church, Stratford City Hall, Gallery Stratford and many of the historic homes throughout the city. Tommy chatted extensively with the Harts during the two-hour tour; he felt that he made a special connection with Jennifer. As the tour wrapped up, Ryan and Chuck took him aside.

"Listen, Tommy, would you spend fifteen minutes alone with Chuck? I'd like you to talk with him, okay?" asked Ryan.

Tommy looked at Ryan. "May I ask why?" he replied, curiously.

"I'd prefer to let Chuck explain. Trust me," he said, smiling with a nod.

Tommy trusted the man more than anyone on the planet. "Okay," he replied.

Chuck put his hand on Tommy's shoulder and led him down Ontario Street. "Thanks for coming. Let me buy your lunch. Anywhere you want!" Chuck immediately put Tommy at ease, one of his special skills.

"Thank you," replied Tommy, quickly considering the invitation to choose where to eat.

Tommy eyed the patrons at Pazzo dining under the shade umbrellas a few hundred feet away on the patio. Chuck caught his young companion's eyes fixated on the trendy restaurant; Tommy didn't need to say a word – thirty seconds later the two took a seat at the last table in the sun.

"You chose the perfect spot, Tommy. Did you know that Timothy Findley used to live right upstairs?" asked Chuck, pointing upwards at the penthouse condominium of the three-story building; the luxurious apartment had a beautiful rooftop terrace with a breathtaking view of Lake Victoria.

Tommy looked at Chuck, a balding man who wore a full gray beard – and stared directly into his friendly blue eyes. "No," he replied, shaking his head, having never heard of him, but not wanting to admit it.

"He spent hours and hours on this very patio. Timothy was one of the original actors when the Stratford Festival opened in the 1950s," explained Chuck. "But he became a writer and that's what he's best known for. Timothy Irving Fredrick Findley. His friends called him Tiff, an acronym of his initials."

Tommy nodded his head. Oh, how he would love to sit on the Pazzo sidewalk patio with Alex for hours and hours and watch pedestrians stroll by – watch the world go by.

"Much of Tiff's work were books about troubled individuals," explained Chuck, reaching in and pulling a book from his bag. "Please take this and read it."

Tommy grabbed the hardcover and read the front, *The*

Last of the Crazy People. "Thank you, Chuck."

"The book has been labelled Southwestern Ontario gothic. You'll find it interesting," said Chuck while putting on his sunglasses. "When you're finished, we'll meet again for lunch and discuss it."

Book in hand, Tommy realized how much he missed reading, recalling the garage-sale books his mother purchased.

"Tommy, it wasn't an accident that Ryan asked you to join the walking tour today. Ryan and I go way back. In fact, the three of us have something in common," he explained.

Tommy cocked his head to the side, intrigued.

"For years, I acted as the facilitator at Choices for Change; before that, I was a group member. And, guess who else used to be a member?" asked Chuck, not expecting an answer. "Ryan Hart."

Chuck let his guest absorb his revelations for a moment before continuing. "Ryan gave me permission to share this with you, but it's up to him to explain anything further."

Tommy considered his companion's divulgence; it simultaneously startled and comforted him. Ryan was the most stable, generous and put-together individual that he knew. What had led him to Choices for Change?

A waitress with a smile on her face arrived and placed their food on the table. Tommy peered down at his balsamic bruschetta on French bread, seasoned with the appropriate touch of peppercorn medley and Oysters Rockefeller, garnished with butter, parsley and lemon.

Chuck removed the top half of his bun and squirted ketchup on his hamburger.

"Everyone has a story, Tommy," explained Chuck, dropping a fry into his mouth. "Everyone is dysfunctional; it's a matter of degree," he said with a huge grin, followed by a soft chuckle. "We come into this world as blank slates; then adults get their hands on us – it's often downhill from there."

Tommy absorbed the chagrin and crooked smile on Chuck's face; the man was serious about his declaration.

"Do you like to play video games, Tommy?"

"I love to," he replied, his eyes lit thinking of the hours dedicated to Killer Comet.

"Have you ever heard of chaos theory?" asked Chuck, certain that he hadn't.

"No, I haven't."

"The science of surprises. Let me give you an example. In the old days, we played pinball machines."

"I've played before," Tommy blurted, thinking of the pinball machine in Robert Hiller's cabin – Tommy ducked as a bullet whizzed by him.

"Okay, great, Tommy; you understand. All of the movements of the ball are governed by the basic laws of science, such as gravity, force and elastic collisions. We should be able to predict exactly where the ball ends up, every time, but we can't; the final outcome is unpredictable. Two balls that are released with the exact same force should behave identically, but they won't. That's chaos theory."

Tommy nodded, "The game wouldn't be fun if you knew the outcome."

"Exactly!" exclaimed Chuck. "But what happens if you shove the machine to manipulate where the ball goes?"

"The game shuts down because you tilted the machine," replied Tommy confidently, remembering how that happened to him.

"Exactly, again. You gained too much of an advantage by shoving that machine."

The two lunch companions looked at each other for a moment, both of them smiling. Tommy felt an unusual connection with Chuck, a strong connection that he hadn't felt since he looked at Robert Hiller on that deck after firing a few rounds of that Glock. That time, it didn't end well.

"Tommy, of all the advice I give you, remember chaos theory. The outcome of your life is unpredictable right now. Figure out what you can do to tilt things in your favour and manipulate your life. That is the key. What that looks like is different for everyone, but I guarantee that the answer is somewhere in your group at Choices for Change. Those who survive, learn to tilt the machine."

Chuck went on to tell Tommy his own tragic history. His father owned a business that manufactured wrist bands, the kind that attaches around your wrist at theme parks such as Disney World or Sea World. His father sold millions over the world each year in every imaginable colour. As the market became more competitive for these bands, his father had to reduce costs; so, he moved his manufacturing plant to Mexico.

On one of his father's trips to Mexico, his son went with him. Chuck was an eighteen-year-old confident and cocky teenager, who was a few weeks away from attending university. Strolling home after a delicious traditional Mexican dinner at an upscale restaurant, he and his father were robbed at gunpoint. While his father was unreservedly removing his wallet from his back pocket to hand it over, Chuck and his teen bravado lunged at one of the two gunmen; the gun fired, sending a bullet out of the chamber that ripped through his father's chest wall and directly into his heart. He died before he hit the ground.

"You can imagine the guilt I felt, Tommy," said Chuck, wiping ketchup off his lip with his napkin. "Not a day passes that I don't regret my actions. If I had done nothing, my dad would still be with me; perhaps he would be on this patio dining with us. My mother became a widow – it was my fault – and I couldn't handle the guilt at the time; it still haunts me."

Chuck explained how his life came to a standstill when his father died; he didn't go to university. Instead, he holed up in his family home, remaining in bed, while his mother nursed his shattered psyche. Nightmares violently shook him out of his sleep with images of his father laying on a sidewalk in a pool of blood. He did not have a full night's sleep for three years, unless he was passed out, drunk.

"Tommy, when you lean back on a chair, balancing yourself on the two rear legs – if you lean back just a little too far – you begin to fall backwards; for a split second, you don't know if you can catch yourself by throwing your weight forward, or, if you'll end up on your ass. Many years followed before I caught myself.

Tommy nodded; he understood that uncomfortable, teetering feeling.

"I still have nightmares, but they're not as frequent or intense. I still have regret and guilt, but I healed. You can recover from emotional trauma; I'm proof of it."

Tommy welled inside. Was a repair possible for Thomas Theodore Henderson? The question constantly occupied him; the answer was elusive.

"Tommy, how is your drinking?"

Silence followed – Chuck sensed the teenager's uneasiness. "It's okay. Don't be ashamed; you're not in trouble. Tell me the truth."

"I'm drinking quite a bit, still. It's not the Harts' alcohol. I would never steal from them, ever," he said, lowering his head. He was ashamed of the beer hidden under his bed at the penthouse, obtained through Dillon's connections.

"Tommy, what is your favourite memory?"

Tommy dipped his last piece of French bread into the leftover butter on his plate. His meal, prepared to perfection with amazing artistry, had disappeared. He wanted to rise, walk through Pazzo's front doors and march through the restaurant until he found the chef, shaking his hand with delight.

"Well done, sir," he would tell him. "That was unbelievable. My compliments!" And then he would slap the chef on the back, "Bravo; I shall return this evening. I wouldn't dare miss any of your celebrated creations."

But Tommy did not rise. Sitting on that patio was not at all what he had dreamt of when he stepped off the bus three months earlier and walked by the merrily chatting patrons toasting each other's accomplishments. That moment summed up his existence best; despite eating the tastiest food in his life on a sunny Saturday with a charming and caring companion, his food tasted bland. The view was bland. His outlook was bland. Everything was bland. Bland, bland, bland – that was his filter on life.

Maybe it was Alex's absence? Who could blame him for keeping that relationship; Alex made him feel better – Alex was always there for him, despite the questionable adherence to the ground rules.

"Tommy, did you hear me? What's your best memory?"

Nobody had ever asked him that question before; he had never considered it. It could have been at Hiller's cabin, shooting the Glock and driving the car around the property – until it all happened. Now, it was his worst memory.

"When I was seven years old, my mother always packed my school lunch. She forbade me from peeking in my bag before lunchtime because I would spoil the surprise. She warned me that I shouldn't expect my favourite every time – and I didn't – anticipating all morning what I might get. Every day I opened my lunch bag to discover my favourite, a baloney sandwich cut into four squares with the crusts carefully cut off. Mom placed a dab of ketchup on each square, as I liked it. Then, it just stopped one day; I had to make my own lunch."

In trance-like oblivion, Tommy didn't hear the waitress ask him if he wanted his water refilled.

"Chuck, in hindsight, I didn't even like baloney. But my mother made something special for me; she took the time to remove the crusts off. For those few minutes, I was the only thing she cared about."

As Tommy recounted the story of the walking tour and his conversation with Chuck to his fellow group members at Choices for Change, he apologized for taking too much time; immediately, the group asked him to continue, so he did.

"Early on Monday morning, two days after the Saturday walking tour and my visit with Chuck, I found a handwritten note that had been slid under my bedroom door."

The note indicated that Tommy's lunch had been prepared and located in the fridge – odd because he always made his own school lunch. Although only 6:30 am, Tommy crept downstairs, retrieved the bag and returned to his room; with his back against the door, his hand pulled out a sandwich – baloney – cut into fours with a dab of ketchup on each piece.

CHAPTER TWELVE

Maybe I'm the Last of the Crazy?

Tommy required three minutes to walk north from the Hart residence on Front Street to reach Lake Victoria, and another two east along Lakeside Drive, before he reached Tom Patterson Island; the city named the two acres after the Stratford Festival's founder. Pedestrian and auto traffic was light, except for modest congestion approaching the island, where artisans had displayed their wares for Saturday's *Art in the Park* festival.

Tommy's feet clacked on the wooden footbridge as he made his way to the grassy paradise. Tranquility permeated the air, unlike last Saturday when the island hosted a wedding and two hundred guests. He shared the island with a young couple at the early hour of 5:43 am, all three arriving at the brink of sunrise.

Tommy sat on an iron bench facing east while the sun rose. As anticipated, the warmer lake water heated the thin cooler layer of air above, creating a hypnotic fog. Slivers of sunshine pierced their way through the mist, fighting for Tommy's attention. Occasionally, language lacks the words to adequately describe evil; equally, it sometimes understates life's beauty. Tommy could not conjure up words to capture the captivating sight before him.

Tommy closed his eyes and began his meditation – slowing his breath and clearing his mind; the tug of war within his mind remained with stubborn obstinance. An epic battle waged, the outcome determining how he viewed himself and the world. Tommy scoured for anything that would tilt the machine – tilt the war in his favour.

After twenty minutes, Tommy pulled Timothy Findley's *The Last of the Crazy People* from his backpack; two weeks had followed since Chuck placed it in his hands. He silently thanked Lake Victoria for giving him strength – for advising him that he could handle a little bit more.

"Shit!" exclaimed Tommy, opening the book's cover and reading the hand-written note on the first page. *To Chuck, to the best healer I know, Love Tiff.*

Why did he give me a signed copy of the book? Tommy now handled the book with extreme care – with the fragility of the moth that he wanted to cup in his hands and send off to magnificent freedom. Even one smudge would blemish the autographed novel's perfect condition; he promised himself to return it quickly – sooner the better.

Eleven-year-old Hooker grew up in a dysfunctional family; after his mother's miscarriage, she withdrew from the family and locked herself away in her room. Hooker's older brother, Gilbert, enjoyed his alcohol and smoking vices, failing as a role model. Their father, Nicholas, struggled to keep the family together; but with increasing dysfunction, Gilbert commits suicide and plunges the family into despair. The story culminates with Hooker shooting everyone in his family, landing him in a psychiatric hospital.

After seven hours of flipping pages, Tommy finished Timothy Findley's book – the murderous and disappointing ending souring him. He had been expecting an inspirational climax. Why the hell did Chuck give him this damn book? Fuck! I thought he was trying to help me; instead, he showed me how poorly life can end.

Tommy considered ripping the autographed page clear from the book before returning it. The thought swirled in his mind as he slammed the book back into his backpack, wondering if it was Tommy Henderson who was the last of the crazy people. It wasn't the craziest of ideas. The sunny clear sky didn't look as bright as it had that very morning, even though it was; and that was a damn shame.

Back in his room, after preparing a delicious quesadilla, Tommy pulled out his laptop computer gifted to him by Ryan. He drafted a resumé, a difficult task given his experience was limited to slugging pet food. Tommy devoted hours, the final product sparse as to special skills, finding it inappropriate to include "barely surviving."

Tommy desired a summer job with more responsibility, a stepping stone to something better, even if he wasn't sure what he was stepping towards. However, dozens of sent resumes went unanswered, his follow-up calls ignored. Discouraged, he gave up, only to catch a break three weeks later. Tommy had applied to a local law firm searching for someone to shred confidential material and to deliver legal documents to other law firms and real estate agents in and around Stratford.

Marvin Kittle, the managing partner of Stratford boutique law firm Kittle Littner LLP, received Tommy's resumé. The straight-laced, no nonsense driven forty-eight-year-old lawyer had proudly accepted the nickname, "Type A." Up at 5:00 am each morning to gobble breakfast and arrive at the office by 5:45 am, Kittle considered his completion of the New York and Boston marathons as two of his greatest achievements.

Kittle had no intention of interviewing Tom Henderson, a high school student with no relevant work experience; the dozen university applicants were far better suited. But Kittle's law clerk mistakenly scheduled an interview, and by the time the lawyer discovered the mix-up, his guilt prevented him from cancelling. He would allow ten minutes with Thomas T. Henderson and then quickly end their meeting.

The interview lasted an hour. Tommy surprised Kittle, exhibiting maturity beyond age seventeen; the teenager presented well, articulate and sharp-minded. Kittle couldn't explain it; he sensed that Thomas Henderson needed the position more than the others, but several considerations existed.

Thomas or Tom, as he was now presenting himself, left the interview with a handshake, confident that he performed admirably; however, Mr. Kittle warned him that many had applied. A decision would be made within the week.

Despite Kittle's pleasant surprise, the man wavered and waffled over his decision, understanding that hiring Tom Henderson came with risk. Applicants put their best foot forward; looks can be deceiving. Firing him and rehiring him would be inconvenient; safer choices existed. What the hell was it about Thomas Henderson? He ruminated about Tom's answer to one of his questions.

"Thomas, why do you want this position at Kittle Littner?"

"Mr. Kittle, have you heard of chaos theory?" Thomas provided a pinball analogy. Without discussing his background, he stared Kittle directly in the eye and told him that the position would tilt things in his favour.

All the world's a stage, mulled Kittle – those very words spoken the prior evening while sitting in plush seats, taking in Shakespeare's *As You Like It* at the Festival Theatre. Unlike the actor portraying the melancholy Jacques, the sadness in Thomas Henderson's eyes requited no acting. Kittle had seen it hundreds of times in his practice. What had happened to Thomas Henderson?

Tom received a call the day following his interview; he was told to report to Kittle Littner's offices the next morning at 8:00 am sharp.

"Be prepared to work your ass off!" directed Marvin Kittle.

Tom embraced his new job, excitement at the step forward. In addition to the several kilometres he already walked weekly exploring Stratford's beauty, he now biked daily across Stratford delivering and picking up legal documents. His fitness improved; the exercise helped to clear his mind.

However, storm clouds rumbled in; his troubling relationship with Alex offset his accomplishments at the law firm. He and Alex went at it hard on a Tuesday night; Tom didn't get to bed until 2:00 am after losing track of time. Infuriatingly, he broke his promise to be in bed early on weekday nights. Tom slept through his alarm the following morning and arrived a half-hour late for work, ashamed at the disapproving glances when he walked through the door. He had let Marvin Kittle down, a man who had taken a chance on him – it served as a breaking point. They all knew; he was sure of it. He would straighten Alex out when he was mentally prepared.

That evening, while lying in his bed and enjoying a quesadilla, Tom watched *Five Epic Battles that Changed the Course of History* on the History channel: the 490 B.C. Battle of Marathon, when the Greeks repelled Persian invaders, the 1066 Battle of Hastings, when William the Conqueror invaded England and defeated King Harold II, the Surrender of Yorktown in 1781, where General Cornwallis surrendered his British forces, and finally, the 1815 Battle of Waterloo, when the Duke of Wellington defeated Napoleon Bonaparte.

Thomas found the battles fascinating, with impressive courage and conviction on all sides; the soldiers never wavered from the principles upon which they fought. Their ferociousness and tenacity on the battlefield proved it.

However, win or lose, carnage found both sides: amputations, blindness, deafness, lost limbs and of course, death. Curiously, the production included no discussion of the emotional consequences such as flashbacks and nightmares. Even the winners were losers – the conclusion was inescapable.

Tom met with Chuck for lunch two weeks after reading *The Last of the Crazy People*. He felt relieved that he hadn't ripped the autographed page out of the book; it would have made for a tremendously awkward lunch, otherwise.

After a strong handshake, the two sat down at Bentley's restaurant patio, packed with tourists and locals; lively laughter and a million and one stories filled the air under the sunlight. Chuck was genuinely pleased to see him, something that can't be faked. What the servers must overhear, thought Tom: stock tips, who was divorcing who, who was getting fired, who was an alcoholic or criminal.

Tom handed over *The Last of the Crazy People* in perfect condition. "Thank you, Chuck," he said, mostly meaning it.

"First things first, Tommy. I shared your baloney

sandwich story with the Harts. I hope you don't mind."

"Not at all," came the reply, a sheepish smile across his face. "Thank you. It was nice; special, but emotional."

After ordering, Chuck quickly addressed Findley's classic. "Well, how was the book?" asked Chuck, eager to hear his young companion's opinion.

"Honestly, I was surprised to receive an autographed book," replied Tom.

Chuck mulled over his response. His reasons were twofold. He wanted Tommy to know that he trusted him with his book and, secondly, he understood that Tommy would want to return the book as soon as possible. It guaranteed they would speak again, soon.

"I knew you would take care of it, Tommy."

"Were the two of you friends?" asked Tom.

"We were. He was an amazing man. We frequently sat on Pazzo's patio, having a meal and watching the world stroll by. It's amazing what the mind can accomplish, hashing life's bumps out with a friend over a few hours. Everyone has a story."

Tom nodded in agreement. Perhaps everyone has a story, but surely not like his own – one that had shaken his soul.

"So, how about the book?" asked Chuck.

"It was well written, beautifully written but I was bummed at the end. It didn't end well for anyone," explained Tom, feeling comfortable enough to be frank. "I was expecting more of an uplifting ending, maybe a *Chariot's of Fire* sort of thing."

Chuck immediately laughed, a deep belly chortle that brought a smile to Tom's face, followed by his own snicker. Chuck had a gift; making Tom laugh was not easy.

"I understand your sentiment, Tommy; maybe I should have warned you. You're absolutely correct - the ending is not uplifting, but I wanted you to read it to appreciate the contrast between you and Hooker."

"What do you mean?" asked Tom.

"Hooker was driven to insanity and murder by his

horrible existence and circumstances. His brother killed himself for the same reasons."

Tom nodded slowly.

"Tommy, you have already made the most important decision in your life – one that I consider courageous and necessary to ensure that you don't suffer the same fate as Hooker."

Courageous. He had never been called courageous; he certainly had never felt so. Quite contrarily, he had been a coward on the grandest of scales. Yes, the grandest of scales. If Chuck knew the truth, he never would have offered such a misguided compliment.

"Tommy, you made the decision to leave your environment, knowing that you were destined to die a slow death, like Hooker. Leaving as a sixteen-year-old kid with nothing but two knapsacks and a desire for a different path – I can't think of anything more fearless. And that, sir, is the first decision that you made that has tilted this battle in your favour."

Tom enjoyed his lunch with Chuck, a man creeping into friendship territory. He had pulled Tom in tightly, wrapped his arms around him and provided comfort without even touching him. Admittedly, Alex had the same quality at their first introduction; this was different, and so much better.

The two feasted, Chuck on a Bentley's favourite, coconut curry noodles, and Tom on a burger and fries. Tom caught himself laughing, and finding the food delicious.

As they finished up, Tom excused himself after an extended handshake and slap on his back.

"I need to be home by 2:00 pm, Chuck, to assist the Harts with some gardening." After completing the sentence, it struck him; he had referred to the Hart residence as home – a first. It felt good.

A month past his eighteenth birthday, Tom met someone. In his opinion, no other woman matched her beauty. Sure, he recognized the cliché, but the thunderbolt struck him with ferocity. The summer student sat behind the reception desk when he delivered an envelope to the law office of Heintzer Simms.

"Thanks," she said, flashing him a beautiful smile. With questionable subtilty, Tom scanned her – blue eyes, long blond hair and a sexy figure contoured behind a blue blouse and tan skirt. The fine-detailed flower-shaped pendant around her neck resembled his mother's.

Tom failed to immediately respond, the lightning strike deactivating his vocal cords and social skills.

"I love your pendant," he finally squeaked after a few awkward seconds.

"Why thank you," she said, maintaining her smile, and noticing his sparkling blue eyes. She gazed down at her pendant, "My mother gave it to me."

Tom nodded and retreated, leaving the office. Arriving at the elevator, he chastised himself for not saying more, or even asking her name. He had never experienced the odd tingling feeling in his stomach before; the intense sensation could remain forever, he determined, the unabating thumping of his heart heard through his chest.

Veronica, back in the office, rubbed her pendant as she was accustomed. What a surprising but pleasant detail for a teenage boy to notice, she mused.

Tom had never had a girlfriend – or kissed a girl. Now six feet tall and in fabulous shape, he had long ago lost his scrawny physique. Limited confidence, desire and gumption all contributed to his lack of experience, but he couldn't deny it – something unfamiliar had been awoken deep inside.

That night, Tom's difficulty falling asleep arose not because of the anticipation of visiting demons; rather, a nameless woman, who he had met once for two minutes, carried the blame. Surely, she was not interested in Tom Henderson; he knew it. How could she have affected him that quickly? Damn, the mind was peculiar – and occasionally in a good way.

The following day, he canvassed everyone at Kittle Littner to determine if anything required delivery to Heintzer

Simms with disappointing results. At lunch, on his own time, he took matters into his own hands and biked to Heintzer Simms. As the elevator reached the fourth floor, second-guessing consumed him; what the hell was he thinking? He took a few steps and peeked through the glass doors of the law office.

The goddess sat there – not absent on a lunch break as he feared; his heart galloped quickly, his eyes stuck on the silver flower pendant. Tom took a deep breath and summoned his courage before pushing open the doors.

He strolled in casually. "Hi, I'm here for a pick-up for the law office of Kittle Littner," he asked her, glimpsing down at her name tag, Veronica.

"I don't think so," Veronica replied with a puzzled look, her eyebrows scrunched. She searched her desk, shuffled papers and appeared frazzled. Then, she picked up her telephone and called six other law clerks to inquire; Tom's guilt accelerated, his ruse causing unforeseen grief. She finally put the receiver down.

"No, nothing for pick-up," she said, shrugging her shoulders. "What was to be picked up? From whom?" Her smile appeared – Tom began to melt; a few more minutes in Veronica's presence and he would become a puddle on the floor.

"Hmmm, I'm not sure," he replied. "There must be a misunderstanding. You must be new here?" asked Tom, acting on his contrived segue.

"I sure am!" she said. "I started three days ago for the summer. I begin university classes in September; I'm saving for tuition."

"I'm Veronica Edwards," she said, extending her hand.

"Tom Henderson. Very nice to meet you, Veronica," he replied, matching her smile, feigning calmness. Her soft, smooth hand grabbed his, sending electricity through him; he hung on longer than necessary.

"I'm sure I'll see you soon, Veronica," he said joyfully. "I'm here two or three times a week."

"Well, until then, Tom," she replied as he walked backwards slowly until she was out of sight.

"Wow," he said to himself, descending on the elevator, pleased he had both kept his composure and did not end up as an embarrassing puddle on the floor.

Work at Kittle Littner progressed well for Tom; Kittle provided increasing responsibility. He self-taught how to use digital legal research databases, a task normally reserved for summer law students. Kittle appreciated the promise in young Henderson; maybe he could help tilt the machine?

When August arrived, Tom questioned his flirting prowess. Although Veronica laughed at his cheesy jokes, her responses indicated nothing more than decency. No reliable clue existed of her interest in him. She would be heading to university in less than a month; he might never see her again. The solution was simple; ask her out, but Tom didn't have the nerve. What's the worst that can happen, he reasoned? She says no; what's the big deal?

But Tom's subconsciousness understood the big deal – the brain is a curious and wonderful organ, complex and mysterious. How was it that they knew to come over the wall and attack when he slept? How was it that they understood every last fear and weakness he had? Veronica's rejection would crush him, his egg-shell exterior crumbling from the assault.

Every time he stepped off the elevator at Heintzer Simms, he intended to ask her out, but it never happened – his past muzzling him. Self-chastising proved ineffective.

One evening in late August, Tom sat with Dillon at his home on a Friday night. Alex attended, as usual; however, despite an uneasy truce, tension existed between the two. While the evening became somewhat rowdy, Tom did not consider it excessive.

Tom laid out his intense feelings for Veronica.

"So, Tommy Henderson has a big-time crush," teased Dillon, laughing. "Well, I happen to be a ladies' man, so I can help you!"

Once Dillon was done razzing his buddy, they put their heads together. The two concluded that Tom would show himself as a bumbling fool if he asked Veronica out in person; the results may be disastrous. They hatched a different plan so brilliant in its simplicity, that Tom didn't understand why hadn't conceived of it himself. Was it juvenile? Yes. Was it immature? Yes, but time dwindled.

The following Monday, Tom arrived at Heintzer Simms in the late morning with only one envelope.

"Good morning," said Veronica, greeting him with her usual beautiful and cheery smile. Tom noticed her knee-length skirt, heart-shaped locket and two small pearl earrings.

"Good morning, Veronica," replied Tom, just as cheerfully. "Just one envelope today. Read carefully who it's for," emphasized Tom through the squeakiness of his voice.

"Okay," she replied curiously, taking the envelope in slow motion.

"Got to run, Veronica. Lots of deliveries today," he said, hustling to the elevator as quickly as possible. He had spent hours on the letter, agonizing and redrafting his words; he did not want to be present when she opened his letter, relieved when the elevator door closed.

Veronica looked down at the envelope.

"VERONICA EDWARDS (PERSONAL & CONFIDENTIAL)"

She tore open the envelope and pulled out the letter. Veronica began to read the handwritten letter. After a minute, she arrived at the last line:

One date? I will be at Revival House Restaurant tonight at 6:30 pm. If you don't come, I completely understand.

Tom struggled to concentrate the rest of the afternoon, hoping that at any moment he would pick up his ringing phone to hear Veronica on the other end; but when he left the office at 5:15 pm, demoralization had come aboard – nothing but silence. He biked home, ran up the stairs two at a time, and flopped on his bed. He read a note left under his bedroom door informing him that the Harts would be home late after a fundraising dinner.

Tom considered the ramifications if Veronica did not arrive at the restaurant. He imagined the embarrassing walk of shame he would endure each time he dropped documents off at the front desk of Heintzer Simms. Perhaps he hadn't thought his plan through. His doubts crept to the surface, keen on explaining that foolishness put him in this position. Why had he raised his hopes?

Tom was about to shower when he heard a knock on the front door; knowing the Harts were absent, he bounded down the stairs and flung the door open.

"Hi, Tom," said Veronica, shocking him; his jaw dropped. "I'm sorry. I couldn't wait until 6:30."

Before she finished her sentence, Tom grabbed her; he hugged her tightly, giving no consideration to the idea that she intended to let him down easily. She hugged him back with equal force; he held her tighter than he had ever held anyone before – he knew that she loved him as much as he loved her. Having waited his whole life to be held like that, Tom did not let go, cherishing every last second.

Tom repeated those magical words in his head, 'I'm sorry, I couldn't wait until 6:30.' Never had sweeter words been spoken to him; Shakespeare could not have crafted anything as divine.

And then they kissed – a soft beautiful kiss – the kind that stays with a man forever. Any attempt to describe the kiss, even by masters of prose, would understate what it meant to Thomas Henderson. But, if forced to, exploding fireworks would suffice.

A scientist would have physiologically described it as a wave of endorphins shooting through his body, but to Tom, it was simply a wave of goodness fighting back against his past. As his mind swirled, he understood true love; he would never let it go.

They pulled back from each other, staring without saying a word, Tom finally breaking the silence, "I can't believe you're here, Veronica."

"I can't believe it took you that long to ask me out," she said, poking him in the stomach. "How many signs could I give you? I was sure you weren't interested," she said, hugging him again.

Hand in hand, the two smitten teenagers walked to Revival House for dinner, although Tom's feet never touched the ground. Three hours later, after incessant talking, laughing and smiling, Tom and Veronica said good night, ending the best day of his life.

Tom felt alive for the first time, his head crashing down on his pillow, full of exhilaration. He briefly had the urge to celebrate with Alex, but decided against it; why take the chance of ruining a perfect day? At least for one night, his demons had no chance of climbing over the wall as he drifted into sleep – repelled by visions of a beautiful smile.

A few weeks later, Veronica and Tom strolled Lakeside Drive on a hot Sunday afternoon with no particular destination. The two stopped under a leafy, mature tree, a few feet west of the Tom Patterson bridge to cool in the shade and escape the thirty-degree heat. Car after car cruised past slowly, keeping time with the casual speed of the river and the few clouds overhead.

Patrons and artists at *Art in the Park* bartered and engaged in delightful chatter. Tom watched a family carefully place a tablecloth over a picnic table, three feet from the water's edge. An enthusiastic game of cricket played at the foot of the majestic Shakespearean Festival Theatre, brought the occasional jubilant shriek. Built in the 1950s at the top of a hill, it stood there with its crown-like roof, overseeing its subjects below.

Tom grabbed Veronica's hand and gently pulled her away from a few wild honey bees that had built a hive in the hollow of the tree, a few feet from them, the honey overflowing from its comb and dripping down the trunk. She smiled and thanked him.

Their relationship blossomed quickly, the two becoming inseparable. When Veronica decided to remain in Stratford and commute to her university classes in Guelph, Tom was thrilled.

Tom opened up to Veronica, describing the history with his mother and most of the circumstances that had brought him to Stratford; but he never told the complete story. He had never told anyone the full story – shame and pain did not allow for it under any circumstances.

Veronica provided her full support. Like Marvin Kittle, she knew Tom could accomplish whatever he wanted in life, although he did not have a plan.

An improved position on the battlefield did not equate with victory. Although an extra battalion, masquerading as love, had shored up the brigade, Tom's battle was far from over. Veronica, alone, could not exorcise Tom's demons. While he would accept all assistance, ultimately this was his fight.

Veronica had raised his relationship with Alex on several occasions, turning the calm waters of their romance somewhat choppier, threatening the stability of the new relationship. Veronica told him without equivocation that no room existed in their relationship for a third; she refused to carve out any space for the negative influence. The ultimatum scared the hell out of Tom.

CHAPTER THIRTEEN

The Break-up

Anxiousness consumed Tom; he ruminated over Alex while staring up at the ceiling from his bed, exhausted after ten hours at the firm, but unable to quiet his mind. Damn it! Alex scared him – the effect on Veronica, his future, and the direction that he was travelling. How was it that the warm blanket that protected him from the icy realities of life, now served as a barrier against all the goodness that wanted to enter?

It was disconcerting how Alex had managed to carve out an ever-expanding place in his life over the years, an insidious erosion – as slow as it took the ocean tides to create The Hopewell Rocks in New Brunswick. It took those tides an eternity to create those lonely, massive rock formations that now penetrated the surface of the ocean waters, a dramatic ending to years of daily, unrelenting assaults against the seemingly impenetrable surface. Those rocks now appeared isolated and unprotected as they faced the turbulent waters and harsh elements, circumstances that Tom wanted to escape.

He was at a crossroads but wondered if he was mentally prepared for the battle. His stomach knotted; he couldn't push a quesadilla down his throat. He had not encountered the uncomfortable sensation since he couldn't take another bite of Muriel's delicious chocolate chip cookie, so many years ago.

Tom remembered those chocolate chip cookies with crystal clarity; he recalled everything about the trial. The scent of Howard King's cologne entered his nose while thinking of his march to that tiny, bare room. Unfortunately, many memories from his youth were just as vivid – the smell of campfire smoke muscled the cologne aside as Tom looked for a non-existent Nile River on the ceiling.

Breaking up is difficult, especially when you have been together that long; did he have the courage to do it? Alcoholism had a stranglehold on him – those gigantic hands had the strength of a thousand men.

"Tommy, grab me an Alex from the fridge!" bellowed his mother nonstop over the years, requesting that he bring her a beer – an Alexander Keith's Pale Ale. Her favourite brand filled the fridge, leaving no space for milk on the shelves.

One fateful day, he grabbed two cans – one for Linda, and one for himself. The first sip kicked off an intense and complicated relationship with Alex. His new, constant companion brought a fogginess that dulled his demons' swords when they came over the wall to attack; however, the irony that Alex carried his own sword, and was now prepared to plunge the cold metal into him was clear. Tom's one-time protector, jilted by his consideration to end it, advanced with a full-scale assault; Alex sensed the teenager's wavering and vulnerabilities – he had never been committed to the break-up before.

Tom closed his eyes, drifting to unconscious sleep two hours later. In World War II, when the Germans proceeded with ten months of bombing raids on England, Brits described the difficulty of falling asleep at night, afraid of the carnage that would arrive overnight. Tom understood.

Alex came while deep in REM sleep – using the cover of night to scale the wall, arm in arm with Tom's other demons; the nocturnal visit had played out hundreds of times before. As Alex scaled up that ancient, stone wall, with a combination of delight and purpose, Tom met Alex at the top.

Alex, with a devilish grin, smiled at Tom's subconscious and reminded him of their inseparability.

"Tommy, I'm here. With me, you can forget that nasty stuff with Hiller; I know how those secrets torment you, but I'm here now, buddy."

For unclear reasons, except that the mind is both a curious and mysterious organ, Alex was not afforded free rein to scale down the other side of the wall.

"You're are not coming over this time, Alex. It's over. This time, I mean it."

Alex's grin disappeared, replaced with pursed lips and

irritation from being challenged.

"No, it's not over, Tommy," replied Alex, sternly. "You're being emotional. We've been through this before; we can work it out, just like the other times."

"It's different this time, Alex. I'm stronger; I'm moving on."

"Move on?" Alex cackled. "You've said that countless times, but couldn't – because you're weak. You're a weak, son of a bitch. So, let me scale down the wall and get this over with."

"It's different, now. I'm sorry, Alex."

"It's not different, Tommy. Who was there for you when nobody else was? Me! Who was there when there wasn't another goddamn person who cared about you? Me!"

"You're not good for me anymore, Alex. I need to move on."

"But Tom, for so many years I've protected you when they came for you – when they came over the wall! Have you thought about that?"

"Every bloody day, Alex. I'm ready to defeat them without you."

"You'll never do it, Tom. You little, wimpy bitch. Because I'm at your side – that's why you have any courage. You're nothing, without me. I lifted your sorry, pathetic ass up off the ground and gave you the strength to leave your mother's house. What about loyalty?"

"It wasn't you, Alex. I wanted you to leave then."

Alex laughed in Tom's face. "That's bullshit, Henderson. I know your dirty little secrets. Have you forgotten that? You'll never get over that without me."

"I've got Veronica now. I don't need you anymore."

"So, Tom, it is that bitch who is getting in between us!"

"Hey, leave her out of it; she's everything you're not. She loves me. She wants me to improve."

"Okay, Tom. I understand you're upset. I'm sorry for what I said about Veronica. This is hard for me, too. Let's compromise; we'll only see each other once a week? We can't throw our relationship away. Look what we've been through."

"We're though, Alex! You've never respected the boundaries I set."

"Listen, I get it. I understand, Tom. How about just one more night, then? For old time's sake."

"It's over. I never want to see you again, Alex!"

"Fuck you, Henderson, you ungrateful asshole. And, fuck that little whore, Veronica. I'm going nowhere!"

Alex took one hand off the top of the wall, slapped Tom across the face and laughed at him. "What are you going to do about it - you pathetic, little man."

With no success, Tom attempted to shove Alex back down the wall. Alex had tightened his grip, smirking at Tom's futility.

Tom's rage had been accumulating for eight years; it shot to the surface with a vengeance. Was he capable? Tom reached out and grabbed Alex's throat with two hands; he squeezed with all his might, veins popping in his forearms.

"That's right, Henderson. You'll have to kill me because I'm not going anywhere," squeaked Alex, his face turning red without oxygen. Alex's hands loosened.

Briefly, Tom considered releasing Alex's neck, but his rage peaked. It was now or never. He maintained the pressure, never letting up. Tom watched the blood vessels in Alex's eyes begin to pop, the beginning of the end. Only when Alex's limp, lifeless body remained in his hands, did he let go, allowing Alex to hurtle back down the wall. Tom stared down at the crumpled body. Had the demon been slain? Suddenly, Alex's body twitched. Tom's relief turned to terror, his expanded eyes staring down, wondering if he had not completed the job; but consciousness intervened before he could make a final determination.

Tom's eyes opened in fear, awoken from his nightmare as he had many times before. Sweat dripped from his forehead. He placed his face into his hands and sobbed, completely exhausted. Tom couldn't catch his breath, his chest heaving in and out.

Pushing himself to a sitting position in bed, Tom looked over at the clock – 3:00 am. Weary, he slid out of bed; it had to be done now. Tom reached under the bed and pulled out a case of Alexander Keith's Pale Ale. Sixteen full cans remained. He picked up the case, opened his bedroom door and tiptoed down the hallway to the bathroom. It takes twenty-two seconds to open and empty a standard 341 ml can of beer into the toilet; after less than six minutes, Tom returned to his room with twenty-four empty cans now in the case.

Tom slid into bed. He laid his head on a pillow and looked up at the ceiling. He considered himself a recovering alcoholic. The carnage from those five epic battles that changed the course of history consumed him. They could add a sixth, he reasoned.

CHAPTER FOURTEEN

The Uninvited Guest

After Tom's high school graduation, he began working full-time at the law firm. He completed an online university degree with Veronica's encouragement – a three-year political science degree while working full-time; the years whizzed by. The busyness focused Tom's mind and served as a positive distraction.

At work, increasing responsibilities such as drafting pleadings and attending to several small claims court matters kept his mind active.

With a degree in hand, Kittle called Tom into his office one Friday afternoon.

"Sit down, Tom," he said, motioning him to a leather chair. Kittle pushed a pile of stacked client files aside, clearing the view to his young employee.

"Listen, Tom. You've been performing remarkably well here," he explained. "We've noticed the steps you've taken to improve yourself."

"Thank you, sir," replied Tom to his mentor.

Kittle proceeded to encourage him to apply to law school, promising a $5,000 scholarship for each of the three years plus a glowing reference letter. Tom exited the office, excited about the possibility.

That evening, he and Veronica sat under an umbrella at the corner of St. Patrick and George Street, dining at The Parlour Steakhouse. Tom quickly raised his earlier conversation with Kittle, the excitement in his eyes reciprocated by his date.

"Of course, you have to go!" exclaimed Veronica. "It's the chance of a lifetime."

Her unreserved encouragement meant everything to Tom. The question about to come off his lips was appropriate – it was time; not one doubt existed.

Looking at his future, Tom reached across his steak

dinner and handed Veronica a box. As she pulled out the ring, Tom asked her to marry him. He had planned something more romantic, but he couldn't wait a minute longer.

"Of course, I'll marry you," she screeched, tears welling. "I love you, Thomas Henderson."

"I love you, too!" he replied, wiping away his own tears.

A man, donning a baseball hat and sunglasses, dined across the room. He observed the two teary-eyed fiancés creating a mild fuss. While the man decided not to stroll over and say hello to his old friend, recognizing that Tom was deep in conversation, a smile formed on his face. Chuck witnessed it all play out; he couldn't have been more pleased that Tom tilted the pinball machine in his favour with something called love.

Tom and Veronica decided on a quick, intimate wedding; they scheduled it six weeks later, in October.

For the next few weeks, the two busily planned their wedding. Tom studied into the wee hours each night for his upcoming law school entrance exams.

Veronica's parents hosted the wedding at their house. The pair exchanged nuptials on two acres in the village of Sebringville at the outskirt of Stratford. Perfection reigned with unseasonably high temperatures, allowing guests to wear shorts and short-sleeve shirts at their casual affair. As smoke wafted from the spit, Dillon, Ryan and Chuck stood at Tom's side while he and Veronica exchanged vows.

Linda Henderson was noticeably absent on Tom's special day. Tom didn't even know if his mother lived in the same apartment, or if she was still alive. Her previous patterns suggested she would have moved on several occasions by now to evade creditors.

While Tom had thought of his mother often, he had not seen her for six years since walking out her door; he harboured no desire to invite her. Had she taken even one step to find him after he left? For the first few weeks after his arrival at the Hart residence, he expected the police to arrive and chastise him for leaving his mother in that manner.

"How could you not leave a note?" the officer would ask him. "Your mother is worried sick; she hasn't slept a wink since you left." Then, the officer would order him to pack his belongings, "I'm driving you back."

But the police did not arrive – and after a few weeks, Tom lost hope. What kind of mother was Linda Henderson? Unfortunately, he knew the answer to that question, but the reasons behind her deficits were as complicated as the brain itself.

After a tearful and emotional goodbye with the Harts, Tom and Veronica moved into their own apartment on Wellington Street, in Stratford, above the Red Rabbit Restaurant. Tom had no appropriate words to express his gratitude to the Harts, a loving couple who literally saved his life. Ryan had tossed him a lifeline and pulled him in from stormy seas, a minute before he was about to go under.

Curiously, Tom never discovered why Ryan attended Choices for Change, but figured someone probably threw him a lifeline once – probably Chuck. Out of respect, Tom never inquired what circumstances brought him to those meetings. He thought Ryan would raise it if he so desired, but it never happened. And that was fine with Tom. A man deserves his privacy, especially dealing with his demons.

The newlyweds decided against an immediate honeymoon. The cost factored in, as did Tom's hectic pace studying for the law school entrance examination courses – the LSAT – and working full-time. He had three months to prepare and write the exams for a hopeful following September admission. Life consisted of three activities: working, studying and taking long walks with his wife throughout Stratford.

When exam time arrived, Tom was prepared. Each of the six sections dealing with different areas of competence was brutally difficult. He did his best, but skepticism crept in as he left the exam room. However, he was now living his life like he wanted – like the Avon River – effortlessly maneuvering over and around those rocks in its way.

Tom's life was moving fast. As his troublesome past became more distant and replaced with better memories, his outlook had become increasingly positive. His sleep improved; the frequency Veronica had to wake from screaming nightmares had decreased. However, his secrets remained in the rear-view mirror, despite speeding away from them as fast as possible.

One morning, Tom awoke to Veronica's absence in bed. Clearing his eyes, she ran from the bathroom with a pregnancy test in her hand; because of her glow, he didn't need an explanation to understand. His eyes opened up as wide as possible with excitement.

"We're pregnant!" she exclaimed.

"Oh my god, Veronica," whooped Tom. "We're having a baby?"

"We sure are, honey," she replied. "Or, shall I call you, daddy?" They hugged tightly – tighter than on their first date. Veronica was in love with a week-old baby.

With a child on the way, Tom and Veronica moved into a small bungalow owned by Veronica's parents, who rented it to them at below-market rent. The finished basement, good-sized backyard, and office for Tom to study in were great; but the glimpse of Lake Victoria one block north from their upstairs bedroom created perfection. Tom watched the water effortlessly flowing west towards Shakespearean Gardens daily, a reminder to forge ahead.

Tom pulled the mail from the mailbox each day expecting to find a letter from the University of Western Ontario, in London, in response to his law school application. Because it was in commuting distance from Stratford, he only applied to one school. They wanted to remain near Veronica's parents.

Tom felt disappointed when he found the mailbox empty. However, Tom's past was about to collide with his present, an ironic clash that would forever determine his future.

CHAPTER FIFTEEN

Collision Course

As the years passed since the *Regina v. Hiller* criminal trial, Jonathon Sussman constantly wondered what had become of Tommy Henderson. He couldn't shake the mop-topped kid who suffered an unfortunate destiny of testifying against a sexual predator. Every time he prosecuted a sexual assault case, or questioned a child witness, his mind wandered to Tommy. The justice system failed his young witness; worse, he had played a haunting role. On good days, Sussman felt that failure of the system was an inherent part of any system run by human beings. After all, humans make mistakes; it was inescapable.

On bad days, his fumbling of the case ate at him with insidious resolve. A vast difference between human error and incompetence existed. Was he ready to have handled that case? With the benefit of hindsight, he easily concluded the answer in the negative. He never would have made those same mistakes in later years.

Hiller's acquittal created a minor bump in the road toward Sussman's trajectory to legal greatness. Although his boss, Roger Tillman, supported him after the acquittal, another two years had passed before the rising star was given another high-profile case. Prosecutions and politics were inseparable; the case created embarrassment for Tillman.

Sussman considered the acquittal more than a professional issue. Both Hiller and the system abused the boy. Surely, Tommy was left with the view that the jurors didn't believe him – that he was a liar; such a heavy anchor must have weighed the boy down. No child should begin life under those circumstances.

Boorish as it was, he was relieved when Hiller killed himself, a befitting karmic ending for the monster. He no longer had to worry when Hiller would prey on his next victim; it had already become one hell of a way to live before his death.

Ten years after the trial, Sussman drove around London on a Sunday afternoon, clearing his head – his favourite way to relax. He took a right on Dundas Street and headed eastbound towards the core of the city. As he slowed for a red light, he drove past a newly-opened diner, *Tommy's Diner*. It couldn't be, he concluded. What are the chances? But his calculations confirmed the possibility.

He completed a U-turn and returned to the diner, expecting to find a smiling Tommy Henderson smiling behind the counter, excited at operating his own business. Tommy would proceed to explain that all that trial stuff was only a minor blip on his way to a successful life.

"Don't give it a second thought," Tommy would tell Sussman after the prosecutor apologized for botching the trial. Tommy would regret that the trial had caused Sussman so much grief and hand him a coffee, "On the house, Mr. Sussman."

Sussman pulled into the parking lot and took a spot in between two other cars near the front entrance. He entered the diner and took a seat at the counter, ordering a coffee to go from a teenager, who looked about eighteen. While the waitress was pouring his coffee, he asked her who owned the diner.

"My father, Tom Fister. Why do you ask?" she said, worriedly.

"No reason. I thought it might be owned by an old friend of mine," he replied.

Sussman left *Tommy's Diner* with his coffee, feeling silly about his unplanned detour. He hopped back into his car and continued touring the city; however, he couldn't shake Tommy Henderson. "Damn it," he said to himself, considering a second detour.

Sussman turned right off King Street and then made a left on William Street, travelling two blocks until he arrived at Shirley Avenue. He slowed – giving himself time to change his mind – but he did not; he turned left and crept along the street, confident that he would remember Linda Henderson's apartment building. He pulled over in front of a grey-bricked, three-story building, second-guessing his decision. Anyway, ten years had passed, making it unlikely that Linda and Tommy remained in the same apartment. Surely, they no longer lived there.

Sussman got out of his car and walked slowly to the front doors; he entered the smelly lobby. Animal urine? Human? His finger scrolled down the list of names, B Adams – 1D, R Anderson - 2D, K Brennan - 3C, F Caruthers - 3F and then L Henderson - 2B. Damn, they still live here, understanding that this was no longer a theoretical exercise.

Was he being too obsessive? Impulsive behaviour and stalking past witnesses were not his styles. He retreated, taking a few steps back towards the doors. "Damn it," he said, stepping forward, and ascending the stairs to the second floor. He had to know. Traumatized children frequently had a disproportionate contact with the criminal justice system later in life.

Sussman found apartment 2B, knocked three times loudly and waited, preparing himself to be invited in by Linda and Tommy for a morning coffee and a muffin. No answer followed. He knocked five more times, this time louder. After thirty seconds, he could hear faint shuffling from within the apartment. He looked at his watch, 11:40 am.

Suddenly, the door opened about eight inches. Linda Henderson, dressed in a raggedy white nightgown, looked out into the dark hallway at Sussman. Straining, she squinted attempting to process his face.

"Hi, Linda."

A few seconds passed while Linda tried to identify her uninvited visitor. "Jonathon?" she finally asked, unsure.

"Yes, Linda. It's Jonathon Sussman," he replied. "I'm sorry for dropping in like this. I was driving by and wondered how you and Tommy were doing," he explained, not anticipating the awkwardness.

"I haven't seen Tommy for five years," she said, her head bowed to avoid eye contact and the light. "He left when he was sixteen. I'm ashamed that I haven't seen or talked to him since. I have no idea where he is or what he's doing."

The revelation smacked Jonathon in the face – it stung. Disappointment engulfed him. He had expected Linda to open the door and invite him in, followed by Tommy's appearance. Tommy would approach him and shake his hand, smiling. His envision was worse than wishful thinking; it was delusional to expect that door to open up and reveal something wonderful.

"How are you keeping?" asked Sussman, hoping for a positive response but not expecting it. She had not aged well, appearing closer to fifty than thirty-six. She remained as thin as he remembered but sicklier. His eyes wandered to the scarring on her left wrist. Woken from a deep slumber and not expecting a visitor, Linda forgot to put on the black velvet wristband that she usually wore to hide the permanent memorial of that desperate night. Linda, seeing her visitor stare at her wrist, quickly hid her hand behind the door.

Linda just shook her head sideways, no, answering Sussman without saying a word. He wasn't sure if she was answering his question or simply indicating that she was in no mood for a conversation.

"I'm sorry, Jonathon. I would invite you in but the place is a mess and I haven't slept much," she said, yawning. "I wouldn't be very good company. But it was nice to see you."

Before he could ask another question, she closed the door, ending their brief interaction. Jonathon walked away, shaking his head in disappointment. "Shit," he said loudly. "Why did I knock on that goddamn door, today?" It was a detour that he would regret for some time.

Despite the setback caused by *Regina v. Hiller*, Sussman's career eventually flourished. He sat as a director on a number of corporate boards and was heavily involved in professional development within the criminal bar. Additionally, he was teaching Introduction to Criminal Law and Sentencing as an adjunct law professor at the University of

Western Ontario in London. He devoted his life to the law, working upwards of one hundred hours per week. He had no time for a social life, preferring his marriage to the law, even if it was extremely lonely.

Although well respected for his courtroom acumen, successfully prosecuting many high-profile cases including two murder cases, some interpersonal issues had arisen within his workplace over the years. Sussman occasionally wondered how far that functional borderline personality apple his father had been diagnosed with, fell from the tree.

Approximately one year after dropping in on Linda Henderson, Sussman sat in his office at the University of Western Ontario. He headed the law school's admissions committee. That particular day, he had to review and select five further law school applicants from fifty for admission. The fifty had tied at the cutoff line based upon a combination of undergraduate university grades and LSAT test scores.

Only one hundred and forty-five students out of one thousand eight hundred applications would enter law school; the competition was fierce, requiring the rejection of many qualified candidates. Sussman agonized over the decision as he reviewed the fifty applications – picking five became torturous because they were practically indistinguishable.

Sussman picked up the forty-second application and read the name, Thomas T. Henderson. It was a common name, he mused; this must be a different Tommy Henderson. It had to be, he concluded, having had already learned his lesson from *Tommy's Diner* a year earlier. Besides, he deduced, Tommy Henderson had left home at sixteen; it wasn't realistic that he would be applying to law school under those difficult circumstances. Finding him in a gutter was likelier.

Sussman reviewed the application carefully. Thomas T. Henderson resided in Stratford, Ontario. He was born on August 6, 1993, which did fit the Tommy Henderson he remembered. He read a glowing letter of reference from a Marvin Kittle.

Sussman flipped to the last page, where applicants

attached personal passport-sized photographs. He stared at the photo. He had difficulty recalling the boy's face from ten years ago, let alone determining whether this photo was him. But the red hair matched the boy he knew.

Sussman turned to his computer and signed into the Crown's secure website. He typed his password, getbadguys123. A search of "Hiller" prosecutions in the last thirty years revealed thirteen. Sussman clicked on Robert Hiller, which brought him to the prosecution case summary. He scanned the brief quickly, arriving at the twentieth line – *Complainant: Thomas Theodore Henderson, D.O.B., August 6, 1993.*

Sussman's arms dropped to his side; he fell back into his chair and looked at the ceiling. Unbelievable! It's him! He had never been more stunned, or relieved – his body tingling with the discovery. Shaking his head, he announced to an empty room, "I only have four more to choose."

CHAPTER SIXTEEN

It's Just Not Fair

"Have you been in front of the new judge, Tom?" asked Mike Dare.

Tom and his colleague stood in the counsel lounge, hurriedly putting their robes on in preparation for court, commencing in three minutes. After rushing from his law office, he only had a few minutes to gown. Three years out from being called to the Ontario Bar, he had built himself a busy criminal law practice.

After graduating from law school, Tom opened his own law practice when, to everyone's surprise, Kittle decided to retire and open up a bed and breakfast on the banks of Lake Victoria. After a distressing assessment from his cardiologist, Kittle knew his heart would survive longer without the stress of a busy litigation practice. With his mentor gone, Tom set off on his own.

Tom loved lawyering - the intellectual demands, stewardship of the justice system and most importantly, the adherence to the highest of ethical standards.

"No, who's the judge today, Mike?"

"Judge Sussman," he said. "He seems okay, maybe a little cranky; but aren't they all," he said, laughing. "He's newly appointed. Apparently, he's a top legal mind out of London," Dare explained, opening his eyes wide in feigned reverence. "I hope we don't disappoint him with our regular legal minds here in Stratford."

"I don't think you're allowed to be a judge until you've lost your sense of humour," said Tom. "I'm sure I read that in the *Courts of Justice Act*."

Tom turned back to Dare, "Mike, what did you say his name was?"

"Sussman. Why do you ask?" replied Dare.

"It sounds familiar. Anyway, I'm not sure we need another cranky judge," said Tom, lightly slapping his colleague's back.

"Are you golfing tonight?" asked Dare, referencing "men's night" at the Stratford Golf Club.

"No, and I doubt I'll be golfing much this season. I'm putting in long hours at my practice; I'm not seeing Veronica and Lucas enough as it is. So, if I intend on remaining married, it will be difficult to fit golf in," said Tom, dryly.

"How is the little guy?" asked Dare.

"Lucas is fabulous; he's changed our lives in so many ways. I like you too much to bore you with hours of little Lucas stories," said Tom.

"Much appreciated," replied Mike, smirking.

Tom opened the door to the courtroom, bowed, and took a seat three benches back. He watched as the new judge, Crown Attorney Denis Barrison and defence counsel Mary Chapman discussed a sentencing date.

The spectacled judge, with short dark hair, scanned the courtroom as he listened to submissions by Denis Barrison. A moment later, the judge's eyes locked on Tom's. Tom smiled slightly to acknowledge the judge, but subtle enough not to interrupt the submissions. The judge looked back towards Barrison.

Sussman, Sussman, Sussman; Tom repeated the name in his head. Why is that name familiar? The judge also looked vaguely familiar, but he could not piece it together.

A few court matters later, the judge inquired if anyone had any quick matters to address before the morning recess.

Tom jumped to his feet and approached the bench. "Good morning, Your Honour," announced Tom. For the record, my name is Henderson, initial T."

"Yes, thank you, Mr. Henderson. I think we may have met, before," said the judge.

While Tom racked his brain as to where he met Judge Sussman, he spoke to the criminal matter of *R. v. Hutton*. "I'm acting as an agent for Julia Wilson, who acts for Mr. Hutton, Your Honour," advised Tom. He went on, "This is the first appearance and I'm asking that the matter be put over to

September 13 to give Ms. Wilson time to review the disclosure provided by the Crown."

"That's agreeable," said Barrison.

"Matter put over to September 13 for either a guilty plea or to set a trial date," ordered Judge Sussman, scribbling his endorsement in the court record. "Mr. Henderson, please advise Ms. Wilson that I will not be granting another adjournment unless there are extraordinary circumstances," he said, firmly.

"Yes, of course, thank you, Your Honour," replied Tom.

Tom bowed, retreated from the bench, and left the courtroom. Perhaps he crossed paths with the judge in Woodstock, where he attended court from time to time.

Tom stopped in the foyer of the courthouse to speak to court clerk Heather Gibbs. They engaged in small talk, complaining about the weather and the City's doubling of metered parking rates.

As Tom said goodbye to Heather, a call of his name from behind interrupted his exit, "Mr. Henderson!"

Tom spun around, surprised to find Judge Sussman coming toward him. "Mr. Henderson, do you have a couple of minutes to chat?"

"Of course, Your Honour," he replied, respectfully – although his time was tight.

"Let's go to my chambers, then," directed the judge.

The request puzzled Tom. *What is this all about?* He wasn't about to question the new judge about his motives, wanting to make a positive first impression.

The two of them climbed the stairs to the second level of the courthouse where the judges' chambers were located. Neither of them said a word until they entered his office and sat down, Judge Sussman behind his desk in a black leather swivel armchair and Tom in one of the two chairs in front. Tom could hear the ornate clock tick on the wall.

"Do you remember me, Mr. Henderson?" the judge asked.

Tom had already searched his memories for an answer,

without success; but he paused for effect, before responding. "Did we meet in the Woodstock court, sir?"

"No, Mr. Henderson," he replied. "That's not it. That's not it, at all."

Tom's answer did not surprise Sussman; he was only ten years old when Hiller's trial went forward, and over a decade had passed.

That cute, childish face was long gone. It pleased Sussman that Tommy Henderson had made something of his life, and was equally satisfied that he played a role in getting him into law school. Without his assistance, Tommy Henderson likely would not have been one of the fortunate chosen five.

Sussman recognized the bright blue eyes; they sparkled and weren't so sad now. But the out-of-control red curly hair had been replaced with the neat and tightly cropped haircut of a professional. He had a man's body; Tommy kept himself in shape. The judge had aged too, but also kept himself in shape with a strict daily exercise regimen.

However, the long work hours had taken their toll on Sussman. He hadn't had one serious relationship since becoming a lawyer. In most ways that mattered, he was a lonely man for complex reasons. As much as he loved the law, the law did not love him back, quite as much.

As he stared at Tom across his desk, he was convinced he would not have recognized Tommy Henderson by appearance alone. He would just have walked by him on the street.

Hiller's trial still haunted him; he stared his error straight in the eye across his desk. The grip of guilt still hung tight.

Tom stared at Sussman. "I'm sorry, Your Honour," said Tom apologetically. "I just can't recall."

"That's okay," the judge replied. "I wouldn't expect you to, Tommy," he said with a smile.

Did the judge just call him, Tommy? Did he hear that correctly?

"How did you enjoy your political science degree?" asked Sussman.

"I really enjoyed it," replied Tom, raising his eyebrows – the bizarre meeting becoming stranger by the minute. Maybe the judge was stalking him, Tom wondered, chuckling inside.

"Tommy, I was the prosecutor in the trial of Robert Hiller when you were ten years old," he stated, matter-of-factly.

The admission stunned Tom, but he did not let on. A few seconds of silence ensued while he absorbed Sussman's curveball. A bullet rang out and whizzed by his head, nipping his ear on the way by.

He looked at Sussman squarely in the eyes. "Wow, that was unexpected."

"I'm sure it is," replied the judge, clasping his hands.

Tom fidgeted with the pen in his hand and glanced at the clock, a signal that he wanted out of that office quickly. He had somewhere important to be.

"I am so pleased to see what you've done with your life," offered the judge. "I have never forgotten you, Tommy. I mean Tom. I mean, Mr. Henderson. I apologize for the casualness, but it's how I remember you. Please take no offence. I remember you as little Tommy Henderson with that mop of red curly hair always being pushed out of your eyes," he explained. "I hope everything has turned out well for you."

"Yes, things have turned out well, Your Honour," replied Tom, not prepared to discuss his early departure from his mother's apartment, unaware that Sussman knew.

"Listen, I have to get back into court because the recess is over; but I want to take you for lunch, sometime, if you're available," offered Sussman. "I want to find out everything that has happened to you since the trial."

"Yes, that would be great," replied Tom, fibbing with a straight face; he had no interest in discussing his past.

Both men stood up and shook hands. Tom opened the chamber door and walked out, stunned that his dark past had returned to pay him a visit.

Tom quickly exited the courthouse after his impromptu meeting, his mind now buzzing after the interaction. He was now late, not having built those lost fifteen minutes into his tight schedule. He jogged to his car, which was fortunately parked directly in front of the courthouse. Nausea set in when he turned on the ignition; under other circumstances he would have taken a few minutes to compose himself. It was not safe to drive, but Tom could not be late for Lucas' appointment.

He pushed through traffic, treating yellow traffic lights as green, attempting to arrive at Dr. Heather Sprott's office on time. He drove too fast with too little focus on the road, unable to stop the swirling in his head. Tom ran a stop sign at the intersection of Huron and Ontario Street, causing another driver to slam on his brakes. Screeching tires and an extended blaring horn snapped him out of his fog.

"Shit," yelled Tom, realizing he was nearly t-boned. He refocused on more important issues – his three-year-old son – whose follow-up visit with Dr. Sprott would begin momentarily. Born at 7:08 am after a sixteen-hour labour, his beautiful seven-pound, six-ounce boy arrived on the planet, the ultimate gift a man can receive. When Lucas entered their world, everything changed; the parents were thrilled.

Veronica was a great mother. She took a leave of absence from work to concentrate on raising Lucas. If manageable, Tom and Veronica hoped she could remain a stay-at-home mom until Lucas began kindergarten.

Six months earlier, Lucas began falling down for no apparent reason. At first, neither parent took notice, because two-year-old children are clumsy and fall. That's what they do. But it soon became clear that something more than usual toddler clumsiness lurked as the frequency of his falls increased. The circumstances caused the Hendersons deep worry, but they remained hopeful no serious underlying health issues existed.

Tom pulled into the clinic and quickly parked; he hurried into Dr. Sprott's waiting room where he found Veronica and Lucas. Lucas played in the corner with some toys and didn't see his father at first.

"Sorry I'm late, hon."

"Don't worry, they're running behind; Lucas' name hasn't been called," replied Veronica.

"I hope we get answers today," said Tom, shaking his head. "This process has been long and frustrating," he lamented. "Why can't they figure out what's going on?" he said, sighing and looking at his son.

"I don't know, but something is going on," said Veronica. "It's not our imagination? Or, is it? I don't know."

"It's not our imagination," replied Tom. "It doesn't mean it's serious."

Finally, Lucas turned around to see his dad; he smiled and ran towards his father, falling down after two steps. He got back up and gave his dad a hug.

Both parents thought the same thing, both looking down at the floor and realizing nothing existed to trip over. They turned to each other, dejected; their shoulders slumped.

"Hi, Daddy," said Lucas.

"Hi, Lucas. Do you know how much Daddy loves you?" Lucas pointed to the sky, which meant to the moon and back.

"Well, I love you more than that," Tom said, grinning at his boy. He gave him another hug and patted him on the head. Lucas wandered back to the toy box, but before he could grab a toy, a nurse entered the waiting room to summon them.

"Lucas Henderson," she announced.

The three of them followed the nurse to Dr. Sprott's office.

"Dr. Sprott will be with you shortly, folks," the nurse said as she left. Tom grabbed a tongue depressor and gave it to Lucas to play with while they waited.

More waiting, lamented Tom. "Hurry up and wait," he complained to his wife. The mountain of paperwork on his office desk momentarily distracted him, quickly replaced by his encounter with Sussman.

"Boy, do I have a story to tell you when I get home tonight!" exclaimed Tom to his wife. "You won't believe it," he said, shaking his head.

"Is it bad?" she asked.

"No, just weird," replied Tom. "I mean, really weird!"

Dr. Sprott arrived. "Hello, everyone. Good to see you," she said, sitting down and opening Lucas' chart.

Dr. Sprott had been practicing family medicine for five years; she had become the Hendersons' doctor after Lucas' birth. At the time, Tom and Veronica joked with each other that they wanted their doctor to be older than them; however, she proved to be excellent and diligent.

Both parents tried to read Dr. Sprott's expression to determine if bad news was coming, but they couldn't guess either way. She maintained her usual expression; Tom hoped that meant good news.

Dr. Sprott looked up from the chart. "The good news is that all the results from the tests are back in," she said. "The results indicate some abnormalities, but the exact issue has not been pinpointed, unfortunately," she explained.

Abnormalities. Tom was not comforted by what he heard; alarm bells rang. Abnormalities were not good. He did not need a medical degree to arrive at his conclusion.

"What kind of abnormalities?" asked Veronica.

"The tests indicate that there may be a neurological basis for Lucas' symptoms," replied Dr. Sprott. "But Lucas tested negative for all of the main neurological conditions that form part of our standard tests. So, I have sent everything off to Dr. Vernon at SickKids Hospital in Toronto. He's an expert in his field; I've asked Dr. Vernon to review Lucas' medical records. His office will contact you for an appointment."

Dr. Sprott closed Lucas' file and looked at the Hendersons. "I wish I had more answers for you, folks; but Lucas' clinical presentation is nothing that I've seen before. I also had my colleague in the clinic, Dr. Santash, review everything to ensure I wasn't overlooking something. He's stumped too."

Tom and Veronica looked at each other, their fear evident. They both felt sick to their stomachs.

After thanking Dr. Sprott, the three left her office. When they reached the parking lot, Veronica turned to her husband, "Tom, can you take Lucas home for me?" she asked.

"Why, aren't you going home?" he responded, concerned.

"Yes, but please do it and don't ask me any questions," she pleaded. "I will be home shortly."

"Okay," said Tom, hugging her.

He strapped Lucas in the back of his car and left, leaving Veronica to drive away on her own.

Veronica drove two blocks and parked at the back of an industrial mall. After looking around to ensure she was alone, she put her head on the steering wheel and began sobbing, uncontrollably. She grabbed a plastic bag from the floor and held it under her face for thirty seconds, but didn't throw up. She sat for a further ten minutes, breathing deeply and gathering herself, finally feeling strong enough to drive home.

The two concerned parents waited every day for a phone call from SickKids Hospital, the unknown weighing heavily on them, making it difficult to think about anything else. What if Lucas' condition worsened while everyone sat around waiting, a concern that Veronica repeated to herself over and over.

Every week, Veronica called the hospital to make sure that she had not missed a telephone call, knowing full well that she had not; she hoped her call would prompt the hospital to give her an appointment date.

"These things take time, Ms. Henderson," was the standard answer given to her each time she called. "We promise that we'll call you as soon as Dr. Vernon has reviewed Lucas' chart."

Tom found it difficult to remain focused on his law practice. Nothing mattered if Lucas was seriously ill, including his law practice. He searched every neurological disorder on the internet, but because so many existed, it was impossible to conclude anything – except that all of them were bad. His son's symptoms fit many of them in the early stages.

Veronica and Tom concluded that Lucas was not improving and perhaps worsening, their imaginations running wild during the torturous waiting period; the worst-case scenarios dominated their thoughts.

One Friday in early July, three weeks after Lucas' appointment with Dr. Sprott, Tom finished a criminal trial in London at 2:30 pm. His long hours preparing for the trial left him exhausted. With the additional stress of Lucas' unknown health state, Tom inched toward his breaking point. Alex crept into his thoughts; he missed his old friend.

Although the jury had just commenced deliberating, an off chance existed that they could render a verdict before the end of the day; so, Tom decided he would stay in London until at least 5:00 pm, in the event that occurred. It was preferable to making the hour-long drive back to Stratford, only to potentially be recalled to London to hear the verdict. Besides, Tom needed a couple of hours to decompress.

He drove to an English pub a block away from the courthouse; rumour had it that it served the best burger in the city. He checked his phone and confirmed no messages from his wife. Ernie's Pub offered Shepherd's Pie and Bangers & Mash as the daily specials.

Tom sat at the bar and ordered a cheeseburger with bacon and a Diet Coke. The middle-aged waitress engaged in some innocent flirting with Tom; that was his interpretation. His wife would agree it was not his strongest skill. Regardless of the waitress's true intentions, Tom exhibited no interest.

Tom could not think of anything but Lucas as he watched some PGA golf on the sixty-inch television behind the bar. After one bite into his burger, an unfamiliar voice from a man beside him at the bar interrupted him.

"Tommy, is that you?" he asked.

Tom looked at the guy; some familiarity existed, but it may have been his imagination. He wasn't sure.

"It's me, from grade five," the man with jet black hair announced. "You know, from Mr. Hiller's cabin," he said, attempting to jog Tom's memory.

Innocence on Trial/Roth

Suddenly, it clicked. A volley of bullets rang out, whizzing by Tom's head; one of them clipped the opposite ear to the one that was nicked in Judge Sussman's chambers. "Of course, George Gerontonis!" exclaimed Tom, forcing a grin – somehow managing to look pleased to see him.

The two old friends shook hands.

"Man, it is good to see you," said George.

"You too," replied Tom. "Shit, it's been a long time."

"Let's move to a table and catch up," offered George.

"Absolutely," replied Tom, although he certainly had no desire. He picked up his food and moved over to a nearby table, where George's features became obvious after a few minutes. He looked the same, except for a thick beard and larger belly. His black hair still stood up straight, like a porcupine.

The waitress wandered over and took George's order, wings and a pint of ale.

George explained that he was a computer programmer, although he was out of work at the moment. He had three children under six and two ex-wives. George drank another two beers while they reminisced about old times, the alcohol relaxing George. About an hour into their reunion, the tone became serious.

"Tommy, it really is good to see you," said George. "I really mean it."

"Yes, it is, George," replied Tom, nodding his approval, but wondering how many others from a past he was trying to escape would show up, unannounced. First Sussman and now George. Unfucking believable, he said to himself.

"Tommy, I'm sorry about the trial when you were a kid," he said, apologetically. "I couldn't believe Hiller killed himself."

Well, there it was – the elephant in the room – finally brought up, to Tom's consternation. He rued having this conversation, adjusting himself to avoid another bullet that whizzed by his chest.

"Me neither," replied Tom, glancing at the bar;

Alexander Keith's Pale Ale was on tap. It had been so long. "It's a hell of a thing, George," said Tom, wanting to return to their trivial discussions of the weather and sports.

"I wouldn't expect you to feel sorry for him – and I understand if you were pleased he was dead," said George, nodding his head. "The damn legal system is full of bloody loopholes and technicalities. My mother told me that your lawyer really screwed up!"

"He wasn't really my lawyer, George," explained Tom. "And no, I didn't want Hiller dead, not at all."

"Well, justice sometimes gets done one way or another," said George. "Maybe you didn't want him dead. I don't know, but at least the pervert couldn't hurt any more kids."

"Ya, no doubt about that," agreed Tom. "You must feel the same way?"

"What do you mean?" asked George.

"You know. You told me that he was grabbing your privates in the big bed," replied Tom.

"Oh ya," said George, followed by a sip of ale. "Well, I was joking about that when I told you," he explained. "Chris and I got together; we wanted to wind you up. I told the police as much after they charged Hiller for touching you, when they were investigating. My mother was so pissed off at me; I didn't blame her."

"I'm glad he didn't get to you, George. Listen, I have to run." Tom put forty dollars on the table. "That should cover mine."

"It's been great to have a visit, Tom," said George, who stood and shook Tom's hand. He handed Tom a piece of paper. "Here's my number. Call me and we'll get together again."

"You can count on it," replied Tom, knowing there wasn't a chance in hell. The two men shook hands again and ended their chance encounter.

Thankfully, Tom did not get summoned back to court that day for a verdict. He texted Veronica to inform her that he had left to return home.

When he pulled into the driveway, Veronica met him at a run to tell him that SickKids had called and scheduled an appointment for the following week. They hugged, both hoping they would soon have answers about their boy's condition. Was a one-week appointment a good sign or a bad sign? Two months later might have suggested no urgency, but one week? So went the speculation when something you loved was at risk.

When the day of the appointment arrived, Tom and Veronica awoke before daylight to drive to Toronto, building in an extra two-hour cushion if traffic was terrible. A constant rain, coupled with a car accident that reduced four lanes to two, turned a two-hour drive into an almost three-and-a-half-hour drive. Dr. Vernon's assistant had advised them that Lucas did not need to come for the appointment, so Veronica arranged for her mother to care for him.

Tom learned from his internet research that Dr. Harold Vernon was a world-renowned pediatric neurologist, which was comforting; but seeing him was very difficult, which made the quick appointment concerning.

They arrived with twenty minutes to spare after parking their car in the underground parking lot, off Chestnut Street. The two walked hand-in-hand into the hospital, making their way to the fourth-floor waiting room. Except for brief small talk, each of them remained preoccupied with their thoughts, trying to forget the knots in their stomachs. Veronica had only a coffee for breakfast because she had no appetite. Tom nibbled on a bagel on the ride to Toronto, but didn't finish it.

Tom felt a vibration in his pocket so he pulled out his phone and read a text from his assistant, Kerri, *How's it going? We are thinking about you.*

Fifty minutes past the scheduled appointment time, the nervous parents were called into Dr. Vernon's office.

"Come this way, Mr. and Ms. Henderson," directed the receptionist. She walked them down a long corridor and into Dr. Vernon's office, a large corner office that was well appointed and professionally decorated. A life-sized diagram of the nervous system hung on the wall, starting with the brain and ending with the superficial peroneal nerve in the leg.

Dr. Vernon, a man in his fifties, wore a lab coat and a stethoscope around his neck. He sat behind his desk when the Hendersons walked in; at first, he didn't look up from what Tom concluded was Lucas' medical records. He had an aura of extreme busyness; Tom concluded he did not have time for idle chit-chat or extended pleasantries.

Tom and Veronica discovered Dr. Vernon's pleasant and compassionate personality; however, a multitude of demands pulled him in several directions. He wanted to devote ample time to parents, discussing their children and the consequences of their illnesses, but insufficient hours existed during the day.

He abhorred delivering catastrophic news to parents, a frequent occurrence in his profession – it wore on him emotionally; he never became used to it. How could you be human and become accustomed to it? His flat outward expression did not provide justice to the empathy that he felt for his patients and their families. Dr. Vernon had dedicated his life to medicine, sacrificing his family life by working sixteen hours a day. He promised his wife he would always have Sunday breakfast with her.

"Please sit down, Mr. & Mrs. Henderson," offered Dr. Vernon, who raced straight to the point, as a man with his hectic schedule was inclined to do. "We have identified Lucas' condition. It is called left hemisphere cerebral dystrophy, known as Remington's disease. I'm confident of this diagnosis. Unfortunately, I do not have good news for you," he said, frowning and removing his glasses.

Tears flowed down both parents' faces, but they remained quiet and attentive. Even though they knew nothing about this disease, Dr. Vernon had already said enough to devastate them.

"I will discuss Remington's Disease and then I will answer all of your questions," explained Dr. Vernon. He went on to explain that Remington's is a rare genetic disorder that usually affects males between the ages of two and five, a progressive degenerative disease of the brain for which there is no cure. The cause is a missing enzyme that breaks down or metabolizes a protein, PNA2a. Without that enzyme, the protein multiplies uncontrollably, and degrades the neurons in the brain, which control all impulses and activity of the whole body. Messages from the brain don't reach the spinal cord.

"Think of a strainer that doesn't allow water through because the holes are plugged with pasta," explained the doctor, solemnly.

Dr. Vernon paused to push the tissue box on his desk towards the Hendersons, who were trying to listen carefully and process what they had heard. God, he hated delivering bad news.

"You have already witnessed some of the symptoms, such as loss of muscle control and problems swallowing," said Dr. Vernon. "Unfortunately, these symptoms will progress and you will continue to see a developmental delay in Lucas. It is likely Lucas will go blind within three years and die within the next five years."

The last sentence hit their ears with the force of a sledgehammer. Veronica bent over and began wailing. Tom felt nauseous; he attempted to stop crying, so that he could listen to Dr. Vernon. Even through their tears, both of them heard very clearly that their son had a death sentence.

"I'm very sorry, Mr. and Mrs. Henderson," said the doctor, sincerely. "Unfortunately, I have little to offer Lucas in terms of treatment."

The parents were dumbfounded; they couldn't believe what they had been told. At least with cancer, you could fight it, but Dr. Vernon offered no hope.

Veronica partially gathered herself, first. "Dr. Vernon, is there any research on this disease?" she asked. "Is there any hope at all?" she pleaded.

"It's a rare disease; very rare, in fact," answered Dr. Vernon. "When a disease is that rare, less research tends to be done on it. I can't offer you any hope and I'm being frank so that you can prepare yourself. I can't and won't provide false hope."

Tom walked over to the corner of Dr. Vernon's office and knelt over a garbage can and vomited.

With his eyes on Tom, Dr. Vernon explained to Veronica that Lucas' condition was chronic and emphasized that, at best, it could be managed, not cured.

"I'm afraid that you will have to address twenty-four-hour care needs for Lucas over time," warned Dr. Vernon. "It might not be in the next year or two, but certainly within the next three to four years. It's difficult to predict. As I said, this disease is so rare there's limited research or case studies to help me guide you."

Tom returned to the desk, with paleness and red eyes.

"Are you sure there's nothing?" asked Veronica again.

"I attended a conference one year ago. As I recall, a Dr. Estrada presented," replied Dr. Vernon. "He practiced neurology in Mexico and had some interest in researching this disease, but I can't remember the details or if he ever actually carried out any research. I do remember something very strange, almost absurd, about Dr. Estrada's presentation, but I don't know why."

Dr. Vernon explained that he did not believe any research was published in the last two years, so no further developments existed in treating Remington's. He promised to immediately contact them if he discovered anything new.

"I will write to Dr. Sprott and give her some ideas on follow-up care for Lucas," he said. "Again, I'm very sorry. I will now excuse myself because, as usual, I am running behind," he said, exiting his office and leaving the two devastated parents.

Tom and Veronica hugged each other from their seats. After a few minutes, they stood up but Veronica's knees buckled and she fell to her knees on the floor.

"I think I might be sick too," she said, her hands covering her face.

Tom quickly retrieved the garbage can and brought it to his wife. He gently rubbed her back, pulled her hair away from her face and put it behind her ears.

"My heart is aching," whispered Veronica.

"I know," said her husband, still rubbing his wife's back.

"Why us, Tom?" she asked, looking up from the garbage can.

Tom started to respond but decided against it; he didn't have an answer that would bring any comfort.

Once Veronica could stand, they held each other tighter than ever before – tighter than their first date. Tom wiped the last tears from his wife's face and grabbed her hand.

They made their way out of SickKids as quickly as possible, escaping the sterile smell and the white walls that were closing in on them, neither of them looking forward to the long, silent drive home.

Two days later, Tom worked from his home office Saturday night, finishing a settlement conference brief that required filing Monday morning. He looked forward to watching a movie with his wife. Although, his son's diagnosis made it difficult to enjoy anything. Tom had been walking in quicksand the last two days, every step seemingly impossible to take.

Before shutting off the computer, Tom performed a Google search before joining his wife on the couch. He typed in *Dr. Estrada left hemisphere cerebral dystrophy*; surprisingly, three results popped up.

Tom clicked on the first, a website for the 19th annual Association of Neurologists conference held in Miami, two years ago. He scanned the first page and clicked on a link near the bottom first page, *Hydrothermal Graphite and Left Hemisphere Cerebral Dystrophy*, and watched as a photo of Dr. Estrada and a very brief summary of his paper appeared. Tom assumed this was the conference that Dr. Vernon referred to.

Tom scanned the page. Dr. Juan Estrada's biography indicated that he was trained in the United States at the University of Florida and specialized in the treatment and rehabilitation of pediatric neurological disorders. He carried out too many studies to count, cerebral palsy, carnosenemia and another dozen at least. He authored two books, *The Regulation of Prolactin Release* and *Drug Metabolizing Enzymes in the Cerebellum*. He was a Fellow of Merit in I.D.V. research, whatever that meant.

Tom clicked on the second search result and discovered something more interesting; with raised eyebrows, he pushed his head closer to the screen. A paragraph summarizing Dr. Estrada's research revealed the existence of a rare Mexican plant created by a one-of-a-kind hydrothermal event. The plant contained a unique enzyme composition effective in the treatment of Remington's disease. The mention of a treatment excited Tom; his heart raced.

Tom clicked on the third search result, scanning quickly and finding mainly a repeat of the first two sites; but a statement at the bottom of the page provided something new – testing had been suspended. What the hell, thought Tom, his heart sinking. Why was it suspended? No explanation was provided.

Tom wrote down the phone number located at the end. He had the urge to call it, but concluded it was likely not Dr. Estrada's phone number; it probably rang to a hospital. Although Tom didn't speak Spanish, he reasoned that Dr. Estrada trained in the United States and probably could communicate in English.

The phone rang six times; Tom was about to hang up when, surprisingly, someone answered on the seventh ring.

"Hola," Tom heard on the other end.

"Hello, I'm looking for Dr. Estrada, please," said Tom.

"This is he," replied Dr. Estrada, in understandable but broken English.

"Hi, I'm calling about your research into Remington's disease. My son has this disease; the doctors here in Canada say he has no chance to be cured and he's going to die."

"What's your name, sir?" asked Dr. Estrada.

"Tom Henderson," came the reply.

"Mr. Henderson, there is a cure. No further research is

needed. Unfortunately, it is impossible to get the material, which would cure your son," he explained.

"What do you mean, it's not available?" asked Tom excitedly, but confused.

"It's a long story, Mr. Henderson. The plant, which holds the cure, is rare and is owned by private hands," he explained. "The land is very valuable and has other uses for which others are willing to pay a lot of money."

"Others, what others?" asked Tom. "And, how much money are we talking about?"

"I can't say for sure; but millions, I think, Mr. Henderson. Millions."

"Well, who owns it? What are their names? I would like to talk with them." Tom could barely contain himself after hearing the word "cure."

"It's not that simple," stated Dr. Estrada. "I have personally tried many, many times to secure the plant. These people do not care about saving a few lives. They only care about money," said Dr. Estrada with exasperation.

"I can't accept that!" said Tom, raising his voice. "My son is going to die!" he said, even louder.

Tom was confused. None of this made sense. A cure existed but it wasn't available? Silence ensued for a minute as Tom processed Dr. Estrada's words.

"Listen, Dr. Estrada. I want to come and meet with you, please?"

"It won't make a difference, Mr. Henderson," replied the doctor. "I promise you, I have tried everything imaginable."

"I still want to come, anyway. Please! Please!" Tom begged.

"I don't know, Mr. Henderson. There's really nothing to talk about."

"Please, my son is going to die. I need to know I've done everything possible to save his life! Surely, you understand that."

Dr. Estrada heard the desperation. All too well, he understood a parent's desire to turn over every stone to help save a dying child.

"That's fine, sir, but unfortunately it will be a waste of your time."

Tom arranged to meet Dr. Estrada at his residence, outside of Guadalajara in two days. He hung up the phone, pulled his credit card from his wallet and purchased an Aeromexico ticket, flight 67L901, seat 16C. After printing his e-ticket, he put his face into his hands and shook his head. He couldn't believe what he had just heard; he couldn't believe that he was travelling to Mexico. Hope existed. He grabbed it and clung it tightly.

Oh shit, Tom said to himself, realizing that Veronica remained on the couch, waiting for him. She had no knowledge of his conversation with Dr. Estrada.

Veronica was not thrilled that Tom was travelling to Mexico, especially alone.

"You shouldn't have bought a plane ticket before discussing it with me first," she said, mildly irritated. In her heart, she knew that he had to make the trip, despite the bizarreness of her husband's conversation with Dr. Estrada. The slimmest of chances must be pursued. What kind of parents would they be if they just gave up on their son?

"Tom, you understand how dangerous Mexico is?" she asked.

"It's overblown and exaggerated by the media, Veronica," he replied, hugging her. "I'm going to Guadalajara, not somewhere like Juarez."

"I need you with me right now," she said, tearfully. But she understood, even if it was all too much.

They put their heads on their pillows that night knowing that hope existed. Maybe it was faint – but it was damn powerful. They had nothing two days earlier in Dr. Vernon's office.

Tom fixated on his conversation with Dr. Estrada and grabbed Veronica's hand underneath the covers. He squeezed it. She squeezed back harder while kissing her husband's forehead.

Tom wished that he could take away his wife's pain. Their love for each other provided comfort; for a fleeting moment, he forgot the ache in his heart and focused only on the love he had for his wife.

Love can push you places where you might not be able to go otherwise, mused Tom. He wasn't thinking of Mexico. Rather, it was a place, deep in his soul, that he feared visiting.

CHAPTER SEVENTEEN

Purpura, or not Purpura, That is the Question

Tom's plane landed on the tarmac at the Guadalajara International Airport two days later, as planned. He arranged for Kerri to clear his schedule and file the settlement brief he completed Saturday night at the courthouse.

The plane ride gave Tom a few hours to think about his discussion with Dr. Estrada. The man sounded compassionate, but the story he told him was both mysterious and puzzling. Tom had no idea what to expect when he finally arrived. Maybe he would meet with the doctor, a three-minute conversation would follow and he would have to return home. Perhaps, he shouldn't have raised his hopes without having any real understanding of what Dr. Estrada explained.

Tom convinced himself the meeting was necessary, even if he did have to turn around. He preferred that outcome over accepting Dr. Estrada's statement that his trip would be a waste of time – better than accepting nothing could be done to save Lucas' life.

"There is a cure" were Dr. Estrada's exact words. A renowned specialist did not have access to it? How could that be?

Tom sent an e-mail to Dr. Vernon on Saturday night, explaining his conversation with Dr. Estrada. Dr. Vernon responded the following day that he had no knowledge of a cure; no published studies existed. He emphasized that it sounded "crazy" to him, warning Tom to be careful of charlatans who promise cures while preying on desperate parents.

Once the plane landed, Tom quickly maneuvered through the crowded airport searching for an exit and a taxi. His only luggage consisted of a carry-on bag. He had not booked a hotel, having had no idea of the length of his stay, or if he would be staying. He thought only about the answers he would receive from Dr. Estrada in a couple of hours.

Guadalajara was a city of over one and a half million people, an urban and modern city, contrasting the rustic image that Tom had in his mind. Tom navigated the throngs of airport travellers until he found a covered breezeway, where taxis had lined up. He hopped from one to another searching for an English-speaking driver with no luck. Only five percent of the population spoke English.

Tom chose a driver that appeared the friendliest and handed the man a piece of paper with Dr. Estrada's address, *Calle San Juan, 16002, Salamanca.*

"Si," said the driver, motioning Tom into the taxi. "Doscientos Pesos, Senor," the driver demanded with an outstretched hand.

Tom opened the door and slid into the back seat. He handed Miguel two hundred pesos, twice as much as the tourist pamphlets suggested, but he had no appetite to challenge or barter with the driver.

Tom calculated the trip to Dr. Estrada's residence might take about forty-five minutes. He preferred their meeting take place at the Guadalajara University Hospital, where he worked, but Dr. Estrada did not provide that option.

Miguel took highway 90D from the Guadalajara International Airport, which was situated fifteen kilometres south of the city center, and headed east. After a half hour, the taxi left the more comforting urban setting of the greater Guadalajara area onto a dirt road, more reflective of Tom's original assumption of his destination.

The driver barely spoke. Tom hoped his silence resulted from the language barrier; but disconcertedly, the smiles had disappeared since Tom handed him his fare.

Tom attempted to create small talk by using popular Spanish phrases learned from an online Spanish dictionary. "Mexico es un hermaso pais!" meaning Mexico is a beautiful country. In response, Miguel cocked his eyebrow, looked briefly at Tom in the rear-view mirror and then refocused his attention on the road. Tom questioned his prior assessment that this driver was the friendliest of the group.

Music blared after Miguel turned on the radio, apparently to signal that he had no interest in idle chatter – furthering Tom's nervousness. With thunderbolt effect, Tom suddenly realized he had no idea of his whereabouts; worse, he had placed his trust in a man whose intentions became more suspect with each revolution of the tires.

Half the sun slipped behind the horizon bringing long shadows and confirmation that darkness was imminent. Why had he taken no precautions? How could he have been so careless? Tom massaged his front pocket, feeling for his wallet and passport. His wife knew Dr. Estrada's address – useless information if he never arrived. His cell phone showed fifteen minutes of remaining battery. Even if he found a power source, his charger had proven incompatible with Mexican outlets at the airport.

The inescapable realization that Miguel could be whisking him anywhere set in. Were they nearing Salamanca?

The driver veered onto a second dirt road. After another kilometre, the taxi wound through the narrow, dirt-covered streets of a dilapidated and sketchy neighbourhood. The confines of a city provided comfort, despite its ramshackle appearance.

"Are we close, Senor?" asked Tom.

In response, Miguel incomprehensibly mumbled something in Spanish. The impulse to jump out of the taxi at the next stop and make a run for it flashed in his mind; however, the idea of scurrying around an unfamiliar area after dark garnered no solace.

Miguel looked in the rearview mirror; frustrated, he shook his head and mumbled in Spanish again – certainly a swear word. A vehicle approached rapidly from behind, prompting the driver to turn the radio off and pull over.

Was this an ambush, wondered Tom? Miguel appeared nervous. "Stay here," he ordered his passenger in almost perfect English.

Tom's heart began to pound, adrenaline coursing through his body. Six hours ago, he relaxed in the comfort of his home; now, he sat unnerved in a dicey and unwelcoming area of south Mexico.

Tom appreciated his helplessness if anyone wanted to rob him, or worse. A sinking feeling that only comes when facing serious peril washed over him.

The driver of the pursuing vehicle exited and marched towards Miguel, who met him halfway. As the man approached, Tom observed his police uniform. Was this development good or bad? Mexican police had a notorious corrupt reputation.

The two men initially talked calmly, their discourse quickly elevating into an argument with raised voices and animated hand gestures. Tom reconsidered opening the taxi door and dashing into a nearby alley. But then what? He couldn't outrun a bullet from the gun secured around the officer's waist. His internal dialogue distressed him. "This is crazy," he whispered to himself.

The police officer took his index finger and pointed it at the taxi driver before sticking it into his chest, pushing Miguel back several inches. The driver did not cower, yelling at the officer and swiping his hand away from his chest. Tom expected the officer to pull out his revolver and shoot Miguel dead for his brazen irreverence, leaving Tom as the sole witness to a roadside murder. Tom understood what happens to such witnesses in Mexico: they disappear.

Then, as quickly as their interaction elevated, it abruptly calmed down. Miguel returned to his taxi and opened the back door to address Tom. "He wants to know where you're going," he asked again in near-perfect English.

He clearly speaks English, concluded Tom with equal amusement and consternation. Why the hell was he hiding it?

"Dr. Juan Estrada," replied Tom. "I'm visiting Dr. Juan Estrada, a doctor in Salamanca about my sick son."

Surprise and relief formed over Miguel's face. "Oh, okay, Senor," he said, closing the door and jogging back to the officer to deliver the explanation. The cop calmly nodded, alleviating a measure of Tom's apprehension. Tom exhaled, now believing this encounter would not end in bloodshed.

Suddenly, the officer began walking towards the taxi with a pronounced limp, opening the rear door at his arrival. A burly man in his fifties, with a stubbled face, ducked his head through the door, "Senor, please thank Dr. Estrada from all of us in Salamanca."

Tom tried not to stare at the long scar running from under his right eye to his upper lip, a disfigurement that arose from an incident beyond a shaving accident.

"Si, I will, I definitely will," Tom replied, smiling.

The door closed. Scarface returned to his vehicle and drove away, allowing Tom to fully breathe again.

Miguel hopped into the driver's seat. "That was very close," he said in fluent English.

"What was that all about?" asked Tom, his heart slowing.

Miguel accelerated, before answering. "It's best not to be stopped in this area very long," he said, scanning his rear-view mirror to ensure they were not being followed.

"He tried to find out everything about you," offered Miguel. "He planned to shake you down; he wanted to rob you – that would have been the best-case scenario. But, because he inquired about your destination, he contemplated kidnapping you. He asked me if you were wealthy."

"You're kidding, right?" asked Tom, shocked at the revelation.

"No. He would have called ahead to a gang; they would have snatched you and paid him a kick-back for the heads up of your arrival," explained Miguel.

"Kidnapping!" bellowed Tom. "Maybe he has called ahead?"

"He would have taken your money if he was going to," replied the driver.

"So, why am I so lucky?" asked Tom.

"Dr. Estrada just saved you," he replied. "He's a hero in this area – a big-shot Guadalajara doctor who could make millions working in the United States but remains in Mexico.

He provides free medical treatment to the locals here in Salamanca. I now recognize the address you gave me as his clinic. That officer told me that Dr. Estrada saved his mother's life."

As Tom watched the storefronts with barred windows go by, he realized the fortune of his narrow escape. He considered directing Miguel to turn around and return to the airport – the smart, safe and reasonable choice; however, the trifecta of rational behaviour would not save his son.

In grade four, Tom watched Kevin Miller incessantly bully fellow student Nick Danson on the playground. Kevin, a year older than both Tom and Nick, uncharacteristically became one mean son of a bitch; nobody understood the reasons. Kevin's eyes carried rage. What the hell had happened to that once friendly kid.

Kevin's schoolyard antics appropriately foreshadowed his later lot in life, when he landed in prison as an adult; he sported a handsome, tear-drop-shaped tattoo under his left eye at his sentencing, signifying to the world that he had killed someone. The young schoolyard bully embraced his nickname, "Miller the Killer." Although pleased that the Killer focused elsewhere, Kevin tended to spread his unwanted attention to all of his meek schoolmates eventually. Tom figured it was only a matter of time before the Killer had him in his crosshairs.

Tom felt terrible for Nick, the gentlest of kids. Kevin tormented him daily by punching him in the same spots on his legs and back, resulting in permanent bruising throughout the school year.

During a Monday morning recess, late in the school year, Tom witnessed the bravest of acts. Miller the Killer's fists pounded on Nick while everyone stood around without intervening. Nick kneeled on the ground, tears in his eyes. The Killer bent over him, mocking him, knowing that nobody would step in to prevent him from inflicting his daily dose of humility and pain.

Without warning and with the precision of a fully trained

ninja, Nick pulled his right arm tight to his body before letting it fly backwards; he released an elbow that connected directly onto the Killer's nose – a thing of beauty. The goddamned smug look disappeared from the Killer's face at exactly the same time as everyone heard the cracking of Kevin's nose. Even the uninterested children playing across the schoolyard looked over when they heard the crunching sound of the Killer's nose echo towards them. Sitting in the taxi, Tom heard the crack as if it had occurred yesterday.

Tom had never seen so much blood. When the Killer dropped to his knees and witnessed the red gusher flowing from his nose, he freaked before sobbing. Kevin stood and rushed into the school, leaving every kid staring at Nick, shocked at his retaliatory exhibition. Tom wouldn't have blamed Nick if he got up and strutted around as the new king of the playground – the boy who had brought Goliath down with one mighty blow and now demanded all of the reverence and spoils that came with it.

But Nick didn't rise up. He stayed on his knees, crying inconsolably, a vision that remained with Tom forever. In hindsight, he understood Nick's reasons – carnage followed the victor, just as it had in *The Five Epic Battles that Changed the World*.

If that elbow hadn't landed directly on the Killer's nose, the Killer would have had that tear-drop-shaped tattoo inked years earlier, because he would have killed Nick Danson. Nick surely knew of the possible consequences. Yet, he let that elbow fly – an act of courage that Tom required, sitting in the taxi.

Tom directed the driver to continue. After three minutes, Miguel pulled in front of a two-story white-stucco building and stopped. The exterior's extensive flaking suggested a decade without fresh paint. Only three feet separated the road from the front door. Tom couldn't decipher the faded signage except for "medico." With squinting and resolve, the number 16002 became visible, unequivocally confirming he had reached his proper destination.

Adrenaline slowly dissipated from his body; however, he decided against relinquishing his hyper-alertness. Tom thanked Miguel and passed him a twenty-pesos tip as a tip.

"Senor. I'm sorry for ignoring you during the ride. Most gringos travelling to Salamanca are up to no good," explained Miguel. "Drugs you know. I hope Dr. Estrada can help your son."

The two shook hands. Miguel drove off with urgency, his squealing tires propelling dirt into the air. At that moment, Tom realized that prudence required keeping Miguel there until he knew Dr. Estrada would receive him. He arrived two hours past the agreed arrival time and his phone was dead.

Tom grabbed the brass knocker and struck the door three times. The lack of response distressed him. Exhausted, and with a near kidnapping fresh in his thoughts, Tom wanted off the streets where he felt like prey. Tom stood in the middle of the Salamanca at 10 pm, searching for a man whom he had never met – a doctor who warned him not to come. What the fuck am I doing here?

Tom knocked harder, but with the same results, knowing that each smack attracted unwanted attention. He may as well have pulled out a blow horn and yelled down the street, "Come and get the idiot gringo."

Tom turned around and placed his back against the door, sliding down slowly until his butt reached the dusty sidewalk. He recalled Dillon's recommendation to always sit with your back against the wall to prevent surprise attacks from behind; he never contemplated needing the advice made in jest.

With face in his hands, Tom cried. He had come a long way, likely for no reason; and now the hope to save his son was disappearing faster than Miguel's tail lights out of Salamanca.

After a minute of feeling sorry for himself, Tom tried to gather himself. Looking around, he realized that he didn't see one person on the street. The neighbourhood of mixed residential and business buildings was completely deserted. Salamanca might as well have been a different planet compared to Guadalajara. He wouldn't describe it as a shanty town, but it wasn't far off.

One lonely flickering street light provided limited illumination, the remaining bulbs broken or burnt out. A stifling breeze stirred up the street's dust and garbage, reminding him of a spaghetti western, where everyone cleared the street. He expected two lonely cowboys to appear, walking towards each other, ready to draw on each other as that cheesy whistling song from *The Good, The Bad, and the Ugly* played in the background. Or, maybe it was *A Fistful of Dollars*. The whistling sound entered his brain, followed by "wah, wah, wah."

Sweat drenched his clothes courtesy of a thirty-one-degree temperature now that he was out of the air-conditioned taxi.

If Tom possessed the locals' knowledge, he would have been terrified. The streets of Salamanca were not safe, gangs protecting their drug turf at night. Whether for target practice, or for his outsider status, Tom would be shot if a gang member came upon him. Life meant little in Salamanca, a key hub in Mexico's billion-dollar drug trade.

Dr. Estrada's commitment to the city, despite the constant danger, produced his hero status with the locals. Unlike his fellow citizens, Dr. Estrada had the option of escaping the mean streets of Salamanca, but he chose to stay.

Tom considered his next step. Option number one: sitting with his back against the door until daylight hoping that Dr. Estrada would find him in the morning. But remaining in the open, exposed, created uncertain dangers; maybe Scarface would return. Option two: slinking into a dark alley; but who knew what he would find hidden in the darkness.

He could randomly start knocking on doors, praying someone would help him. But what if he knocked on the wrong door? Anyway, what local would welcome an unknown pale gringo off the street who did not speak Spanish at this hour? Desperation set in – the variety that Scarface implanted in him two hours ago.

Suddenly, the front door of 16002 Calle San Juan flew open, shocking Tom; he jumped to his feet, swung around and faced a man standing 5' 4" tall in the doorway. They stared at each other with surprised looks.

"Mr. Henderson?" asked the man, cocking his head to the side with a rippled forehead.

Tom immediately recognized Dr. Estrada's voice from their telephone conversation.

"Yes, I'm Tom Henderson," he replied, his surprise transitioning to relief. "Please tell me you are Dr. Estrada."

"Si, Mr. Henderson. Come in quickly, please. It's not safe out here," he emphasized in a hushed tone, pulling Tom in and shutting the door. "Follow me," directed Dr. Estrada, instructions which Tom willingly followed. Ascension up a flight of stairs brought the pair into a small but tidy and comfortable apartment.

A lean one-hundred-and-thirty-pound Dr. Estrada presented as a well-kept man who wore tiny glasses on his nose. A thin dark moustache and a shaved head bookended two soft brown eyes; he appeared tired and sad – consequences of a busy medical practice and watching dozens of children die in your care over a long career. Dr. Estrada learned early that if he saved ten children, but lost one, the one consumed him. The lost child always won the battle for his thoughts, the devastating ending seared into his mind.

"Sit down, Mr. Henderson. Honestly, I never believed that you would actually come; when your 8 pm arrival time passed, I didn't give it a second thought," he explained.

Dr. Estrada noticed Tom's red eyes; he knew his guest had been crying. "Te ves como una mierda,", announced his host, which was met by a blank stare. "You look like shit," repeated the doctor in English.

"Trust me, I feel like shit," replied Tom.

"Mr. Henderson, I'm so sorry. My wife and I were sleeping," he explained. "We wondered if we heard knocking but concluded we were dreaming; strange noises exist in this neighbourhood."

Tom nodded, his eyes expressing his understanding.

"My wife finally made me check," he said. "I'm pleased I did because these streets are dangerous," he said with his hands raised in the air. "How long were you out there?"

"It doesn't matter," replied Tom. "I'm relieved to be indoors and to have met you. Please call me Tom."

"And I'm Juan," said the doctor, smiling at his guest. Juan extended his hand and they shook.

"I practice medicine on the main floor and live up here," said Juan, who quickly interrupted himself. "Where are my manners? Are you hungry, Mr. Henderson?"

Tom didn't want to impose, but hunger understated his condition. "Actually, I'm starving, Juan."

"Sit down and relax. I'll prepare you something," said the doctor.

"Something very simple, please Juan. I'm not here to impose."

A woman appeared from a bedroom, offering a friendly and warm smile to their guest. The petite woman wore her hair pulled back into a ponytail; her half-open eyes affirmed an interrupted sleep. She threw a shawl over her nightgown, appearing unperturbed by the late-night intrusion, perhaps accustomed to the irregular and unpredictable schedule of a world-renowned pediatric specialist.

"Hello, Mr. Henderson," she said, extending her hand. "You have come a long way to see my husband."

"I have come a long way, but I can assure you it's for a very good reason," replied Tom.

"This is my wife, Rosetta," said Juan, who retreated to the kitchen but continued to listen.

"My husband told me about your son," she said, mixing sugar and cinnamon with coffee grinds before starting to brew. She caught Tom watching, "Are you okay with a traditional Mexican coffee?"

"Of course, thank you," came the quick reply.

"I'm very sorry to hear about your son," offered Rosetta. "What's his name?"

"Lucas. He's just," cracked Tom's voice, preventing him from completing his sentence. He continued a second later after composing himself. "He's just so young," he said. "Please excuse me," apologized Tom, embarrassed about displaying his emotions in front of the Estradas. "It's been a long day," he explained, proceeding to describe his travels since he landed in Guadalajara.

"Capullo!" exclaimed Juan, calling Scarface an asshole after listening to Tom. "I know the officer. He patrols this area and is beholden to the Lozano cartel. That scar resulted when he tried to shakedown the wrong person three blocks from here, two years ago."

Juan looked at Tom and shook his head in disbelief. "You've no idea how close you came to being kidnapped tonight!" exclaimed Juan, continuing to shake his head in frustration.

Actually, Tom knew. "I have you to thank for saving me, Juan. You're respected and appreciated in your community."

Juan carried a steaming bowl of lentil soup and a coffee to Tom, who immediately put a spoonful of soup into his mouth. "Thank you, it's delicious." Then he took a sip of the spicy coffee.

After he finished eating, Juan and Rosetta invited Tom into their living room. The juxtaposition of the Estrada's modest abode against his world-renowned professional standing spoke volumes about Dr. Estrada's character and values.

"I grew up in this neighbourhood, four blocks from here," explained Juan. "Childhood friends and acquaintances surround me. This is my home."

Juan accepted a coffee from his wife; he thanked her, but she had already disappeared into their bedroom.

"I spend most of my time at the University Hospital in Guadalajara, but I live here and run a free medical clinic Tuesday and Thursday afternoons. "I have treated the police officer's mother. Unfortunately, he has fallen far from the tree; I believe that is your English expression," said Juan. "Tom, these streets were safe when I was young. "Our clinic has been broken into six times over the last year for the medications."

Tom listened carefully, thankful for Juan's hospitality, but wanting answers to the questions he had come for.

"I know you didn't travel to Mexico to hear about me," said Juan, reading Tom's mind. "Tell me about Lucas."

Tom described Lucas' symptoms and Dr. Vernon's diagnosis given. "I'm desperate to save my son."

"I'm very sorry; I understand why you've taken this journey to see me," replied Juan. "Any good father would."

Rosetta, also a doctor, returned and sat. The two hosts proceeded to describe a tale that could have been the basis for a Hollywood movie – and it was true.

The Estradas re-filled their coffee cups, told their guest to relax and then provided the answers he sought.

Located three kilometres northeast of Salamanca, at the base of the San Palapal Volcano, lies a sixteen-acre, two-kilometre-deep, one-of-a-kind geological deposit.

"I literally mean one-of-a-kind in the world, Tom," emphasized Juan.

Goldstar Corporation, a micro-cap mining company, discovered the deposit within the thirty-square kilometres to which it had geological rights. Ironically, Goldstar searched for gold when they found it; initially, the company had no idea of its importance.

"In time, with testing, Goldstar understood their find – and became very excited; they found a graphite deposit, Tom, but no ordinary graphite," explained Juan wide-eyed, palms to the ceiling.

Rosetta explained that regular graphite originates from a sedimentary process – over millions of years organic material in the ground is transformed by heat and pressure into graphite. When removed from the earth and processed, this graphite is left with many impurities from different minerals and compounds that were mixed in with the organic material. The impurities are essentially baked in; although graphite is useful for many commercial applications, such as automobile batteries, its value is relatively modest.

"Goldstar found hydrothermal graphite, an important distinction," said Juan after taking a drink of coffee.

He explained that millions of years ago, a two-kilometre-deep magma chamber exploded upwards by volcanic activity pushing carbon fluids through the earth to the surface. The carbon fluids were so hot, one hundred percent of the impurities found in regular sedimentary graphite were burnt off. The fluids then cooled quickly, leaving the fluids to emerge as a completely pure form of graphite – the first of its kind on the planet.

Rumours spread of Goldstar's discovery; the locals became excited at what the deposit might have meant economically for the region – mining and processing jobs. But only a select few knew exactly what had been found.

"Graphite is known for its strength and heat resistant properties, which is why it is used in batteries, lubricants and coatings for products that are subjected to heat; but its effectiveness is limited by the impurities embedded within it," explained Juan. "Now Tom, because this new graphite has absolutely no impurities, its strength and heat resistant properties are extraordinary – off the charts. For example, the range of ballistic missiles is limited by the heat caused by friction on the nozzle as it flies through the air. It can only fly so far, and so fast, before the heat warps the nozzle affecting its flight accuracy and range."

Tom did not notice Rosetta re-filling his coffee cup because of his fixation on Juan's story. Juan leaned in and looked at his guest squarely in the eyes.

"Those same missile nozzles coated with Goldstar's graphite can travel twice as fast and twice as far. Can you imagine the importance to military forces around the world? This new graphite can withstand 5000-degree heat without losing its strength, he explained.

Tom nodded, appreciating the value of hydrothermal graphite. "A short-range ballistic missile becomes a long-range ballistic missile," offered Tom.

"Exactly," replied Juan. "What if China, or any superpower, or even North Korea, have missiles that fly twice as far as the Americans?" asked Juan, rhetorically. "This is a big deal, trust me."

Tom did trust Juan, even though he had only met him an hour ago. The doctor had the ability to pull you in quickly and immediately make you feel comfortable. Chuck had the same ability.

Juan explained that Goldstar eventually disclosed that this unique graphite was worth one hundred thousand dollars an ounce compared to five thousand dollars for regular, sedimentary graphite. Goldstar's corporate value shot up from two million dollars to an eye-popping six billion dollars.

"Tom, two Goldstar directors mysteriously disappeared before the share price zoomed ahead, assumed murdered, and Goldstar suddenly had a new majority shareholder – a company controlled by the Lozano cartel."

"That's quite a story, Juan; unbelievable. How does the cure fit in to this?" asked Tom. "I'm confused."

"The Lozano cartel tightly controls the graphite deposit," explained Juan. "It's well guarded; nobody can approach it. The surface area is mostly nondescript; the deposit is not exposed at the surface, starting fifty feet below the surface."

Rosetta explained that the deposit's surface is covered with a previously undiscovered variety of Purpura jatasium, a plant native to Mexico; but this variety's appearance differs to the Purpura jatasium that botanists know of. It has brilliant purple leaves; however, the significant difference – the leaves' composition includes a unique enzyme never found on Earth before.

"Given that the plant is only growing on the surface of the graphite deposit, its growth is surely associated with the volcanic evolution of the area," explained Juan. "For the same reasons the graphite is special, this special plant developed from the hydrothermal event."

"So, the cartel only values the graphite deposit; they

don't care about the plant?" asked Tom.

"Correct," replied Juan.

Rosetta re-filled Juan's coffee and stroked the back of his head, which drew a soft smile from her husband.

"Wow," said Tom, releasing an extended sigh. "How do you know all of this?"

"I'm a doctor, yes, but I am a scientist at heart," Juan replied. "I have sources, but that discussion is best left for another day, my friend," he said, patting Tom on the knee.

"How does the Purpura jatasium fit into all of this?" inquired Tom.

"There are two problems, Tom. "When the graphite deposit is eventually mined, all this unique Purpura Jatasium will be destroyed for good. Although it's a perennial flower, it's fragile and in extremely limited quantity."

Tom learned that the jatasium's enzyme could metabolize the protein currently replicating uncontrollably in Lucas' brain; the plant's enzyme was virtually identical to the one missing in Lucas' body.

"I know this for a fact, because I have treated two children with Remington's disease, and they both completely recovered," said Juan. "There's absolutely a cure, not one doubt about it."

Juan explained that there are other varieties of the jatasium genus throughout Mexico, but they do not have this enzyme. "I've tested them all!"

"So, why can't we just grab the plant, if it's the graphite that is valuable?" asked Tom. "Clearly, the cartel doesn't care about the jatasium."

"Well, now we arrive at the root of the problem," said Juan. "The cartel won't allow anyone near the deposit; a barb-wired fence completely surrounds the property. Heavily armed guards and security cameras monitor the grounds."

Juan explained that he discovered the plant by accident when hiking in the area. A wrong turn led him to the back of this graphite-laden property. Juan recognized the species; but because of the colour and texture, he knew he had discovered a new variety. "I had never seen such a vibrant purple! I grabbed a few leaves for research. This occurred well before Goldstar discovered their hydrothermal graphite."

"My research shocked me. I found a cure," Juan explained, delight in his eyes.

However, when Juan returned to the graphite deposit to retrieve more plants, armed guards prevented his access; he couldn't get within two kilometres of the jatasium. Juan explained to the unfriendly guards that he only wanted to gather the curative plant, but was chased away on two occasions and warned that if he returned again, he would be shot.

"I've tried other channels to get the plant without success," sighed Juan.

"What other channels?" asked Tom.

"Again, stories for another day," replied Juan, smirking. "I tried unsuccessfully to harvest more enzyme from the remaining small quantity of jatasium in my possession. I didn't have enough."

Tom sat, thinking momentarily before he addressed Juan. "Why doesn't the cartel just give up the plant if it means nothing to them?"

Juan explained that the cartel wants no attention brought to that area. If the presence of a miracle plant became known, the government would be forced to step in and prevent its destruction. This would create a delay or even prevent the mining of the property.

Tom absorbed the tale, dumbfounded that a cure existed a mere three kilometres away; he could not accept that it was out of reach, despite Juan's explanation.

"We have no friends in the Mexican government," lamented Juan. I made a few phone calls and received a stern warning to stop if I wanted to continue to practice medicine in Mexico. Those with power and money eliminate anything or anyone that threatens either. Do you understand?"

Tom did – but there had to be a way, he mused.

"I'm sure you appreciate what goes on in Mexico," said

Juan. "The Lozano cartel are concerned that someone will interfere with their valuable resource. I'm confident that a fierce chess match will turn bloody at some point. Those two dead board members are proof of it."

"You can bet the Americans are involved, somehow," said Tom. "They have to be."

"To answer your question, yes; the cartel could easily give up the plant, but we're not dealing with reasonable people. They are ruthless killers, who wouldn't waste one thought on a dying child. Most of them probably wouldn't shed a tear over the death of their own mother, if it was in their financial interest," said Juan.

"So, that's what we're dealing with," said Tom, pondering.

"Yes, sir" replied Juan, shaking his head, again in frustration.

Tom concentrated for a minute, exposing a furrowed brow to his hosts. "What if they were offered money for the plant? Certainly, that's the cartel's language."

"Maybe, I don't know," replied Juan, shrugging.

Rosetta motioned to her husband to follow with her into the bedroom.

"Give us a few minutes to talk," said Juan as the two excused themselves. Tom heard muffled discussion behind the bedroom door, which developed into a mild argument.

The Estradas emerged from the bedroom; Juan spoke, "Tom, I may have a way to contact those controlling the graphite deposit. I can't tell you who, how, or why to protect you, but I can try," he said. "I make no promises, but I will try, if it's your request."

Tom replied quickly, "Oh, it is. I will do anything. Absolutely anything! I will be forever grateful!" And, Tom meant it. He would do anything to save his son's life, a comforting resolve.

"Do you have a figure in mind for payment?" asked Juan.

Tom hadn't considered it. He and Veronica had modest

savings. Maybe they could fundraise?

"I'm not a rich man, Juan," he said, scrunching his shoulders. "But whatever it takes. Do you have a suggestion?"

"I have no idea that they will even deal with us, but it has to be significant enough to grab their attention. A million dollars, perhaps? I'm not sure," admitted Juan.

"Well, offer them one million dollars, then," instructed Tom. "I will get the money somehow." But he had no idea how he would come up with a million dollars. Veronica's parents were middle class and comfortable; however, they wouldn't have anywhere near a million dollars.

Juan told Tom that this process would not happen overnight, if it occurred at all. Working through dangerous channels, where undesirables walked in the shadows, had to be navigated carefully.

"Let's get some sleep and we can talk again in the morning," said Juan. "You can spend the night here. My brother drives into Guadalajara every day; he can drive you to the airport tomorrow in daylight."

Tom's phone had long ago died, so Juan sent a text to Veronica advising her that he was fine and would be returning to Canada tomorrow. She had become fraught with worry when she had not heard from her husband.

As Tom fell asleep, he tried to process all he heard at the Estrada residence. If he woke in the morning and discovered he had dreamt of this trip, he wouldn't be surprised. But hope existed – a glimmer – and that was all he could ask for. Tom slept restlessly on a couch much too short for his frame; morning arrived quickly.

At daybreak, without breakfast or a delicious Mexican coffee, Tom said goodbye to the Estradas with hugs and thanks. He caught a ride back to the airport with Juan's brother, Enrique, finding the daylight trip pleasant. Tom listened to Enrique's entertaining stories about Mexico and Juan's childhood, while admiring the countryside's rugged beauty and the many cacti that filled the landscape.

Tom used the three-hour wait before his departure to

conjure up ways to raise one million dollars. Maybe, fundraising? The goal was daunting, perhaps out of reach.

Exhausted, Tom pulled into his driveway at 2:00 am, thankful he had not fallen asleep on the way home from the airport after nodding off a couple of times. He felt like a character in a spy novel, pushing through the front door and crawling into bed without taking his clothes off.

Veronica turned over, "I missed you."

"Me too," replied Tom, hugging her tighter than usual.

"How did it go?" she asked.

"I'll explain everything in the morning but there's hope," he said.

"Hope is all I need," she said softly.

After an insufficient six-hour sleep, Tom awoke to his wife's beckoning.

"Come and eat, Tom," she yelled.

Tom descended the stairs and shuffled towards the kitchen table where a wonderful breakfast awaited him. His half-closed eyes took in the steam rising off his eggs. "Looks delicious!"

"Lucas is still in bed," said Veronica, handing him a coffee.

"Thank you. We should start making this with sugar and cinnamon. In Mexico, they mix it in prior to brewing – delicious and spicy."

"I'd love to try it, Tom."

"Thanks for breakfast. I'm starving," said Tom as he sat down at the kitchen table.

While eating, he recounted his eventful trip, although he left out Scarface and his almost kidnapping; he need not worry his wife more than necessary.

The story stretched their imaginations – the Mexican drug cartel, Purpura jatasium and hydrothermal graphite, but they had no reason to question Juan Estrada. Tom considered Juan compassionate and honourable, a better man than Tom Henderson. After all, it was he who had contacted him. What would Dr. Juan Estrada have to gain by concocting such a wild tale? Nothing. No other reasonable answer existed. Juan didn't even want him to come.

The Hendersons prepared to fundraise immediately. It wasn't clear when, or if, Juan would contact him, but they assumed the best.

Veronica would focus on fundraising while Tom maintained his practice. She would call the local newspaper to run a story about Lucas, emphasizing his need for expensive life-saving medication not available in Canada. Juan warned Tom never to raise the graphite deposit publicly or his back channels would close faster than a Venus' Fly Trap.

Tom finished his breakfast and waited for Lucas to awake before heading to the office; he hadn't seen enough of him lately. When 9:00 am arrived, he peeked in his room, purposefully banging the door to rouse his boy.

"Come here, buddy," said Tom softly, snuggling in beside his son. "I missed you."

Lucas turned around and hugged his dad while kissing him on the cheek.

"I love you, buddy," whispered Tom into his son's ear as a few tears rolled down his cheek.

Why is this happening to us? How much can I take?

Tom drove to his office and settled in. He still had a busy practice to run; three dozen messages waiting to be returned. But before he did anything, he made two very important calls.

Four weeks had passed and Tom still hadn't heard from Dr. Estrada – a tortuous wait. What channel was Juan was working through? The Lozano cartel likely did not have an office number that you called to schedule an appointment.

In the fifth week, Tom called Juan, promising the doctor that he loathed bothering him, but he and his wife's anxiety compelled him to reach out. Each passing day meant Lucas was a day closer to death. Juan responded with his usual patience, advising Tom that the process was in motion, but unfortunately, he had nothing to report.

"It's a very delicate situation," explained Juan.

As Tom said goodbye, Kerri stepped into his office, smiling.

"A civil matter?" she exclaimed, placing a letter in front of her boss to sign. "You haven't handled a civil matter since you became a lawyer. Are you crazy?"

Yes, thought Tom – likely the last of the crazy people, thinking of Timothy Findley's book and poor old Hooker; like the boy's final destination, Tom did not rule out ending up in an insane asylum. The pressure pushed him in that direction.

"I scanned the contingency fee agreement," advised Kerri.

Tom smiled at her. "Criminal law doesn't pay the bills very well," he explained. "Besides, I feel like broadening my horizons, so I will give it a shot."

"Okay, boss; whatever you say," she replied. "Good luck!"

Tom spent the evening drafting a civil Statement of Claim to commence a personal injury lawsuit on behalf of Lawrence Wheeler. Mr. Wheeler claimed the sum of five million dollars for pain and suffering, lost wages and treatment expenses resulting from a slip and fall on an icy Stratford sidewalk.

Mr. Wheeler suffered a concussion after striking his head on the cement; his severe post-concussion syndrome symptoms included serious and disabling migraine headaches. Wheeler claimed he would never be able to work again. And, given his young age of twenty-five, his future lost income would be significant. Tom never would have taken on such a case previously, but Wheeler was a former client. When the opportunity to earn a large fee presented itself, Tom had to take it, given his anticipated expensive purchase in Salamanca.

The contingency fee agreement determined legal fees based on a percentage of a court award or settlement – 33%, the maximum allowed by the Law Society of Ontario. The agreement provided that legal fees would be zero if Tom couldn't secure anything for Mr. Wheeler.

Tom's primary challenges: he knew almost nothing

about civil litigation and secondly, civil matters could drag on for years. His son could be dead by then.

He addressed the first issue by researching every night about civil litigation procedures and evidentiary matters; Tom borrowed two legal textbooks from the local law association's legal library. His extensive reading helped him determine the experts that he required to advance Wheeler's future wage loss claim.

Tom also called a law-school friend who specialised in civil litigation. Andrew Murray invited Tom to ask questions, but warned Tom he was in over his head.

"There's too much to learn in a short time, Tom," said Murray. "And, you have no civil trial experience to rely upon."

Tom agreed with Murray. Still, he believed he knew enough to muddle his way through; however, because of the significant damages claimed, a fierce defence from Stratford's liability insurer would be presented. Tom knew it – and it unnerved him.

After a few hours, Tom completed his pleading. At 9:00 pm, he left it on Kerri's desk with a note to have Wheeler's Statement of Claim issued at the courthouse the next day.

CHAPTER EIGHTEEN

Amicus & Ven

Amicus dropped his keys on the table and walked across the carpet to the other side of the room and closed the curtains to ensure not a sliver of light penetrated. Two minutes later, he heard the expected soft knock on the door.

"Come in," whispered Amicus, opening the door no wider than necessary.

Ven stepped in quickly, without saying a word. Amicus looked both ways down the hallway and then closed the door quietly behind Ven, before taking Ven's coat and throwing it onto one of the two beds in room 322.

Both of them felt the tension and excitement, neither knowing which was the more powerful emotion of the two.

"Thanks for coming," said Amicus.

"I've been waiting to see you all week," replied Ven.

"Did anybody see you?" questioned Amicus.

"No, I don't think so but it's difficult to be sure."

Amicus grabbed Ven's hand and placed it over his heart. "Can you feel how fast my heart is racing?" he asked Ven.

"I can; mine's racing twice as fast. Here, feel it."

Amicus' hand trembled as he moved it towards Ven and placed it over Ven's heart. Indeed, he could feel it pounding. Amicus had never engaged in anything like this before – he understood that everything was at stake.

If either Amicus or Ven possessed ambiguity about crossing the Rubicon, they overcame it. Standing in the room, they had now moved past the scheming stage. Both of them had the entire week to cancel this rendezvous but neither did, both of them sure that the other would cancel at the last minute when cold feet got the upper hand. Surely, clearer heads and moral minds should have prevailed before it got this far.

But here they were. Were they actually going to allow this to happen?

"We shouldn't be doing this," lamented Ven.

"Of course, we shouldn't," replied Amicus. "But sometimes you have to do what feels right, not what is right."

Amicus took his hand away from Ven's heart and caressed Ven's cheek. "And this feels so right," swooned Amicus.

"It does, but we're both risking so much," said Ven, reluctantly acknowledging that the risk elevated the excitement in the room.

"Come with me," urged Amicus, grabbing Ven's hand and walking to the bed. Amicus took his hands and gently wrapped them around Ven's waist, until Ven quivered at his touch. As they stared deeply into each other's eyes, neither of them could hold back any longer. Neither of them had to wait or anticipate any longer.

They kissed passionately. Once Ven felt Amicus's sweet lips, any hesitation melted away with all judgment.

Amicus laid Ven down on the bed – the fight now over for both of them – willing losers in their moral battle; they made love in room 322 for the first time. And with that ill-advised encounter, Amicus and Ven began attending Stratford's Queens Inn once a week on Tuesday afternoons.

CHAPTER NINETEEN

Consensus Ad Idem, Not!

Kerri popped her head into Tom's office. "A Dr. Estrada is on line two."

He immediately picked up the phone, "Juan, is that you?"

"It is, Tom," came the reply. "I have good news and bad news for you, my friend," he said matter-of-factly. "The good news is that the Lozano cartel will deal with you; they'll sell the plant."

"That's great, Juan!" Tom replied excitedly.

"It is, but now the bad news," said the doctor, cautiously.

"Okay, tell me, Juan."

"Tom, the price is two million dollars."

"Two million dollars!" shouted Tom.

"I know. I know. But that's their demand; they're not the negotiating type, if you know what I mean."

"I do know, but how will I raise two million dollars? One million was impossible."

"Let me give you some more good news," said Juan. "The cartel understands that you will have to raise the money, so they are giving you nine months to make payment."

"Well, isn't that generous of the cartel," replied Tom, sarcastically. "Such a benevolent organization. This is so goddamn ridiculous."

"I'm sorry, Tom."

"I appreciate everything you're doing," replied Tom, feeling guilty for shooting the messenger.

"Tom, there's one final thing I have to tell you and it's very important, so listen carefully," said Juan with trepidation.

"Go ahead, Juan."

"I was not the person who made the face-to-face contact with the cartel," he explained. "The Lozano cartel views this as a deal that must now be fulfilled, rather than an offer contingent on whether you can come up with the money."

"What are you trying to say?" asked Tom, nervously – his voice quietening.

"They view it as a contract that must be fulfilled," explained Juan.

"But I never made any such deal," said Tom, exasperated. "No meeting of the minds; no consensus ad idem."

"Of course, you didn't, but we're not dealing with ordinary business people here," said Juan. "The cartel does not deal with alleged contract breaches in court, where you can make such an argument," Juan warned in a concerned voice. "Their remedies tend to be more permanent, and definitely more violent."

"Oh my God, Juan. What have I gotten myself into here?" asked Tom.

"I'm sorry. I didn't see this coming," he said, apologetically.

Tom did not respond.

"Are you still there?" asked Juan.

"Yes, Juan. You've been incredibly helpful; thank you. I'll keep in contact with you about how much money I can raise."

The two men said goodbye and Tom hung up the phone. The worried father clasped his hands behind his neck. How was he in a position to be killed by the Lozano cartel if he did not come up with two million dollars? This must be a bad dream. It had to be, because you couldn't make this up, he lamented – a vision of his body dangling from a Mexican overpass intruding his thoughts.

Tom got up and closed his office door. He sat back down, opened his desk's bottom drawer and felt around but could not find what he was looking for. He missed Alex; would one quick visit be that harmful?

Two days later, Tom awoke in the middle of the night, 2:30 am, to his son's crying. He looked over at his wife, who was not stirring, so he dragged himself out of bed and shuffled down the hall to Lucas' room. He slowly pushed the bedroom door open to find Lucas sitting up in his bed.

"Daddy, sick," Lucas cried out, softly.

Tom sat down beside his son and rubbed his back before feeling his sweaty and alarmingly hot forehead. He picked his son up and walked down the hallway to his bedroom. "Veronica," whispered Tom, raising his voice after receiving no response, "Veronica!"

Veronica raised her head off her pillow, slightly. "What is it?" she asked, groggily – her eyes barely open.

"Lucas is burning up. I mean really burning up!"

Veronica reached up and put her hand on Lucas' head. "Oh my God, Tom!" she exclaimed. "We need to get him to the hospital, right away. There's no sense even taking his temperature; he's so hot," she directed. "Let's go!"

Veronica jumped out of bed and threw on yoga pants. She left Lucas in his pyjamas and carried him out the front door to meet her husband, who had already started the car. She jumped in the front seat with her whimpering and lethargic son in her arms.

Tom called ahead on his cell phone to the Stratford General Hospital emergency department to alert them of their impending arrival.

Thankfully, empty roads allowed Tom to race at twice the speed limit. In four minutes, he pulled with screeching tires in front of the emergency room doors; Veronica pushed the car door open before Tom fully stopped, and rushed through the emergency room doors with Lucas in her arms, leaving Tom to catch up.

A tall thin man with glasses wearing several days of stubble entered the emergency room.

"I'm Dr. Plaine," he said. "We've been waiting for you."

"Put the boy there," said Dr. Plaine, pointing to a gurney. The doctor performed a cursory examination on Lucas' still body. He quickly found a faint pulse, before placing his stethoscope on Lucas' chest. Dr. Plaine and an orderly whisked Lucas away, the doctor bellowing back to the parents that he would return to talk to them after carrying out some tests.

After an agonizing forty-five-minute wait in the stark emergency waiting room, Dr. Plaine reappeared. "Come with me, please," he said to them. They followed him through double doors, down a hallway, and past the X-ray room until they arrived at the Intensive Care Unit. Several nurses and clinicians hurriedly performed their duties.

They entered room 607, a private room within the thirty-bed unit, where Lucas lay in bed receiving intravenous fluids.

"He's stable," said Dr. Plaine, hovering over his patient. "He's sleeping," offered the doctor, alleviating Tom's concern that he was unconscious.

"I accessed both Dr. Sprott's and Dr. Vernon's electronic records. Lucas' illness is complex. I'm sorry," he said, sincerely. "I just got Dr. Vernon out of bed to discuss Lucas. Luckily, I connected with him at this hour. We're waiting for test results, but it's clear Lucas has a serious brain infection," explained Dr. Plaine. "He has encephalitis, inflammation of the brain; I've prescribed a cocktail of antibiotics."

"What does this mean, Doctor?" asked Tom.

"Frankly, it's very serious," responded Dr. Plaine.

"So, what now?" asked Veronica.

"His condition has become septic; the infection is in his bloodstream. Lucas' body has released chemicals to fight this infection, but the body's response has been too strong creating an imbalance and causing inflammation."

"And what does that mean, Doctor?" asked Veronica, her face turning white.

"We're trying to prevent septic shock, which can trigger a dramatic loss of blood pressure, multiple organ failures, and unfortunately, death. We have flooded Lucas's body with antibiotics to try and prevent this.

"Oh my God, Tom," said Veronica, putting her head into his chest.

Tom wrapped his arms around his wife. Their thoughts mirrored each other – could this be it? Dr. Vernon provided a death sentence, but at least they had years. Perhaps they only had days, or worse, hours until Lucas died. The weight of that possibility crushed them.

"We may transfer Lucas to SickKids in Toronto," explained Dr. Plaine. "That may be the best place for him; I won't know until around noon today. I want to see how he responds to the antibiotics."

Tom looked at his watch, 4:10 am; they would not know the plan for several hours.

"You should be prepared that the infection will be difficult to get under control," said Dr. Plaine, an ominous warning that penetrated their inner cores.

"What are you saying?" asked Veronica.

"His condition is very fragile," he replied. "There's a waiting room you can stay in, but, unfortunately, you can't remain in here."

Dr. Plaine extended both parents a comforting pat and left the room, leaving Tom and Veronica alone to embrace, tears streaming down their faces. It was too much for both of them.

They both stood over Lucas's bed, peering down at their innocent son, wondering if he would ever open his eyes again – wondering if they might have to say goodbye.

"This isn't fair, Tom."

"No, it certainly isn't," he replied. Lots of things aren't fair in life, Tom concluded, musing about what life had dealt them. Surely, he had received a disproportionate share, he lamented, looking at the tubes and lines attached to his son.

Tom had a court hearing in only a few hours. How would he be prepared, physically and mentally? Exhaustion permeated his body. He sent Kerri a text directing her to contact the court and request an adjournment.

Tom hugged his wife, consoling her as best he could. He teetered at the edge – one gust of wind away from being blown over the cliff and hurtling to a very dark place he once patrolled. And, it scared him. The bullets rang out, but he had neither the will nor the strength to duck, fortunate that the projectiles only whizzed by him and did not permanently lodge into his soul.

"We've been hugging each other for the wrong reasons lately, hon," said Tom, wiping her tears.

"I love you," she said. "How did I get so lucky to have you in my life?"

They situated themselves in the tiny I.C.U. waiting room and drifted to sleep, searching for a brief respite from their emotional toil; although sleep had proven to be an ineffective shield, in Tom's view. Rather, night combat provided a distinct advantage for the aggressor, the darkness hiding its next move.

At 5:30 am, a "code blue" shocked Veronica from her sleep. She shook Tom. "Wake up," she said in a voice too loud for a hospital, but he had already awoken. Tom felt a pang of fear and adrenaline shoot through his body, the same sensation that occurs when you are driving home to your family and you hear an ambulance siren blaring away; you wonder if that ambulance is on its way to your house. The Hendersons watched a team of doctors and nurses dash down the hallway past the I.C.U. waiting room with a crash cart.

The parents leapt from their chairs and pursued the team directly to Lucas' room; the ambulance arrived at Tom's home. A nurse stepped in front of the scared parents, preventing entry into their son's room, "I'm sorry. You'll have to wait out here."

Their faces pressed on the door's glass window, the Hendersons eyed the team frantically working on Lucas. The boy's eyes remained closed while a doctor intubated him. Electric paddles were applied to his chest, delivering a blast of electric current to his heart to treat his life-threatening cardiac dysrhythmia.

The Hendersons fixed their attention on the heart monitor, which now indicated a beating heart, causing their panic to slightly diminish. After a few minutes, the nurses and doctors surrounding Lucas began to relax, their faces losing some tension.

One of the doctors turned around; he stepped into the hallway after seeing the stunned and frozen faces looking through the door.

"I'm Dr. White, the attending doctor tonight. Are you Lucas' parents?" he asked, knowing they must be.

"Yes," they responded in unison.

"Dr. Plaine will return in a few hours," he said. "Lucas appears stable at the moment but we're monitoring closely. His body has been battling the infection; this stressed his heart," explained Dr. White.

"Is he going to be okay?" asked Veronica, clasping her hands.

"If we can get the infection under control, the stress on his body will be reduced," replied Dr. White. "He's a very sick little boy, right now."

After a half-hour, they breathed easier, yet knowing if his heart stopped once, it could stop again; Lucas was losing the battle.

At 6:30 am, Tom drove to his office for a few minutes, knowing that Lucas was in no immediate danger. When he arrived, he answered e-mails and left instructions for Kerri on a number of client matters.

Tom looked at his desk's bottom drawer, but knew what he desired was not there. He signed a few cheques Keri had left for him before returning to the hospital.

The hospital arranged for an ambulance to transfer Lucas to SickKids Hospital in Toronto; and at 10:00 am the ambulance left with Veronica riding in the back with her son, who remained lethargic, but was now awake. Tom followed in his car, giving him ample time to ponder what kind of man he was. The question was fair and difficult; but he couldn't answer it – when an answer is that painful, willful blindness is required to keep your sanity.

Once the Hendersons settled Lucas in at SickKids, they decided Veronica would remain in Toronto and Tom would return to Stratford. Tom hated the arrangement, but he had to try and keep his law practice and the house of cards he had built afloat. Rent, staff wages and operating expenses continued to accumulate, whether he was there are not.

Besides, he had the Wheeler case, which he needed to win if he had any chance of paying the cartel, although it was such a long shot, he might as well have purchased a lottery ticket. Those were the odds that he faced – two million dollars appeared unattainable, but he had no choice but to try.

At least Wheeler's litigation was moving ahead, even quicker than Tom had hoped for. Tom had been served the defendant's Statement of Defence from a well-heeled Toronto Bay Street lawyer, Mark Dietz, who officially represented The City of Stratford on paper; but in reality, he took instructions from the city's liability insurer. The Statement of Defence contained boiler-plate language, which simply denied everything allegation; it offered no real indication of whether the defence might succeed.

After two conversations with Dietz, Tom realized the lawyer had a mountain-sized ego, who believed the litigation world revolved around him. This process would not be easy.

Examination for discoveries, a pre-trial process that provided an opportunity for Dietz to question Wheeler under oath in the presence of a court reporter at Tom's office, proceeded a month later – quicker than usual. Andrew Murry characterized it as lightning speed for a significant, personal injury case. Likewise, Tom could question the city's representative. This discovery step allowed both lawyers to determine what the other side's evidence would likely be in trial.

Prior to Wheeler's examination, Tom and his client spent two straight days in his office preparing for the important day. Tom listed two hundred questions that Dietz might ask Wheeler and simulated the upcoming examination by bombarding his client with questions. Tom asked him the same questions in every way possible, tried to trick him, and raised his voice attempting to fluster his client. Then, after Tom finished, they repeated the questioning again; Wheeler was not thrilled about the overkill, but he followed his lawyer's instructions.

Tom and Wheeler scoured his medical records, line by line, until his client knew every entry, word and comma perfectly.

Wheeler impressed Tom, an uneducated man, yet savvy and intelligent; he was ready for Dietz's onslaught.

Tom believed the issue of liability was airtight. His client slipped on ice; the city's disclosure documents suggested that despite terrible winter conditions, the city had not salted or sanded in the seven days prior to his fall. Wheeler stated that the ice was at least an inch thick, confirmed by the two ambulance attendants who had arrived on the scene to assist him.

As such, Tom reasoned that only the extent of damages – what the final dollar figure would be – should be at issue, rather than whether damages should be paid at all; however, Dietz did not appear to be the type to concede anything.

As expected, Wheeler performed well at his examination – almost too good. His polished answers appeared rehearsed occasionally, but Dietz never tripped him up, which frustrated the opposing lawyer.

Tom examined the city's Manager of Infrastructure and Development, the department that maintains the city roads and sidewalks. Unlike Wheeler's examination, which lasted seven hours, Tom only needed thirty minutes to examine Nathan Horner. Horner explained that the city divided its inspection, salting and sandy responsibilities into thirty zones; a maintenance worker, assigned to each zone, had the responsibility to continuously inspect and apply salt or sand as needed in the assigned zone.

Horner provided sworn evidence that three months prior to Wheeler's fall, the zones were rejigged, and for unclear reasons, someone omitted the corner where Wheeler fell in the transition; no maintenance worker was assigned to this particular corner. Horner agreed the corner had not been maintained by error. Once Tom heard the admission, he stopped asking questions – liability had been proven.

The steady march towards Wheeler's trial continued. On the brilliant advice of his colleague, Andrew Murray, Tom brought a motion for summary judgment – which he was certain to lose, in part. Tom devoted a weekend to research the steps required to bring a summary judgment motion before the court.

By way of a summary judgment motion, a party to the litigation could ask the court for a final ruling on issues such as liability or damages without the need for a formal trial. A motion judge provided rulings based upon sworn affidavit evidence filed with the court, rather than oral evidence. Generally, the judge would make a final decision regarding a particular issue, if the decision was so obvious the judge felt no trial was required. Tom filed a transcript of Horner's questions and answers from his examination in support of his motion.

When Tom brought the motion, Dietz simply conceded the liability issue rather than fighting it, but Dietz argued that a trial was necessary for Wheeler's significant damage assessment. Although Tom argued for a summary judgment on Wheeler's damages as well, he knew a trial would be required for that issue; not surprisingly, the judge ruled as such. However, one significant benefit arose from bringing the summary judgment motion – thanks to Murray's suggestion; the judge immediately set Wheeler's trial date, bypassing dozens of other civil litigation matters waiting on the trial list. This prevented his client's matter from languishing, while other matters proceed before his. Whether luck or genius, Tom didn't care.

Tom now had a trial date set five months into the future, August 6th, a full six weeks before the cartel's nine-month deadline. While pleased about the unusually quick court date, securing two million dollars seemed formidable.

Tom prepared night and day for the trial, periodically travelling back and forth to Toronto. He pushed his other clients aside, focusing solely on Wheeler.

Lucas fought off the original infection, but suffered a

second one; Dr. Vernon had a concerned look on his face, when he discussed the setback.

Carrying on at the office, when he desired to be in Toronto with Lucas and his wife proved challenging. It had become clear that he was in over his head with the Wheeler trial. He had to be at his best, but his heart remained in Toronto. What if Lucas died when he was not there? How could he live with himself?

Tom struggled with the anticipated complex evidentiary issues. Dietz forewarned Tom Dietz that he would challenge his doctor as not properly qualified to give evidence as an expert on post-concussion syndrome. Tom appreciated that it took more than a medical degree to be qualified to give expert testimony on specialized medical issues. He would be calling Dr. Crane, who had extensive experience with head injuries, to provide evidence on Wheeler's post-concussion syndrome.

Dietz told him that he would argue that Dr. Crane's experience only qualified him to give evidence on trauma to the head, and that concussion syndrome fell into a totally different field of medicine. Dietz would argue that the research on concussions and medical developments, including the understanding of post-concussion syndrome, was occurring rapidly; only doctors who focused their practice in this area were up-to-date and qualified to give opinions.

Tom contemplated that his expert would be permitted to give expert evidence. A ruling rejecting his expert would devastate his case; it would collapse without calling expert medical testimony. Murray advised him that personal injury cases were won or lost based on a battle of the experts. Which expert opinion did the judge prefer?

Tom paid eighteen thousand dollars, drawn on a line of credit, to have medical experts assess Wheeler and prepare their reports. He did not have the deep pockets of a large insurer behind him to hire the very best.

Meanwhile, Dietz planned to fly Dr. Franklin in from California, a renowned expert in post-concussion syndrome. The cost to hire the team doctor for the NFL's San Francisco

49ers professional football team would be prohibitive, out of reach for a small-town lawyer.

Dietz repeatedly told Tom – mocked him – that the trial judge would prefer a world-renowned expert over his unknown doctor. "Give it up now, Henderson," he said through laughter.

In the lead-up to a trial, a lawyer wonders which judge has been assigned to the trial. Presiding judges have their own styles, personalities and bent toward the admissibility of evidence; they have their own approaches to life. They are human beings, after all. Some judges exhibited more compassion and might unconsciously be persuaded to find in favour of a sympathetic plaintiff on certain issues.

Although no mention that a defendant had insurance could be raised at trial, judges, unlike juries, knew when an insurer responsible for paying any damages was likely in the background. Of course, a judge would know that a municipality had a liability insurer that would be paying any damages. Perhaps, this knowledge created an unspoken advantage for Tom, although he couldn't count on it.

Non-legal factors could play a role in a judge's decision, consciously or not, although a judge would never admit so.

Usually, judges were assigned on a rotation basis but occasionally, a particular judge was chosen to hear a case because his or her schedule allowed for it, or because of expertise in an area of law. Generally, a random rotation presented the best optics of fairness; however, no requirement existed to rotate because all judges were considered unbiased and independent.

When court clerk Rosemary Adams brought Judge Sussman the trial list for the upcoming civil litigation trials, she handed it to him and asked, "Your Honour, shall I assign judges as I normally would?"

He looked up and down the list at the twelve matters scheduled for trial. *Lawrence Wheeler v. The Corporation of the City of Stratford* was last on the August trial list, which commenced in three weeks. Thomas T. Henderson, counsel for the Plaintiff and Mark Dietz for the Defendant, read Judge Sussman.

Rosemary remarked to her boss, "I don't think I've ever seen Mr. Henderson on the civil matter trial list. He only practices criminal law," she said, surprised.

Sussman sat pensively for a moment, crossing his arms – and then looked up at Rosemary, "I've been busy lately and this trial could be long. I could probably use a break but assign me to the Wheeler case, please. Let's see how good a lawyer Mr. Henderson is," he said to Rosemary, handing her back the trial list. "Please randomly assign the rest of the matters as usual," he instructed.

"Yes, Your Honour," she replied.

Tom stayed the weekend before the trial in Toronto with Veronica and Lucas, thankful to take a break from his trial preparation. Lucas's condition remained the same, awake and talking; but his stubborn infection had him running a high fever, taxing his diminutive body every minute of the day.

Tom returned to Stratford Sunday morning to meet Wheeler for last-minute preparations before the commencement of trial the following morning. Wheeler arrived at noon; they reviewed his anticipated testimony again and discussed trial strategy. After Wheeler left four hours later, Tom reviewed his notes and updated his litigation plan. Alone with his thoughts, the nerves set in, stalking his vulnerabilities. Game day approached, and the stakes were high for Tom, both as a father trying to save his son's life and as a lawyer wading into unfamiliar waters.

The next morning, Tom entered the courtroom at 9:15 am, forty-five minutes before the 10:00 am start time, unpacked and settled in at the plaintiff's table, situated to the right of the judge's bench. Tom took a deep breath and looked around the room, trying to calm himself.

Because the trial would only address damages, he hoped it would only last a week, but it still meant being away from his family far too long.

Mark Dietz arrived ten minutes later, entering the

courtroom with an arrogant swagger, appearing put out when Tom extended his arm to shake hands. He wouldn't have looked out of place in a spaghetti western, slowly walking down the dusty streets of Salamanca, preparing for a gunfight.

With a serious expression, Dietz looked at him. "It's not too late to take the five- hundred-thousand-dollar offer."

Tom stared at him with his bravest face but didn't respond.

"My client has made a formal offer, Tom," he said. "You know that if your client does worse than our offer after the trial, he's responsible for all of our legal fees from this point on, even if he wins something," said Dietz.

Deitz's explanation of this elementary legal cost principle in civil litigation, learned in the first year of law school, shoved Tom's inexperience in his face; Dietz meant it to be condescending – mission accomplished.

Dietz had already taken great delight in bringing Tom's misstep of electing to proceed with a trial by judge alone, rather than with a jury, to his attention. "What were you thinking, rookie!" he said, perplexed but pleased.

Jury awards were generally higher than judge awards; jurors were inclined to be more emotional than a judge. Even more so, jurors were manipulated far easier than a veteran litigator who had risen to the lofty position of a judge.

"You'll get less, Tom. Last chance to settle before the trial starts," warned Dietz. "Otherwise, you may want to call your own professional liability insurer, now, for not recommending that your client accept it."

"Thanks, Mark, but I'll take my chances," replied Tom. "If you can get to three million, we can have a serious conversation," said Tom loudly, feigning confidence.

Dietz laughed at him. "Come on. You know you'll never get that. Take the offer and get something for your client. Let's save a week of our lives and a whole lot of money," he said. "The cost consequences will bankrupt your client," said Dietz; "and your client will be suing you for not advising him to take this offer. And trust me, my client will vigorously pursue the collection of its costs," he promised.

"Can't do it, Mark. My guy will never work again. Listen, I'll give you a break," offered Tom. "Offer me two million seven hundred and fifty thousand and I'll see what I can do," he said, smiling.

Dietz smirked and replied, "You're a dreamer, Henderson." Dietz turned away and walked back to his table, shaking his head and mumbling to himself.

Tom walked over to the court clerk. "Who is the presiding judge for the trial, Rosemary?" he asked.

"Judge Sussman," she replied as she put a jug of water in front of the judge's chair.

Thankfully, Wheeler arrived on time; Tom brought him to a private meeting room for a last-minute pep talk and to calm him down.

"I'm nervous," said Wheeler, his hands shaking.

Tom decided against telling Wheeler that he felt the same way. Instead, he put his hands on the front of Wheeler's shoulders and said confidently, "Everything will be fine. You and I have been over this a thousand times. I know it's stressful but we will get through this together," he said. "Take a deep breath and let's get in there and do it."

Tom walked back to the counsel table with Wheeler, maintaining his air of confidence.

"All rise," announced the court clerk. "In the matter of Lawrence Wheeler and The Corporation of the City of Stratford, the Honourable Judge Sussman of the Superior Court of Justice presiding."

The judge bowed, his action reciprocated by those in the room.

"You may be seated," said the clerk.

"My notes from the pre-trial judge indicate that this trial will take approximately four days," said the judge. "Are counsel still in agreement with that estimate?" he asked.

Tom and Dietz nodded their heads.

"Are there any preliminary issues before opening statements, gentlemen?" asked Judge Sussman.

The lawyers handed a joint document brief to the clerk, agreeing that everything in the document brief was being admitted for the truth of its contents. After discussing a few other preliminary matters, Dietz addressed the final one.

"The defence is challenging that Dr. Crane is an expert of the subject matter of post-concussion syndrome," explained Dietz. "The defendant's position is that Dr. Crane is not qualified to provide expert evidence on post-concussion syndrome in this trial," he explained.

"Mr. Dietz, you are certainly entitled to a voir dire on this issue and I am completely open-minded about the issue," said Judge Sussman. "But I have read Dr. Crane's resume and on the face of it, he does appear to be qualified."

Take that Dietz, you putz, said Tom to himself.

"Thank you, Your Honour. I request the voir dire," said Dietz, his furrowed forehead expressing confusion at the judge's comment about Dr. Crane's experience. How could he be perceived as an expert on the face of it, wondered Dietz?

Dietz followed through on his threat to take issue with his expert. Tom should have researched if a court had ever qualified Dr. Crane as an expert in post-concussion syndrome; the answer would have been in the negative. However, Sussman's preliminary views comforted him.

Both counsel provided their opening statements, which lasted an hour each.

Tom explained to Judge Sussman how the court would hear evidence from Mr. Wheeler, who would testify about his injuries, symptoms and the impact his injuries had on his daily activities and ability to work. As well, the Plaintiff's father and former girlfriend would testify. The Plaintiff would adduce evidence from Dr. Crane, subject to the outcome of the voir dire, about the effects of the Plaintiff's concussion, and post-concussion syndrome.

Lastly, the court would hear testimony from future care cost specialist, Dr. Ronald Hanover about Mr. Wheeler's future care costs, such as treatment and medication. His estimate, based upon an expected life span of a further forty-seven years, would total approximately three million dollars. And finally, the court would hear from an economist who will estimate the present value of Wheeler's past and future wage loss claim at 2.9 million dollars. Additionally, Tom advised the judge that his client sought pain and suffering damages in the amount of $300,000.

Dietz followed with his opening statement and listed his witnesses which, not surprisingly, would contradict the plaintiff's witnesses in respect of damages. Tom jotted down the figures that Dietz submitted that his witnesses would testify to regarding damages, a number totalling about $375,000.

Dietz presented confidently with a polished delivery. His esteemed career covered three decades defending injury claims for insurance companies; the man was comfortable on his feet.

After opening submissions, the judge carried out a two-hour voir dire regarding Dr. Crane's qualifications.

Tom submitted that Dr. Crane was an expert on post-concussion syndrome and that Dietz's argument was really who was the more qualified expert. Dietz repeated the same argument to Sussman that he had previously given Tom. Unfortunately, Tom found Dietz's argument effective; however, Judge Sussman gave no indication of which way he was leaning after hearing the arguments.

After the voir dire submissions were complete, the judge recessed court and retired to his chambers after advising the parties that he would take an hour to consider his ruling.

After the judge left, Tom turned to Dietz to make a smart-ass remark but decided against it. He might need an ounce of goodwill from the man in the future, although Dietz likely did not have had that capability. Poking Dietz could interfere with an opportunity to settle, although that possibility looked slim, now that the trial had commenced.

"You made effective submissions," offered Tom to Dietz, reaching deep to appear sincere.

"I certainly did. This could be a quick exit for you," replied Dietz, puffing his chest. "You should have taken the offer," he gloated.

As promised, the judge entered the court an hour later to make his first ruling of the trial.

"After having heard the submissions of counsel and reviewing the resume of Dr. Crane, I am satisfied that Dr. Crane is an expert and the court makes that finding. Dr. Crane shall be permitted to testify," ruled Judge Sussman.

Dietz jumped to his feet when he heard the ruling. "Your Honour," he said, bewildered.

"Sit down, Mr. Dietz. I have made my ruling," he said sternly.

Dietz sat down, not attempting to hide his irritation.

Go on, Dietz. Piss off the judge at the beginning of the trial, thought Tom.

"Gentleman, it's 2:10 pm; I don't want to start evidence today, so we will begin at 10:00 am tomorrow," stated Judge Sussman.

On the way out of the courthouse, Tom heard Dietz talking to his client around the corner. "I have no idea where that ruling came from," he said. "I'm shocked."

Tom drove back to the office and returned several telephone messages, relieved that he had survived the first day and kept Crane in the ball game. He scanned his e-mails and responded to a few.

His mind turned to his son as he worked at his computer, heartbroken that his son was fighting for his life while he sat there in his bloody office. He picked up the phone and called his wife; he needed to hear her voice. Lucas remained stable. At least he wasn't worse.

Tom admitted to Veronica that he was tired and stressed, but the idea of seeing her soon would keep him going. He was ashamed that he needed an emotional boost from his wife, when it was he who should be strong for her.

Tom put his dinner of leftover chicken and pasta into the office microwave and set it at two minutes. He found a stool, opened the top cupboard in the kitchen, and felt around until he found what he was looking for. Tom filled his coffee cup, took a few gulps and waited for the buzz. Just one to calm the nerves, he said to himself, ashamed at the weakness.

Wheeler arrived at his office at 6:00 pm as they agreed. Over the next three hours, he prepared his client again for his examination-in-chief and Dietz's cross-examination. Wheeler appreciated the extra preparation this time, now understanding the stress and intimidation of a trial.

While the trial was about damages and a battle of the experts, all of the experts' assumptions needed to be based on facts presented as evidence in the trial. Judge Sussman needed to believe the extent of Wheeler's disability and what he could or could not do, if he was going to accept Tom's experts regarding his wage loss and future care costs.

The contentious issues of damages involving number crunching, assumed costs, inflation rates and wage rates would all come after Wheeler testified. Tom wondered if the tide had turned in his favour, given the ruling on the voir dire, but he didn't want to get ahead of himself. Yes, the judge had ruled that Dr. Crane was qualified to give an opinion on post-concussions and their effects on Wheeler. This certainly did not mean he would believe anything Dr. Crane testified to, or would prefer his evidence over Dietz's expert, Dr. Franklin.

Nevertheless, Tom felt more confident and admittedly, he also enjoyed the pleasure of observing Dietz's face when Judge Sussman made his voir dire ruling. However, an important question remained – would he get to see it again? Wheeler hadn't been awarded a damn penny yet.

Tomorrow would be a very big day indeed. Deitz would be attempting to destroy his client.

After a restless sleep, fighting demons, Tom arrived early at court the following morning. His back hurt, fueled by the tension. Despite Dietz's view, Tom preferred a judge-alone trial; jury trials often came with a dog and pony show requiring theatrics from the lawyers. At least he did not have to worry about becoming a fine actor.

Tom called Wheeler to the stand as his first witness and asked him questions for five hours, broken by a fifteen-minute morning recess and one-hour lunch break. His examination-in-chief proceeded smoothly. He asked non-leading questions in a slow and methodical manner, bringing Wheeler through from the time when he fell until his present state. Like Wheeler's discovery testimony, he answered his questions confidently; importantly, he appeared believable.

Wheeler testified that he walked along the sidewalk to the variety store when his Kodiak boots slipped out from underneath him on ice that was hidden by a light dusting of snow, causing him to fall backwards and strike the back of his head on the ice.

"I remained on the ice, unconscious, for several minutes."

The paramedics arrived ten minutes later, loaded him into the ambulance and rushed him to the hospital with the sirens blaring away. Wheeler testified that a few hours after his fall, he ran to the bathroom at the hospital to vomit. He developed an agonizing headache and the emergency-room doctor admitted him overnight for observation.

Wheeler testified that he became very sensitive to natural and indoor lighting, which bothered him terribly and required him to wear sunglasses inside and outside. While on the stand, he received permission from Judge Sussman to wear them in court, to Dietz's chagrin.

Wheeler explained to the court that his most debilitating conditions were his lack of focus and short-term memory loss. His head felt fuzzy all the time; because of forgetfulness, he frequently missed doctors' appointments until his rehabilitation therapist provided him with an electronic diary to keep track of his schedule.

Wheeler became teary when explaining how he was unable to work and had become depressed because he felt unproductive and useless. Also, because he didn't socialize any longer and had no motivation to leave his apartment, he had lost touch with his friends. The isolation further weighed on him, causing a vicious circle, mentally. Mostly, he filled his days sitting in the apartment with the lights off and the curtains closed. He had become a different person – the strain of his condition caused the breakdown of his long-term relationship with girlfriend Michelle Arden.

Wheeler detailed a long list of activities that he performed before that he couldn't do anymore: recreational hockey and baseball, poker night, dancing, bowling, meeting friends at the pub, fishing, snowmobiling, grocery shopping, mowing the lawn, snow shovelling and housekeeping.

After finishing his questions, Tom was pleased. Now, the question was whether Wheeler would survive cross-examination.

"Thank you, Mr. Henderson," said Judge Sussman. "Mr. Dietz, you may begin your cross-examination of this witness," directed the judge.

"Thank you, Your Honour," replied Dietz.

Dietz stood up and began his cross-examination. Dietz's client, the liability insurer, spent twenty thousand dollars on private investigators, who attempted to follow Wheeler and catch him performing activities that were inconsistent with his professed disability. The investigators usually sat in their vehicles all day, doing nothing but waiting, because Wheeler barely left his apartment. When he did leave, they observed him walking slowly wearing sunglasses, accompanied by his father every time. To Dietz's consternation, the private investigators obtained no footage of Wheeler's activities that suggested he was exaggerating his symptoms or his disability. Dietz would have eaten Wheeler alive on the stand if the surveillance had shown him partying with his friends at a bar, playing golf, or even being away from his apartment for extended periods. But Dietz had nothing.

The surveillance corroborated Wheeler's testimony. No reason existed for Dietz to use the surveillance as evidence because it would just bolster Wheeler's case and his credibility. Because Dietz did not use it, the rules of civil procedure did not require Dietz to provide a copy of the surveillance video to Tom.

However, Tom knew the surveillance must exist.

Andrew Murray advised him that because of the injuries involved and the amount being claimed, every insurer would use private investigators. All injured plaintiffs were prone to some exaggeration.

But Dietz commenced his cross-examination at a disadvantage – he had no ammunition to pierce Wheeler's testimony. Dietz knew that Tom would be calling Wheeler's father and his ex-girlfriend who would likely corroborate all of Wheeler's difficulties. Dietz had little to attack Wheeler's veracity; the defence lawyer pounded away with repeat questions, attempting to tie the plaintiff in knots and confuse him. He asked the same questions in different ways, trying to catch Wheeler in an inconsistent statement, but to no avail. Wheeler remained steady and consistent, the endless preparation now evident, although he had slightly less polish to his answers on account of his nervousness.

When Dietz sat down after completing his cross-examination two hours later, Tom smiled internally, thrilled with how Wheeler had done on the stand. He had won half the battle.

Court resumed the following morning with Wheeler's father, Nigel, who testified how significantly the head injury had affected his son. He explained that his son used to be an outgoing and friendly person, but had since become solemn, grumpy and depressed. Nigel testified that it was heartbreaking witnessing his son moping around his apartment continuously. And while he loved his son, Nigel wondered how long he could continue to be his caregiver and housekeeper.

Dietz cross-examined Nigel and tried to push him into agreeing he would say anything in court to help his son including exaggerating his symptoms. Nigel convincingly disagreed with Dietz's suggestion, "If I thought my son was exaggerating in any way, I would not support him. I was born on a farm, where hard work and honesty made up the backbone of a man's soul. I swore on a bible when I got on this witness stand and I take my oath very seriously, sir."

And with that, Dietz advised Judge Sussman that he had no further questions and sat down. Dietz must have regretted cross-examining Nigel; the man's effective testimony exuded honesty and only helped Wheeler's case.

Tom then called Wheeler's ex-girlfriend, Michelle Arden. The attractive woman wore no make-up to court and had her hair pulled back into a bun. She wore a floral-patterned floor-length dress which, combined with the bun, suggested she drove in from an Amish farm.

Tom had interviewed Michelle to prepare her for the trial; her court presentation was markedly different from her attire during their initial meeting. The mini skirt, high heels and tank top were purposefully replaced with a more conservative look. Also, she toned down her irreverent and bombastic personality, replaced with a measured and calm demeanour.

Michelle testified that she and Wheeler had been dating for about six months when Wheeler had his fall on the ice. She explained that they were in love and had even talked about marriage. After his injury, she supported Wheeler as he tried to work his way through his problems; but his personality changed.

"He became despondent and aggressive. We argued frequently and then, emotionally, he kept pushing me away," she testified. Michelle said that the relationship soured and ultimately came to an end when Wheeler broke it off after a particularly nasty argument.

Tom turned his witness over to Dietz for his cross-examination. Perhaps having learned his lesson after cross-examining Nigel, Dietz proceeded gently with Michelle. Dietz asked several questions to explore Wheeler's personality before he fell and the types of activities he pursued before the fall; she provided answers consistent with the evidence Wheeler and his father gave the court. Dietz finally sat down, again, without damaging Wheeler's case.

"Gentlemen, we will adjourn for the day and return tomorrow morning at 10:00 am," ordered Judge Sussman.

Tom and Wheeler walked out of the courtroom and into the hallway. Wheeler started to smile; seeing his client's lips begin to curl up, Tom immediately put an end to it. Wheeler knew the testimony went well, but Tom knew better.

"This isn't over yet," Tom said. "We still have to get through the expert testimony and I think there will be some speed bumps tomorrow, so let's not get ahead of ourselves, okay?"

Tom raced back to the office and threw a frozen pasta dish in the microwave before calling his wife. "It's going well so far, hon; there's reason for some optimism."

"I'm so proud of you, Tom," she said.

"It's not over yet, Veronica. Tomorrow will be difficult with the experts but I'll do my best."

Veronica explained that Lucas' condition was the same, stable, but serious. In reality, his condition had slightly worsened. Lucas' temperature had elevated and he had reverted to constantly sleeping, but Veronica decided against sharing that with her husband. He did not need the added pressure at this critical juncture of the trial.

Tom dictated a few letters to clients, returned three telephone messages while he gobbled down his dinner, and then called Dr. Crane to prepare for the next day.

The following morning, at 10:00 am sharp, Judge Sussman entered the court.

"All rise," announced the court clerk.

The judge walked in, bowed, and took his seat.

"Please call your next witness, Mr. Henderson," said Judge Sussman.

"Yes, Your Honour," replied Tom. "I call Dr. Stephen Crane to the stand."

Dr. Crane took his place on the witness stand. After putting his hand on the bible and taking his oath, he looked at Tom.

With carefully planned questioning, he brought Dr. Crane through his credentials and the books and papers that he had authored. Crane then took an hour discussing post-concussion syndrome from a medical perspective – a form of brain injury. He explained that those individuals who suffer a concussion go on to have numerous and widely varied symptoms.

"The brain is fickle; with identical trauma, two people could have completely different symptoms," said Dr. Crane.

Dr. Crane testified that the symptoms described by Mr. Wheeler, including headaches and difficulties with concentration, were all associated with post-concussion syndrome. After examining Mr. Wheeler in person, and reviewing the plaintiff's medical records, he offered the court his diagnosis, "Mr. Wheeler suffered a concussion and went on to develop post-concussion syndrome. These symptoms are likely permanent, given their severity this far removed from the injury date."

"Those are my questions for Dr. Crane," announced Tom.

"Your witness, Mr. Dietz," directed the judge.

Dietz poked around non-contentious issues for a half-hour until he got to the crux of the issue.

"Isn't it true, Dr. Crane, that many people who suffer a concussion, never go on to develop post-concussion syndrome?" asked Dietz.

"Yes, that's true. Most don't," he replied.

"And it's true that it is not known why those individuals with post-concussion syndrome persist with symptoms?" asked Dietz.

"I agree with that statement," replied Dr. Crane.

"And is there a specific test that can be completed to determine that a person has post-concussion syndrome or the extent of their symptoms?" Dietz asked.

"The symptoms are mainly subjective," replied the doctor.

"So, someone could exaggerate their symptoms and it would be difficult to know that they were exaggerating?" suggested Dietz.

"It could be difficult," he conceded.

"Dr. Crane, you would agree with me that symptoms can improve over time," asked Dietz.

"Yes, that's correct," responded the doctor.

"And you are aware that symptoms can improve even a year or two after the injury occurred, correct?"

Tom now realized where Dietz was going with this line of questioning.

"Yes, I'm aware," Dr. Crane answered.

"So, it's fair to say that Mr. Wheeler's symptoms are not indefinite and he may improve or even recover?" asked Dietz.

Dr. Crane paused and did not answer, formulating his answer.

"Dr. Crane," Judge Sussman said. "I require an answer, sir."

"Well, improvement is possible, but it is unlikely Mr. Wheeler will completely recover, although the possibility exists," he testified.

Tom exhibited no reaction; he knew that answer could significantly impact the assessment of damages. He could hear Dietz arguing in final submissions that Wheeler was not totally disabled – he would be able to work in some capacity in the future.

Tom had brought Wheeler's claim quickly. Dietz would argue that Tom should have waited at least two years to determine how well he recovered. Yes, the litigation proceeded prematurely, but Tom didn't have two years. Dietz let Dr. Crane's answer sink in, overjoyed that the value of Wheeler's claim just tanked.

Dietz announced that he had finished questioning this witness and sat down with a pompous look on his face, a look that Tom wished he could slap off from across the room.

It was now 3:00 pm; Judge Sussman recessed court for the day and ordered everyone to return at 10:00 am the following morning.

After the judge left the courtroom, Tom said goodbye to Wheeler. While he packed his binders and documents, Dietz wandered over to his table, strutting with the confidence of a victor. Tom felt like ripping Dietz's head off his shoulders and advising him that he was an asshole, but he refrained.

"Do yourself a favour and talk to your client," said Dietz. "I know my client's previous offer has been withdrawn, but why don't I see if I can convince my client to settle for three hundred thousand," he suggested. "There's not a chance the judge will award damages based upon a permanent lifetime disability," he said, emphatically. "Your client needs to accept that he'll have to work again; my client is not providing him with a lifetime pension plan!"

Tom stared at Dietz and responded confidently, "Can't do it, Mark. My guy is never working again so I can't recommend that to him. We'll have to play this out."

Under normal circumstances, Tom would have accepted Dietz's invitation to resolve the matter, but he needed a lot of money to save his child's life. Of course, a lawyer who put his own needs ahead of his client's needs betrayed the most fundamental duty owed to a client, but he couldn't think about that, right now. He needed to prepare for tomorrow, which would likely be the last day of the trial.

The following morning, exhausted and drained, Tom arrived five minutes before the commencement of court, much later than his usual arrival. He did not sleep well the previous night. His wife finally confessed to Lucas' deteriorating condition; the news weighed on him. Tom entered the courtroom with a less-than-ideal state of mind.

Dietz agreed to allow Tom to simply file his detailed and extensive expert reports that provided opinions on wage loss and treatment costs, without calling the authors to testify.

Dietz explained to Tom that he believed the reports were useless because they were based on wage loss and treatment needs lasting Wheeler's whole life.

"There's no chance the judge will accept a lifetime disability. Go ahead and file them with Sussman. I don't need to cross-examine these experts. You're getting two or three years of disability, tops. You got in over your head, Tom. Competent counsel would not have brought this matter to trial this soon."

Andrew Murray had cautioned him about bringing Wheeler's case too soon for these very reasons. Tom decided against pummeling Dietz and calling him a capullo. He created a fist with his right hand, and then released his fingers when common sense prevailed. Besides, he was thankful to simply file his reports. He agreed that Dietz could simply file his expert wage loss and future care reports as well.

Wheeler's smile from two days ago disappeared when he overheard Dietz's comments; he was not pleased. Perhaps the wheels had not fallen off but they were awfully wobbly. Tom didn't have time to calm his client down as Dietz's medical expert was about to commence testifying.

Tom rested his case. Dietz advised the court that Dr. Franklin would be his only witness given that both parties had agreed to file their economic loss reports in lieu of calling the witnesses to provide oral testimony.

Dr. Franklin performed amazingly. Within a few minutes, his history impressed everyone. Dietz took twenty minutes detailing his witness's extensive professional biography: board certified in traumatic brain injury and forensic psychiatry, trained at Harvard and Berkeley, member of the clinical and forensic faculty at University of California, and authored four books on brain injury and post-concussion syndrome. In addition, he wrote forty published articles on post-concussion syndrome. UCLA's post-graduate doctoral program in brain injury used his textbook for the program.

Wheeler shot Tom a quick glance as if to say, "we are so screwed." With those credentials, how could anyone not accept a word that was about to come out of this doctor's mouth?

Dr. Franklin explained that the research-based understanding of post-concussion syndrome has been developing rapidly. "It is defined as a syndrome because there are many symptoms, or a collection of symptoms. Despite the research, it's not entirely clear why some people have severe or more prolonged symptoms than others. However, it's clear that those suffering the condition generally improve over time."

He explained that while recovery or improvement varies within the first two years, it is expected that an injured person will continue to improve or start to improve during this period.

"Dr. Franklin, eight months have passed since Mr. Wheeler's fall," said Dietz. "Please look into the future at the two-year anniversary of Mr. Wheeler's injury and advise the court what you would expect, in terms of improvement, if any," asked Dietz.

"Based upon Mr. Wheeler's testimony and the medical records I have reviewed, I would expect his symptoms to improve by fifty to seventy-five percent over that period," he answered. "I estimate that his chance of not improving at all would be five percent; his chance of completely recovering by the two-year anniversary is twenty-five percent. However, the most likely outcome is a fifty to seventy-five percent improvement."

Dr. Franklin took a drink of water, before proceeding. "If the injured person gives his or her brain time to rest, significant recovery will occur in almost all cases," he explained. "Rest and time are the most important factors in recovery."

"And, if Mr. Wheeler's symptoms improved by fifty to seventy-five percent, please tell the court your opinion on disability," Dietz requested.

"Although Mr. Wheeler would still have symptoms, he would not be disabled," testified Dr. Franklin. "With or without the use of medication, his symptoms would be manageable, and although there may be some inconvenience and discomfort, those symptoms would not be disabling. He'll be able to work."

"Thank you, Dr. Franklin," said Dietz. "I have no further questions."

"Your cross-examination, Mr. Henderson," said Judge Sussman.

Tom stood up. How could he poke holes in Dr.

Franklin's testimony? He had no idea. "Dr. Franklin, you can't be absolutely sure that my client will not be permanently disabled, can you?"

"No, that's why I said a five percent chance existed that Mr. Wheeler would not improve," he replied. "If I was one hundred percent certain he wouldn't be disabled, I would have said there was a zero percent chance he would have improved."

Tom stood, thinking for a moment. He did not know what to ask next.

"Mr. Henderson?" said Judge Sussman as the seconds passed.

Tom felt hot and uncomfortable, his face becoming flushed. He was freezing; he knew it, but didn't know what to do about it.

"Mr. Henderson, are you okay?" asked the judge.

He couldn't think of one further question to ask; he looked foolish, standing at the podium, saying nothing. Then, Tom blurted out, "No more questions for this witness, Your Honour," and proceeded to sit down beside Wheeler.

"Dr. Franklin, you are excused," said Judge Sussman.

Dr. Franklin stepped down and walked out of the courtroom. Dietz raised his eyebrows, stunned at Tom's ineffective cross-examination, almost feeling sorry for opposing counsel – but compassion was not his style. Dietz grinned slightly, enjoying every minute of his expert's powerful testimony and his adversary's final debacle.

Tom couldn't believe his ineffectiveness during the most important case of his life. Why didn't he tell the judge that he wasn't feeling well and ask for a recess to gather himself?

Both lawyers made final submissions to Judge Sussman in the afternoon, each of them taking about two hours to review the evidence and argue the positions of their respective clients. Final submissions were rarely significant in the final determination. The judge had heard the evidence and was unlikely to be swayed by final arguments at this point. Usually, judges had their minds made up once all of the evidence was completed.

Judge Sussman thanked both counsel and their clients. "Counsel, thank you for your professionalism throughout the trial," he said. "You have both made able and strong arguments, serving your clients well and giving the court a great deal to consider."

"All rise," announced the court clerk. His Honour left the courtroom and ended the trial.

Tom turned to Dietz and extended his hand to him. "Congratulations, Mark. You are a strong advocate; I don't want to face off against you, again."

"Thanks," replied Dietz. "Listen, can I speak to you privately for a minute?"

"Sure, let me walk my client out, first," replied Tom.

He walked Wheeler out and told him there was nothing to do but wait; Tom would call him once he received the judge's decision. They shook hands and Wheeler left his lawyer to return and speak with Dietz.

Tom walked back to Dietz's table, "What's up?"

"I'm sure you realize that it did not go well for you with Dr. Franklin. My client has authorized me to make an offer of two hundred and fifty thousand dollars to settle. Talk to your client and get this settled. You might only receive a judgment around one hundred and fifty thousand, depending on how the judge views it."

Tom looked at Dietz and politely said, "Mark, I appreciate the offer. I really do, but I have to decline."

"Don't you need to obtain instructions from your client before responding?" he asked. "It's his decision, not yours."

"I have instructions from my client, Mark. Have a safe drive back to Toronto."

CHAPTER TWENTY

Judgment Day

Tom immediately drove home from the courthouse, packed a bag and sped to Toronto to be with his wife and child. He sent an e-mail to Kerri informing her that he was taking a few days off, time that he couldn't afford to take right now, but he couldn't afford not to either. Tom had a two-hour drive to reflect on the trial; he did not relish the experience. Loneliness blanketed him while heading east on Highway 401, thinking about his day, thinking how he had frozen when it counted the most. The sickness he felt had no organic cause; however, some optimism existed.

He hit rush-hour traffic on the Gardiner Expressway, which ran parallel to Lake Ontario in south Toronto. While he inched along, he took in the fantastic view to his right; seagulls danced and weaved with each other over the lake without a care in the world. He knew a swallow with a similar disposition once.

Tom carried worries worse than the brutal, bumper-to-bumper traffic in front of him. That's what perspective taught him – thinking of Janice Thorton – which he often did. He chuckled, thinking of Duncan; he didn't realize Duncan was a dog until ten minutes into her story. Janice and her daffodil – he could hear her like it was yesterday.

Tom found Veronica fast asleep in a chair, five feet from their son. He leaned over Lucas' bed and kissed him on his warm and flushed cheek. He looked peaceful, despite the tubes and deadly battle waging within.

Pulling up a chair beside his wife, he sat down and gently rubbed her back; her touch energised him. Love shot through his arm and comforted him in a way that words could not accomplish. Veronica opened her eyes and smiled at her husband.

"I missed you," she whispered.

"Not as much as I missed you," replied Tom. He felt

better looking into her eyes, a sure sign he was madly in love.

"How did the trial go?" she asked.

"Let's talk about it later, okay?" he replied.

Veronica nodded and grabbed his hand. They strolled to the Delta Chelsea Hotel on Yonge Street, two blocks away, and spent the night together. The hospital promised to call immediately if Lucas' condition changed. They both felt guilty about leaving the hospital but they needed to hold each other without listening to doctors being paged or hearing one more code blue.

After two days with his family, Tom faced reality and returned to Stratford, attempting to keep his practice alive. With Wheeler's trial out of the way, and no plans to ever handle another civil matter again, he could again focus on criminal matters.

Tom hoped to receive the court decision soon, so he could gauge where he stood in securing the jatasium. Veronica had raised about one hundred and seventy-five thousand dollars in donations so far, a generous sum, but nowhere near the two million required to secure the one-of-a-kind plant. No plan B existed to obtain the plant, so Tom, despite his atheism, prayed like hell that his Hail Mary pass would be caught.

Dr. Vernon warned the Hendersons that Lucas' condition remained fragile. A delicate stalemate between the dangerous invader and Lucas' immune system ensued. Unfortunately, an extended fight favoured the infection, a relentless foe that did not give in easily.

Three weeks after the trial, while working at the office on a Friday night, the fax machine hummed at 6:00 pm. Tom scanned the first page and knew immediately it was Judge Sussman's judgment coming through. His son's fate rested on the thirty pages that slowly accumulated on the tray in front of him.

The issue of liability had already been decided. What would Sussman order for damages? Tom read the pages as they came off the fax machine. The first page came through, which stated the style of cause *Lawrence Wheeler v. The*

Corporation of the City of Stratford. As usual, the majority of the decision and bulk of the decision reviewed the evidence given and the positions taken by each of the parties.

Tom had to wait until page twenty-nine dropped onto the fax machine's tray, which contained the summary section of the judge's final conclusion on damages. Every personal injury lawyer skipped to this section first.

In Summary, I find the Plaintiff, Lawrence Wheeler is entitled to damages as follows:

Pain and suffering............$175,000
Future Wage Loss............$2,340,000
Future Care Costs:..........$2,100,638
Interest due......................$300,438
Legal fees........................$600,467

Total............................$5,516,543

As such, I make an order for judgment in the amount of $5,516,543.

Tom couldn't believe his eyes. He read it twice, then three times, unable to control his elation. A scream heard outside on the sidewalk two stories below flew from Tom's mouth. He whooped in delight, performed an uncoordinated jig, and collapsed to his knees in relief. His wife cried uncontrollably when she received the fabulous news from him a minute later.

But Dietz flattened Tom's jubilation like a pancake when the defence lawyer served a Notice of Appeal two days later, freezing the judgment until the Ontario Court of Appeal heard the appeal, a process that could take years. Unlike Tom, Dietz went ballistic when he received the judgment. In the analysis section, where he read that Judge Sussman preferred the evidence of Dr. Crane, he threw a full cup of coffee against the wall. He yelled numerous expletives at the judge, profanities heard on all levels of the multi-floor Bay Street firm.

The appeal seriously curtailed Tom's plans. Not only would the appeal delay receiving any settlement funds, but after reading Dietz's appeal brief, he became concerned that it might be successful; the arguments for significantly reducing the extent of damages were convincing.

Tom waited for a few days before he called Dietz so that he would not appear eager.

"Listen, Dietz, why don't we meet to discuss the judgment," he suggested.

"Why would I, Henderson?" asked Dietz. "No offence to Judge Sussman but I'm not sure what trial he presided over. On second thought, I say that with offence to His Honour because that judgment was ridiculous," complained Dietz, unable to hide his disdain.

Nevertheless, Dietz agreed to meet with Tom the following week, which Tom viewed as a good sign, because it meant that Dietz might still be motivated to resolve matters.

After consulting with Andrew Murray, Tom realized that he was in a better position, legally, than he had initially understood. Significantly, Dietz's Achilles heel was proving that Judge Sussman committed an error in law. Even if the appellate court would have come to different conclusions based on the facts, such as how long Wheeler would be disabled, a successful appeal required more. A trial judge is entitled to prefer the evidence of one witness over the other. The Ontario Court of Appeal could not overturn a decision on that basis; only if it were found that Sussman applied a wrong legal test, such as the standard of negligence or the burden of proof, would the appeal succeed.

But even if Dietz's appeal failed, Tom couldn't wait for another year because Lucas might be dead. Tom might be dead too, at the hands of the Lozano cartel. Tom and Veronica went from very high to very low in a matter of days, an emotional rollercoaster.

A great deal rode on his upcoming meeting with Dietz,

who agreed to meet him on the condition that Tom travel to his Toronto office at First Canadian Place on Bay Street. Sure, Henderson won the trial but Dietz now exercised his leverage of time and Sussman's suspect decisions to his full advantage. Andrew Murray advised him that the liability insurer would formulate its strategy based on cold-hearted business decisions.

"This isn't emotional for them, Tom; it's about money," explained Andrew. "Whatever you do, don't let Dietz think you're desperate. He'll smell it miles away."

Two days later, Tom made his way to Toronto to meet Dietz, using the drive to contemplate how he would approach his meeting with the Bay Street lawyer. Should he be cocky and confident, trying to make Dietz beg him to take less? Or, should he appear agreeable and make it clear that he was willing to take substantially less than Justice Sussman's award. Both strategies had their risks. Too reasonable and Dietz would smell blood and low-ball Tom; but if he presented as inflexible, Dietz might order him back to Stratford and let the Court of Appeal sort it out in a couple of years.

Tom parked on level three of the underground parking lot and scaled a set of stairs to First Canadian Place's lobby, an impressive, modern building in the middle of Toronto's financial district. Many of Canada's largest law firms and corporations called the building home.

Tom strolled across the marbled floor in the well-polished foyer to the first of two elevator banks. He scanned the directory - Bank of Montreal, Brookfield Properties and Loblaws until he found Levitson, Dietz and Mirvin LLP. The firm marketed itself as an international law firm with a website that described itself as one of the oldest law firms in Canada; in 1939, Stuart Levitson founded the firm, a man who eventually became the Premier of Ontario. Its clients included Fortune 500 companies and governments from all over the world.

Although he would never let on to Tom, the trial's outcome extremely upset Dietz. The international insurer paid the firm millions in legal fees each year; the optics that Dietz got his clock cleaned by some rube from Stratford handling his first civil litigation case were embarrassing. Dietz wanted to save face with his very important client.

But even though Dietz had some ammunition for his appeal, he understood the challenges he faced persuading the Ontario Court of Appeal to reduce the award. The court could not overturn Judge Sussman's findings of fact; he hoped that Tom did not fully appreciate this.

Dietz would play hardball with Henderson, but he had firm instructions to settle the matter if he could negotiate a significant reduction in the award.

The elevator door opened on the forty-fifth floor, occupied entirely by Levitson, Dietz and Mirvin LLP and their two hundred and twenty lawyers, who practiced law in forty-three countries. After Tom checked in with the receptionist, he relaxed on an Italian-leathered sofa and read a complimentary newspaper while sipping a cup of coffee. The entire place smelled like money. Money, money, money. A lot of money. The waiting area had all the trappings that you would expect to make the captains of industry comfortable when visiting the prestigious Bay Street firm: fresh coffee, News Day and Business Week magazines, bagels, croissants and muffins.

After twenty minutes of waiting, it became clear to Tom that Dietz was making him wait on purpose, sending a message that Dietz was in no hurry to deal with the matter – psychological warfare. Dietz didn't realize that nothing existed more unnerving than watching your child die, so waiting had no effect on Tom. Instead, he reflected on Janice and Duncan, and the daffodil.

Ten minutes later, Dietz slowly waltzed into the waiting room, sporting his three-thousand-dollar navy-blue-pinstriped Armani suit. He approached Tom and feigned his regrets, "So, sorry, Tom. I couldn't get off the phone with a client in Switzerland."

Tom had an intrusive thought of accidentally spilling his coffee on Dietz's Italian suit and then reacting with an over-the-top apology, but he came to his senses.

"Oh, were you late, Mark" Tom responded, looking at his watch. "I had no idea."

Dietz smirked. "I've been backed up all morning. Follow me. I've booked one of our board rooms."

Tom followed Dietz down a long hallway with expensive artwork adorning the walls. Offices to his right looked to the south with a view of Lake Ontario, although they were not close enough to see the dancing seagulls. The two lawyers entered one of the twelve boardrooms.

"Have a seat," said Dietz.

"Thank you."

"What can I do for you, Tom?" asked Dietz.

So, Dietz was going to play the "I don't care or have a care in the world attitude" to its full extent, mused Tom. He strategized quickly and decided he would respond with the "I know what you are doing" approach.

He smiled at Dietz. "Well, I drove to Toronto to find out what you wanted for your birthday, Mark. Also, I really wanted to know if you had sesame-seed bagels in the lobby," said Tom, smiling. "I'm disappointed you didn't provide whipped butter," he said, facetiously.

"That's very cute," replied Dietz, keeping a straight face. "But listen, I'm very busy, so what do you have to say."

No softening from Dietz with that approach, thought Tom. He gambled with a more aggressive approach. "Well, Mark, if you don't know why I'm here, then both of us are wasting our time," he said, straightening his back and fixing his best miffed look on Dietz. "You just had a five-million-dollar judgment rendered against your client, so you know damn well why I'm here; if you want to try and resolve it, let's try – but maybe your client would rather have that judgment sitting on its books for a few years. I don't care. Just tell me and I'll be on my way."

Dietz took it all in, now the one deciding how to respond. The game of chicken worked both ways.

Tom upped the ante, "My days as counsel for Mr.

Wheeler are numbered. Andrew Murray has agreed to represent Wheeler as appellate counsel if the matter can't be resolved," advised Tom, a clear lie meant to pressure Dietz.

Dietz's mind churned with the revelation. He relied on Tom's inexperience as an advantage proceeding with the appeal. Now, he would have to contend with a well-respected and experienced personal injury lawyer.

That cheesy whistling song from *The Good, The Bad, and the Ugly* entered Tom's mind, or, maybe it was *A Fistful of Dollars,* followed by, "wah, wah, wah." Memories of the dusty mean streets of Salamanca intruded his thoughts. He stared down Dietz in full-bluff mode, pushing back hard. Seconds ticked by; Tom waited for Dietz's response and his oversized ego. Was he about to be sent packing?

"Relax," said Dietz, in response. "You and I both know that every ruling went your way in the courtroom. Sussman made some reviewable errors, which will be reversed by the Court of Appeal. Having said that, my client has some interest in getting the matter resolved. Let me grab my file and I'll be back in a minute."

Tom leaned back in his chair and sighed after Dietz left the room. He closed his eyes and let the tension dissipate.

Dietz returned a minute later; the two immediately got to work, reviewing the areas that Dietz perceived were reviewable. They agreed on some issues, and agreed to disagree on others. After two hours of back-and-forth discussion, Dietz excused himself, explaining that he needed ten minutes.

After twenty minutes, Dietz returned to the boardroom and sat down. He wrote something down on a pad of paper and then ripped the sheet off the pad. After folding it, he handed it to Tom.

"This is absolutely the best that I can do," said Dietz, looking sincere; however, identifying a wolf in sheep's clothing had its challenges.

Tom took the paper and unfolded it, *$3,600,000 inclusive of costs and interest.* He screamed inside with excitement, yes, yes, yes! His heart skipped a beat. Outwardly, he maintained nonchalance, a straight face to ensure he did not appear too eager. "Don't let Dietz think you're desperate. He'll smell it miles away." Andrew Murray's advice had served him well. Wheeler wanted his money yesterday and had already given Tom instructions to settle at whatever figure he felt was reasonable.

"That's a hell of a haircut," said Tom, frowning to express his displeasure. "I'm not pleased with it, but it is my client's decision, so give me a minute and I will call him for instructions." He excused himself and walked to the lobby where he pretended to make a call. He felt like doing a jig, but did not. Although he did take one bite out of a bagel and place it back on top of the others.

Tom had a firm offer; he couldn't risk negotiating any further. He returned to the boardroom five minutes later and extended his hand to Dietz, "We have a deal."

Tom waited for an hour while Dietz's assistant prepared the settlement documents to finalize the matter. After executing the release and settlement memo, the two lawyers shook hands.

"You'll have the money in your trust account in two days," promised Dietz.

Tom called his client to advise him of the settlement, before rushing back to his Stratford office, pleased as hell that he had negotiated a deal. But he had some calculating to do, and his odyssey was far from over.

CHAPTER TWENTY-ONE

Whatever Happened to that Cool Guy?

Wheeler arrived on time at Tom's office, two days later, at 7:00 pm as they had arranged.

Tom was fond of Lawrence Wheeler – intelligent, charming and fun to be around, the kind of guy that could have great success in life; but Wheeler exemplified underachievement. He reminded Tom of a popular high-school student who was good-looking, physically developed before his peers, and always had a beautiful girlfriend on his arm. Seemingly, he had every advantage – destined for success.

Twenty years later, at your high school reunion, you realize he hasn't changed since he was eighteen, complete with the same juvenile sense of humour, and still playing video games in his parents' basement, with no evidence that he has matured at all. Everyone who envied him in high school scratches their heads and asks themselves, whatever happened to that cool guy?

Wheeler filled himself with excuses – not to do something, why he was late, or why he couldn't keep a job. He quit jobs because his "boss was a dick" or "somebody wasn't fair to him."

Tom considered Lawrence Wheeler a lovable louse with a great personality, as contradictory as it sounded. If he devoted as much energy to get himself ahead as he did to outwitting the system, success would find him; but you can't change hard wires.

Tom got Wheeler off on two previous criminal charges, once for cheque forgery and another on petty theft charges. The very convincing Wheeler lied over and over on the stand at his criminal trials; on both occasions, the judge accepted the believable Wheeler's testimony and found reasonable doubt. Interestingly, when Dietz examined Wheeler at his discovery, he asked him if he had ever been convicted of a criminal charge. Wheeler answered no – the truth. Perhaps, asking him if he had ever been charged criminally was the appropriate question.

When Wheeler arrived at Tom's office, he greeted Tom with a huge smile on his face. "I can't believe it! I can't believe it!" exclaimed Wheeler. They sat down at the firm's modest boardroom table after Tom locked the front door and ensured they were alone in the office.

"We did it!" screeched Wheeler.

"Yes, we did," replied Tom, pleased but not overjoyed like Wheeler. Until Lucas recovered, he would not celebrate.

Wheeler grabbed the certified cheque that Tom handed to him. His client looked down at the cheque payable to Lawrence Wheeler for one million, eight hundred thousand dollars.

"That's beautiful," said Wheeler, kissing the cheque, and then raising his hands in the air. "I've never seen that much money in my life," he said, eyes wide.

"Me neither," said Tom, half-chuckling.

"Fifty percent. Exactly as we agreed" said Wheeler, nodding his head in approval.

"Absolutely. A deal is a deal," replied Tom.

"Listen Lawrence. Neither of us can ever bring this up for as long as we live," emphasized Tom. "Never mention this to even one other person. Do you understand? Don't mention this to your friends or girlfriends. Don't brag about it to anyone. If you do, these things have a way of coming out," he warned. "And if it does, we'll both be doing five to ten years in the penitentiary," Tom said, firmly. "Do you understand?"

"Sure, man. This secret is ours," replied Wheeler. "I can't spend this money in prison, after all," he said, laughing. "You have to admit, I acted great!" boasted Wheeler. "I even had my own father fooled. I should receive an academy award," he said, laughing again.

"You did great, Lawrence," replied, Tom, conflicted.

"I hit my head harder than I wanted to though, Tom," explained Wheeler. "That goose egg took weeks to heal; but it probably helped that the emergency room doctor documented it, right?"

"It did," replied Tom. It was true – that goose egg was the only objective indication that Wheeler struck his head hard. Why in the world would it cross anyone's mind that he faked his fall with swelling of that size on his head?

"I memorized all the concussion symptoms," bragged Wheeler. "Nobody caught on, not even the doctors hired by the insurance company. I fooled the private investigators too, but it's hard to stay indoors for seven months. I went stir crazy."

Tom nodded his head, yes.

"The only thing I regret is breaking up with Michelle. We were discussing marriage," said Wheeler with a whiff of melancholy.

Tom put up his hands to stop Wheeler from talking. "Listen, you held up your part of the bargain. You did great. But this will mean nothing if we end up going to jail. And I don't mean six weeks. I mean for a long time," said Tom. "So, let this be the last time either of us mentions this to anyone, even between us, okay?"

"Absolutely," replied Wheeler. "My lips are now officially sealed."

"And remember Lawrence, just because your case is settled, be smart; don't start working or doing activities you shouldn't be able to," Tom warned. "You can bet the insurer will ask the police to start a criminal investigation if they suspect anything."

"I understand. Don't worry," replied Wheeler. "With almost two million in the bank, I shouldn't have to work again."

The two men shook hands and Wheeler left the office.

Tom committed a serious crime – he was a criminal who had not been caught, at least yet. Pulling it off brought a cocktail of emotions, each fighting for supremacy. However, his desperation matched Piscine Molitor, the starving boy who lamented that "hunger changes everything you thought you knew about yourself." So does the thought of losing your child. Tom would not wish it on anyone.

Unfortunately, Tom would worry for the rest of his life that Wheeler would start bragging to the wrong person and he would receive a knock on the door from the police, someday. He accepted the risk – one that he had to take.

Tom hatched his nefarious plan after he could conceive of no legitimate way to raise the money for the cartel. Donations would fall well short of the unfriendly and unsympathetic Mexican vendors' demands.

So, Tom conceived a fake slip and fall injury scenario; he called Wheeler to gauge his interest, tiptoeing around his plan at first. However, given his past involvement with his client, he believed Wheeler would find a potentially huge payday alluring. Wheeler was the ideal co-conspirator – smart enough to pull it off and unethical enough to want to pull it off. It was the kind of agreement that was not reduced to writing; a handshake sealed the deal.

Tom drove around the city looking for the optimal place for Wheeler's fake fall. When the corner of George Street and Wellington Street went unmaintained for several days, and he witnessed pedestrians stumbling and having difficulty walking over the slippery terrain, he settled on the spot. Fortuitously, Tom observed the owner of one of the retailers fronting the sidewalk slip and shake his head in frustration with the conditions. The man made an excellent witness, when interviewed by the liability insurer.

"Hurry, Lawrence, get to the corner before they salt it! It's a mess right now and liability on the city will be obvious," he directed to his partner in crime. "Fall in broad daylight when witnesses can observe the icy conditions when they come to assist you. This will also make it easier for the ambulance attendants to document the conditions."

Tom told Wheeler to pretend he was knocked out and not to come to until either bystanders or the ambulance attendants arrived.

He gave Wheeler a list of concussion symptoms and told him to fake vomiting during the first couple of days. "Light sensitivity, short-term memory loss and constant headaches; those are the three most important conditions, Lawrence," instructed Tom

"Private investigators will tail you. If you're caught, even once, doing something inconsistent, the big payday is over!" emphasised Tom.

Tom chose post-concussion syndrome – a serious and legitimate injury without tests to prove objective findings; Wheeler's subjective complaints would be enough. No doctor could rule out his injury with testing.

Tom now had one million eight hundred thousand dollars from the settlement, plus two hundred and eighty thousand dollars from donations, for a total of just over two million dollars. He now had more than enough money to satisfy the cartel. But, getting the money to the cartel and securing the jatasium presented his next challenges. Tom had no time to rest given that the clock was ticking on Lucas' life and apparently his own, according to Juan. Tom had nine days left before the nine-month deadline ended.

Tom called Juan and arranged to meet him the following morning at the Guadalajara airport after booking a red-eye flight that very night. Juan told him that he and his brother would pick him up at the airport, which Tom appreciated; he did not look forward to another taxi ride or dealing with another capullo on this trip. Juan provided him with the combination for an airport locker to pick up an important package on arrival.

"No, Juan, I can't. I won't!"

"It's important Tom; it's necessary," said Juan.

Juan surprised Tom when he laughed at the method of payment. Naively, Tom assumed the money would simply be wired to the cartel's bank account.

"No, Tom," said Juan. "This has to be a cash transaction," he explained. "Money-laundering laws and the threat of accounts being frozen – they don't want the money to be traced."

"How am I supposed to carry around two million dollars

in cash?" he asked Juan.

"Just like the movies, Tom. In a suitcase," replied Juan, laughing nervously.

"Okay, Juan, I will figure it out, I think," he responded, not finding the circumstances as amusing as Juan.

Tom and Veronica decided that she would attend his law firm's bank in the morning and arrange for the transfer of the money to the bank's affiliate in Mexico. He would meet Juan and his brother at the airport at 10:00 am; then, they would drive him to the bank to retrieve the cash before travelling to the graphite deposit to make the exchange with the cartel.

Tom made record time getting to Pearson International Airport in Toronto, assisted by quiet roads and the late hour. As with his first trip to Mexico, he only brought a carry-on bag, ensuring that he did not have to navigate the long baggage check-in lines. When Tom found his seat on the plane, exhaustion took hold; he reclined back and closed his eyes, searching for demon-free sleep. He began mentally preparing for the following day, telling himself that he was ready to face anything head-on, knowing that he needed to be strong for Lucas.

Four hours later, Tom awoke from his sleep by a shake of the arm.

"Mr. Henderson," said the voice. "Mr. Henderson, we're about to land," said Amanda, the flight attendant.

"Thank you," said Tom, opening his eyes, but feeling nauseous from a lack of sleep. His back hurt because of the awkward position he spent the night. Amanda brought him a bottle of water without asking.

"Thank you," he said, twisting the top and taking a drink.

Tom looked at his watch, 7:40 am local time, an hour behind Toronto. Good, the flight would be landing on time. He pulled out his phone and confirmed Veronica had not provided any updates.

After a smooth landing, Tom disembarked and made his way to customs and border protection security, where a burly agent hassled him. The gruff man wanted to know why he had returned to Mexico; the agent became skeptical of Tom's explanation that he planned to meet a neurologist, regarding his son. After several minutes of back-and-forth discussion, Tom googled Dr. Estrada's image from the Guadalajara University Hospital website on his phone, and showed it, which satisfied the man.

As instructed by Juan, Tom made his way to the storage facility in the lower level of the airport and found locker #655. Inconspicuously, he looked around before dialling the combination, 32-34-19, that Juan gave him. The locker door popped open, but before reaching in, he swivelled his head a second time to ensure nobody was watching him, although surveillance cameras hung everywhere, including above him. Tom stuck his hand in the locker and felt around until he found, a small black leather case.

He slowly pulled it out and quickly stuffed it into his pants as casually as possible, knowing that it contained a 9 mm handgun, courtesy of Juan's friend, who had left it for him.

It was the first time that Tom had possessed a gun since the target shooting on Robert Hiller's property as a child. Juan told him that it would be loaded but he decided against verifying that in a busy airport – too many eyes existed. Surely, he would land in a Mexican jail if caught with an unregistered gun. He bristled at the length of sentence he might receive.

During their conversation last night, Juan insisted that he have a gun. Tom resisted but Juan became emphatic, so he relented. What kind of danger was he walking into? Shooting a gun off Hiller's deck as a child was one thing, a gunfight with ruthless cartel members was quite another.

"Tom, you will be carrying around two million dollars in cash and meeting with a dangerous drug cartel," Juan said. "You need a gun!" he implored.

"But won't they check me for weapons when we make the exchange?" asked Tom.

"Yes, but they mainly care about wiretaps," he said.

"They will not be surprised that you have a gun. Trust me, I know of what I speak."

Tom did not tell his wife about Juan's strong recommendation because he couldn't put that worry on her. He pushed the nightmare scenario of making Veronica a widow and Lucas dying from his thoughts; he needed to stay focused and see this journey through.

When Tom departed Stratford, he squeezed her tight before leaving the house, considering that it could be the last time he saw his wife.

"What's up?" Veronica said, pulling back after sensing he wanted to tell her something.

"Nothing," he said. "I'm just worried about all of us."

Tom scanned around for Juan and his brother with no luck; however, forty-five minutes remained until the specified pick-up time. So, he grabbed a coffee and a bagel at one of the airport restaurants, unaware that he was being watched. He only took one bite of his bagel on account of nausea that had not completely vacated, but he did manage to get his coffee down.

After paying for his food, he walked to the pick-up zone and sat on the bench, watching for Juan in the thirty-three-degree heat and listening to the Spanish chatter. Tom preferred the comfortable air-conditioned airport, but his ride would arrive shortly. He felt for the gun case to ensure it remained discretely secured in his pants.

At 10:01 am Tom received a text from Veronica, *transfer complete - no change with Lucas*. The Mexican affiliate now had the money; great, one less worry.

"Where the hell was Juan?" The doctor oozed responsibility; he wouldn't be late, the tardiness making him nervous. Traffic delays? Yes, possible, but of all days, he lamented.

At 10:35 am, with no sight of Juan, Tom called Juan's cell phone number but his call proceeded directly to voice mail. Where was he? He stood up and paced around, hoping to alleviate his impatience and growing paranoia.

"Mr. Henderson," came a male voice from behind.

Tom swung around to face a man he did not recognize. "Yes," replied Tom, pushing his head toward the man with a surprised and curious look.

"I'm Carlos, Juan's cousin," said a six-feet-two-inches-tall hulk who weighed close to two hundred and thirty pounds. He wore jeans and a tight black t-shirt that clung to his torso, leaving no doubt that he lifted weights. A shaved head, goatee and wrap-around sunglasses, which prevented any eye contact, completed the intimidating package. Tom noticed an expensive watch on his left wrist.

"Nice to meet you, Mr. Henderson," said Carlos, extending his hand.

Tom did not reciprocate, leaving Carlos hanging. "Where's Juan?"

Carlos smiled at him. "Mr. Henderson, Juan has been delayed; he asked me to pick you up."

"What do you mean, delayed?" asked Tom, sternly.

"He had an emergency; nothing to worry about," replied Carlos. "He asked me to take you to the bank and then transport you to make the buy. Juan will meet us at the exchange location."

"I don't believe that story for one minute," replied Tom, teetering between incredulity and the urge to run. Without a doubt, Juan would have called him if the plan had changed.

"What kind of emergency, Carlos?"

"Why don't we talk about it on the way to the bank?" responded Carlos. "We don't have much time."

"Listen, I'm not going anywhere Carlos, or whatever your name is," said Tom, raising his voice with an unwarranted hint of bravado.

"Please calm yourself, Mr. Henderson," requested Carlos. "It's not a good idea to attract attention, especially with that gun tucked in your pants."

The gun comment pushed him back onto his metaphorical heels; he thought quickly, but zero preparation went into this development. *Damn it, I haven't even left the* airport yet and I'm dealing with this curveball, he said to himself.

Did Carlos know that he had the gun because he was following him, or did he know because he had put it there for Juan? How was it that he ended up in Mexico with a gun in his pants talking to a goon named Carlos, who wanted to take him to retrieve two million dollars and then meet with a drug cartel? You couldn't make the absurdity up, Tom repeated to himself.

Tom looked around the airport and felt the walls closing in on him, running through all of his options hastily. He couldn't walk over to the police officer standing at the Aeromexico customer service counter and ask for help. Maybe, he should just run somewhere, anywhere? But this would not get him any closer to securing the jatasium.

Surely the cartel authored this ruse, concluded Tom; or could it have been Juan? How much did he really know about Juan, anyway?

"Mr. Henderson, I don't want to alarm you," said Carlos. "But I'm about to tell you something that is slightly concerning. It's important that you do not react; keep a straight face, or better yet, smile, because I don't want them to suspect that I've told you, okay?"

"Who is them?" asked Tom through clenched teeth.

"Mr. Henderson, if you want to live, please start listening to me and smiling," suggested Carlos. "I'm Juan's cousin," he repeated. You must trust me if you want to live," he implored.

"Where does Juan live, Carlos?" asked Tom. "Tell me exactly where he lives."

"Calle San Juan, 16002, Salamanca, " replied Carlos.

"Who is Juan's wife?"

"Rosetta; she's is a doctor. Juan is a neurologist and he works at Guadalajara University Hospital," responded Carlos, somewhat convincingly. "And your child, Lucas. will die if you don't receive the jatasium plant."

Tom looked at Carlos, realizing the cartel would have all

of this information. Was he walking into a trap? Probably. But his choices included bad, worse and awful.

"Okay, Carlos. I believe you. Let's go."

"Good," replied Carlos. "We're being watched this very minute by a member of the cartel, who I caught following me on the way here. I'm guessing the cartel wants to be sure that you arrive with the two million dollars and keep up your end of the bargain. Come with me and I'll drive you to the bank."

Reluctantly, Tom followed Carlos to a black sedan, parked a minute away near the arrival platform. They both got in and Carlos sped off.

"What bank, Mr. Henderson?"

"It's Banco Santander on Morelos Avenue," replied Tom, feeling like a prisoner. He considered Andrew Murray's advice, "Don't let him know you're desperate. He'll smell it miles away."

Tom sat in the front passenger seat as Carlos made his way to downtown Guadalajara in about fifteen minutes, where traffic thickened in the core of the city. Carlos snaked his way in and out of the busy downtown, a mixture of historic cultural and modern office buildings.

Carlos pulled out a cigarette, lit it, and started tapping on a Jesus Christ figurine dangling from the rear-view mirror in unison with the music playing on the radio. He appeared too relaxed for a guy being followed by the cartel, not once looking around or checking his rear-view mirror – strange for a guy observant enough to catch the cartel following him to the airport.

"You're very relaxed for a guy being followed by the cartel?" Tom said to Carlos.

Carlos looked at his passenger. "It's never a good idea to show fear, not anytime, but especially not with these guys. There's no sense making them jumpy when all they're doing is making sure the money gets there."

"I'm glad you're relaxed, Carlos," remarked Tom. "It makes me feel better."

"Good, Tom. Very good. Maybe you want me to hold

that gun for you?" asked Carlos.

"No thanks," came the reply. He was not giving up his gun, although certainly, all two hundred and thirty pounds of Carlos could just take it from him if he wanted.

Carlos continued to move slowly through traffic. The sweltering heat had both of them sweating, but Carlos had his window down; his left hand hung out the window dangling his cigarette, allowing the cool air to escape. Tom began to complain, but he didn't want to inhale smoke either, so he didn't bother saying anything.

Finally, Carlos pulled over in front of the bank, thirty minutes after they left the airport.

"I better go in with you," said Carlos.

Tom didn't reply but he didn't object either. The two men entered Banco Santander. Tom approached the customer service desk after taking ten steps across the terrazzo floor.

"Good morning. My name is Thomas Henderson."

A beautiful and petite brunette looked up from her chair. "Mr. Henderson, good morning," she replied, cheerily. "We've been expecting you. The manager, Senor Estevez, will meet with you, shortly. Please have a seat and enjoy some coffee."

Carlos and Tom took a seat in the reception area.

"So, where did you get two million dollars?" asked Carlos. "That's a lot of money!"

"I'm a hitman. I killed someone for it, so you better be nice to me," replied Tom.

"You're a funny guy," said Carlos, laughing loudly. "Seriously, where did you get it?"

"I'm not kidding," replied Tom, straight-faced.

Just as Carlos was about to ask him for the third time, Sr. Estevez exited his office from the rear of the bank. The distinguished gentleman walked across the tiled floor and approached Tom. "Mr. Henderson, it's a pleasure to have you in our bank today," said the manager, with an extended hand.

"Thank you," replied Tom.

"Please come to my office, Mr. Henderson." The two

men started walking away, bringing Carlos out of his seat to follow.

"Carlos you can wait here," said Tom. "I can do this on my own." Then, he stepped back to Carlos and whispered in his ear, "Better to have a lookout, anyway."

While he and the manager walked to the rear of the bank, Tom looked back at Carlos and pointed at his own eyes, and then at Carlos as if to say, "I'm watching you."

Sr. Estevez's huge and expensively furnished office at the corner of the bank screamed money, like Dietz's firm. The manager invited Tom to sit down in one of the two black leather chairs situated in front of his large hand-crafted desk made from a rubber tree.

Sr. Estevez, a tall and graceful man, resembled Ricardo Montalban. An expensive three-piece navy-blue suit and impeccably polished tegus lizard dress shoes confirmed his affinity for the finer things in life.

"A coffee, Mr. Henderson?" asked Estevez.

"No thank you, sir," replied Tom.

"Sr. Henderson, I have to admit I'm puzzled by the request I received from your bank in Canada," he said. "We don't even keep two million dollars cash in the bank, normally. I had to make special arrangements to obtain that kind of cash first thing this morning; I'm surprised we were able to accomplish it, frankly. Is it true you want to walk out of this bank with two million dollars in cash?" he asked, bewildered.

"It's true," replied Tom. "I wish I could explain, but I can't. I'm not sure you would believe me, anyway."

"I'm sure you appreciate the danger you are putting yourself in, Sr. Henderson," he warned, eyes wide open. "This is Mexico, not Canada. I love my country, but things are done a little differently here."

Given that he had a gun tucked in his pants and that Carlos was waiting for him in the lobby, waiting to take him to the cartel, Tom wished he could share the irony with Sr. Estevez.

"I appreciate your concern, but I'm in a hurry so, if I could get the money that would be great, please," said Tom, anxiously.

"Sr. Henderson, like Canada, Mexico has reporting requirements when someone is withdrawing this much cash; it's money laundering legislation. I'm obligated to make certain reports of cash withdrawals in excess of one hundred thousand dollars. I only bring this to your attention in the event that these reports might cause you inconvenience from a tax reporting perspective.

He had already hatched a plan to avoid paying taxes, but he agreed, that such a reporting could raise red flags in Canada. Tom sent up a trial balloon, "I understand that occasionally, a donation can go a long way to ensure that certain reporting is not done?"

"Sr. Henderson, we do have such a program, now that you raise it. I almost forgot about it. Ten thousand Canadian dollars is the standard donation." And with that, Tom immediately called his wife and had Veronica wire another ten thousand dollars to the bank.

With that unexpected and unsavoury business behind him, Estevez stood and retreated to a closet behind his desk that hid a walk-in safe. He dialled the combination, swung the door open and returned thirty seconds later dragging two large grey suitcases on rollers behind him.

"Holy shit," said Tom when he saw the two oversized suitcases, bulging at the sides.

"Two million dollars is a lot of money, Sr. Henderson, even when using the largest denomination," he explained. "There's one million in each suitcase."

Tom hadn't contemplated what two million dollars in cash would look like. He grabbed the two suitcases, which thankfully were equipped with wheels.

"No charge for the suitcases, Mr. Henderson," said Estevez, an ironic gesture given he had just greased his newest client for ten thousand dollars.

"Thank you, Sr. Estevez. You have been very helpful,"

said Tom, extending his hand to the bank manager.

"You're most welcome, Sr. Henderson," replied Estevez. "Is there anything else I can do to assist you?"

"No, there isn't, but thank you," replied Tom, grabbing the suitcases to begin his exit. Then, he stopped and turned around to face Estevez. "Actually, Sr. Estevez, there is something you could do for me."

"Of course, Sr. Henderson, what is it?" he asked.

Carlos occupied himself in the waiting area, flirting with the receptionist, Maria. She had no interest, but humoured the man as an occupational hazard. While Carlos leaned over her desk, asking her to dinner, Maria took a telephone call and listened for a few seconds. She put her hand over the receiver, "Carlos have a seat and I'll be over to talk to you in a second," she said, accompanied by a wink and a smile.

He sat down as directed, impressed with his prowess. Carlos placed his hands behind his head, reclined back on the soft leather loveseat and glanced at Estevez's closed office door and the drawn blinds covering the floor-to-ceiling glass wall. A couple of minutes later, Maria brought Carlos a coffee.

"You're the most beautiful girl in Guadalajara, Maria," swooned Carlos.

Maria refused to give Carlos her phone number but she promised that she would call him, if he provided his number.

Carlos looked again at Sr. Estevez's office, impatiently. Weren't the blinds open when they arrived? He couldn't be sure. Peering at his watch, he realized that they had been in the bank for forty-five minutes, so he asked Maria to check on Tom.

Maria slowly walked back to Estevez's office, knocked on the door and entered, only to return a couple of minutes later.

"I'm sorry, Carlos," she said, shrugging. "Sr. Henderson is not here."

"What!" cried out Carlos. He jumped from his seat and raced back to Estevez's office, barging in without a knock, startling the manager.

Carlos grabbed him by the shirt and growled, "Where is he?"

"He left through the back door," replied Estevez, pointing. "He said you were to meet out back with the car."

Carlos bolted out the back door and onto the busy street, looking both ways, but Tom was long gone. With a frustrated shake of his head, Carlos ran back into the bank and out through the front doors to his parked car, slamming the dashboard with his hands in anger. How would he explain this to his boss? It could mean his life. "Hijoputa!" he yelled in his native Spanish. If he had said it in English, anyone within three hundred feet would have heard him yell "motherfucker."

After thanking Estevez for having Maria run interference on Carlos, Tom took the extra few minutes to escape through the back door and flag down a taxi. Now, safely in the back seat with his two suitcases, he pondered his next move.

"Where to, Senor?" asked the driver.

That was a very good question. Where to indeed, the possibilities percolating in his mind as he placed each of his hands on his precious cargo.

Meanwhile, while Tom contemplated his next step, Juan, his wife and Juan's brother stood at gunpoint in the Estradas' apartment in Salamanca – the perpetrators someone other than members of the Lozano cartel.

When Tom previously inquired with Juan about "back channels," Juan did not explain. "Stories for another day, Tom," he said. The Estradas' son led a local gang that engaged in Salamanca's illicit drug trade; he also had close ties with the Lozano cartel, which resulted in a bitter falling out between them, years ago.

Juan told Javier that he had brought dishonour to the family name and helped destroy the neighbourhood. Agonizingly, Juan provided an ultimatum to his son – leave his criminal life behind, or he could have no part in their lives. It had been years since they had contact.

During Tom's last visit, when Juan and Rosetta excused themselves and retreated to their bedroom, unbeknownst to

Tom, he heard them arguing about Javier. Rosetta had proposed to her husband that Javier contact the cartel about purchasing the jatasium; she suggested they invite their son to discuss it, given his contacts with the cartel. Juan vacillated, wondering if contacting their son would violate their principles.

"Isn't saving a boy's life more valuable than our principles, Juan," pleaded Rosetta.

So, Rosetta extended an invitation. Surprisingly, Javier met with his parents and agreed to contact the cartel and facilitate a trade, one million dollars cash in exchange for five pounds of jatasium. Juan explained to his son that many children's lives could be saved, including a young boy named Lucas Henderson.

Javier easily met with the cartel's representatives; he negotiated the jatasium's sale price, and a five percent commission for his efforts. However, the cartel only demanded one million dollars, rather than two. Javier hatched a plan – he told his father the cartel required a two-million-dollar payment, rather than the correct figure – and schemed to pocket one million dollars for himself. It would be the easiest score of his life.

The plan appeared simple. Javier and his thugs would take the two million dollars from Tom Henderson and keep one million dollars for themselves. Javier would personally deliver the other million dollars, less his five percent commission, to the cartel in exchange for the plant. He would then provide the plant to his father. Nobody would be wise to his double-crossing, and he would be one million dollars richer.

In order to disrupt his father's plan to pick up Tom at the airport, Javier had one of his hoodlums, Luis, go to Juan's apartment and hold them hostage. Luis incorrectly, but purposefully, identified himself as a member of the Lozano cartel when he arrived, deflecting blame for the intrusion.

Luis did not allow any of his captives to use their cellphones, which prevented Juan from warning Tom. Javier sent his underling Fernando, who misidentified himself as "Carlos," to pick Tom up at the airport and confiscate the two million dollars. The cartel had not followed Fernando; his story was a complete fabrication.

So, at gunpoint, Juan, his brother and Rosetta, mistakenly believed the cartel had stormed their apartment, oblivious that their son's treachery resulted in their predicament.

Tom instructed the taxi driver to circle the city core while he contemplated his next move, unsure what to do next. Tom appreciated the absurdity of driving around with two million dollars in cash, and having no ability to contact Juan or the cartel. But why would he want to contact the cartel? It appeared they were attempting to rip him off. Or, maybe he should blame Juan?

After fifteen minutes of aimlessly touring the historic district of Guadalajara, Tom decided to check himself into the downtown upscale Marriott. Luckily, the top floor's presidential suite was available for two thousand dollars a night. Importantly, only staff had access to the top floor; Tom wanted tight security. He had no idea who may be following him or trying to track him down. A further dozen calls to Juan's phone went unanswered.

What the hell was going on? None of it made sense. Maybe the best course of action would be to get back on an airplane and get the hell out of Mexico, but that decision meant certain death for Lucas; he just couldn't do it. He would rather die than return to Canada without the jatasium, recalling Nick Danson's perfectly timed elbow to the face of Miller the Killer, the most courageous act that he ever witnessed.

Tom entered the hotel room and shoved his two suitcases under the bed, with less than an eighth of an inch to spare. Then, he walked to the window and looked down from the thirty-first floor at the bustling traffic below. Now what? He had to do something, but what? He lay down on the bed and stared up at the ceiling in total quiet. Unlike in apartment 2B, he could not find the Nile River.

The urge came on – a gust of wind blew in and pushed Tom to the very edge of the cliff. He resisted, but his desperation had unlimited strength; he couldn't hold it in any longer. Shame enveloped his body as the tears rolled, a pathetic, uncontrollable release. Where was his strength? Where was his inner Nick Danson?

Why hadn't he been brave as a child? Why didn't he just say no? He could have refused. Why? Why? Why? If he had just said no, he would have been able to sleep all these years. Now, he had to push them back, night after night, when they came over the wall for him. A volley of bullets whizzed by, shot from a machine gun. Maybe, one would rip into him and tear him to pieces; he deserved it.

At age ten, Linda told Tom that he would run out of tears if he cried too long, a notion that he clung to on so many nights; but his mother lied. Physiologically, tears were endless, exhaustion the only chance for reprieve. Tom considered pulling the covers up over his head to hide from the world; only the vision of his son in a hospital prevented the act.

After a half-hour, Tom gathered himself and hopped off the bed. He left the room, leaving the suitcases under the bed, and made his way down to the lobby and then out onto the street where he flagged down another taxi. He jumped in the taxi and gave the driver Juan's address. "Let's go, senor," he ordered, handing him two hundred pesos.

Although Tom had decided that he would travel to Juan's apartment, he was unsure what he would find. Was it wise to go? He had no other options. Resolutely, he decided he would either leave Mexico with the jatasium, or leave in a coffin. He pulled the gun from his pants; yes, it was loaded. Juan couldn't be behind this. Why would he provide him with a loaded gun? Tom tossed the gun case on the taxi's floor and tucked the gun in his waist at the back of his pants.

After a thirty-minute drive, and without Scarface's interference, he arrived in Salamanca, thankful for the daylight.

"Approach slowly, senor," he told the driver as they

rolled towards Juan's apartment, looking for any suspicious activity. Everything appeared damn suspicious, his head flicking from side to side, scouring the street. Tom stared at the street vendor hawking gorditas and tamales, concluding he presented no threat; however, it reminded him of his hunger. Other than the one bite of bagel at the airport, he had not eaten all day. Tom noticed a car parked in front of Juan's apartment but he didn't see another soul besides the street vendor.

Tom asked the driver to pull up behind the parked vehicle. Once stopped, he cautiously waited in the taxi for several minutes. Finally, he handed the driver another one hundred pesos and asked him to wait for fifteen minutes, having learned his lesson from his last visit.

Tom exited and walked over to Juan's front door, knocking twice, without a response. Déjà vu washed over him. He knocked harder, angrily, with the same result. As he was about to turn around and place his back against the door, it opened quickly. Shockingly, he faced Juan.

Tom expected Juan to start apologizing profusely and explaining that this was all an innocent misunderstanding. Wasn't it tomorrow you were supposed to arrive, Juan would ask him? Then, he would slap Tom on the back and invite him up for some great conversation and delicious Mexican coffee.

But before Tom could say a word, Juan put two fingers to his lips and shushed him in the quietest of voices, cocking his eyes upwards, a signal that he had company. But who?

"Please come up, sir," said Juan in a regular voice. "I normally don't see patients today, but I will make an exception," he said as the two men ascended the stairs and entered Juan's living room. Luis had ordered Juan to answer the door and bring whoever was knocking back upstairs.

"If you don't do exactly as I say, I will put a bullet in her head," threatened Luis, pointing at Rosetta with his gun barrel.

The two were met at the top of the stairs by Luis, a short, muscular man, pointed his weapon at the duo. Rosetta sat on a chair in the corner beside her brother-in-law, scared and weary, her eyes red from crying.

By now, Fernando had summoned up the courage to call Javier and explain to him that Tom had given him the slip, so he didn't have the money. Javier, in turn, called Luis and told him to keep watch for Henderson, in the event that he showed up with the money looking for his father.

"Sit down, Mr. Henderson," ordered Luis, waving his gun at Tom.

Tom realized the misstep of coming to Juan's apartment.

"Where is the money, Mr. Henderson?" asked Luis.

"I don't know what you're talking about," replied Tom.

In response, Luis immediately smashed the butt end of his gun down on the side of his head, sending him violently to the floor – a blow that opened up a cut above Tom's left eye, which started bleeding heavily.

"If I have to ask again, I will shoot all of you dead, right here," warned Luis.

Rosetta cried out, "Just tell him, Mr. Henderson," she pleaded. "He will kill us!"

Tom, dazed, attempted to pick himself up off of the floor. After managing to push his body up, he collapsed onto the sofa. Luis put the end of the gun to Tom's forehead and growled, "Tell me where the money is now or I'm pulling this trigger."

Still groggy, Tom attempted to formulate a response through the haze.

"Listen," said Tom, slowly, putting the palm of his hand up towards Luis. "I have the money and it's safe, but hidden," he explained. "I'm the only one who knows where it is. If you shoot me, nobody will ever find it, especially not you. I've come to Mexico for the jatasium; if I can't leave with it in my hands, I don't care if you put a bullet in my head."

Tom envisioned a fortunate housekeeper at the Marriott pulling the two suitcases from under the bed the following morning when he didn't show up to check out of the hotel. He imagined her astonishment when the briefcase clicked open and she saw all that cash.

"Give me the money, Henderson, and I'll get the

jatasium for you," said Luis. "It's that simple."

"I'm supposed to trust you after you've pulled this stunt," exclaimed Tom. "There's no way I'm giving up the money without somebody putting the jatasium in my hands. And, if that's not good enough, go ahead and shoot me!" he yelled out at the top of his lungs, blood trickling into his eye.

Of course, Tom didn't want a bullet in his brain. While his obstinance wasn't exactly a bluff, the stakes were slightly higher than in Dietz's office when he negotiated the resolution of Wheeler's case. Would he even hear the crack of the gun before the bullet lodged in his brain, or would it be lights out without knowing that had happened? How long would it take for Veronica to discover that he had been shot dead in Salamanca?

It is surprising what does and does not go through your head when you think you are about to die. Time stands still, allowing you to process a lifetime of memories in an instant. What raced through Hiller's mind when he slung that rope over that beam and made that fateful decision? Was he as scared as Tom, or had the alcohol dulled his faculties? Tom had never decided if courage or cowardice pushed Hiller to his self-imposed death. Either way, his desperation matched Piscine Molitor. Even though Luis hadn't pulled the trigger yet, bullets whizzed by his head for the second time that day.

Tom felt relief, at least momentarily, when the lights didn't go out. Luis believed he would rather take a bullet than give up the whereabouts of the money. He did not relish explaining to Javier that he killed the only person who knew the location of the money. Having had listened to Javier rant about Fernando's incompetence and the beating he planned as a consequence, he exercised some restraint.

"If you want the money, don't lay another hand on me," warned Tom, displaying a cockiness despite his relatively weak position. After all, a man fuelled by cocaine and fear had a gun pointed to his head.

"Think about what you're doing," said Tom. "All I need is the plant."

"Okay, what are you proposing?" asked Luis, begrudgingly.

"Well, firstly, who the hell are you?" asked Tom. "Who do you work for?"

Luis paused, unsure how to respond, but confident that Javier would kill him if he told the truth.

When Fernando told Javier that he had lost Henderson, Javier went ballistic, less so because of the money and more so because Javier now worried about his own life. Javier arranged the deal with the cartel – one million dollars for five pounds of jatasium – packed and delivered in a cooler of ice. The time and place for the exchange were set; if Javier did not show up with the money as agreed to, the cartel would cut his tongue out, torture him and then publicly hang his body as a warning to others. The cartel had its own interpretation of habeas corpus, a method that Lady Justice would not approve of.

After Tom's verbal act of defiance, Luis sent Javier a text to let him know he had Henderson at his parents' house but not the money, which partially relieved Javier.

"I'll be there in fifteen minutes. Hold him!" ordered Javier, in response.

Luis decided that he would do nothing until Javier arrived, thankful he did not have to extricate them from their botched plan.

Twenty minutes later, when Javier walked through the apartment door, Juan and Rosetta's hearts sank when it became obvious their son concocted the betrayal within the four walls of their home.

"What are you doing here, Javier?" asked Rosetta, wondering where she had gone wrong raising her son.

Javier ignored her and walked directly to Tom, who remained seated on the love seat. "Listen, Henderson, I want the money and I want it now." Javier pulled out his own gun and pointed it at him, his hand shaking from overwhelming anger.

"Put the gun down, Javier!" yelled Juan at his son. "What are you doing?"

"Shut up," he replied to his father, without looking at him.

Tom repeated the same message to Javier that he gave to Luis - that if he died, he would never see the money.

"Well, if I don't get the money, I'm dead so I might as well take you with me," warned Javier, keeping the barrel pointed at his temple.

"What's it going to be, Henderson?" asked Javier. "I'll give you to the count of three to tell me or you're a dead man."

"How could you do this, Javier?" screeched Rosetta. "We didn't raise you this way," she shouted through her tears.

Javier straightened his arm out to within one inch of Tom's head, the muscles in his trigger hand twitching in full view. Javier could bluff too, except that he wasn't.

One!" yelled Javier. "Two!" yelled Javier.

By this time, Tom had reached behind his back and put his hand on the gun tucked in his pants, thankful that he had ditched the leather case in the taxi. He began to swing it in front of him, intent on firing before Javier said "three."

Before Javier had the chance to say three, four men burst into the apartment, three of them brandishing guns. Unlike the imposters in the room, these men were actually members of the Lozano cartel, sporting buzzcuts and dressed in black suits. They wouldn't have looked out of place strolling the halls of Dietz's law firm at First Canadian Place or sitting around Goldstar's boardroom at its annual meeting.

Jorge, the tallest of the four, and the only one without a gun in his hand, took charge. Jorge looked at Javier angrily; they clearly knew each other.

After Javier realized that he could not make the pre-arranged meeting with the cartel on time, he called Jorge to explain the unfortunate developments. He rationalized that his chances of survival improved by providing a heads-up, rather than being a no show. Jorge demanded to know Henderson's location; Javier had no choice but to tell him

Jorge spoke first, "Who is Henderson?"

"I am," said Tom, wiping blood from his face.

"Where is the million dollars as agreed to?" asked Jorge firmly, in a manner that demanded respect.

Million dollars? Tom looked at the Estradas. Why did he not say two million dollars?

"I have it and I want to exchange it for the jatasium," replied Tom, respectfully.

"I thought you did too. We've been waiting for you; you didn't show," replied Jorge. "I don't take kindly to be kept waiting, Mr. Henderson."

Javier stood there, silent, understanding his perilous predicament. When Javier greedily hatched his scheme, he did not consider the possible contingency now before him. He had deceived the cartel. He knew Tom Henderson would pay two million dollars, a deadly omission. If the cartel learned of the betrayal, Javier might as well shoot himself to prevent the torture that was sure to follow. Misrepresenting yourself as a Lozano cartel member was alone, enough to find yourself hanging from a highway overpass.

"I can take you to the money right now," said Tom, emphatically. "It's safe in Guadalajara hotel. The million dollars is in a suitcase. I promise, there's no problem."

"We have the plant in the truck, packed in a cooler with ice as agreed. Let's go now," ordered Jorge.

"I want Dr. Estrada to come, please," requested Tom. "He needs to take the plant to his lab at the university and prepare it to be shipped."

"Fine, the two of you can come," replied Jorge.

"I will come, too," said Javier.

"No, you won't. Your job is complete and you can forget about your commission," responded Jorge, irritated.

Javier had no way of explaining that Tom had two million dollars without admitting to his own duplicity.

Juan, Tom and the four men dressed in suits loaded into Jorge's decked-out red Hummer and headed towards Guadalajara. Jorge broke the initial awkward silence when he addressed Tom, "Tell me about your son's disease."

He described Lucas' condition and how the jatasium

would save his life.

"I'm sorry to hear that. I'm a father too and it would break my heart. This is just business, you understand," he said apologetically.

"I know," replied Tom.

"My name is Jorge."

"Nice to meet you, Jorge," said Tom, not appreciating the absurdity of that comment.

After a thirty-minute drive, Jorge pulled up to the front of the Marriott. Tom, Juan and Jorge exited the vehicle. Jorge walked around to the rear of the truck, opened the hatch, and pulled out a blue cooler. The three of them entered the hotel, took the elevator to the top floor without saying a word and then made their way to the presidential suite.

When Tom opened the door and they entered, Jorge joked, "One million dollars is clearly too low of a price given the style in which you travel, Mr. Henderson. Even Juan looked around with raised eyebrow, surprised at the ostentatious suite, wondering how Tom ended up in the presidential suite.

Tom briskly walked into the bedroom with Jorge on his heels. Tom positioned his body in between Jorge and the bed as he bent down to pull one of the suitcases out, hoping that it would come out smoothly without pulling the other one out into Jorge's view. He grabbed the handle and pulled very slowly, thankful when it emerged without disturbing the other. Tom threw it on the bed, opened the latches and watched as one million dollars came into view.

Jorge flipped through a few of the tightly packed bundles of cash and performed a mental calculation in his head by counting the rows.

"It's all there," said Jorge, handing Tom the cooler. Juan came over and opened it, looked inside, and then nodded his approval.

"It's a pleasure doing business with you, Mr. Henderson," remarked Jorge, who promptly left the suite without a goodbye.

Tom and Juan stared at each other before hugging, neither of them needing to say a word, both of them now knowing they were safe.

"We've done it, Juan," exclaimed Tom, peering down at the vibrant purple leaf that could save his son's life.

"We have my friend," replied Juan, grabbing Tom's arm with a squeeze.

Tom kneeled down and yanked the other briefcase out into the open.

"I need to get to the hospital, quickly; processing is required to get this into an acceptable form to send across the border for your Canadian doctor," explained Juan.

They hurried down to the lobby, where Tom checked out, while Juan secured a taxi in front of the hotel. The two men jumped in the back seat and headed to the hospital, a drive that would only take ten minutes.

"Juan, we need to make a quick detour," said Tom, directing the taxi driver to Banco Santander.

"Okay, but hurry, the ice is melting in the cooler."

When the taxi pulled up in front of the bank, Tom disappeared into the stone building with the suitcase and returned fifteen minutes later. He had not considered that Sr. Estevan would have to run all the cash through their counting machine before depositing the money back in his account.

Once Tom returned to the taxi, they continued to University Hospital. In ten minutes, Juan opened the door and stepped onto the sidewalk with the cooler. Tom joined him to say goodbye.

"Juan, I don't know how to repay you. You've put your life at risk for my family; I don't have the proper words to express my gratitude."

"I know you would have done it for my family," replied Juan.

Tom wasn't sure, but he hoped so.

"I better get going," said Juan, impatiently. "I will contact you once I have shipped the jatasium, okay?"

"Okay," replied Tom, who handed the doctor an

envelope.

"What is it?" asked Juan.

"Just a thank you note. Open it later. One last thing, Juan," said Tom, pulling the gun out of his pants and slipping it into the cooler. "Please take care of this for me."

"Of course. I'm just glad you didn't have to use it," replied Juan, having no idea that Tom had been a half-second away from putting a bullet into his son. The two men shook hands before Juan rushed off to his lab to prepare the jatasium.

He unlocked his office door and entered, plopped the blue cooler down on the floor and placed Tom's envelope on his desk. Juan opened the cooler and removed the jatasium, packed exactly as he had instructed.

The extraction of enzymes from plant tissues, rich in phenolic compounds, could be complicated because these compounds can prevent or severely hinder the process. Juan washed the leaves, dried them with a blotting method and then cut the plant leaves into small pieces, before placing them into a Waring laboratory blender for two minutes. He maintained the temperature of the material – known as homogenate – between four to eight degrees, which would maximize the yield. Juan removed the homogenate and added a binding agent, polypeptide solution, and then incubated the mixture for an hour.

Finally, he put the homogenate into a centrifuge, which separated the enzyme from the rest of the mixture, producing the final product for Lucas. Juan placed the enzymes, now in liquid form, into a sterilized plastic container before freezing it.

When done, Juan sat down and took a big breath. He exhaled, finally able to absorb the day's events. His disappointment in his son wrenched his soul; Javier terrorized his family for money, a new level of depravity. Their relationship permanently ended today; no repair existed for the rupture – his boy had died in his eyes.

Juan picked the envelope from the desk, grabbed a letter opener and sliced it open to find a piece of paper. His eyes bulged; he looked a second time to ensure his eyes were not deceiving him. With excitement and bewilderment, Juan's hands shook. He held a bank draft, drawn from Banco Santander, payable to Dr. Juan Estrada in the amount of five hundred thousand dollars.

A handwritten note accompanied the cheque, *Thank you for all you have done, Juan. Given the deep discount I received on the jatasium, I hope this will help you personally and with your research. Your friend, Tom.*

Juan wiped away a tear. He rarely cried, but even the most stoic man can be moved emotionally to a place he does not go often. Juan had given his entire career to his detriment; Tom's generosity overwhelmed him.

After saying goodbye to Juan at the hospital, Tom continued on to the airport to board the first flight home. He considered giving Juan the full extra million dollars, but kept the remaining half million for income taxes. He had planned to evade those taxes, but Tom figured he had engaged in enough criminal behaviour for one year. Ironically, a tax evasion charge was likelier than anyone ever finding out about his phoney lawsuit.

At the airport, he waited on standby and luckily caught a flight to Toronto, ninety minutes later, excited about putting his feet back on Canadian soil and hugging his family.

Once he had stuffed his carry-on bag into the overhead storage bin and settled into seat 16B, he prepared for a relaxing flight home. He watched a complementary movie for a few minutes, trying to wind down. Later, when he squeezed up the aisle and entered the lavatory, he finally understood the strange looks he had received; the deep cut near his temple required stitches and a streak of blood remained on his cheek.

After returning to his seat, the flight attendant asked him if he wanted a beverage. He scanned the menu that she provided him, chuckling when located the flight's feature – Alexander Keith's Pale Ale. If a time existed when he deserved a beer, it was now.

"Diet Coke, please," requested Tom, not missing his old

friend.

About fifteen minutes prior to touchdown, he awoke with the announcement to fasten seat belts as the pilot began his descent into Toronto. Tom looked down at his phone and saw a text from Juan, *Package complete - to arrive tomorrow at 11:00 am at SickKids Hospital. I'm not sure how I could ever properly thank you!*

"You already have, my friend," said Tom softly.

Tom sent his wife a text, updating her on his arrival and the jatasium delivery.

Three hours later, he walked through the SickKids' front doors. He found his wife sleeping in her usual chair in Lucas' room, curled in a ball; he decided not to wake her.

He stood over his sleeping boy. "It's coming, Lucas, it's coming," he said, quietly. "Keep fighting," he said, clasping the bed railings and shedding a few tears.

Veronica stirred; she cracked open an eye to see her husband at Lucas' bedside, prompting her to get up and sneak over. She put him into a bear hug from behind, before kissing his cheek. "I missed you," she said. "It's going to work, Tom. I feel it in my bones."

"Yes, it is," he replied.

Tom turned around and hugged his wife tightly, which she reciprocated in kind.

"What happened to your head?" she asked, alarmed.

"I'm fine. I'll tell you all about it later, or you can read it in my upcoming bestseller," he said, chuckling. He stared into her eyes. God, he loved her. He looked down at his son and recalled Chuck telling him that he would find the answer at Choices for Change, and perhaps he did; however, with the evidence in, Tom made an irrefutable finding – the two people in front of him tilted the game in his favour.

"I can't believe that the jatasium is actually on its way," Veronica said, her eyes beaming with amazement.

"I still don't believe it either," replied Tom. "I won't believe it until that package arrives tomorrow, International Courier Services between 10:00 am and 11:00 am."

Tom fell asleep at 8:00 pm, curling up on an uncomfortable bench in the I.C.U. waiting room for a deserved thirteen hours. Veronica urged him to go to the hotel to rest, but he couldn't; he had to be nearby.

Although feeling improved the next morning, one good sleep would not restore his strength and energy. His left eye had turned purple, almost as bright as the jatasium; but Tom didn't care now that he was safely home.

Tom and Veronica enjoyed hospital cafeteria breakfast while focusing on the clock that read 9:12 am, knowing that the courier would arrive in less than an hour. After breakfast, they hung out at loading dock number twelve, reserved for courier arrivals and deliveries. As the minutes ticked past 10:00 am, they became anxious.

When 11:00 am came and went, Tom called the courier company and was told the package should arrive within the next few minutes. Before he hung up, the courier van arrived. The driver placed a cooler in the hospital shipping clerk's hands. Dr. Vernon had left strict instructions to bring the package to his office immediately upon arrival.

Dr. Vernon informed the Hendersons that he and Dr. Estrada had spoken earlier that morning to discuss treatment and dosages. The parents returned to Lucas' room, and within an hour Dr. Vernon appeared.

"Okay, folks, let's see what happens," said Dr. Vernon, who added the enzymes to the IV solution bag.

Dr. Vernon explained that he required forty-eight hours, and maybe longer before he could gauge improvement. The doctor took blood samples to establish Lucas' baseline levels.

Tom took a few days off from work to keep vigil over his son, mixed with long naps and full-night sleeps with his wife. The parents had every reason to be hopeful, but until the doctor confirmed that the enzymes were breaking down the proteins in his brain, they wouldn't celebrate. If it didn't happen, it would be the letdown of a lifetime.

Dr. Vernon re-did the blood tests at 8 am the following morning and said he would have initial results in three hours.

Dr. Vernon appeared excited, but he kept his enthusiasm measured in front of the Hendersons.

The pair waited as patiently as possible, given the circumstances, knowing they were on the cusp of knowing if their boy would live or die. They talked, played cards, brought each other coffee and completed crossword puzzles to busy themselves, the pins and needles hurting. The anxious parents silently read magazines when Lucas' eyes opened.

"It must be working, Tom!" screeched Veronica to her husband as they turned and hugged in disbelief. "Could this actually be happening?"

"Maybe miracles can happen," replied Tom.

An hour later, Dr. Vernon walked through Lucas' door wearing a smile. "His protein levels are down by fifteen percent. I can't believe it," he declared. "I really can't believe it!" He marched to Lucas' bedside to assess the groggy child. "It's not often a doctor gets to witness this. I have enough enzyme to treat every child with Remington's disease for the next two hundred years!"

In tears, Veronica and Tom leaned over and hugged their son. If they had looked behind them, they would have seen a third person in tears; but by the time they turned around, Dr. Vernon had left, uncomfortable with showing such emotion.

SickKids discharged Lucas three weeks later with a complete recovery, which still had Dr. Vernon shaking his head in disbelief. He and Dr. Estrada were already collaborating on their journal article to make the treatment known internationally; surely, a handful of children existed who needed the enzymes to battle the disease.

CHAPTER TWENTY-TWO

Homecoming

Tom had neither seen nor spoken to his mother since age sixteen, a separation that was either a blessing or a tragedy. Tom concluded it was both.

Lucas had been home for a month after his discharge from SickKids Hospital when Tom made the decision to see his mother, assuming he could locate her – assuming she was alive. They had unfinished business; he felt strong enough for the first time in his life to address it with his mother. However, many a skydiver confidently boarded that plane, certain that they would jump, only to stare out that open door into the abyss and lose their nerve.

As Sussman had done years earlier, Tom decided that he would first try their old apartment, giving himself almost no hope that he would find his mother in the same apartment. On a Saturday morning, he made the hour-long drive to London, not contemplating that he would find his mother that day, which made the trip easier – because a reunion didn't feel real. Mentally, he had it planned; he would knock on the apartment door, find a new occupant, and then have lunch at a local eatery before returning home.

However, he must not have totally ruled out the possibility, because he rejected Veronica's invitation to join him, knowing the conversation he needed to have with Linda must be done privately.

Tom would have preferred seeing his mother somewhere else, having no desire to return to apartment 2B – he didn't have sufficient armour.

Linda's life froze in time when her son left to find his own way in the world, her apartment becoming a time capsule that Tom was about to unlock. When she opened her door that Saturday morning, shock took control of both of them equally. His mother's frailty smacked him in the head, reminding him of the missing years. Linda wondered when her little boy had become a man; perhaps hallucinations had invaded.

Bullets rang out, whizzing with a ferocity. They both ducked at the same time.

His mother looked much older than her age, her long black thick hair replaced with a thinner and greyer version. She hunched over; her eyes had been in the dark too long, her pupils unable to adjust to the light.

"Hi, Mother."

Linda pulled him into the apartment and hugged him tightly, then pushed him back to look at her boy who had become a man without her. It had been so long.

"You're so handsome!" she said, stepping back and looking her son up and down. "It's so good to see you," she said, using all of her emotional energy to keep herself together. "Come in, please, and sit down," Linda said.

"Thank you, Mother."

"I always knew you were smart," she said proudly. "A lawyer, too. It must have been all those books I bought you as a child."

Tom was silent, not knowing what to say. *How did she know I was a lawyer?*

"I saw your name in the newspaper a few times," she explained.

"I have a beautiful wife, Veronica, and a three-year-old boy, Lucas." He pulled out his phone and showed his mother some photos.

"Oh, they're beautiful; he looks just like you. You've made a good life for yourself, Tommy."

Silence followed. There was so much to say; there was nothing to say.

"That's a heck of a lot more than I can say about myself," Linda said, sheepishly.

Again, more silence.

"I have ovarian cancer," she blurted out. "I don't have much time left, maybe a few months, maybe a little more. The doctors can't be sure," she explained, rubbing her pendant in between her fingers.

The woman in front of him had become a stranger. He did not know how to console her; he did not know if he wanted to.

"Maybe it's Karma?" she offered. "By coming here today, you have fulfilled my final wish," she said. And, she meant it.

Should he raise it? He wanted to. Adrenaline coursed through his body. But his mother was about to die. Was it worth it? Maybe it was too cruel? He had come for answers; he deserved answers. Damn it, he deserved answers, irritated that the internal debate raged. Bullets whizzed by.

Linda had no desire to discuss it; the secret could follow her into her grave. She preferred it. She stood from the table, took two steps and prepared an instant coffee for her son, without asking Tom if he wanted one. She placed it in front of him, pleased to play hostess. Tom took a sip; it tasted awful. Damn, it tasted awful.

"Thanks, Mom. It's delicious."

Did his mother know that he knew of Hiller's suicide? After all, his knowledge came courtesy of his eavesdropping on Sussman's visit. She never raised it with him.

Finally, Tom gathered up his nerve. It was time.

"We killed that man, Mom," he said calmly and unpassionately. He used the same tone when he ordered a coffee at a drive-through.

Linda did not respond. Despite her son's mild tone, he might as well have pulled out a blow horn and put it to her ear because those words came out like a clap of thunder so forceful that it shook the ground. To describe the quiet that followed as stunned silence was apropos – not an ounce of embellishment.

"And, you made me part of it," Tom said in the same tone. "I was only ten years old," he said. "What were you thinking?" he asked, tears now filling his eyes. A decade of pain raced for the exits.

Just as she couldn't find the appropriate words so many years ago, she couldn't find them today. "I attended his funeral," she said. I couldn't tell you about his suicide. I couldn't put that on you," she explained.

"I haven't had a full night's sleep since he killed himself, Mom," said Tom, wiping away tears.

"Neither have I, Tommy, but I deserved it. You didn't."

"What were you thinking?" he asked.

Linda took a moment before responding, "I did something unforgivable that I can't take back, although I've wished every day that I could."

She wiped away her own tears. "I was a sick person. I still am. I'm sure you knew it – the depression, the anxiety, my alcoholism, my drug addiction and my broken heart."

Linda knew her son wanted more, but anything she had to offer would come up well short of satisfactory. "I wish I had something better to say," she said. "We were being evicted again; I didn't want to move again. Desperation changes who you are, Tommy. I wanted a settlement. They should have settled." Linda coughed into her sleeve and took a drink of water.

"A curse has followed me around since then; I deserved it all and more. I know you were just a boy; I shouldn't have involved you in my plan. I should never have made you tell those lies about Mr. Hiller."

"We might as well have murdered him," said Tom, shaking his head. "With our lies, we destroyed an innocent man. The ridicule and shame we heaped on him; only a rope could save him. He was a good man. He was good to me."

"I know, Tommy," replied his mother, lowering her head in shame.

"I couldn't get proper counselling; I couldn't tell anyone the goddamned truth," explained Tom, raising his voice.

"That's why I haven't tried to contact you all these years," replied Linda. "You were better off without me in your life. Moving was the best thing you ever did for yourself. Just look at what you have done with your life." Linda took another sip of water. "I was a poor mother; I'm sorry. I've been given the ultimate punishment for my sins. I deserve it. I look forward to it."

Silence allowed Tom to absorb his mother's explanation.

"I had many more years on this earth than Robert Hiller. How fair is that?" she asked, rhetorically. "I've never asked for forgiveness because I didn't deserve it. To be honest, I've been rotting away, waiting to die."

"But why, Mom? I've never understood." Tom began to cry. "We killed a man!"

"I killed him, Tommy. You were just a boy; I told you what to do and what to say. And for that, I'm so sorry." Linda reached out and grabbed her son's hand. "You can't blame yourself."

"I still don't understand why, Mom."

Linda took another drink and looked at her son. "I was a single mother. My depression wiped away rational thought. When you told me that Hiller molested George Gerontonis, I saw dollar signs. Listen to me, Tommy. I'm not making excuses. You've come for an explanation and I'm giving it to you, as poor as it is." Linda began crying harder. She placed her hands over her eyes.

"Tommy, when you told me that Hiller groped your friend George, dollar signs flashed in my eyes. We had nothing. I thought the school board would quickly settle if you said he molested you, too," she explained.

Tom couldn't look at Linda anymore; he lowered his eyes.

"I know it sounds stupid, but I didn't want the police involved or criminal charges to be laid. I believed they would just pay me off to get rid of me. I know how naive that sounds when I say it out loud; the school board told me that they had to call the police," she explained. "I didn't think it would go that far; I started a snowball rolling that I couldn't stop."

Tom looked up at his mother, still crying.

"I knew I could be arrested for making it up so I continued with the lie," she said. "And, because of what you told me about George, he deserved to be punished anyway. Jonathon Sussman pleaded with me to continue; he didn't want him abusing other kids. Neither did I.

"Oh mother, I had lunch with George a few years ago. Hiller never touched him; he made the accusation as a joke."

More stunned silence followed as the ramifications of her son's words sent a dagger into her already perforated soul. "Oh my God," she said faintly and then proceeded to put her face in her hands.

Tom stood up from the table, took three steps, and opened the apartment door. He turned his head back and scanned the apartment – bullets whizzed by. Then, he gave his mother his attention, "Listen, Mom, I'm really sorry you're sick."

Tom closed the door after stepping into the hallway. He leaned his back against the wall and stared at the flickering light on the ceiling. The stench overwhelmed him, giving him every reason to escape quickly, but he froze. Did he have any right to judge his mother? She had been as desperate as he had been - as desperate as Robert Hiller in those final seconds. And, if you asked Lester Mobey, as desperate as Piscine Molitor, the starving boy adrift in the Pacific Ocean.

Janice Thorton flashed in Tom's mind. You couldn't be "more desperate" than someone else. You were either desperate, or you weren't, a perspective he never had any ambition of gaining.

On the drive home, Tom thought of only one thing – how Robert Hiller had lost the lottery of good luck in life.

CHAPTER TWENTY-THREE

A Midsummer Afternoon's Meeting

Amicus arrived early at the Queen's Inn after Ven agreed to meet him in their regular room at 2:00 pm on Tuesday afternoon. He arranged a delightful assortment of Ven's favourite fruit and cheeses, and then grabbed a bottle of water from the mini-fridge before sitting on a corner chair. As usual, the closed curtains prevented any light from entering.

Despite their many afternoons in that very room, Amicus felt nervous. The two used nicknames – Amicus, Latin for friend and Ven, Danish for friend – when contacting each other to remain anonymous and prevent their relationship's discovery.

Self-reflection can be a bitch, lamented Amicus, finding himself stuck somewhere between D.H. Lawrence's *I never saw a wild thing sorry for itself* and the understanding that those birds were still sad when they dropped their frozen dead from that bough.

Amicus heard the familiar light knock on the door, walked over and let Ven in, a pattern that was now well into the double digits. They embraced for a minute. It's hard to fake passion, concluded Amicus, as he let go for the final time.

"Thanks for coming," said Amicus.

"Of course," said Ven.

"Have you been well?", asked Amicus.

"I suppose I have. It's all relative," replied Ven.

Amicus grabbed Ven's hand and walked Ven to a corner table and two chairs.

"Sit down and enjoy," urged Amicus. "I brought your favourites."

Ven sat down and looked over the assembled food, appreciative that Amicus had gone to the trouble.

"You know that I love you, right?" asked Ven.

"I do know," replied Amicus, but offering nothing more to Ven's disappointment.

They sat down and had a few bites, although Amicus was not hungry.

"What you've done for me can't be measured," emphasized Amicus; he meant it.

"Sure, it can. It's measured in a life," replied Ven. "I would do it again."

Ven, sensing the inevitable, peered at Amicus. "Is this beautiful lunch a peace offering?" asked Ven, not receiving an immediate response. "I did what I did because I love you," said Ven.

"The course of true love never did run smoothly Hermia," replied Amicus, referring to Ven's favourite Shakespearean play, *A Midsummer Night's Dream*.

"And why do I fear I'm in the shoes of Lysander today," lamented Ven, appreciating that this would be their final meeting. "I always knew you didn't love me," asserted Ven with regret, knowing it is difficult to fake passion.

Tom paused before responding; he would not deny the truth. "Listen, Jonathon. I need to put my life back together," explained Tom. "I know it sounds selfish, especially after what you've done for me."

"I understand, Tom. I knew it would end someday. I really did."

"How can I ever thank you?" asked Tom. "You risked everything to help me through the most difficult time in my life."

"Lucas' well-being is the only thanks I need," he replied, "but I will miss this hotel."

And with that final exchange, Jonathon stood and exited the room for the last time.

Tom left a few minutes later but, unlike Jonathon, he would not miss that hotel room. Despite his admiration for Jonathon, he detested the sight of it. He promised his son that he would do anything for him – to do anything to save his life – and that is exactly what he did. He had seduced Jonathon with a purpose and had hurt him terribly today. The guilt weighed on him.

Resolutely, Tom decided he would not leave anything to chance in winning Wheeler's trial and securing a large enough award to pay the cartel. Half of Tom's plan included Wheeler, and half included Jonathon Sussman. Sadly, and ironically, Tom had learned how the legal system could be manipulated from Linda; but unlike his mother, he had beaten the system that he had sworn to respect. Painfully, he accepted that the apple hadn't fallen far from the tree.

Surprisingly, Jonathon risked everything for him; however, a man would do almost anything for love. Jonathon had a weakness, like his father before him. Harshly, after Tom attended that first lunch with him, he knew it could be exploited.

Nevertheless, it was fair to ask what went through Jonathon Sussman's mind, although the answer would be elusive. Lester Mobey had the best answer, even if unsatisfactory: the human brain is a curious and wondrous organ, magnificent but mysterious, evolution's magnum opus, a masterpiece really, except that it is so fragile, imperfect, narcissistic and prone to severe lapses in judgment. It is a chameleon of sorts, just as capable of manipulation and deceit as a means to survival as it is of love and tenderness as a means to survival. It will be whatever it needs to be.

The following morning, Tom and his family walked to Lake Victoria for a picnic. The sun shone, the birds chirped and Lake Victoria reflected with perfection.

Tom strolled along the pathway, adjacent to the river's edge, with Veronica on his left and Lucas on his right. Peace carved out a spot in his soul, but those bullets had taken their toll – the scars undeniable. He resembled Lester Mobey's car following the repairs required because of the accident that killed his wife. He looked like new on the outside with a fresh coat of paint, but clunky sounds emanated from under the hood, and he shimmied when he went too fast. But, if you looked closely, excitement had found his eyes – similar to Chuck's when he discussed Stratford's history, or Benjamin Hunt when he discussed safari animals.

Lucas threw a stone in the river and giggled when it splashed. As the ripples spread, Veronica grabbed Tom's hand and kissed him on the cheek. A bystander wouldn't have noticed the simple peck – but it was the kind of kiss a man never forgets. It reminded Tom that he won the lottery of good luck.

CHAPTER TWENTY-FOUR

Animal Kingdom

The Komodo dragon, the largest living lizard in the world, has patience unlike any other predator, except humans. Notorious stalkers, such as the lion or cheetah, become impatient with hunger and attack with a flurry of violence, relying on speed and strength to bring their prey down.

The ambush predator waits for its prey, using stealth and camouflage to attack the unsuspecting prey that never saw it coming.

The Komodo Dragon's bite appears trivial to its much larger prey when afflicted, the prey dismissing the superficial affliction, unimpressed with the lizard's predator prowess.

Unbeknownst to its prey, a poison lies within the saliva of the Komodo Dragon, deadly, but very slow acting. That superficial wound won't heal, festers and eventually becomes infected. The lizard follows its future meal for weeks as it becomes weaker and weaker until it does not have the strength to defend itself. Ironically, the downfall is so slow, the victim doesn't even know it is occurring until it is too late.

Kevin Miller was not always known as Miller the Killer. Anyone that knew the usually outgoing and friendly boy would have described him as passive, having never laid a hand on anyone. His parent's divorce was difficult, made more so, when his father moved several hours away and their time together diminished.

When Kevin's mother mentioned her son's troubles to his grade five science teacher, the empathetic and understanding man promised that he would keep a careful watch over the young boy. Better yet, his teacher suggested a few visits to his cabin would surely cheer her son up.

"I've got a pond, pinball machine, bicycles, horseshoes; all the boys love it!" exclaimed Robert Hiller.

Kevin's mother quickly accepted the invitation, desperate to assuage her guilt from the divorce. She would do anything to make her son happy, including overlooking the warning signs.

When George Gerontonis' father died, his absence left a crater-sized hole in his life; the gregarious man with a swashbuckling laugh could not be replaced. In hindsight, George's mother erred when she let her son look at his father's body at the hospital, giving him one final time to see his father – and hopefully have closure. But that high dose of electricity that surged through his body caused his father to burn in a way that no son should ever witness.

George's crafty conscious mind could block the images, even if a bullet whizzed by occasionally; but his subconscious could not fend off the memories, his mind as defenceless as the Persians when the Spartans attacked at night. Tom feared the nocturnal nightmares, scared to put his head on the pillow.

George's mother found a sympathetic ear in George's science teacher, who agreed to keep an eye on her struggling boy. Mr. Hiller had a great idea.

"Why doesn't George come to my cabin? Lots of activities and many boys to occupy his time!" offered Hiller.

George's mother accepted the invitation, desperate to push the darkness away from her son and replace it with sunlight. She was willing to do anything, including overlooking the warning signs.

Hiller had a plan, a tried and tested methodology. He appreciated the delicacy of these matters; he had to be careful, showing the patience of the Komodo Dragon. It was a curse to have these urges, he lamented. "Why can't I be like everyone else," he said to himself.

After he had gathered the vulnerable, he identified his primary target – the weakest in the pack who would muster up the least fight. If you were lucky, like Tommy Henderson, Hiller ruled you out – because you raised a red flag; you might not be compliant, or worse, you might tell. Your devotion to the brother lacked sufficient enthusiasm.

When Hiller stalked his prey, he counted on the boy's oblivion to the numerous and successive minor afflictions that formed part of the master plan. Those first pats on the leg followed by successive hugs appeared innocuous, at first. What about the touching in the big bed? Inadvertent touching explained it – plausible if you wanted it to be.

"George, give me a hug, young man," demanded Hiller, after praising the boy's driving capabilities.

By the time the victim reached the final stage of treachery, that boy was attached to a wolf in sheep's clothing who had replaced his missing father.

"I will give fifty dollars to whoever walks to the bottom of the ravine and back alone," offered Hiller, as he sat with the boys around the campfire near midnight, fresh off a discussion about his war buddies and their extraordinary bravery. The boys looked down the ravine and the wooden planks embedded in the hillside to serve as stairs, the bottom few invisible on account of that pitch-black darkness. As Hiller expected, indeed wanted, nobody accepted the offer, each of the boys staring at a ravine full of imaginary predators ready to pounce, unaware of the irony.

Hiller made his second offer, "Okay, twenty dollars to whoever will walk to the bottom and back with me."

At the bottom of the ravine, where the ultimate betrayal occurred, Hiller relied on a cocktail of concealment to keep his dark acts secret: the brother code, the tower of brotherhood, the friendship, but mainly, the shame.

A year prior to Tommy's attendance at the cabin, Kevin Miller trekked down the ravine with Hiller six times – the dark secrets finally eating him. The once passive boy became a bully, tormenting children on the playground until Nick Danson finally let that elbow fly, stripping the Killer of the only way he knew how to deal with his pain.

When George Gerontonis made his way down those steps for the first time, he believed that he just made the easiest twenty dollars in his life, unaware that it was the most expensive walk that he would ever make. After a few weeks, George's mother demanded to know the cause of his despondency.

Finally, George relented and broke the brother code, breaking down and telling his mother everything. The mother and son embraced each other while they cried.

A police constable attended the next day to briefly interview George. Once she understood the complaint, she expressed her regret and advised that a detective would be out to see them. But fate made an appearance between that first visit and the second visit from the detective – George observed fellow students incessantly tease Tommy Henderson about being abused by Hiller.

"Did you get diddled today?" yelled the students, one of many verbal assaults that landed on the boy with a thud. On a Thursday, George watched Tommy wander off behind a portable to escape the arrows. George peeked around the corner to find his friend kneeling and crying, alone in his torment. Why would anyone put themselves through that, wondered George?

When the detective arrived to obtain a formal statement, George's story had changed.

"Sorry, it was a joke," explained George to the detective, lowering his eyes. He had been dared by his friend, Chris, to tell that crazy story.

Both the detective and George's mother knew her son was now lying, but the detective had no choice to record his false statement. Prosecuting Hiller became impossible; George's flip-flopping of versions would always result in reasonable doubt said the prosecutor, Jonathon Sussman.

Curiously, George's possibly exculpatory statement or any reference to him never ended up in the disclosure provided to Lester Mobey; instead, a hand pushed that document through a shredder.

Coincidence had George finding Tom at Ernie's Pub in London more than a decade after Hiller's trial. George interrupted his drive to an Alcoholics Anonymous meeting to grab a pint and figure his life out after a second failed marriage and losing another job. Apparently, he had anger issues; but nobody understood his relentless nightmares. Fending off demons nightly as they scaled the wall came with a toll.

One unexplainable phenomenon puzzled George. All these years later, he recalled with crystal clarity exactly how many steps it took him to climb from the bottom of the ravine up to the cabin after Hiller first snatched his innocence – forty-one. However, he had never counted them. How was that possible? Lester Mobey had the answer: the human brain is a curious and wondrous organ, magnificent but mysterious – undoubtedly evolution's masterpiece.

-THE END-

About the Author

Stephen Roth is a Canadian lawyer who resides in the charming and captivating city of Stratford, Ontario, Canada, home of the world-renowned Stratford Festival. Influenced and inspired by the numerous artists, writers and actors that have called Strafford home, including esteemed writer and former resident, Timothy Findley, Stephen used a COVID-19 slow down to switch from writing legal briefs to penning his first novel, Innocence on Trial.

Stephen proudly incorporated the alluring and trendy aspects of his home town as a backdrop to his first novel. Whether Lake Victoria, the banks of the Avon River, or the busy downtown patios of Pazzo Taverna and Fellini's Restaurant, Stephen believes each and every reader will be drawn to visit Canada's best-kept secret.

Stephen's follow up novel, The Perfect Season, inspired by the French-English strife in Cameroon and his family's love for the Detroit Tigers, will be published in mid-2022.

Printed in Great Britain
by Amazon